Pl...   my Everything

About the Author

Katie Marsh lives in south-west London with her husband and daughter. As well as writing novels she has a career in healthcare, and *My Everything* was inspired by the bravery of the patients she met while working in stroke services.

Katie loves strong coffee, the feel of a blank page and stealing her husband's toast.

You can follow her on Twitter @marshisms or visit her website at www.katie-marsh.com

KATIE MARSH

My Everything

HODDER

First published in Great Britain in 2015 by Hodder & Stoughton
An Hachette UK company

4

Copyright © Katie Marsh 2015

A CIP catalogue record for this title is
available from the British Library

Paperback ISBN 978 1 473 61363 8
Ebook ISBN 978 1 473 61362 1

Typeset in Plantin by Palimpsest Book Production Limited,
Falkirk, Stirlingshire
Printed and bound by Clays Ltd, St Ives plc

Hodder & Stoughton policy is to use papers that are natural, renewable
and recyclable products and made from wood grown in sustainable
forests. The logging and manufacturing processes are expected to
conform to the environmental regulations of the
country of origin.

Hodder & Stoughton Ltd
Carmelite House
50 Victoria Embankment
London EC4Y 0DZ

www.hodder.co.uk

For Max and Evie

One

Hannah wakes up with a piece of toast stuck to her face.

She opens unwilling eyes and realises that the lights are on. She is fully dressed. Her teeth are unbrushed. Exhaustion oozes from every pore. She peers at the clock on the wall and closes her eyes again in despair. It's 2 a.m. This day of all days isn't meant to start like this. It's supposed to be different. The start of things to come.

She rubs her aching neck as she pulls the soggy toast from her cheek and drops it onto the plate. Her phone is shuffling through the more embarrassing realms of her playlist and she hastily presses pause. Her body feels like it belongs inside a chalk line at a crime scene. She levers herself up on her elbows and surveys the marking laid out across the kitchen table.

'Damn.' She's managed to knock her wine glass over in her sleep and now Year 10's essays on *Macbeth* look as if they have been liberally spattered in blood. She wonders if she can get away with saying she did it deliberately to bring the play to life. She imagines her students' sceptical expressions and very much doubts it. Their teenage antennae are on a constant hunt for scandal of any kind, and she suspects the school rumour mill will despatch her to the Priory before the week is out.

A text bleeps its arrival. Steph is in the middle of a marking marathon too.

Has he been home yet? Have you told him? x

Hannah taps out her reply. No and no.

Steph texts straight back. But you will? Promise?

Hannah exhales. Yes. Otherwise you'll kill me. And I'd quite like to see the next series of *Scandal*.

Good luck. You can do it x

As Hannah pushes her chair back she hits the spoils of her latest doomed attempt to walk past a bookshop without buying anything. She reaches down and strokes the smooth comfort of the front covers, tempted to stay up all night losing herself in someone else's story. Then she remembers what she is going to do today, and she reluctantly stands up, exhaling slowly to calm the nerves clutching at every breath.

Tom. I'm leaving you. She feels a skewer of fear at the thought of saying the words out loud. Of seeing his mouth opening and his eyes narrowing as he prepares to attack her for one final time. It's one of his talents. Email. Voicemail. Good old-fashioned shouting. He always knows how to hurt.

She takes the plate to the overcrowded sink, squeezing it in beside an empty can of baked beans and a dirty pan that is busy generating some new kind of life form.

Later. She'll deal with everything later. She switches off the lights and unbuttons her grey dress as she climbs the stairs. She stops in surprise at the bedroom door as she hears the rasp of her husband's breathing. She had assumed he was still at the office. Another deal. Another night apart.

She slides quietly beneath the duvet.

'Why didn't you wake me when you came in?'

Tom's only answer is a snore.

Scratch.

Hannah pulls the pillow over her head.

Scratch.

She can still hear it. She sticks her head out and looks at the clock. 4:30. She is raw from lack of sleep.

There it is again.

She turns over. 'Tom, can you be quiet?' Her voice comes out as a croak. 'I'm trying to sleep.' It would be so wonderful if he actually listened.

Fat chance. Instead he starts mumbling. His voice is breathy and slurred.

'Sh. Sh. Sh. Shtuck.'

Reluctantly she leans towards his side of the bed. She peers through the darkness and sees a figure on the floor. Great. Clearly he's been busy with whisky rather than work. Again. She reaches over and prods him but gets only a moan in reply.

'For God's sake.' She rubs her aching eyes with her hands.

'Shtuck. Hellllllmeeeeee.' Wearily, she reaches over and turns on the bedside light. She looks down at him, blinking in the sudden brightness.

Something is wrong.

Horribly wrong.

Tom is lying on the floor, his body contorted, eyes wide and pleading as they meet hers. His face is ashen and lopsided, his distorted mouth straining to form words that Hannah can't understand. She watches, horrified, as his right hand pushes feebly against the wooden foot of the bed. *Scratch.* His left hand is curved beneath him at

3

an impossible angle, his fingers pulled upwards into a misshapen beak.

Something terrible has happened. Hannah's pulse spirals and she stumbles out of bed and instinctively reaches down to try to pull him up. She strains every muscle but his body is a dead weight and he slumps back down to the carpet. She winces as she hears him groan, worrying that she has made things worse. Her mouth is dry and panic threatens to choke her.

They need help.

'Don't worry, Tom.' Her fingers shake as she picks up her phone to dial 999. 'Don't worry. It'll be OK. You'll be OK.'

If she says it enough times she might believe it.

Her call is answered instantly and her voice wavers as she asks for the ambulance service. Saying the words out loud makes this shockingly real. Tom's eyes are pure terror and she reaches down to stroke his dark hair. It's baby soft. It's been so long since she has touched it.

A male operator asks her the questions she has only ever heard on TV. What has happened. Who. When. Where. She controls the shake in her voice as she answers, and he tells her that an ambulance will be with them very soon. She finds herself wondering who the operator is. What he looks like. Whether he can tell her what the future holds.

Maybe it's better not to know. She hangs up and stands frozen for a moment, until she hears Tom mumbling a word that could be her name. She folds herself onto the floor and cradles his head in her lap, blocking out the future and trying to give him whatever comfort she can. She takes his right hand in hers and he clutches her fingers and they wait together for whatever comes next.

His hand feels cold. Heavy. Like responsibility.

Two paramedics arrive minutes later – a man and a woman whose names she instantly forgets but whose faces she will remember for ever. She follows their green uniforms up the stairs and into the bedroom.

'What's wrong? What's happened to him?' Hannah is starting to shake and crosses her arms tight across her chest in a vain attempt at comfort.

The woman's chestnut ponytail flicks behind her as she kneels down next to Tom. She barely looks old enough to buy alcohol but her unruffled concentration steadies Hannah as she takes Tom's pulse. 'I'm not sure yet. I'll just examine him.' She stares at his face. 'Hello, Tom. How are you feeling?'

'Sh. Sh. Shtuck.'

'OK.' The girl nods as if he is speaking normally. 'I'm just going to do a couple of tests so we can start to make you more comfortable. Can you raise your arms please?'

Hannah holds her breath. *Come on, Tom.*

His right arm rises but his left remains at his side.

Hannah wills it to move.

Nothing.

Hannah turns to the man as panic starts to rise. 'Is he going to be OK?'

He looks at her with unwelcome news in his eyes. 'Tom's face is drooping. Together with the speech and movement issues, it looks likely that he's had a stroke. We'll need to do further tests to confirm.'

'A *stroke*? Oh God.' She tries to force away tear-stained

memories of her childhood babysitter dribbling in a hospital ward.

'We'll get Tom to hospital as quickly as possible.' The man's voice is steady. Designed to reassure.

'OK.' She is struggling to focus. Her mind is shouting STROKE and her breath is coming in gasps. She digs her nails into her palms to keep the tears at bay. 'Can I come with him?'

'Of course.' He drops his eyes tactfully to the floor. 'You might want to get dressed first though.'

She looks down at her minimal pink T-shirt. Yes. Getting dressed is a good idea. She pulls the first clothes she finds from her wardrobe and goes into the bathroom to change.

She is still fumbling with her jeans as she walks out to see that Tom is in a portable chair and the paramedics are carrying him down the stairs. His short hair is drenched in sweat. His eyes are blank and his waxen face lolls to the right, cruelly contrasting with the energy and joy of the man in the wedding photos on the walls, punctuating his descent. Tears prick her eyes at the shock of seeing him so helpless. So mortal.

She must help him. However she can. She throws her coat on and pulls her bag from its peg in the hall before running out of the door. As she pulls it shut she catches a glimpse of someone reflected in the dark glass of the living room window. The flashing blue lights of the ambulance illuminate the curly hair exploding from her head. Her white face. Her terrified eyes.

It takes her a second to realise that the woman is her.

The ambulance screeches through south London streets and ten minutes later they are outside the hospital. It is clear that every second counts.

Tom is in danger.

Tom might die.

She can't think about that. As the door opens Hannah steps down onto the tarmac, bracing herself against the whip of the January wind. The paramedics swiftly wheel Tom's stretcher towards the red ACCIDENT AND EMERGENCY sign that glows ominously through the darkness. Hannah reaches out and takes Tom's hand as they pass a skeletal man standing by a large NO SMOKING sign. He is puffing defiantly on a cigarette and gives her a wink as she strides past. The gesture is so inappropriate she is tempted to slap him in the face.

No time.

The paramedics push Tom into the hospital and a tall man with stubble as dark as his eye bags strides towards them. He is tucking his tie into his shirt and Hannah sees the exhaustion beneath his smile.

'Hi, I'm Dr Malik, the stroke consultant on call. You're . . .?'

'Hannah.' He is already talking to the paramedics as they push Tom along the corridor. Words volley back and forth. Cerebral artery. Possible haemorrhage. Each one only serves to make her more afraid.

Tom is the silent eye of the storm. She squeezes his fingers but he doesn't even react to that any more. His eyes are now closed and she can see him shutting down right in front of her. She won't let him. She summons the strength she knows he needs and leans closer until her mouth is near his ear.

'Hang in there, soldier.' It's an endearment from old times and his lids flicker open in response. For a second their eyes connect and she feels hope surge. Then his lids close.

7

'Tom?'

Nothing.

'*Tom?*'

No. She won't let this happen. She turns to the paramedics, but they are already pushing Tom through a set of cream double doors labelled RESUSCITATION ROOM. She is about to follow but Dr Malik stops her. As the doors close she has a brief glimpse of bright lights and smells the metallic tang of blood. Bile rises in her throat and she takes a deep breath as Dr Malik steps towards her.

'We're going to take your husband for more tests. Then I'll be able to come back and tell you more.' He indicates some grey plastic chairs. 'Wait here please. You can call someone if you need to.'

'I . . .' But he's gone.

She is alone.

It's terrifying.

She sits down and discovers that the chair has been ergonomically designed to give her a slipped disc. She springs back up and stares at the flaking wall in front of her. The colour resembles Tom's face the morning after a bad kebab.

She thinks of him lying there. Powerless.

She clenches her fists.

Come on, Tom.

'All right, darling?'

She spins round as the smoker from outside lands heavily across two chairs. He leans towards her and she is enveloped in an unappetising cloud of stale spirits.

'No. I'm not all right.' She steps away from him. Suddenly being alone doesn't seem so bad.

He coughs and phlegm crackles in his chest. 'Is that your husband in there?' He indicates the cream doors with his head and leans back, spreading his legs wide. Hannah averts her eyes from the unfortunate hole in his jeans.

'Yes.' Her voice is high and strained.

'Been married long?'

She looks towards the double doors, desperate to know what's happening behind them. 'Five and a half years.'

He nods. 'Never made it that far, myself.'

Hannah can't say she's surprised.

Hannah jumps as Dr Malik pushes through the doors. His face is stamped with a gravity she doesn't want to understand.

'Come through, Hannah. We're ready for you now.'

'Good luck.' Her companion gives her a thumbs up. 'He'll be fine.'

'I hope so.'

Talk about clutching at straws.

She takes a deep breath and follows Dr Malik into the resuscitation room.

Coaster from Coco's Diner, Soho

Summer 2006

He was drinking a malted milkshake when he met her. Hannah. She was a waitress in a fantastically short skirt, her black curls pulled back unwillingly beneath a pink baseball cap. All he wanted to do was reach out and set them free.

She was so animated. So full of giggles and chatter. So out of his league.

Looking around, he thought most of the men in the diner were in love with her – including those who were the other way inclined. He was just the quiet student in the corner. Whenever she served him he found himself hiding behind his law books, any confidence dissolving into sweaty mumbles and a terrible urge to pun.

But he bided his time and drank so many overpriced milkshakes he had to work extra hours at the pub. And make a new notch in his belt. And then one day his patience was rewarded. He was arriving at the diner when she came out for a fag break. He said hello and held out his Union Jack lighter. A chance to impress her. To connect. At last.

The lighter didn't spark.

He tried again. Nothing. He could feel panic rising. Then she put her tiny hand over his to steady it and the flame burst into life. And she looked at him. Really looked at him. Wide brown eyes examining his face. Red lips curving into a smile. She was so close he couldn't think straight. Marlboro Red scented the air. It was now or never.

His mouth was moving. Apparently it was forming words. 'I've never fancied a girl in a baseball cap before.'

Not his finest hour. A pause yawned between them, long enough to age him by a decade. He dropped his eyes. Shit. He'd blown it. Then . . .

'I've never fancied a guy who can't light a cigarette before.' Her tone was so deadpan that he looked up at her face again. Checking. He saw a glint of mischief in her brown eyes as she exhaled a predictably perfect plume of smoke. 'I was wondering how many more visits it would take to get a conversation out of you.' She smiled. 'It's been a long campaign, soldier.'

He dared to exhale. 'Well, I wanted the moment to be right.' A shrieking hen party strutted past them bent on some serious Soho mischief. He grinned. 'You know – just the two of us.' A pigeon flapped above them and he became aware of a warm wetness on his forehead. He touched it with his hand and groaned. 'Obviously the pigeon shit wasn't part of the plan.'

She started to giggle and then threw her head back in an uninhibited roar of laughter. And he looked at her and began to laugh with her and he promised himself that he was going to do everything he could to get this amazing girl. Everything.

Two

As she walks through the resuscitation room, antiseptic claws at Hannah's throat. She blinks as her eyes adjust to the neon lights and she sees Dr Malik turn to her, running a hand through increasingly disorderly hair.

'Can you confirm when you first noticed the symptoms, Hannah?'

She searches for an answer, but all she can think about is Tom's body on the floor. His eyes closing. His left arm glued to his side.

She shakes her head to try to force the images away. She must remember. She must help.

'I don't know. About an hour ago, I suppose.'

'And do you have any idea when they started?'

'No.' She feels as if she is failing some kind of test. 'I'm so sorry. He was sound asleep when I went to bed at two.' Behind a pink curtain to her left she catches a glimpse of a man rasping into an oxygen mask as though every breath were his last.

'And would you say he is generally fit and well?'

'I guess so. He plays football. And runs. Sometimes. Or he used to, anyway.' She feels a pulse of frustration. She should know more. Be able to say more. The truth is, in the last few weeks she has spent more time talking to her newsagent than to her husband.

'Does Tom smoke?'

'Yes. Well, not much.' They walk past shelves stacked with tubes and needles. 'More in the last few months.'

'And has he had any recurring symptoms recently?'

She struggles to think. 'Like what?'

'Headaches? Clumsiness? Forgetfulness?'

She thinks back. 'He gets a lot of headaches when he's hungover.'

'And how often is that?'

'Pretty much every day recently.'

'And you're sure he'd been drinking? Before the headaches?'

'Yes.' She nods, though uncertainty jolts her. She never bothers to ask any more. 'Why?'

Dr Malik doesn't answer and she follows him to the end cubicle, where she sees a figure in a pink hospital gown on the bed. A tangle of wires is attached to his chest and a black monitor bleeps out his vital signs. A nurse in a dark blue uniform is lowering an oxygen mask over his face, talking to him quietly as she pulls the strap over his head.

Hannah is about to walk on when she sees that Dr Malik has stopped and is pulling up the metallic slats at the side of the patient's bed.

She looks at him again. He has dark hair and a wedding ring.

It's Tom.

She raises a hand to her mouth as a sob explodes from her throat. Tom isn't human any more. He's all wires and veins and limbs. This can't be the same man who whooped her over the threshold. Who spent their engagement party concocting lurid purple 'Hantinis' in a cocktail shaker. Who drove through the night in an ageing Ford

Escort to bring her a 'first day of teaching' hamper of cake, Stilton and Amaretto.

Suddenly she can only remember the good times.

'Let's go.' Dr Malik starts to manoeuvre Tom's bed into the corridor. A bearded porter takes over the steering so Dr Malik can focus on his patient. The nurse stays at Tom's head as they push him through an assault course of abandoned trolleys, cardboard boxes and hulking metal cages stacked full of sheets.

Hannah jogs to keep up. 'Where are we going?'

Dr Malik lifts Tom's left arm up but it falls down. 'We're taking him up to the CT scanner to see what's happening in his brain.'

Hannah's stomach plunges. 'What are you looking for?'

They enter the lift. The heavy grey doors close and it starts to judder upwards at an infuriatingly slow speed.

Dr Malik checks Tom's pulse and then raises his eyes to Hannah's face. 'Strokes happen when the blood supply to the brain is cut off, either by a blockage in an artery or a bleed in the brain. Do you see?'

Hannah swallows. 'I think so.'

'Good.' He nods. 'The CT scan will show us which one – if either – has happened to Tom.'

Hannah is twisting the strap of her handbag so hard it is cutting into her palm.

Dr Malik is looking at Tom again. 'Once we can see what's happening we'll know how to treat him.'

'OK.' Hannah stares at Tom as the lift finally deigns to reach the correct floor. His stillness terrifies her. She thinks back to their last argument – the energy of his anger as he paced around her pointing out her long list of flaws. Naïve. Selfish. The same old list. Looking at him lying inert on the stretcher, she finds herself wishing he was shouting at her now. Wishing that he could.

Dr Malik helps to steer the trolley out. They turn yet another corner and enter the radiology department. The reception area is dark and uninviting.

Dr Malik keeps moving. 'Please wait here, Hannah.'

'No.' Her hands ball into fists. 'I want to be with him.'

He shakes his head. 'I'm sorry. You can't come through.'

'Please?'

'The radiation levels are too high. You'll have to wait outside, I'm afraid.' He drums his fingers impatiently on Tom's chart. 'We have to take him in now – every second is vital.'

'OK.' Her shoulders slump as Tom is wheeled away and she is left alone again.

It's eerie out here. She walks towards the water dispenser but there are no plastic cups. Her stomach rumbles. She checks the time on her phone. Five thirty.

She hears the scanner being switched on as she scrabbles through her bag in search of something to eat. She eventually unearths an old jumbo pack of Maltesers and pulls it open. The chocolates have been squashed out of shape but the sugar comforts her and she pops another into her mouth. Then another. Then one more. Suddenly she's cramming them in, trying to block out the sense that her world is about to shatter. Nine. Ten. Eleven. She closes her eyes and her world reduces to chocolate and the crunch of honeycomb between her teeth.

Soon she hears footsteps and Dr Malik approaches and sits down next to her.

'Hannah.'

'Yes?'

'The scan has confirmed that Tom has had a stroke.'

She can't accept it. 'But he's only thirty-two.'

Dr Malik shakes his head. 'I'm afraid that doesn't make any difference. The blood flow is blocked to the part of his brain that controls his left side, and we can see a small area of damage on the scan.'

'Oh God.' Hannah's hands are clasped together so tightly she can't feel her fingers any more.

Dr Malik continues. 'We don't know what time symptoms started, so the best treatment we have is to admit him to the stroke unit and monitor him carefully. We'll be taking him up in a minute.'

He gives her a taut smile before turning and striding off. Hannah sits staring at the floor, the final Malteser melting slowly in her palm. She closes her eyes and tries to remember how to pray.

When they wheel Tom out of the scanning room Hannah leaps up and takes his hand again. It's ice cold.

The lift reluctantly transports them upwards, and on arrival Tom is pushed towards yet another set of double doors. Hannah looks up and sees that they are entering the stroke unit.

Dr Malik is back. 'We're going to look after Tom in here for now.' He gestures to the darkened ward behind him. 'We'll monitor him intensively and the nurses will make sure he's stable.' The ward is full of breath and night-time rustling. He gestures to a nurse behind the reception desk. She comes out and helps to push Tom into the bay on their left.

Dr Malik leans towards Hannah, speaking in a low voice.

'We're just going to set Tom up in a bed and get him settled. Please can you wait here?' He gestures towards a door labelled QUIET ROOM. 'We won't be long.'

'Why?' Hannah feels a pulse of anger. 'I should be with him.'

'We just need a few minutes. Then you can come through.'

Once again Tom is surrounded by people while Hannah is left by herself. She walks to the window and looks down at a forbidding floodlit sculpture in the courtyard below. She thinks of all the calls she needs to make and the bad news she has to break and feels like banging her head against one of its twisted metal spikes.

She can barely acknowledge what's happening herself. She has no idea how to tell other people.

She sits back down and pulls her phone out of her bag. She takes a deep breath and dials Julie's number. As the phone rings she imagines Tom's sister disentangling herself from whichever man she is dating this week. Not that she expects an answer – Julie has a strong track record of committed unconsciousness till noon.

A voice surprises her by drawling down the line. 'Yeah?'

'Julie. It's Hannah.' She tries to keep her voice calm. Comforting.

It doesn't work. Julie has an appetite for disaster. She can find it in even the happiest of situations. 'What is it? What's wrong?'

Hannah lowers her voice still further. 'I'm afraid Tom's in hospital. He's had a stroke.'

'*What?*' Julie greets the news with a cough that belongs in a TB clinic. 'Is he . . .? Is he still . . .?'

'Yes, Julie. He's still alive. He's stable now and they're going to monitor him overnight.'

'Shit.' Hannah hears rustling, and the repeated click of a lighter failing to work. 'SHIT.'

'Julie?'

Hannah hears the sound of a hand slapping against skin. A man indignantly grunting. Julie's bedfellow is not going to be allowed to sleep for much longer.

Julie's voice, to whoever it is, is sharp. 'Look, can you make this bloody lighter work?'

A deep voice. 'It's six a.m., Jules. Go back to sleep.'

Hannah rubs her eyes, trying to release the ache of tension clamped across her brows. She hears more grunts. Then Julie again. 'I'm having some really bad news here, can you just sodding do something and light me a fag?'

Hannah sighs. 'Julie?'

'Yeah, just a second.' Hannah hears frantic clicking again. 'It doesn't bloody work, just sort it out will you? My brother's just had a stroke, OK?'

Somehow Hannah doesn't think the relationship will last much longer. She takes a deep breath. 'Listen, things are bad, Jules, but the good news is that they've already got him on the stroke unit where they can monitor him and give him the treatment he needs.'

'So he'll be all right?'

'I don't know.' Hannah feels overwhelmed by exhaustion. 'I have to go now, but come up here as quickly as you can. Please?'

'But the car's knackered. I don't know—'

Hannah cuts in. For once Julie will have to sort herself out. 'Take the train or something. Anything. We're at the stroke unit at King's Lane Hospital. I'm sorry but I really do have to get back to Tom.'

'OK.' Julie's voice sounds suddenly frail. 'Give him my love. Please?'

'I will. See you soon.'

She hears the sobs starting as she hangs up.

When Hannah is allowed through to the ward Tom is caged in a bed, surrounded by beeps and needles. A clear IV bag hangs from a stand above him. Fear churns in her stomach as she sinks into a chair at the side of the bed and reaches out to hold his hand.

Dr Malik leans against the bed and looks at her. He speaks in a low voice. 'The next twenty-four hours are really important. We'll be watching for complications and trying to find out why he had the stroke and how much rehabilitation he will need.'

Hannah watches Tom's breathing. In. Out. She feels that if she looks away even for a second it might stop.

She feels the tears start to fall.

'How long can I stay here with him?'

'Take as much time as you like.'

'Thank you.'

As he leaves she turns to Tom and is struck by how young he looks. The semi-darkness wipes away his corporate frown lines until he's the man who couldn't take his eyes off her in a Soho diner. Happy days . . . She raises her eyes to the ominous lines on the monitors as tears slide down her cheeks.

She is overwhelmed by how much they have lost.

She becomes aware of a faint pressure on her fingers and looks down to see that Tom's right hand has closed around hers. His eyes are also full of tears. She hasn't seen him cry for years.

Tom. Oh Tom.

She caresses his face and waits silently until his eyes close. As his breathing deepens she thinks about what she was going to say to him today. The words that she has been building up to for weeks. Months.

She drops her head into her hands and whispers a plea into the sighing darkness of the ward.

Nobody hears.

Receipt: £35.75, Rainbow Bar

Summer 2006

Their first date ended in a gay bar.

'This isn't exactly the romantic atmosphere I was going for.' He felt himself sliding off his leopardskin stool and tried to use his elbows to clamp himself to the tiny metal table.

'I don't know what you mean.' Hannah shrugged off her leather jacket and ran a hand through her exuberant curls. A smile lifted the corner of her glistening lips. He was desperate to kiss them, but every time he'd plucked up the courage to try she seemed to take a sip of her drink or a bite of her food.

It was driving him crazy.

Hannah sat daintily on her stool. 'What could be more romantic than drinking toxic margaritas out of a fluorescent pink bucket?'

'True.' He nodded. 'It's what movies are made of.' He sipped through his straw, averting his eyes as chests considerably more manly than his own leant against the bar beside them. 'It was more the music I was thinking about.'

'What?' She pulled an exaggeratedly shocked face. 'And there was me thinking you'd asked the DJ to play it specially.'

He shook his head as A-ha's 'Take on Me' pumped through the speakers. 'I'm afraid not.' He put his hand on hers, feeling lucky when she didn't flick it away.

Her fingers were warm against his. 'Typical law student. You're probably too busy taking yourself seriously to appreciate a good old-fashioned pop song like this one.'

He rolled his eyes. 'And you're too much of a frivolous English student to know any better.' He shook his head with mock solemnity. 'And if you're a fan of this crap, then I'm afraid I might consider it grounds to cross your name off the list for date two.'

'Really?' She leant forward and he had another chance to appreciate the view provided by her low-cut pink top. 'And who else is on this list? Who's my competition?'

He raised his eyebrows. 'Too many candidates to mention, I'm afraid.'

She pulled back. 'I see. So all those nights you couldn't do last week – when you said you were busy working at the pub – you were out with other women?' Her tone was mischievous, but he saw a flicker of concern in her eyes before she dropped them to the table. 'I suppose it's good to know where I stand.'

He couldn't tell if she was being serious.

He leant forward to take her hand again, only for the stool to do its best to foil him. He teetered precariously before gaining his balance. Cool, Tom. Cool.

'Believe me, Hannah, there are no hordes of women in my life. There's my mum. My sister. And I quite like the woman who sells me my Saturday paper, even though she keeps showing me pictures of her endless grandkids. But that's about it.'

Hannah kept her gaze lowered. 'Really?'

'Really.'

She raised her head and took a sip from her straw. He was so relieved to see her smile. 'I wasn't really worried, of course.' She shook her head. 'I mean, obviously I'm besieged by admirers everywhere I go.'

He suspected this was true. But he also saw that she had absolutely no idea. It only made him like her more.

He tried to flex one of his biceps. It didn't oblige. 'Well, I'll beat them all up. Obviously.'

She leant towards him. 'Obviously.' She opened her eyes wide. 'Now that would be a sight for sore eyes.'

'Would it?' He feigned a cool he utterly didn't feel.

'Yes.' She arched an eyebrow. 'Anyway, what would I be missing out on? If I didn't make the cut for date two?'

He zipped his fingers across his mouth and shook his head.

'Oh, I see.' The disco lights caught the silver pendant at her throat. 'You're doing your mysterious thing again.'

'That's right.' He leant towards her. His lips were nearly on hers. At last.

'Is your phone vibrating, or are you just pleased to see me?'

He took a second to realise he wasn't kissing her yet.

'Oh, right.' He took out his phone. 'It's just my mum.' He switched it off and put it back in his pocket.

'This late?' Hannah looked concerned. 'Are you sure she's OK? You can call her back if you like.'

'She's fine. She just likes to say hello when her shift ends.' He braved reaching out to stroke Hannah's hair. 'Now let's get back to that man of mystery stuff. I was enjoying that.'

She placed a finger on his lips. 'Shut up and kiss me.'

So he did. She tasted of citrus and hope.

Take That started to play. He didn't even notice.

Three

'I'm fine.' Julie nods decisively. 'Totally fine.'

Hannah looks at the bin by Tom's vacant bed. She counts how many empty cans of Diet Coke it contains.

Four.

It's 9 a.m.

Julie is not fine.

'Are you sure?'

'Yes.' As Hannah watches, Tom's sister reaches into her pocket and pulls out a bar of chocolate. With her shaking hands and constant caffeine consumption, Julie reminds Hannah of a panicking GCSE student rather than the twenty-three-year-old she really is. Any minute now she'll pull out a can of Red Bull and the picture will be complete.

'Would you like some water, Jules?' Hannah indicates the plastic jug on the tray over the bed. 'It's boiling in here.' She feels sweat prickle beneath her armpits and tries to put her tea down to shrug off her cardigan. She can barely find a space among the cards and presents that cover the white cabinet by Tom's bed. 'Get Well Soons' mingle with chocolates and flowers, and Tom's firm has outdone itself by sending a Selfridges fruit basket that is roughly the size of a Labrador. It is crowned by a pineapple wrapped in an offensively cheerful turquoise bow and encased in silvery layers of plastic that crackle to the touch.

Hannah rolls her eyes in frustration. Tom's colleagues clearly have no idea how bad things are. A week after his stroke Tom is still so exhausted he can barely chew, let alone wrestle with the finest efforts of the Selfridges gift-wrapping department.

'No.' Julie is losing her fight with the chocolate bar. 'I don't want any water.' She impatiently tries to rip it open with her teeth. 'Damn it.' She leans forward and throws her head into her hands.

'It's all right, love.' The man in the next bed lowers bushy eyebrows in concentration as he struggles to eat his morning cornflakes. Milk drips down the front of his blue striped pyjamas as his right hand jerks upwards, keeping a tenuous hold on the spoon. The waxy yellow of his skin contrasts cruelly with the oppressive pink walls of the stroke unit and strands of white hair splay sideways from his head as if making a feeble bid for freedom.

'Morning, John. How are you?' Hannah gives him a smile as Julie turns in his direction. For a hideous second it looks like Julie's going to launch into her fourth major explosion since arriving here.

'Dandy.' John's smile is lopsided. He loses his fight with the spoon and orange flakes splatter across his grey hospital blanket. He jerks his head awkwardly from side to side and his piercing blue eyes twinkle in their direction.

'Things could be worse, love.' His throaty chuckle belongs at a pub lock-in. 'At least you're not wearing your breakfast like me.'

Julie presses her lips into a semblance of a smile. Hannah knows she isn't keen on interruptions and steps in before Julie can speak. 'But you do it with such style, John.'

'Don't I?' The old man indicates the milky mess on his lap. 'I'm all style, me. In the old days I'd—'

'Yes. Well. I just need a moment. Sorry.' Julie stands up and draws the green stripy curtain between the beds. Hannah mouths an apology to John as he disappears.

'God. There's no privacy in here. At ALL.' Julie looks around resentfully at the other occupants of the four-bed bay. Hannah briefly considers having the word 'sorry' tattooed across her forehead. It might save some time.

'I mean, I just need some space to process this, you know?' Julie resumes her battle with the wrapper. She rips it open and breaks off two dark squares of chocolate. She pops them into her mouth without offering any to Hannah. No surprise there.

'I'm just really worried, you know? If Tom can tear his . . .' Julie curls a strand of hair around her finger, staring at the grey ceiling panels for inspiration.

Hannah helps her out. 'Tear his carotid artery?'

'Yeah, yeah.' Julie nods impatiently. 'I was about to say that.' She exhales. 'If he can do that and have a stroke then maybe . . .' Her eyes widen and she peters out.

Hannah stays silent as she tries desperately to think of something to say. Something comforting. Something true. She knows what Julie is thinking. What Julie is fearing.

She knows she would be fearing it too.

Julie puts more chocolate into her mouth. 'Then maybe . . .'

Hannah tries to help. 'Maybe it might happen to you too?'

Julie nods. 'Yeah.' Her voice is tiny. Hannah sees the shadows beneath the wide green eyes. The way Julie is chewing on her lower lip. The fear. The need.

Hannah opens her mouth, only to see Julie balling the wrapper up and hurling it viciously at the bin.

The moment is gone.

'Anyway. No point thinking about that.' Julie stands up and starts pacing around Tom's bed. 'No point at all.' She moves fast. To the window. Back. To the curtain. Back.

Hannah frowns as she feels her daily headache making an entrance. She reaches up and presses the flats of her hands against her forehead in a fruitless effort to keep it at bay. She inhales deeply and smells stale breakfast and antiseptic lemons. She craves a field or a vase of flowers. Even the hospital car park full of south London's finest fumes would be refreshing right now.

She looks at Julie. 'Let's remember the good stuff. OK? Tom's stable. He's starting to speak. He knows who he is.' She swallows. 'The doctors keep saying he's doing well.'

Julie snorts derisively and draws her tall frame up to its full height. Even in her highest heels Hannah would need a ladder to reach her clavicle. 'Sure. That's just what they said about my mum. So that means exactly bugger all.'

Hannah has no answer to that. Instead she stares at the rumpled sheets on Tom's bed, remembering the waking hell of that endless night. Even now Tom is stable she can't stop watching him. Can't be caught off guard. As days become nights become days she watches his chest as it rises and falls, his mouth as it tries to form words, his limbs as they start to try to move again. If she stops looking even for a second it might happen again. She can't let it.

She is guilty enough already.

Julie pivots and her boots squeak against the floor. 'What would you know about it anyway?' Hannah sighs as Julie stalks to the window, staring at the inspiring view of a concrete wall. She is used to being the target of Julie's rage. She's had a lot of practice. 'It's not like you actually bothered turning up when Mum was ill.'

Hannah opens her mouth to defend herself. Closes it. In over a decade of trying she has never succeeded in getting Julie to see her side of the story. The heat of a hospital ward is hardly going to encourage her to change her mind.

Julie flicks her long dark hair. 'Can you lend me a tenner?'

'Another?' The word comes out before Hannah has a chance to stop it.

'Yeah.' Julie crosses her arms across her chest, her green jumper stretching even tighter across her body. 'I need some more food. To keep me going in here. This isn't exactly easy for me, you know.'

'Yes. I know.' Hannah feels like pointing out that she's not having the time of her life either. She hasn't slept since she found Tom, unable to close her eyes without seeing his body jack-knifed on the floor. Now he's stable they won't let her stay past visiting hours any more, so she spends the nights at home staring at the clock, drinking her way steadily through the hours until it's time for her to come to the hospital again.

Her eyes sting and she runs a hand over her face. Her skin feels tight and dry. She can practically feel herself ageing.

She takes a deep breath. 'Can't you use the cash machine downstairs?'

Julie looks at her like she belongs in a bin. 'I just need

a tenner.' She taps her thigh anxiously. 'You two are so loaded, lending me a tenner can't be a problem, can it?'

Hannah restrains herself yet again from lecturing Julie about terrifying mortgages, or the fact that her midnight Googling has revealed that half the people who have a stroke never work again.

She tries a different tack. 'I could get you something from the café. I'm about to head there for breakfast.' She smiles. 'We could go together?'

Julie considers this for all of a nanosecond. 'No.' She shakes her head. 'You go if you want to. I don't want to leave him. It's too—' There's a sob in her voice and she runs a hand over the bed as she tries to collect herself. Her eyes glisten and she gulps a deep breath. She smooths the pillow with her hand and speaks as if to herself.

'When we were little I used to make him play doctors and nurses every day after school. No matter what. I was obsessed with *Home and Away* so he always pretended to be this Aussie doctor on a surfboard – Dr Monk.'

Hannah nods, not wanting to speak and break the spell.

Julie pulls the sheet up straight. Hannah sees the tenderness on her face and can imagine her as a little girl dressed up in her nurse's outfit, watching the door as she waited for her beloved big brother to come back home.

Tom has always said how close they were back then.

Julie sighs. 'He was always running in and saving the life of my teddy or my Barbie before leaping on his pretend surfboard and shooting away.' She smiles and her whole face lifts. 'He got really into it. Or at least he said he did. He used to play with me for hours. Even when he had footie practice to go to. Or a girl he wanted to see.' She wipes her eyes with the back of her hand. 'He loved his footie.' Her voice breaks. 'I wonder if he'll ever play again?'

'Of course he will.'

'You can't know that.'

'No. But I believe it.' Hannah reaches out her hand and places it tentatively on Julie's arm. 'He can get better, if anyone can.'

Julie stays silent. Hannah keeps trying. 'Look, I know how you must be feeling, but—'

Julie snatches her arm away. 'No. You don't.' Her face hardens. 'You have absolutely no idea. I don't even know why I just told you all that. Look, I just need a tenner, OK?'

Sighing, Hannah gets out her wallet and hands the money over. 'There you go.'

Julie takes it without a thank you. 'I'll pay you back.'

Hannah is absolutely certain that she won't. 'Sure.'

Julie frowns. 'Don't you believe me?'

Hannah raises her eyes to the ceiling. Her patience is fraying rapidly and if she stays here she might well say something she regrets. 'I'll just go and grab breakfast.' She picks up her bag and starts to walk away.

The strident voice follows her. 'What's your problem, Hannah?'

My husband had a stroke. On the day I was going to leave him.

For a wild second Hannah thinks she's said the words out loud.

She swallows them back down and keeps walking. John winks as she passes his bed, his face grey and pained. She does her best to smile in return.

'Just in time, Hannah.'

Hannah quickens her step as she sees that Tom is back

from his shower, his dark hair wet and combed back from his face. Julie has disappeared again, presumably in pursuit of sugar. Or nicotine. Or both.

Sandra stands beside Tom, wearing the white top and dark blue trousers of the physiotherapy team, her hand resting on the back of his wheelchair. His tracksuited body is bolstered into place with pillows that are nearly as white as his skin, and his left arm lolls uselessly across the armrest. The grey and black bulk of the wheelchair is reminiscent of the era of the steam train and the thick grey wheels are in possession of an extremely forceful mind of their own.

'Are you ready to help him back into bed, Hannah?' Hannah suspects that it would take a machete to remove the relentless smile from Sandra's face.

'Absolutely.' Hannah is getting good at lying.

'I.' Tom inhales. 'Can do it.' He pronounces each syllable carefully. He still slurs when tired, but his words are getting clearer every day. As is the fact that he is sullen. Angry.

Lost.

Hannah has never seen him this defeated. She bites her lip to stop the tears she knows he hates. She can cry them later.

'Not quite yet, Tom.' Sandra shakes her head. 'Soon you can. But we just need to build up your strength a little more, all right?'

Tom grunts.

'Great.' Sandra has a robust negativity filter. She must need it in here. She looks at Hannah. 'Ready to transfer him? Remember you're supporting his weight while he reaches across from the chair to the bed. OK?' She presses a button and lowers the hospital bed until it is level with the wheelchair.

'OK.'

'Stand on his left side, please.'

Tom's bare feet look strangely vulnerable as Hannah moves into position. His grey tracksuit bottoms flap mournfully around his ankles.

'Good. Now get ready to steady his torso with your arms as he pushes to stand.'

Hannah circles her arms loosely round his body.

'Now, Tom. Push up using your right arm. Hannah, steady him if he needs it . . . that's right!'

It doesn't feel right. Hannah is boiling hot and her right arm is helpfully reproducing the nervous tremor she gets whenever she has to carry more than one drink in the pub. She can feel Tom shaking. Struggling.

She stands beside him, feet planted wide, straining to stop him falling. He's barely eaten anything in hospital but she still doesn't think she can support him. Behind the curtain cutting them off from the next cubicle she hears John retching. She knows how he feels.

Sandra's crisp voice continues. 'Well done, Tom. You're up. Now look across and grab the bed with your right hand. Hannah, get ready to block his knee with yours.'

'What?'

Sandra sees her confusion. 'You know. Support his left knee with yours if it buckles.'

'OK.' She moves her leg and glances at his face. It's ashen. His arm flails limply in mid-air as Hannah becomes aware of sweat dripping incessantly between her boobs. Her right eye starts to water.

'I—'

At last his hand clasps the bed.

'Well done, Tom!' Sandra claps her hands together. 'Now put all your weight on that arm and slide your bum across from chair to bed. Hannah's here to support you.'

Hannah fears her ability to help will be severely limited by an imminent back injury. She summons her remaining strength. 'Come on, Tom. We can do it.'

Sweat beads on Tom's forehead as he pivots across and lands heavily on the bed. Sandra moves to stop him keeling to the left and grins, showing extraordinarily straight teeth. 'Nice work.' Tom turns away and Hannah sees a tear rolling slowly down his cheek.

Sandra's voice is still set to CHEERFUL mode. 'So that's how to get Tom back into bed.'

'Great.' Hannah stretches her aching arms over her head. 'Easy-peasy.'

'And on and off the loo.' Sandra nods with satisfaction. 'We can practise that next.'

'Yippee.' Hannah realises the words have come out more sarcastically than intended as she receives a reproving glance from Sandra.

The physio rapidly moves on. 'Now that Tom's stable we're starting a full programme of therapy to help him regain his physical skills.' She waves a hand. 'Like shaving, sitting, cooking . . . And soon we'll get him up on his feet. Walking with a frame.'

Tom sighs. Hannah puts her hand on his shoulder but he shrugs it away. She feels the familiar thud of failure. She has no idea how to help him.

He looks up at Sandra. 'Want to . . . talk to . . .' He indicates Hannah with his head.

Sandra flicks impatient eyes to her watch. 'OK.' Her white trainers squeak as she turns. 'Back soon.'

Hannah looks at Tom.

'What is it, soldier?'

He keeps staring at the ceiling. His words come out spasmodically, as if even his mouth has turned against him. 'Don't. Don't call me that.'

'Sorry.' She holds the glass out for him again.

He pushes it away with his right hand. 'I can't even drink. Not without you.' Anger flares across his face.

She winces, and puts the glass down on the table.

'I know it's hard, but—'

'Hard?' He looks at her incredulously. '*Hard*? Look at me.' Tears of frustration well up in his eyes. 'I can't piss. Can't shave. Can't even bloody sit up.' His face contorts with rage as he looks at his cards and presents. 'One minute I'm a lawyer with a—' His face is grey with exhaustion but he pushes on. 'With a sports car and now I'm someone who gets fucking fruit baskets.' He reaches out and does his best to push the offending object to the floor. 'I don't even like fruit.' The basket refuses to move but all the cards start to cascade downwards, forming a colourful mosaic of false hope on the floor. Hannah stands, staring at the pain on his face, desperate to fix it.

'Shit.' His tears are flowing now. 'Why did this happen?' Hannah gets a tissue from her pocket and silently wipes them away. 'And why am I crying?' He closes his eyes as if to hold the tears back. 'I never cry.'

Her voice feels tight. 'I don't know.'

'Of course you don't bloody know.' She is horribly used to the rage in his eyes. She's been living with it for months. Before the stroke he'd said it was because of her. Her selfishness. Her neediness. Her mistakes.

Now it's not her fault and yet somehow she feels even worse.

Tom's still trying to talk, though his voice is increasingly strained. 'I don't know why I'm saying this. You can't . . . do anything.'

'I know, Tom. But all we can do is concentrate on getting you better.'

'Better?' He practically spits the words out. 'I'm not getting better.' His eyes are bleak as they meet hers. 'Face it. This is it. I'm a cripple.'

'No, Tom.' She desperately searches for the right words. 'You're not a cripple.'

He lifts his left hand with his right. Lets go. Watches as it falls down to the bed. 'Yes I am.'

'No.' She shakes her head. 'The doctors say—'

'Doctors.' He dismisses them with one shake of his head.

'Come on, Tom.'

He doesn't listen. 'No.' He gestures to his inert left-hand side. 'This is it. Lucky you.'

Guilt pierces her and she tries to take his hand. 'No, Tom. I—'

'Hello mate.' A deep voice cuts into their conversation. 'What's that bloody awful tracksuit? Don't you know grey isn't your colour?'

'Nick.' Hannah has never been more delighted to see him.

'Hey, mate.' Tom frantically wipes away his tears as his best friend walks towards the bed.

A tiny flicker at the corner of Nick's mouth is the only sign of his shock at seeing Tom. Nick is tall and broad in his navy suit. He looks almost offensively healthy amidst the grey hair and mumbling of the ward.

'Wow, you're really lowering the average age in here, Tom.' He leans in and speaks in a whisper. 'I've always said you were an old git at heart. Did you bring your slippers?'

Tom very nearly smiles.

Nick turns to Hannah. 'How are you?' He puts his hand on her shoulder. 'I bet you're doing a great job looking after this nightmare patient.'

Hannah frowns. 'I don't think so.'

'I do.' Nick holds her eyes. 'A great job.'

Hannah bites her lip to keep the tears away. 'I don't know about that.' She picks up her jacket. 'I think I'll go and get some air. Leave you to it.'

'Good plan.' Nick sits down in a chair next to the bed. 'Now, Tom, you've got three choices of reading matter. A: miracle stories about stroke survivors. B: the latest John Grisham. Or C: *The Times* sports section.'

A smile twitches across Tom's face. 'Stupid question. C.'

'OK.' Nick opens the paper with a flourish. 'But if you're going to make me read about bloody Spurs then I may have to ram that ridiculous pineapple where the sun don't shine.'

Hannah checks her phone as she walks away.

Another new text has arrived.

I miss you.

She leaves the ward and leans against the wall by the lifts, staring at the words.

I can't stop thinking about you.

She touches the screen for a second, her fingers itching to reply.

No. Not now. Not any more.

She deletes the texts and walks on.

A 2p coin

September 2006

'So . . .' Hannah smiled at him as she pulled the purple duvet around her. Her breath clouded in front of her mouth in the chill of her tiny room. 'What do you want to be? In your wildest dreams?'

He ran his hand down the smoothness of her thigh. 'Here.'

She laughed and arched across him to reach the packet of cigarettes on her bedside table.

'I don't think staying here would earn you much money.' She placed something cold and round on his chest. 'That's about all I can afford to pay you.'

He looked down to see a 2p coin. 'Hmmm. I thought you were posh?'

She grinned. 'Not that posh.'

He sighed. 'Well, that's not exactly the starting salary I'm looking for when I graduate. I'd like to be able to afford food.'

She smiled as she placed a cigarette in her mouth and lit it with the Union Jack lighter that had somehow become hers. She exhaled. 'You'll just have to work part-time for me then. I'll pay you in favours. Like a queen.'

'Fine by me.' He curled an arm around the warmth of her body. 'I've always thought you had a regal way about you.'

She giggled. 'How my mum would laugh if she heard you say that. She always says what a clodhopper I am.'

'Does she?' Tom saw a familiar line start to cut across Hannah's forehead. The 'mum' frown.

'Yep.' Hannah nestled into his chest. 'She loves telling people how clumsy I am.'

He heard the sigh in her voice and tried to cheer her up. 'What does she know? She's obviously never seen you dancing on a table after downing your body weight in white wine. You'd fit right in at the Royal Ballet. Or whatever it's called.'

The smile returned to Hannah's face and he felt a glow of satisfaction. 'True.' She turned her head towards him, eyes wide. 'But seriously. What would you be? If you could be anything?'

He gently caressed her forearm. It was not something he ever thought about. Apart from a brief dream of playing football for England, it had always been law. Ever since he'd met that barrister on the train to Bristol when he was thirteen. The guy had given him a can of beer and talked about how he was changing the world. Righting wrongs. Protecting the little guys.

The life he described sounded exciting. Fulfilling. A world away from drinking cider in fields and a mum who stared out of the window every night wishing his dad would come back.

'Go on, tell me.' Hannah prodded him.

He sucked in his stomach as he pulled her closer. Since they'd started dating his running regime had been reduced to the occasional dash to the newsagent's for fags or beers. Every morning he woke up full of jogging intentions, but then couldn't tear himself away from her.

He wound one of her curls around his finger. 'What do I want to be? In my dreams?'

'Yeah.'

'I'd quite like to be an international layabout. With a yacht. And my own personal island.'

'Sounds exciting.' She took another drag. 'Where would you go? In your yacht?'

'Everywhere.'

'Wow, that's quite a voyage.' She giggled. 'Can I come and be a layabout with you?'

He smiled at how casually she mentioned the future. 'Of course. I'll even chuck in a few bikinis and give you the key to my luxury cabin.'

She nodded, satisfied. 'I think I'd enjoy a luxury cabin.'

'I bet you would.' He leant over and kissed her.

She broke away to stub her cigarette out in the misshapen brown ashtray made for her by one of her endless male friends. The ashtray reminded Tom of the craps his dad's terrier used to do after devouring the contents of the kitchen bin, but Hannah was devoted to it.

She leant back on the pillows. 'And in real life? Why law?'

He grinned. 'Because you make loads of money.'

She made a face. 'Really? Isn't there more to it than that?'

'Of course.' He bit back a sharper retort. Her friends were all going into charities or becoming musicians after university. Easy to do when you have ongoing access to the bank of Mum and Dad.

He pushed the thought away. 'That's not the whole reason. It's interesting. And competitive.'

'That'll suit you, then.' She rolled her eyes. 'I saw your face when Spurs lost last week.'

He flinched at the memory. 'I was fine with that.'

'No, you weren't. It took you three pints to be able to get a sentence out.' She leant up on one elbow. 'And even then you insisted on having a hotter curry than anyone else. Just to prove yourself.' She upturned his palm and kissed it. 'But seriously. What kind of lawyer do you want to be? Like Atticus Finch? Fighting the good fight? Or like . . .' She screwed up her face. 'Gordon Gekko?'

He gently shook his head. 'He was a banker.'

She punched him gently on the arm. 'Oh, come on. You know what I mean. One of those city slicker types.'

He loved to tease her. 'Honestly? I don't know what kind. I just want a pair of those red braces.'

'Shut up!' This time she hit him with a pillow. 'I hate those things.'

'Why? I'd be sexy in them!' He dodged away as she pillowed him again. Then he grabbed her and rolled on top of her and the laughing stopped and nothing else mattered but them.

Afterwards he pulled her head onto his chest, dark curls fanning out against his skin. He felt peaceful. Whole.

'So what do *you* want to be?'

Hannah's voice was muffled by the duvet. 'When I grow up?'

'Exactly.'

She waved a hand around in the air. 'Take a look around. What do you think I want to be?'

He surveyed the room.

He pointed in the direction of a spider plant dying a lingering death on her desk. 'I hope you're not aiming to be a gardener.'

She shook her head. 'Not if you paid me. Which you wouldn't. Next guess, please.'

He slowly examined her walls. Fairy lights hung from a shelf straining under the weight of more books than most people read in a lifetime. The dark spines of Penguin classics were stacked next to the muted greys and greens of textbooks on practical criticism. An A4 notepad lay open on the desk with illegible violet scrawl across its pages. Books were piled in the tiny sink. Books were stacked on the floor.

He rubbed his chin thoughtfully with his fingers. 'Ooh, I don't know. Could it have something to do with books?'

'Wow.' She giggled. 'You could be on *Mastermind*.'

'True.' He nodded. 'Specialist subject: stating the obvious.'

She tutted. 'Try harder.'

'Do you want to be a novelist?'

She shook her head. 'Too lonely. Try again.'

'Publishing?'

'Thought about it.' She ran her fingers lightly across his chest. 'But *wrong*.'

'Damn.' He sighed. 'Teaching?'

'Third time lucky.' He felt her stiffen. 'Don't tell Mum, though. She's still hoping I'll have a personality transplant and become an accountant like her.'

Tom raised an eyebrow. 'Not likely?'

'God, no.' He felt her shoulders tense as she answered. 'First there's the maths thing. Not for me. But secondly she's *miserable*. All she talks about is traffic and taxes. Why on earth would I want to be like her?'

'OK.' Tom made a mental note never to bring up her mother again. 'So why teaching?'

'Tricky one.' She kissed his cheek. 'Because everything I say always sounds like a massive cliché. But I helped out on a summer camp a couple of years ago – for disadvantaged kids. And I loved it. That lightbulb moment when they understand something.' Her whole face glowed. 'Amazing.' She shrugged. 'Of course, you only have about two of those moments a week, but if you make the difference for just one kid then it's all worth it.' She smiled. 'And I am a bit of a book fan . . .'

'You don't say.'

'So talking about them all day seems like a pretty good deal to me.'

He smiled. 'So you have a vocation?'

'Yeah.' She grinned. 'I guess I do.' She sank back into the pillows and looked up at the world map taped onto the ceiling. 'And it's a bloody good way of funding my travel habit. The world's my oyster.'

He gazed at the map, seeing the way a large number of countries had been coloured in with a pink highlighter. 'Are those the places you've been to? The pink ones?' He turned his head towards her, scared by how much he didn't want her to leave him. Already. They'd only been together a few weeks.

'Yep.' She nodded. 'Only the rest of the planet to go.' She smiled. 'Tanzania's the place I really dream about. Ever since Dad got me a book on the Serengeti when I was little.' She sighed. 'But I'll go anywhere. I want a passport so full there's no room for stamps any more.'

'Right.'

His passport barely had any stamps at all.

She chewed at a hangnail. 'I'm going away this weekend, actually.'

'You are?'

'Yep. Just me and a few friends.'

He resisted the urge to ask if any of them were male. 'Where are you going?' His attempt at nonchalance sounded distinctly falsetto.

'To Spain. For a music festival.' He felt her eyes on him. Wide. Enticing. 'I'd really love it if you came. We're leaving tonight.'

Just like that. This was how Hannah operated. Last minute. Seat of the pants. Do. It. Now.

Frustration kicked. 'I don't know . . .' He was due to head home to his mum's this weekend and his bank account was already at full stretch.

'Your phone's ringing.' Hannah pushed herself up and swung her legs out of bed. 'I'll go pee.'

He loved the way she didn't try to be polite. The way she blew her nose as loudly as he did and talked about farting and could devour a chicken leg in under a minute. She was more earthy than other girls he'd been with, who would slide out of bed at dawn so their make-up was perfect by the time he woke up. Those girls made him feel dishevelled. Disorderly.

Hannah made him feel at home.

He kept watching her as he answered his phone.

'Tommo?'

'Hey, Jules.'

Hannah pulled on a long silk dressing gown that belonged in one of the black and white films she loved so much. She slipped out of the room and Tom sank back against the pillows.

'How's it going, Jules? Top of the class again this week, little sis?'

'Shut up.' Julie was embarrassed by her academic prowess even though it had landed her a scholarship to a school with its own polo field. 'No chance of that. Everyone's so clever in my class. It's even worse this year, now we're doing our exams.'

He felt a fierce stab of protectiveness and pride. 'Yeah,

43

well, it's easy for them to be clever when Mummy and Daddy have been force-feeding them Jane Austen from the minute they were conceived.'

'Whatever.' She sighed. 'Anyway, I just wanted to check what time you're heading home tomorrow. Mum's worrying about whether it'll clash with her shifts and she says you haven't returned any of her calls.'

Guilt needled him. 'Yeah, sorry about that.'

'We can't wait to see you.' Her voice was high. Girlish. He should see her more often. Go back to Somerset and take her out. He missed hearing her talking about the stories she was writing or following on behind her as she took him on her latest adventure walk around the Somerset woodland just behind their estate.

Julie's voice bubbled with enthusiasm. 'I've got so much planned. And I've got some history homework I'd really like your help with.'

He pictured her twirling the phone cord between anxious fingers, wearing her favourite blue tracksuit with her long dark hair brushing her shoulders.

'I'm sure you don't need my help, Jules.' He took a sip of water from a glass by the bed, wincing as he realised it was vodka. 'I have a feeling you'll do just fine without me.'

His sister's voice quavered. 'But you are coming home, aren't you? It's been ages.'

Hannah's phone beeped and he saw a text light up the screen. He couldn't help it. He had to look.

Hey Han, can't wait for our trip tonight. I'll bring the car, you bring the entertainment. Kisses, D.

Damian. Her ex. Tall and arrogant, with a wallet big enough to match his ego. Tom swallowed, pushing the phone away as Hannah came back into the room.

'Tommo?' His sister's voice faded into the background. He watched, transfixed as Hannah took off her dressing gown. Pale skin. Amazing arse. She had no idea how beautiful she was.

His words came out in a rush. 'I'm sorry, Jules, I can't come any more.'

'Really?' Julie's voice was tiny and he felt a stab of guilt. 'Why's that? I made your favourite lasagne and everything.'

He wavered, but one look at Hannah made everything clear.

'Sorry, Jules. I've just got so much study to do.'

'OK.' Julie's voice was hoarse with imminent tears. He heard a sniffle and then she rallied. 'Just make sure you buy me a penthouse when you're earning your millions in the city. Deal?'

He grinned. His little sister would be OK. She always was.

'Deal. I'll be down to see you soon. I promise.' He relaxed into Hannah's smile as she got back into bed. 'Love you.'

Hannah gazed at him as he hung up. 'So, are you coming?'

'*Sí.*' Tom buried the remains of his guilt in a long kiss. Right now he didn't care about home. He didn't care about all the study he hadn't done. When Hannah was this close he didn't care about anything but her. '*Sí, señorita.*'

She pulled away. 'Well, with Spanish like that on board we're going to be unstoppable.' She ran a hand down his cheek. 'I'm so happy you're coming.' She held his gaze for a second, her face serious. Then she smiled. 'I might actually have missed you.'

He felt excitement bubble inside him.

'Glad to hear it.' He picked up the 2p coin. 'I'll bring this too. Just to make sure we can really party.'

She grinned. '*Viva España.*'

Four

'Seriously? My brother has a stroke and *this* is what you do to me?'

Hannah recognises the voice and her heart sinks. She walks out of the lifts and sees a long dark ponytail by the window at the opposite end of the corridor. It is swinging from right to left at an alarming speed as its owner shouts into her phone.

Hannah walks unnoticed towards the physiotherapy gym, but can't help overhearing Julie's side of the conversation. In fact Julie's voice is so strident she suspects there are residents of Brighton who might be unintentionally tuning in.

Julie's voice rises higher. 'I can't believe this. I worked – like – really hard for you. And now you're firing me?' Expletives fill the air. A woman getting into the lift quietly cups her hands over her daughter's ears. Hannah watches as Julie pauses for essential oxygen intake. Then she starts swearing again.

Hannah has learnt by now that it is best not to approach the raging Julie, so instead she carries on walking towards the gym. Julie has been a barista in Costa Coffee for all of six weeks. It's her third job in a year. All of them have been AMAZING until the point where Julie is fired or decides to conduct a searing affair with a married colleague with absolutely no intention of leaving his wife.

Hannah sighs as she reaches the door. She pauses with her hand against the glass, dropping her head and taking a breath. Seeing Tom in here makes her want to punch the world for doing this to him. When he's in bed he looks like everyone else – whole. Human. In the gym he is set apart. Stripped bare. Sometimes she can barely watch as he tries to walk, his every faltering movement illuminated by the harsh neon lights above him.

God knows how *he* must feel.

She grits her teeth and pushes open the door.

Tom is in the middle of the room. Struggling. Staggering. His grey T-shirt is drenched and his face is stone. He is trying to take steps across the green rubber floor, supported on both sides by Sandra and her equally bouncy sidekick Amy.

Tom's head is down and his face contorts as he tries to move his left leg forward. Hannah balls her fists. It seems so cruel to do this to him. They should just let him lie. Let him recover. He isn't ready for this.

She looks away, staring through the big windows that look out across the London skyline. She can see the Houses of Parliament across the river. Buses on the move. A black speedboat cutting along the choppy grey waters of the Thames. In front of it she spies a pleasure boat full of tourists in bright yellow lifejackets. Even from this high up she can see them pointing. Laughing. Living.

She looks back at the gym. At Tom's world. One step. Two.

'You're doing really well, Tom.' Amy catches him as he keels to his right. Her arm is wrapped firmly around his shoulder. 'Now, let's just get back over there.' She indicates the blue raised plinth in the corner of the room.

Tom does his best to shake his head. 'Can't.'

'You know that word doesn't work in here, Tom.' A strand of auburn hair escapes from Amy's bun. Her white trainers squeak against the floor and the veins in her narrow arms stand out as she supports his weight. 'The more you move now, Tom, the sooner you'll be walking by yourself. OK? And I know how much you want that.'

'Can't.'

'Just try.' Amy's cheerful tone belongs on a breakfast radio show.

'OK, OK.' Tom tries again. Another tiny movement. Sandra supports him on the other side, keeping an eye on his failing left leg as it drags behind him, sabotaging every step.

Tom glances towards Hannah and she sees absolute despair in his eyes. Then he looks down. Away.

Hannah knows he is ashamed. He has always hated showing weakness. She thinks of the time that he fell off his bike and broke his wrist – how he had popped paracetamol throughout the night and only gone to A&E when he'd been unable to grip his handlebars the next morning.

She wants to say something. To make him feel better. To be the movie version of herself – leaping onto the wooden steps in the corner and making a resounding speech that inspires Tom to believe in himself again. She opens her mouth. 'Well done, Tom.' Her words sound ridiculous. Meaningless. They fall dully into the clammy sweat of the air.

She shakes her head and curls down onto the floor, next to stacks of grey walking frames and a black plastic bin full of rubber exercise balls.

The door opens and shuts behind her. She doesn't turn, assuming that it will be an angry Julie looking for her favourite human target. Hannah could do without that right now. She just wants a minute of peace. A minute to adjust.

'Tom's doing well.' Hannah looks up to see that Dr Malik is standing next to her. His arms are folded and his eyes narrow as he watches Tom.

'Really?' Hannah stands up again and leans towards him, keeping her voice low.

'Yes.' Dr Malik nods earnestly. 'He's only been on his feet a few days and he's already regaining his centre.'

'What do you mean?' Hannah looks at Tom's feeble steps, struggling to see any kind of centre at all. As he moves he keels constantly to the left, his face wearing a grim expression of resignation as his leg fails to take his weight.

Dr Malik points at Tom. 'He's starting to compensate for his weakness by pulling more to the right. Look. Sandra is giving him less support than she was when he started.'

'Are you sure?' Hannah tries to see a difference. Fails.

'Yes.' He scratches a hand over his stubble. 'It's not even baby steps yet. But it's progress.'

Hannah tries to take comfort from his confidence. 'I hope so.' She watches as Tom finally reaches the plinth. He has only taken about ten steps and looks ready to drop.

Sandra helps to lower him onto a bench and holds up some water for him to sip. His chest heaves up and down and sweat sticks his hair flat. Hannah thinks of the way he used to vault over fences or shoot across the football pitch and for a second the contrast stops her breath.

Sandra puts the water down again. 'Now Tom, how about we do some sitting to standing?'

'Sadists.' Tom's face is hollow. Pale. A muscle flickers in his cheek.

Sandra laughs as if he's just pulled off a killer gag in a comedy club. 'I don't know what you mean.' She nudges him with her hand. 'Now, come on. If you can't stand up, you can't go home.'

'Home?' Hannah feels the world screech to a halt. The hospital is bad enough. She has absolutely no idea how they will cope at home. Home has stairs. Awkward corners. No comforting professionals to tell her what to do. She turns to Dr Malik and the words rush out before she can think. 'Isn't it a bit soon?' She speaks louder than she intended and darts a look at Tom, hoping he hasn't heard. He is drinking his water and doesn't react.

'Not at all.' Dr Malik shakes his head. 'We start planning for discharge as soon as patients are admitted.' He presses his lips together. 'Tom will be moving independently before too long. Two, maybe three weeks? If he keeps pushing himself.'

'Three weeks?' Hannah feels faint and leans back against the wall for support. 'But it's only ten days since it happened.'

'I know.' Dr Malik nods. 'But Tom is young and healthy. He has every chance of a good recovery. Especially if he's at home with familiar things around him and . . .' He turns to Hannah and she feels the pressure of his expectation settling on her shoulders. 'And familiar people. He needs his loved ones around him. Helping him to adapt to his new circumstances.'

Hannah stands silently, suppressing a violent urge to cry. She wants to help Tom. She wants to be the Hannah that he needs.

She just wishes she knew how.

'He's already said he wants to get home rather than going to inpatient rehabilitation.' Dr Malik jangles the change in his pocket. 'But then he must have discussed that with you.'

He hasn't. 'Discussing' things isn't one of their talents. Hannah stares at her feet.

Dr Malik folds his arms. 'I know it doesn't seem like it, but Tom's one of the lucky ones.'

'Really?'

'Yes.' He looks her in the eye. 'The stroke was in the right side of his brain, and it only affected the left-hand side of his body. His arm. His leg. His movement. Physiotherapy will really help with that.'

'What does that mean? He'll totally recover?'

'We would expect to see some improvement.'

'I see.' She exhales. *Some improvement*. It could mean walking. Could mean a wheelchair for life. She wants definites. Facts. Things to count on.

Dr Malik continues. 'But his language skills are largely unaffected. That's a huge advantage.'

Hannah knows she ought to feel grateful but it's so hard while watching Tom trying to stand up. Failing. Trying again. Failing. The loss is too great. Too visual.

'Can you give me any idea of what we should expect, Dr Malik?' She is dreading his answer. 'From now on?'

He shrugs. 'Hard to say. It affects everyone differently.'

'Any clues?'

'We'll discharge him home with physio support.' He eyes Hannah. 'Your house will be fitted with ramps, grab-rails for him – adaptations so he can settle back in.'

'I see.' Hannah droops against the wall. Ramps won't help to rebuild their relationship. Won't help them to look each other in the eye.

Dr Malik puts his hand on Hannah's arm. 'He's determined. And he's young. Things are as positive as they can be.'

Hannah looks back at her husband.

'Come on, Tom. By yourself now.' Sandra stands back.

'No.' His voice breaks and he slumps sideways on the bench. 'Can't.'

'Yes. You can.' Sandra's voice brooks no refusal. 'Just try. You can do it, Tom.'

Hannah watches as Tom pushes himself slowly to his feet. He stands for a glorious second. Wavers. Staggers. Is caught and lowered back down.

'And again.' Sandra could enjoy a second career as a drill sergeant.

Tom shakes his head, speaking between gasps. 'You. Are. *Evil.*'

Sandra smiles. 'That's what they all say. But the harder you work, the less time you'll have to spend with me in here. The community physios you'll see at home are much nicer than me.'

He readies himself for another push. 'I don't believe you.'

She shakes her head. 'So cynical. Already. And you've barely even started. Now.' She looks at him expectantly. 'Stand up.'

Hannah looks at her husband. Standing. Teetering. Falling. Pushing upwards. Wobbling. Swearing. Falling.

Again. And again. And again.

It's the bravest thing she's ever seen.

A ticket to Tottenham Hotspur v
Charlton Athletic
December 2006

'So where's Mum pretending to be this year?'

Julie leant forward as she peered intensely at the pick 'n' mix display. She frowned thoughtfully before flipping open a plastic lid and scooping several white mice into her orange paper bag.

She straightened back up. 'She said she was going to work. Extra shift at the Premier Inn. They always need extra cleaners at this time of year.'

Tom added a couple of red shoelaces to his growing bag of sweets. 'Didn't she say that last year?'

'Yeah.' Julie eyed the cola bottles, her expression as intense as a NASA scientist at a space shuttle launch. 'But, of course, we both know what she's really doing.'

She looked at him sideways and they shared a quiet nod of understanding. Today their mum would be marking the anniversary of their dad's departure by crying in the pub where they'd spent their first date. She did the same every year. Half a bottle of gin later she would stagger home, climb into bed and then revert to her normal calm self the next morning.

Tom sighed as he dropped a Chomp into his bag. Every year she lied about where she was going and every year he and Julie lied about the fact that they knew, while quietly asking Mick the barman to keep an eye on her.

Meanwhile Tom and Julie were following their own

tradition. *Mary Poppins* and pick 'n' mix. As Julie tried to decide between lemon sherbets and chocolate eclairs, Tom remembered how he had watched the Christmas fairy lights blinking on and off as the shouting had begun in earnest in the kitchen. Then the crying. When the door-slamming started he had dragged his six-year-old sister out of the house and run into the local cinema with absolutely no plan apart from trying to stop her crying. *Mary Poppins* was playing. Perfect.

He had kept his arm round Julie and fed her sweets until her tears had stopped, hating his dad with all his might. Somehow Tom had known that this time his dad would stay away. This time he was never coming back.

Now every year they did the same thing. Thank God his dad had left in the Christmas holidays. Mary and her spoonful of sugar were always somewhere to be found.

'Hello Julie.' A blonde girl with incredibly tight jeans appeared beside them. She had heavily made-up eyes and her red lips stretched into what might have been an attempt at a smile.

'Sacha.' Julie straightened up, pulling self-consciously at her tracksuit top. 'Hi.'

Sacha's eyes ran down over Julie's outfit. Then upwards. They clearly didn't like what they saw. 'What film are you seeing?'

'Just . . .' Julie gave Tom a glance that begged him not to reveal the truth. She scuffed the floor with her trainer. '*Dreamgirls.*'

'Oh ya.' Sacha arched an eyebrow. 'I saw that last week. 'S'OK.'

A boy appeared, a red rugby shirt stretched tight across his chest.

'Hi, Rob.' Tom felt a pang of concern. Julie appeared

to be visibly shrinking in front of the two new arrivals. She was twisting a strand of hair in nervous fingers and was slumping downwards as if ashamed of her height.

'Hey, Julie.' Rob pushed his mop of blond hair out of his eyes before hooking his arm round Sacha's shoulders. 'Our film's about to start. See you.' He turned and steered them both away towards the man checking tickets by the stairs.

Tom looked at his sister, who looked like she was about to cry. 'Who were those two charmers?'

Julie stared at the ground. 'Just people from school.'

'Well, they seemed a bit—'

'Stop it, Tom.' The anxiety on her face surprised him. 'I don't want to talk about them. Not today. OK?'

'OK.' He nodded. 'No problem.'

'Thank you.'

He wanted to get the smile back on her face. 'How about we get you an extra-big portion of Astro Belts?'

'No.' Her eyes still lingered on the spot where Sacha and Rob had stood. Her hand fiddled with the zip of her tracksuit. 'I should probably go easy.'

He hated the self-doubt in her voice.

As they joined the pick 'n' mix queue he tried to think of something to say. 'How's English going at the moment? Written any more killer short stories?'

She smiled and the world was right again. 'No. I've been concentrating on maths.'

'Oh yeah?' He handed their bags over to be weighed. 'What are you planning now? Investment banker? Engineer?'

'No.' He loved her seriousness. 'I thought I might become a doctor.'

He turned to her. 'Oh my God, Jules, you'd be brilliant.'

She flushed. 'Only if I manage it. It's a lot of work.'

He had so much faith in her. 'You can do it. Look at the way you got into your school. No training. No special coaching. Just straight in on a full scholarship.'

Her face had fallen again. 'Yeah. Well. It's a shame I . . .'

He watched her. 'What?'

'Nothing.' She shook the thought away. 'I'll just need to do really well in my GCSEs.' He paid for the sweets and she took her bag and delved in, coming up with a cola bottle. She bit into it. 'Shall we go and watch Mary?'

'Sure.' He walked with her towards the ticket gate.

Her face was bright again. 'And then later we can eat baked beans and you can read me Biggles like we used to do.'

He felt the creep of guilt. 'Sorry, Jules, but I have to go back to London tonight.'

'You do?' The sadness was back. 'Why? To work?'

The trust on her face made him feel even worse.

'No. It's Hannah. She's got us tickets to a Spurs game. Tonight.'

'Oh.' Her eyes were clouded. Hurt.

He tried to talk his way into feeling better. 'And I know we always go home together, but this year I was hoping you wouldn't mind if I headed straight back to London after the film?'

She stayed quiet as the sounds of the cinema ebbed and flowed around them. The shake of popcorn. The squeals of a child.

Guilt kicked him in the stomach. 'I mean, I can stay if you want me to.'

Her face was setting into marble. Then she shook her

head. 'No. It's OK. I'm fine. You go back, Tom. If it makes you happy.' She even managed a smile. 'Hannah must be quite something.'

He nodded. 'Yeah. She is.'

Julie flicked her dark hair out of her eyes. 'Well, then. I'm glad you're happy, Tom. Really glad.'

As she led the way across the thick black carpet towards the cinema, Tom wondered if he should change his plans. He pulled out his phone, but then he thought of Hannah and pushed his doubts away.

Julie would be OK. She always was.

Five

'**E** at something.'

Hannah keeps typing. 'I just need to finish sending this.'

A large slice of pizza appears in front of her laptop screen.

'Go on.' Her best mate waves it towards her mouth. 'You know you want to.'

'In a second.' Hannah pushes it away. 'I have to send in these bloody lesson cover plans.' She finishes typing and presses send. 'Phew.'

The pizza reappears. This time a Post-it lies on its bubbling cheesy surface. *Eat me.*

'Hang on, Steph. I just want to check the email's actually gone.' Hannah checks her outbox. 'Right. Done. Hopefully that means evil Margaret has no excuse to harass me for the next twenty-four hours.'

Steph's long blonde hair flies as she vigorously shakes her head. 'I doubt that'll stop her.' She carves up the rest of the pizza and divides it between two plates. 'I miss Oliver. He was my kind of boss.'

'I know.' Hannah pushes herself up from Steph's sofa. 'He actually made me feel like I was good at teaching.'

'Yep.' Steph shoves a pile of magazines and books to one side and puts the plates on the table. 'It's been a while since I felt like that.'

Hannah hears a small click as she stretches her arms above her head. She feels old. Haggard. 'You'd have been way better as head of department, Steph. *Way* better.'

Steph reaches into a cupboard and pulls out two enormous wine glasses. 'I know.' She sloshes half a bottle of white wine into each one.

'Did I ever tell you what my mum said about it?' Hannah reaches out and takes a glass.

'No.'

'She said that I should have gone for the job.' Hannah takes her first sip. 'That it would have been the perfect step up the career ladder. That I should have factored it in to my five-year plan.'

'What bloody five-year plan?'

'Exactly.' Hannah thinks of her mum's rigid expression and gets a familiar urge to hit herself on the head with a blunt object. 'It's not like I'm aiming at being a head of department anyway. I'd hate all that paperwork.'

'True.' Steph nods. 'I bet Margaret laps it up though.'

'I bet she *loves* it.' Hannah shifts her neck from side to side, trying to ease the ache across her shoulders. 'It probably turns her on. I bet her ideal night is tucking herself up in bed with a Key Stage 3 spreadsheet and a glass of sherry.'

'And don't forget the "Teach yourself Mandarin" CD playing in the background. Just for added frivolity.' Steph puts her glass down on the table and pulls out one of the mismatched wooden chairs. 'Let's eat something. You look like shit.'

'Thanks, Steph. Just what I needed to hear.' Hannah sits down and runs a finger over one of the slices on her plate. She feels her stomach heave and rapidly lifts her hand away.

Steph flicks her fringe back from her face. 'Han, you've spent the past couple of weeks locked in a hospital surrounded by pensioners and illness. You were never going to emerge looking like you belong in a L'Oreal advert.'

Hannah arches an eyebrow. 'I think it's safe to say I never look like I belong in a L'Oreal advert.'

'Bollocks.' Steph takes a hearty bite of pizza. 'They'd love you. The only thing holding your modelling career back is your height. Or lack of it.'

'Cheeky.' Hannah sips her wine. 'I'm of average height, I'll have you know.'

'Yeah, right.' Steph seems to find this far too funny for Hannah's liking. 'Even in six-inch heels you can barely reach your own doorbell.' She pushes Hannah's plate towards her, and her eyes are suddenly serious. 'Now please. Eat something. You're looking so thin.'

'OK.' Hannah picks up a slice of pizza and takes a bite. For a second she's worried she won't be able to swallow, then she tastes the tomato and the tang of the pepperoni and her mouth fills with saliva. She chews and swallows and tears off another huge mouthful with her teeth. Her stomach gurgles with gratitude.

'That's more like it.' Steph leans back in her chair. 'Now we're getting your blood sugar levels back up you can tell me how you are.'

Hannah doesn't want to talk about how she is. She quickly takes another mouthful, so that all she can manage is a shrug.

'That tells me bugger all.' Steph sips her wine.

Hannah swallows. 'Well, what am I meant to say? That I'm having the time of my life?'

'No.' Steph shakes her head. 'Because you're the world's worst liar so I wouldn't believe you.'

Hannah crams more pizza into her mouth. Eating is easier than talking. Easier than facing the future.

Steph leans forward, her voice softening. 'How is he? Any better?'

Hannah shakes her head. 'No. He can't use his left-hand side. At all. Which means he can't dress. Shave. Shower.' She stops. The list of things he can't do is endless.

She looks at the table. Then back at Steph. Words don't help. They only underline what's been lost.

'God, I'm so sorry, Han.' The sympathy stamped across Steph's face only makes Hannah feel worse.

Time for more wine.

Steph runs her finger round the rim of her glass. 'So what are you going to do?'

'What can I do?' Hannah finds that her appetite has vanished again and throws the pizza back on her plate. 'I'm going to take away all the stuff I've moved into your spare room and carry it home and unpack it. Then I'm going to try to help Tom get better. Oh, and for added fun –' she spits the words out bitterly '– I'll carry on doing my shitty job with my shitty boss breathing down my neck because my results aren't good enough. Even though she's given me all the bottom sets, while she swans off and teaches the easy classes who – surprise, surprise – are all predicted A stars.'

Steph's mouth curves bitterly. 'It's not fair.'

'I know.' Hannah blinks back the angry tears that are constantly threatening to fall. 'But none of that matters now.' She thinks of Tom when she left him today. Being wheeled off to the toilet by a nurse. 'If you could see Tom . . . it's just so sad.'

'I bet.' Steph puts her hand on Hannah's. 'But it's not just sad for him. It's so tough on you too.'

'It's tougher on him.'

Steph sighs. 'Yeah, but—'

'But nothing.' Hannah realises she has finished her wine. She has had a hangover every day since the stroke. A new personal best. 'I wouldn't wish what he's going through on my worst enemy.'

Steph arches an eyebrow. 'Not even on Margaret?'

'Not even on her.'

Steph stands up and gets another bottle of white wine from the fridge. 'Well, just tell me you haven't done anything stupid, like cancelling your placement.'

'Of course I cancelled it.' Rain starts to tap against Steph's window and an empty Sainsbury's bag blows against the glass. Hannah sighs. She's a long way from Tanzania. She might never get to go there now. She pushes her glass towards Steph for a refill. 'The doctors say they have no idea how long Tom's recovery will take – I can't exactly bugger off for a year, can I?'

'But Han – this is the job of your dreams.' Steph sits down and unscrews the top of the bottle. 'You were so excited about it you even persuaded me to come with you.'

'I know.' Hannah sighs. 'Though I think not getting the head of department job made you more persuadable.'

Steph shakes her head. 'I am never persuadable.'

'Good point.' Hannah takes another slice. 'Well, you can email me and tell me all about it.'

Steph sloshes more wine into Hannah's glass. 'But it's only February now. Things might change. He might make a miraculous recovery.'

'I don't think so. He can't even walk, for God's sake.'

Steph slumps forward onto her elbows. 'This is just so *shit*. After all the crap of this past year with him – I can't believe this is happening.'

Hannah drinks again. 'Me neither.' She bites her lip, then realises something. 'Oh my God. You're not angry with me, are you? I mean, now I'm not coming with you?'

'Course not. I'm just sad. For you.'

'Because you know I'm really sorry.'

'Han—'

Hannah couldn't stop. 'And I can pay you rent for this place for a month or two if you like – now that I'm not moving in, I mean.'

'*Han.*' Steph adopts her detention expression. 'Stop.' She shrugs. 'You not moving in gives me the perfect opportunity to find a wildly inappropriate flatmate on the internet. You know? Someone who drinks all my gin and decides to show me their body parts in the small hours.'

'Oh God, now I feel even worse.'

'I'm kidding.' Steph grins and her blue eyes gleam. 'And of course I'm not angry. Not with you, anyway. I'd give Fate a good slap in the face, though.' She wipes her fingers on a piece of kitchen towel. 'But thank God you hadn't told him yet. About leaving him. Can you imagine?'

Hannah shudders. 'No. I can't.'

Steph sips her wine. 'At least that's something to be thankful for.'

'Yeah.' Hannah rolls her eyes. 'Whoop.'

Steph nods. 'And does he know about the other thing?'

Hannah shifts in her chair. 'What other thing?'

'You *know*.' Steph picks a mushroom off a slice of pizza and pops it in her mouth. 'What happened after your party.'

Hannah feels her cheeks flush. 'Oh. That.'

'Oh. *That.*' Steph narrows her eyes. 'Or rather oh – him. Raj.'

'No.' Hannah feels a rush of guilt. 'Tom doesn't know about him.'

'Is he still texting you?'

'Nothing in the last couple of days.' Hannah exhales. 'He's back in Brighton now anyway – doing supply teaching there again. Trying to get back with his ex, I think. He won't get in touch any more.'

'Really?' Steph's eyes widen. 'He was all over you. And so tall. And dark. And those cheekbones? Wow.'

Hannah sighs. That party feels like a lifetime ago. Another Hannah. Another life. 'Sounds like you're the one who fancied him.'

'Not my type.'

'No?'

'No.' Steph stands up and puts her plate in the sink. 'You know me. I only like men who look like they could do some serious damage in a rugby scrum.'

'Good point.'

'Plus he's not Australian. Or about to leave the country. Both of which seem to be key criteria for me.' Steph runs the tap.

'Which might be why you're still single.'

'Maybe.' Steph nods. 'Though I like to think it's because I'm choosy.'

'You carry on telling yourself that.' Hannah picks up her glass and stands up. 'I'd better get upstairs and start packing before I get so drunk I can't move. I said I'd go and see Tom again at seven and it's already nearly six.'

'Can't you have a night off from visiting?'

'No.' Hannah starts to walk towards the hall. 'It's weird.

After all those months of shouting at me or avoiding me, now he seems to really hate it when I'm not there. Keeps asking where I've been. What I'm doing. He's still quiet, but he cries now. And he keeps reaching out and holding my hand. Like it's some kind of lifeline.'

'Maybe it is.' Steph stands up. 'Let me help you pack.'

'No, it's all right.' Hannah turns in the doorway. 'I think I need to do this by myself.'

Steph looks like she's about to argue, but then nods in acceptance. 'OK. But I'm here if you need me. And I have chocolate. And gin.'

Hannah smiles. It feels unnatural. As if her mouth has forgotten how. 'Thanks.'

She walks along the narrow hall to the stairs at the end, thinking about how different she had imagined this moment would be. Two weeks ago she had thought she would be running up the stairs to Steph's spare room, full of relief at finally being free. Free from Tom's toxic take on her faults and failures. Free from the pain of seeing herself through his eyes.

Now all that hope is behind her.

She climbs the stairs and pushes open the door. She looks at the double bed in the corner, her breath catching as she sees the bright patchwork of pinks and blues on the duvet cover. It looks so warm and cosy – so much more inviting than the grey and black sheets that Tom likes at home. She sits down on the edge of the bed, remembering the night Steph had bought them for her. She had called them the 'Bollocks to Tom' bedsheets, and promised they would always be here waiting for Hannah whenever she finally decided to leave.

Hannah looks around, seeing her ancient teddy propped up against the window and her Elmo slippers sticking out from under the chest of drawers. Her eyes fall on the copy of the Tanzania *Lonely Planet* lying on the bedside table. She reaches out and takes it, running her fingers over the pages that she has spent so much time with while planning her big adventure. She finds the cluster of newspaper articles pushed into the middle of the book – tales of smiling children and singing tribal songs under the stars. She's been collecting them for months.

Once, she had been ripping one out of a Sunday paper when Tom had asked her what she was looking so happy about. She hadn't told him. She knew he'd only laugh at her. Tell her what a dreamer she was. How she should shape up and get in touch with reality. *Stop dreaming, Hannah. Get real.*

She opens the book and sees a dedication in Steph's writing.

To my amazing friend Hannah who deserves all the fun that she is about to have. This is your year, S x.

As she reads the words Hannah's tears start to fall.

Half an hour later she wipes her eyes and quietly puts the book in the black rucksack hanging on the back of the door. She moves around the room, taking shoes out of the wardrobe and clothes from the drawers until there is no sign that she had ever planned to live here.

She leaves the sheets. She won't be needing them now.

As Hannah reaches the stroke unit an alarm is screeching. Staff are running. Running towards Tom's bay.

Adrenaline surges through her. Tom must be dying. Fear grasps her and pushes her feet into action. Slowly at first. Then more quickly. She starts moving with everybody else, her hand grazing against the white trolley that Dr Malik is pushing in front of him.

'Can you step back please?' Dr Malik flings the words back at her over his shoulder. Hannah comes to a halt but she can't stop looking. Tom's curtains are closed. She feels bile rising. He can't die. He can't. She catches her breath as her mind plays a spool of images. Tom's face alight as he moves in for a kiss. His mouth wide as he celebrates a goal on the football field. His dark hair spiky against Sunday morning pillows.

Her Tom.

Then she blinks as she sees the team pulling open the curtains of the cubicle next door. It's John. Not Tom. She takes a deep breath. Her heart surges.

Everyone in the bay can hear what's happening. The thin curtains do nothing to disguise the fact that the smiley old man's heart has stopped.

'We'll defibrillate now. Charging.'

'Clear.'

Hannah walks slowly past the cubicle, thinking of John's kindness and humour. She slips in to see Tom. She is so grateful he is still alive. Still here. Still in with a chance.

'Hannah.' Sweat beads on Tom's forehead.

'Tom.' She steadies her breathing as she focuses on his face.

'The poor guy.' His eyes are wide with panic. 'He was all right, you know? We talked about cricket. And Spurs.' He closes his hand around hers. 'And how pretty you are.'

Hannah strokes his face. 'Sssshhhhh.'

'CHARGE.' Dr Malik's voice is rising.

Tom frowns. 'Don't do that, H.'

'Do what?'

'Brush it off. You're beautiful.'

'But—'

'H, I'm so sorry.'

'What?'

'CLEAR.' The sound of paddles connecting. Then silence.

'I just wanted to say . . .' His eyes are fixed on her and she can feel the weight of his heart in her hands. 'I saw your face when Sandra talked about me going home. When you were talking to Dr Malik.'

Guilt rushes in again. 'Tom, I—'

He holds up a hand. 'And I need to say . . .' He looks behind her to the riot of cards and presents on his bedside cabinet. 'That you can leave me if you want to.' He drops his eyes. 'I mean, I wouldn't blame you.'

She swallows. 'Tom—'

'No, listen.' She gazes at him. 'Hannah, I know I've been a bastard. I knew I was hurting you. I could see how you stopped smiling. And laughing. And talking. I knew how sad I was making you.' He swallows. 'And I'm so sorry.'

The words she has been waiting so long to hear. Words absent from so many silent breakfasts. From the yawning gaps between box sets and from every lonely car journey with him sitting right by her side. She remembers the way her flaws had become weapons that he turned on her every single day. As if his problems were her fault. Always her fault.

Her anger is still there. Still burning. Despite the stroke. Despite his apology. She knows she has to overcome it. For him. For them.

'CLEAR.'

Tom's mouth trembles as he speaks. 'Hannah, I don't

know what to say. When I had the stroke I thought I would never get to say anything to you. Ever again.' He swallows and then raises his eyes. She sees love. It terrifies her. 'And then you were being so great, but I was still so angry. About the stroke. How unfair it was. And you were the only person I could fire at. You know?'

She puts her hand over his. His face is flushed and his hand is shaking. He needs to stop. To rest.

'Tom—'

He carries on as if she hasn't spoken. 'But now I can tell you. And . . . I know I'm not the man you married. He could pick you up. Cuddle you. Look after you. Make you a cup of tea – he wasn't . . .' He gestures towards himself. 'This.' He blinks a tear away and the need in his eyes makes her want to cry.

'But I know I haven't been that man for a long time. I've been so shit to you and I hate myself.' He sighs. 'And I know that you have—' He stops, his eyes keeping a desperate hold on hers.

'That I have what?' Guilt makes her voice sharp.

He opens his mouth. Closes it. 'Nothing. But I wouldn't blame you if you've had enough. If you don't want to stay. I'll get through it.'

He stares at her and she sees a courage that she has long forgotten.

She leans down and kisses him on the cheek. 'It's OK.'

'No.' His right hand lifts and falls again. 'I should have made more of it, H. More of – us. Of life.'

'You still can.' She kisses his fingers. 'When you get better.'

'Do you think I will?'

'Yes.' She sounds so much surer than she feels. 'And I'll be here. All the way.'

A tear trickles down his cheek. 'Really? Despite everything I've done? How can you want to stay?'

'I do.' She nods slowly. 'I do want to stay, Tom.' Disbelief still flickers across his face. She can see her words are not enough. He needs to believe in her. To believe in their future.

She runs a hand through his hair as she prepares herself for the lie he needs to hear.

'I love you, Tom.' She reaches down and plants a kiss on his lips.

With this kiss I thee convince.

With this kiss I thee deceive.

'I'm not going anywhere, Tom. OK?'

The relief on his face is a price worth paying for her dishonesty. 'Thank you.'

She pulls back. 'But there's one condition.'

The panic on his face breaks her heart.

'What's that?'

'That you don't give up, Tom. No matter how hard it is. You can get angry. Cry. Shout. But you can't give up. Ever.'

'OK.' He nods, then reaches up and caresses her face as if it is the most precious thing in the world. 'You're amazing, H. You're . . .' he reaches his right arm round her, '. . . my everything.'

She pulls him close so he can't see her face.

'Time of death 19:10.'

Batman mask
January 2007

She was pouring tequila when he first told her he loved her.

'*What?*' She slopped the liquid into the final shot glass on the kitchen table and blinked at him, eyes sparkling behind her mask. Screams came from the living room but he ignored them. All that mattered was telling her how he felt.

He raised his voice to be heard over the Capital FM mega-mix that blasted bravely out of the tinny stereo. 'That wasn't quite the reaction I was hoping for.'

She shook her head and nearly dislodged the feline ears that stuck arrestingly out of her curls. 'I'm not sure I heard you right. I'm wondering if it's the tequila talking.' The black whiskers painted on her cheeks rose as she smiled. 'Either that or you're overwhelmed by my Catwoman costume.'

'Well, it is pretty damn spectacular.' He kissed her. 'But seriously, you must have worked out how I feel by now.'

'Maybe.' She rested a hand against his chest. 'I know you're very fond of my body parts. The note you left in my bra this morning gave me an inkling.'

He smiled. 'I'm glad you liked it.'

She hunted around in the cupboard for some salt as she quoted his words. '*Dear bra, please look after these puppies. They're very precious to me and I plan on spending a lot of time with them.'* She poured the salt onto a plate. 'How could I not like that?' She walked round the table and laced her hands round his neck. 'But you're not exactly big on declarations of affection, Tom. It's been over six months and the most you've ever said is that you like having me around.' She stood on her tiptoes and gently pushed the mask on top of his head before kissing him on the lips. 'But then maybe it's one of the reasons I like you so much. You keep me guessing.'

'Like me?' He felt panic start to surge. 'Only *like*?'

She shrugged. 'Well, if you whirl that cape at me a few times this evening I might raise it to something more . . .' She smiled. 'More enthusiastic.'

'Oh really?' He raised an eyebrow. 'There's a promise you'd better keep.'

'Ellison!' A brawny green arm landed heavily around his shoulders as his flatmate Nick arrived in the kitchen with a giggling Superwoman in tow. She was a classic Nick choice – tall and blonde with a strong tendency to giggle when no one had made a joke.

Nick slapped him on the back. 'Where's this bloody tequila then?'

'Coming up, Mr Incredible Hulk.' Hannah gestured to the glasses.

'Great.' The shot glass looked ridiculously small next to Nick's broad rugby-player chest, which was exposed to the waist and painted a violent shade of green.

'Any lime?'

Hannah held up a Jif Lime bottle. 'Erm . . . will this do?'

Nick had reached the stage of drunkenness where the next mouthful was all that mattered. 'Yeah.' He picked up the bright green bottle and squinted at the label, looking as if he was about to swig it down.

Hannah gently removed it from his fingers. She picked a glass and held it high. 'Cheers.'

'Yeshhhh! Cheers!' A lone She-Ra spoke up from the kitchen floor, before keeling sideways into oblivion again.

'Cheers!' They all performed the obligatory drinking and wincing routine.

'More!' Tom could feel the alcohol rushing through his bloodstream. He slopped another round into the glasses. 'To Hannah. Thank you for organising this shuper-heroes party.' He staggered slightly. 'Shit. I think I'm pissed.'

'Not as pissed as that bloke Damian.' Nick downed his shot and grabbed a beer from the pile in the sink. 'He's asleep in the bath cuddling a loo roll. Who invited him, anyway?'

'Me.' Hannah shrugged. 'His date got cancelled so he needed cheering up.'

Tom bit his tongue. He hadn't exactly been delighted when Damian had arrived. Especially as he hadn't even had the decency to bring any booze.

Nick shook his head. 'Well, he's a typical Cranbourne boy. Can't take the pace.' He turned to Superwoman. 'We used to annihilate them at rugby, you know.'

She giggled. Predictably.

'OK, posh boy.' Tom could feel the tequila singing in his veins. 'No one wants to hear about your sporting triumphs. Fastest nerd at prep school, weren't you? The egg and spoon race, wasn't it?'

'Cheeky bastard.' Nick punched Tom jovially in the shoulder. Tom had to concentrate very hard to avoid flinching. 'If only you'd known me back then.' He drew himself up tall. 'I'll have you know my egg and spoon victory was written up in the school newspaper.' The kitchen lights highlighted the green dye in his normally blond hair. 'It was legendary.'

'Yeah, yeah.' Tom grinned at him. 'For you, maybe. But somehow I doubt the rest of the world took much notice.'

Nick rolled his eyes. 'Is that the chip on your shoulder talking? Was this when you were shivering round a candle and dreaming of owning shoes?'

'Hilarious.' Tom opened his mouth to say more but Hannah got in first.

'How about we go and wake up Damian? Get him away from that loo roll?'

There was general drunken agreement that waking Damian up would be a Very. Good. Idea.

Tom was about to join the stampede when he felt a hand curling round his.

'Psssst.' Hannah stood on tiptoe to whisper in his ear. 'I love you too, Batman.' She gently kissed his lips. 'Even if you are my arch-enemy.' She ran her hand down his cheek. 'Though you'd be even better if you played the guitar.'

'I'll work on that.' He kissed her and joy leapt inside him.

'You'd better.' She sashayed out, twirling her tail over her shoulder in a way that made him want to tear off her catsuit with his teeth.

He was about to follow when he heard his phone ringing. He picked it up from the Ikea bookcase that had been leaning suspiciously to the left ever since he and Nick had constructed it after one too many beers. They blamed the instructions. Naturally.

'Hello?' He heard whoops and a squeal coming from the bathroom. He hoped Damian was getting an unpleasant awakening.

'Tom?'

'Mum?' He heard the fear in her voice and reached up and pulled the mask off his head, throwing it onto the table.

'What is it?'

A beat of silence. 'Love . . .' Her voice broke.

'Yes?'

'It's—'

'What?' Down the corridor he saw a sopping Damian emerging from the bathroom. His long hair was dripping and he was leaning heavily on Hannah's shoulder. Her cat's tail was already acquiring a soggy droop. Jealousy burned through him but he blinked it away.

'What is it, Mum?'

'It's Julie.'

It took him a second to understand. Nothing was ever wrong with Julie.

'What is it, Mum? Can I speak to her?'

'No.' His mum dissolved into sobs. 'She's not here.'

'Where is she?'

'I don't know.'

'Mum.' His throat was dry. 'It's nearly midnight. What's happened? Why don't you know where she is?'

'Because—'

'What?' He moved the supine She-Ra with his foot and pushed the kitchen door shut to try to block out the boisterous party shrieks.

'Because she's gone.'

'Gone where?'

'I don't know.' Another sob and then the rustle of a tissue.

He felt a pulse of terror. Tabloid images raced through his mind. Girls abducted. Bodies in woods. Manhunts.

He pressed the phone hard to his ear.

'How long's she been gone?'

'Since this morning. She only went to the shop. I've called all her friends and the police and now I don't know what to do.'

Fear froze him.

'And I was wondering whether she might have come to see you?'

He wished he were more sober. His brain wouldn't work. 'Why, Mum? Why would she have come here?'

'There's something she wants to talk to you about.'

'Is there?'

His fear became anger when he looked down and saw She-Ra keeling over and puking onto his shoe. He stamped away towards the filthy kitchen window, still stained from Nick's latest explosive attempt to cook spaghetti bolognese. He looked out across the street towards the rumbling sound of the trains pulling into the tube station. He looked for her. Her dark hair. Her purple tracksuit.

Nothing. Instead a siren wailed a few streets away and he could see that the man in the opposite flat had just started watching porn with his curtains open.

Just a normal Saturday night.

Except Julie was out there. Somewhere. Fifteen years old. Alone.

He took a breath.

'Look, Mum. Try not to worry. I'll give her a call. And I can come down to you if she doesn't turn up.'

She would. He knew it.

She had to.

77

'OK, love.' His mum's voice broke into a sob. 'But call me if you see her. She did really want to talk to you.'

'I will. She'll be OK, Mum. I promise.'

All he heard as he hung up was sobbing.

He dialled Julie's number, closing his eyes and pressing his hand against his forehead as he heard her voicemail kick in. He could see her face in his mind's eye – smiling that mischievous smile as she recorded her message. He'd done a month of extra shifts to get her that phone for Christmas. Now he only hoped she'd have the sense to use it.

'*Hi. This is Jules. You know what to do.*'

She sounded so young. Fear churned in his stomach. 'Jules? It's me. Where are you? Can you give me a call when you get this? It's urgent. Thanks.'

When he had hung up he picked up the nearest glass and drained it, shuddering at the sickly sweetness. Hannah had clearly been at the Amaretto again.

He stared at his phone, willing it to ring as his mind unhelpfully replayed scenes from *Crimewatch* and slasher movies in a relentless loop.

It had to ring. Had to.

It never did.

Six

'Watch it!' Tom holds up his right hand to shield himself.

'*Stop.*' Hannah tries desperately to halt the wheelchair before it slams into a bollard. As usual it ignores her.

Tom's leg coincides with the concrete before the chair bounces backwards, doing its best to take out Hannah's kneecaps in the process.

She leans down to him. 'Shit. I'm so sorry, Tom.'

He doesn't reply. Hannah waits, dreading his rage.

'Oh well.' He turns his head. 'At least you hit my left leg this time. It's not like you can do any more damage to that one.'

She looks at him. Sees the corner of his mouth rising upwards. Feels herself start to smile. 'God, I'm really shit at this aren't I?'

'Yes.' He nods. 'You really are. And there was me thinking you driving my Mini into a hedge was going to be our worst ever driving experience.'

'Excuse me.' Hannah rubs her bruised kneecaps. Her one-swim-a-month regime really hasn't put her in great shape for pushing the world's heaviest chair out of the hospital and around the South Bank. 'That hedge came out of nowhere. And the car's steering wheel was faulty if you ask me.'

'Sure it was.' Tom sounds entirely unconvinced.

'There you are.' Julie reappears. She thrusts her phone back in her pocket and a frown darkens her face above the collar of her green coat.

'Are you OK, Jules?' Hannah asks. 'No bad news I hope?'

'I'm fine, thanks.' Julie's voice is clipped. Angry. She shoves one hand in her pocket and looks around. She points at the ice cream van optimistically parked at one end of the square. 'Would you like an ice cream, Tommo?'

Hannah wonders whether Julie has failed to notice the vicious February gale slicing through them. She reminds herself yet again that Tom's stroke has been a shock for Julie, so it's too early to expect her to act like a Normal. Human. Being.

Tom speaks but his words get lost as a little boy screams past on roller shoes, hotly pursued by sweating parents who are clearly regretting ever letting him near them. Hannah leans forward as she awkwardly manoeuvres the wheelchair away from the evil bollard, until her mouth is next to the red ski hat that covers his head.

'What was that, Tom?'

He does his best to turn his head towards her. 'Not Cornetto weather. Let's keep going. As long as you promise to actually look in front of you from now on.'

'OK, OK.' Hannah breathes deeply as she fights to turn the wheelchair round. She pushes harder as the pavement starts to slope upwards, her breathing quickening as she takes the strain. It's her fourth outing with Tom and she is still showing no sign of developing any arm muscles whatsoever.

'We could go to that coffee shop.' Hannah is so breathless she can barely speak. 'The one we used to go to. With all the scooters.' She keeps pushing, wondering how she hasn't noticed how uneven London pavements are before. The incline makes her feel every pound of Tom's twelve-stone frame and she is leaning so far forward she's practically horizontal as she forces the chair along.

'Scooters?' Julie rolls her eyes. 'Bit tactless, isn't it? I mean it isn't like Tommo's going to be hopping back on two wheels any time soon.'

Hannah prickles with embarrassment. 'Oh God. I hadn't thought. Sorry.'

'Don't be stupid.' Tom swipes ineffectually at his sister. 'Jules is just being a cow. It's a great idea, H.'

Hannah realises Tom is standing up for her. It feels unfamiliar. Unsettling.

They turn the corner and her stress levels surge as she realises there are hundreds of people in front of them, all heading towards the London Eye and the river. She can smell the doughnut stand by the riverbank and see a big passenger ferry chugging off across the Thames.

She launches into the crowd. A large group of Japanese tourists turn their cameras in unison towards the skyline to snap a choice shot as the wheelchair hits the cobbles. The chair judders towards the group, and Hannah wishes yet again that it had a horn.

She steers around the edge of the crowd, constantly changing direction to get through the people that surround them, apologising to Tom as the chair reverberates across the uneven stones. The shock jars her hands as they grasp the handlebars and the wheelchair seizes any opportunity to veer off and hit people in the backs of their knees. Or hands. It's not picky.

Just as a street performer dressed in gold strides past them, the chair escapes Hannah's grip and races off to collide with a bin that is overflowing with sandwich wrappers and used copies of *Metro*.

She runs to catch up. 'Sorry.'

'Be careful!' Julie shakes her head.

Hannah's had enough of Julie's constant sniping. 'Look, I'm doing my best here. It's bloody uneven and the steering on this thing is shit.'

Julie tuts. 'It's fine if you know how. Let me do it.'

Hannah has seen her driving a car. Terrifying. 'Are you sure that's a good idea?'

'Oh, come on.' Julie puts her hands on the handlebars and edges her aside. 'I used to push Mum around the place all the time. I doubt NHS wheelchairs have changed much since then.'

Hannah shrugs and gives in. She could do with a break. She stretches her tired arms over her head and watches as Julie navigates her way irritatingly easily through a group of teenage girls, who appear to be dressed for a Mediterranean beach party. She can see the goosebumps on their shivering orange limbs and smell biscuity fake tan in the air.

Julie narrowly avoids mowing down an old man on crutches and turns triumphantly. 'See?' she shouts. 'It's easy!'

Hannah is very glad she can't see Tom's face.

Julie comes rapidly to a halt as one of the teenagers moves into her path at the last minute, gazing intently at her shiny pink mobile. Julie coughs. Loudly. 'Excuse me.'

'What?' The girl looks at her. Flicks her eyes to Tom. Flicks them away. Hannah sees a glimpse of something like embarrassment.

Tom speaks. 'You walked in front of us.'

The girl ignores him and talks over his head to Julie. 'Whatever. I was on my phone, yeah? Not my fault.'

Julie's mouth twists. 'Yeah, well look where you're going next time.'

The girl shrugs. She still doesn't look at Tom.

Julie wheels off again and Hannah catches her up. 'Do you want me to beat her up for you?'

Julie laughs and Hannah thinks how young she looks when she smiles. 'No thanks. I don't think that would have a happy ending.'

'Fair enough.' Hannah nods as they move onto the smooth concrete path that runs along the river. Big Ben looms on the opposite bank, its hands poised just before the hour. The Houses of Parliament reach up to grey skies. Tourists surge everywhere. Cameras glint in the bleak sunlight and cups of tea are clasped in freezing cold hands.

Hannah leans down to Tom. 'Are you OK there?'

'Sure.' As he speaks his left foot falls off the footrest and starts to scrape along the ground.

'Wait up.' Julie flicks the brakes down on either side of the chair. 'I need a pee.' She heads off towards the loos by the park.

Hannah kneels down by Tom's left leg and is conscious of jeans and skirts and leggings swirling around her. She looks up and sees belts and handbags walking past with only the occasional child to make her feel part of the world again. She feels tiny. Irrelevant. How Tom must feel every time he is taken out in his chair.

He gazes forward as she lifts his foot gently back into the footrest. She kisses him on the forehead. 'Nearly there.' She looks at him appraisingly. The wind has brought a faint colour to his cheeks.

His eyes gleam with unexpected mischief. 'Might have some whisky in my coffee at this rate.'

She smiles and straightens up again. 'You can have a double.'

'And a cigarette?'

'Don't push it.'

They both laugh.

Hannah tries to remember when that last happened. She can't.

'Great.' Tom yawns as Hannah puts his coffee on the table. The yellow cup looks way too small to even begin to fight his evident exhaustion. 'Where's the sugar?'

'Here.' Hannah pushes a mug full of gold paper cylinders towards him.

'Thanks.' He picks one up. Stares at it. Tries to hold it and rip it open using only one hand.

'I'll do it.' Julie picks up a packet.

'No. I'm fine.' Tom frowns as he raises it to his mouth and tears it open with his teeth. 'See?' He looks at them triumphantly, only for the packet to slip out of his fingers. Sugar spills down his front. Hannah leans forward to brush it off but he pushes her hand away.

'I'm fine.'

'OK. Sorry.' She sits back in her chair, feeling a familiar pulse of failure. She wishes she knew how to help him.

Julie quietly opens another packet and empties it into Tom's coffee. 'Do you want me to stir?'

'No.' A muscle flickers in Tom's cheek. 'I can still manage that, thanks.'

'Good.' Julie sips her hot chocolate. 'Don't want you getting lazy.'

Tom flinches as a woman hits his head with her

handbag as she swings the door open. Hannah watches as the woman looks down, observing that she sees the wheelchair before she sees Tom.

'Oh! I am *so* sorry.' She leans over him and Hannah notices a flake of croissant on her cheek. She speaks slowly and loudly, as if talking to a lost tourist searching for the train station.

Tom's cheeks glow red.

'No need to shout.' Julie's green eyes flash. 'He's perfectly capable of understanding you.'

'Yes. Of course.' The woman flushes with embarrassment. 'Well, I really am sorry. It's just you're a bit close to the door.'

Tom sighs. 'Don't worry about it. It's fine.' He looks around the cluttered café with its upturned wooden crate tables and battered armchairs. The gaps between them are blocked by baby buggies, shopping bags and rucksacks and Julie's earlier attempt to ram the chair into a far corner had not ended well. He meets the woman's eyes. 'There wasn't really anywhere else to park.'

Hannah knows from the way he sinks down into his coat that it isn't fine at all. She can see him shrinking. Trying to become invisible.

She'd want to be invisible too.

'If you're sure.' The woman lifts her hand in an awkward wave. Then she pulls her handbag higher on her shoulder and heads out into the crowded street.

Hannah's spirits droop. The café is full of bubbling, giggling people who all make Tom look smaller. Sadder. In the hospital he blends in but out here everyone notices him. They all stare for a beat too long, before jerking their eyes away and compressing their lips into a taut line of sympathy. Then their steps quicken as they move away from Tom's tragedy and escape back into their lives — nights in the pub or picking the kids up or the presentation they have to give the next day at work.

There's no escape for Tom.

Hannah exhales and takes a half-hearted mouthful of hot chocolate. It burns her tongue. Of course.

Sandra the physio keeps saying these outings are meant to be fun. *A chance for Tom to reacclimatise before he comes home. For you all to get used to things.*

Instead they leave Tom sapped and sad, while Hannah goes home and raids her ever-decreasing stash of booze. She's down to the Limoncello now. Each mouthful makes her grimace but she still drinks it on the sofa while watching trashy TV and eating cereal out of the packet. She wakes up in the small hours with her shoes on and muesli scattered across her body.

Classy.

She winces as another person brushes against Tom on their way past. 'I'm sorry, Tom. Maybe this place wasn't the best idea.'

'It's OK.' Tom sips his coffee. 'It's good motivation to get out of this damn thing as quickly as possible.'

'Great idea.' Julie leans forward and steals more cake. 'And I think I can help you with that.'

'Yeah? How?' Tom eyes his sister. 'Have you got some kind of magic wand in that bag of yours?'

Hannah watches Julie nervously. Her decisions have a tendency to be dramatic and involve large amounts of cash.

'I'm going to move in and look after you. When Hannah's back at work.' Julie smiles and puts her hand over Tom's. 'It feels like the right thing to do.'

Hannah blinks. Julie puts a very noble spin on being fired. She wonders again about mentioning the phone call she'd overheard, but decides against it.

She leans forward. 'But I thought you were going back to Bristol? To Zac?' She catches a flicker of uncertainty on Julie's face. 'That's what you told me.'

'Yeah, I know.' Julie shakes her head dismissively and her dark hair fluffs around her face. 'But I decided that my big brother was more important.'

Hannah feels worry knotting in her belly. Tom needs someone reliable. Focused. 'But it's a lot of work.'

'So? I can do it.' Julie's lower lip sticks out. 'I did it with Mum.'

'Yeah, I know but—'

'Are you saying I can't handle it, Hannah?'

'No.' Hannah takes a mouthful of cake and wonders why every conversation with Julie feels like it should come with a pair of duelling pistols. 'I just wondered about Zac, that's all.'

'He'll come up on weekends.' Julie avoids her eyes. 'And why should I make my decisions about him, anyway? Haven't you heard of feminism?'

'Yes, of course I have, but—'

'There you go then.' Julie takes another chunk of cake and nods decisively as she takes a bite. Her eyes flick away from Hannah's as she chews.

Hannah watches her carefully. There's something else going on. She's sure of it. She is about to ask more when she sees the smile on Tom's face.

'It'll be good spending some time with you, Jules.' He finishes his coffee and lowers the cup carefully to its saucer. 'It's been a while.'

'Yeah.' Julie nods. 'But don't get any ideas. I'm not being your personal slave or anything. There'll be no bloody fanning you with palm leaves or rubbing your temples with scented oils.'

Tom smiles. 'Thank God.' He puts his hand on his sister's arm. 'And thank you.'

Hannah knows that he's always wondered how to mend things with Julie. It's clear that he thinks this is his chance.

He squeezes Julie's arm. 'I have to say I wasn't looking forward to loads of strangers manhandling me around.'

'Yeah. Well.' Julie takes the final bit of cake. 'You'll just have to put up with me instead.'

Hannah shifts in her seat.

'OK, if you're definitely moving in for longer I'll shift all the crap off the sofa bed in the study for you.'

Tom frowns. 'Why can't she go in the spare room?'

Hannah swallows. Waits a second. 'Because it's better if you're in there, Tom.'

His smile disappears. 'Why?'

Hannah hates the disappointment on his face. 'Because it's on the ground floor with a toilet next door. It'll be much . . .' She stares at the wheelchair. 'Much easier. No stairs.'

'Oh.' His face falls. 'Right.'

She can't meet his eyes. Sharing a bed with him right now would feel too close. Too intimate. Too false.

She reaches out and puts her hand over his.

'Just till you're back on your feet again, Tom. We'll make it work. The three of us.' She summons a smile for Julie. 'We'll have Tom fit in no time, won't we?'

'Sure.' Julie grins. 'You'll be running the marathon by April, Tommo.'

'No.' Tom's face is serious. 'I'll be bloody winning it.' He looks at them both. 'Me and my girls. Together. What a team.'

Hannah forces herself to smile.

She doesn't feel like she's part of a team.

She has never felt so lonely in her life.

Photograph of a birthday cake
in the shape of a football

March 2007

Tom stared at the girl who had answered the front door.

'Jules?' Mum had said on the phone his sister had changed 'a bit' since his last visit. He had forgotten her talent for understatement.

'Hey, Tommo.' Julie shivered as the cold outside air hit her, then she did a twirl. 'What do you think?'

'Wow.' He blinked as he surveyed her again. Her long dark hair had been cut shorter round her face and her legs were clad in skintight jeans he hadn't seen before. Black DM boots encased her feet and a silver pendant in the shape of a dagger dripping blood hung round her neck. 'You look . . . great.'

She didn't. Not to him. He preferred her in tracksuits with a novel in her hand.

'Thanks.' She grinned. 'Are you coming in, or what?' She fiddled with the clutch of dark leather bracelets tangled round her wrist.

'Of course.' He stepped in and held his arms out for a hug.

Her eyelids glittered silver as she stepped into his embrace.

'Happy birthday, Tommo.' Her hair still smelt of apples and he held on, strangely afraid to let her go.

She pulled away first. 'Let's shut the door. It's freezing out there.'

He stepped further into the tiny hallway, taking comfort from the dull green wallpaper and the objects lined up on the hall table. The pig he'd made at primary school before he realised that animals had legs. The key to the shed attached to his mum's lurid Blackpool key ring – a rare present from his dad. It infuriated Tom that she still refused to throw it away, nearly two decades after he had left them.

He breathed in. Mr Sheen with overtones of cat. He looked down to see the animal weaving round his legs. 'Hello, Lion.' He squatted on his haunches and ran his hand over the thick ginger fur. He looked up at his sister. 'He looks well.'

'I'm glad one of us does.' A frown creased her pale forehead.

'What do you mean?' He stood up again. 'Are you OK?'

She sighed and shook her head. 'It's nothing. Doesn't matter.'

'Are you sure? Because it looks like it does matter.'

She didn't meet his gaze.

'No. Everything's great.' She flicked a strand of hair out of her eye.

Tom didn't understand the awkwardness between them. He tried again. 'So. What's with the image change?'

She shifted self-consciously and he knew that he had said the wrong thing. 'Thought it was time I stopped dressing like a kid. I'm nearly sixteen now.'

She looks about twenty to Tom. He wished she were little again. Things were easier then. He knew what to say. How to make her feel better.

'How's Hannah?' She folded her arms across her chest.

'Great.'

'That's good.' Her voice was flat. 'Was she busy today, then?'

'What do you mean?'

She turned and walked into the living room. 'You two seem to be joined at the hip. Whenever I call, you say you're off to meet her. I thought there was no way she'd miss spending your birthday with you.'

'She had a family thing.'

'Oh.' She nodded. 'I see.'

He felt a stab of frustration and put his hand on her arm. 'What are you getting at?'

'I don't know, Tommo. I just thought she might – not want to meet us.'

'Where did you get that idea?'

A shrug.

'Jules, you haven't even met her. She's not like that. She's amazing.'

'So you say.'

He felt a beat of frustration. 'Have I done something wrong, Jules?'

She shook her head. 'No. It's just—'

'What?'

'There's just a lot going on.' He saw tears in her eyes and his conscience started to mutter. 'I miss talking to you, Tommo. Seeing you. That's all.'

He felt a rush of guilt. He knew he should see her more but he was overstretched. His exams. His job at the pub. Sending money back home. Paying his rent.

And then Hannah. His silver lining.

He hugged Julie again, pulling her close in a silent apology. 'Well, I'm here now.'

'Yeah.' She nodded and then dropped into the squashy embrace of their mum's favourite armchair. Tom sat down on the ancient sofa, leaning against the corduroy cushions that his mum had bought just after his dad walked out. He doubted it was a coincidence that they were the colour of shit.

He rubbed a hand through his hair and leant forward to examine the pile of schoolbooks balanced precariously on the coffee table.

'What are you reading at the moment?'

She shook her head. 'Nothing.'

'Really? But you're always reading.'

She chewed fervently on her thumbnail and didn't answer.

He tried again. 'How's school? GCSEs soon.'

'It's all right.'

'And your mates there? How are they?'

She shrugged. 'What mates?'

Worry seethed inside him. 'I thought you were happy at school.'

'Yeah, right.' Her mouth drooped downwards. 'I fit right in with the polo set.' She picked her sleeve with nervous fingers. 'They just love my council-estate chic.'

She had always had friends. Had been fighting them off since her first day at primary school. He frowned. 'It was always going to take a while to settle in, I suppose.'

Julie cut in. 'I've been there a year and a half now, Tommo.'

He stared at her, shocked by the despair on her face. 'Can I help?'

She waved a hand dismissively. 'No. It'll be OK. I just – miss my old mates.'

'I see.' Tom had reservations about her old mates. Particularly about Gary. The one she'd run to last January. The one Tom would rather like to punch.

'But—' He stared at her. 'You're still getting good

grades, aren't you? I mean the whole idea of you getting that scholarship and going private was to help you get better teachers.'

'Yeah.' She bit her lip. 'They're OK.'

'Good.' He relaxed. 'Still on for medical school, then? Like you said?'

She frowned. 'That was a long time ago.'

'It was only Christmas.'

'Whatever.'

The word dismissed him. He leant against the arm of the sofa, hearing the familiar creak and crack of the old leather. Her tautness threw him off balance. He felt clumsy. Wrong. He remembered the way she used to throw herself at him when she was very little, clamouring to be carried. The way she'd imprisoned him in her play tent, protesting loudly when he had to break out to go to school. The way she gripped his hand as she asked for one more story before bed.

He missed that closeness. He missed his sister.

Now she uncrossed her legs and leant forward, clearly making an effort to lighten the mood. 'How are things going with you, anyway? All set for your final exams?'

He felt a familiar kick of fear in his stomach. There were too many books. Too many cases to remember. Too many codicils and torts and not enough time for his brain to absorb them. 'Kind of.' He exhaled. 'I think so. I've been revising like crazy.'

'You'll be fine.' It was such a relief to see her smile. 'When do they start?'

'Beginning of May.' He gulped. 'So make sure you send me your cleverest vibes.'

'I will.' The familiar mischief was back in her eyes. 'I know how much you need them.'

'Cheeky cow.' He threw a cushion at her. Missed.

'See?' She lobbed one back at him and hit him full in the face. 'Even my throwing is better than yours.'

He laughed. 'OK. So you're a hundred per cent better than your sad git of an older brother.' He shrugged. 'I admit it.'

Her face was suddenly serious. 'But you'll look after me, right?' She hugged her knees to her chest. 'When you've got your big job in the City?'

She looked so intense that he didn't want to tell her that he currently had absolutely no job prospects whatsoever. Everyone else already had training contracts. Nick. Jim. All his mates. Not him.

He brushed the thought away.

'Of course I will. I'll look after both of you. Just like I do now. You know that.'

'Good.' Her smile was back. 'And obviously you'll need my help too. With your big cases. I'll be your own personal Erin Brockovich. Minus the boob tubes.'

He grinned. 'Deal.'

He heard a muffled thump from upstairs. 'Is that Mum?'

Julie suddenly seemed intensely interested in her own feet. 'Er . . . yeah.'

'Isn't she still at work? She said she was doing daytime shifts now.'

'She's—' Julie broke off.

'What?'

He could see the confusion on her face. She shook her head. 'Sod it. I'm not meant to tell you this, but she's off work at the moment.'

He stiffened. His mum hadn't missed a day's work in over twenty years. 'Jules? What's happening?'

Her eyes were huge. 'She won't let me tell you.'

'Tell me what?'

Julie's face crumpled. 'She's ill.'

'Ill? Like, flu? Or . . .?'

Julie closed her eyes 'No, not bloody flu.' She shook her head. 'If only. Why don't you just go upstairs and see for yourself?'

He ran to the stairs.

His mum wasn't in her bedroom. The room was tidy and calm just like it always was. Her stripy nightie was folded on the grey cotton pillowcase and her latest library book was lying on the bedside table.

'Mum?' He heard a clunk in the bathroom. Then a gasp.

'Mum? Are you OK?' Panicking, he turned the handle of the door, grateful for once that she'd never got round to fixing the lock. The door opened easily and he walked in.

An old woman was standing in front of him.

She had no hair. No colour in her cheeks. No flesh to fill out the clothes that were hanging from her body.

Nausea rose to his throat. 'Mum?'

She held up the chestnut wig that was hanging from her hands and tried to smile.

'I can't work out how to get this thing to stay on.' Her voice was tight with uncried tears.

He was frozen. 'Mum?'

'Hello, love.' Shame surged through him as she evaded his eyes. It was as if she didn't feel she was good enough for him. 'I wanted to look nice.' He saw how her hands were shaking. 'I didn't manage it. I never get anything right.'

He walked over and hugged her. She had never felt this frail.

'Mum.' He fought for breath. Is it—?' He couldn't bring himself to say it out loud.

Cancer.

'Yes, love.' A sob shook her narrow shoulders. 'I found a lump and now I'm having chemo.' She pulled away from him. 'Don't cry. It'll be OK.'

He didn't deserve the love in her eyes. He should have known. Should have been here.

She patted him on the cheek.

'But—' He ran his hand through his hair. 'Why didn't you tell me?'

She turned back to the sink and wiped up an imaginary bit of dirt with her fingertip.

He stepped forward. 'Mum? Why didn't you let me know?'

He heard a voice behind him. Julie stood in the doorway. Arms crossed. Face full of sadness. 'Because of your exams. She wanted to keep quiet till then. I said she was too sick – that she should tell you – but she wouldn't listen.'

Guilt pierced him.

He couldn't stop shaking. 'But I can help. I can postpone for a year and—'

'No.' His mum drew herself up and bravery was stamped in every line on her face. 'No. I won't let you.'

She took out the tissue that was permanently lodged in her sleeve and dabbed her eyes. 'You've worked too hard.' She flinched with pain and Julie stepped forward and caught her in what was clearly a well-practised gesture.

'Are you OK, Mum? Do you need some water? Tea? A lie-down?'

He watched his sister gently caring for their mum and thought of them alone in this house. Coping. Protecting him.

Shame slapped him.

'Mum. I—' Tears pricked his eyelids. 'I'm so sorry.' He tried to talk but all that came out were sobs. 'I can—'

His mum was beside him now. Her hand was in his. 'It's all right.'

He couldn't speak.

He felt her arms close round him. Heard her quiet intake of breath. 'Now, I've made you a nice cake for your birthday. A football. Just like you had when you were little.' She pulled back and he saw the pride behind her smile. 'Shall we all go and have some?'

She was comforting him and it broke his heart.

He did his best. Took two slices. Chewed. Swallowed. Chewed. Swallowed.

Every morsel made him want to choke.

Seven

'I thought you was dead, Miss.'

'Sorry to disappoint you, T'shan.' Hannah looks at the glossy pout of the girl in the third row of desks.

'Nah you dick.' A blond boy unfolds himself from the seat behind T'shan and flicks his fingers against the back of her head. Justin and T'shan are the current 'it' couple of Year 11. Romance is showing every sign of being dead.

He exhales through his teeth. 'Wasn't her, innit? Was her husband.' He rolls weary eyes. 'You so dumb.'

T'shan appears to find his words enticing, and flicks him a glance that belongs in a lap-dancing club. He smiles the smile of a boy who doesn't have to lie about losing his virginity. Hormones cloud the air.

Hannah raises her voice above the scrape of chairs and the thud of books to address class 11C.

'Right everybody. Today we're going to—'

The door opens and Hannah is sure she can feel a chill in the air.

Margaret.

'Mrs Ellison. Can I have a word?'

Since Margaret's arrival Hannah has learnt that the answer to this question is never 'no.'

'Of course.' She walks towards the door and then turns back to the class. 'Get your books out, please. We're looking at *Macbeth* today.'

The complaints begin.

'Come on, guys. It's my first day back. Play nice.'

She turns her back on the chorus of unwilling groans and walks out of the classroom, closing the door behind her.

She attempts to assert herself. 'What is it, Margaret?'

Margaret pulls at the white cuff of her shirt so that it rests perfectly straight across her wrist. 'I'm about to depart for a conference and thought it was important to see you before I left.'

'Oh? Why?' Hannah stares at the grey scarf round Margaret's neck and gets a strong urge to ask her how she manages to keep the ends tied at such perfect right angles. She imagines Margaret standing in front of her mirror, measuring the angle carefully with a protractor.

She blinks the image away. 'Have I forgotten to do something?'

'No, no.' Margaret shakes her head. Her short dark hair doesn't dare to move. 'I wanted to see how you were.'

Hannah feels the absolute impossibility of being honest. She was woken at 2 a.m. by an old nightmare about being chased around London by an incompetent assassin with a very blunt knife. At 4 a.m. she'd given up on sleep and spent the rest of the night overdosing on Stephen King. Now she feels gritty. Drained.

'I'm OK.'

'Are you sure? You must have had a difficult time recently.' Margaret unfolds her arms and for a horrible second Hannah thinks she might be about to move in for a hug. It would be like embracing an ironing board.

She takes a step back. 'I'm fine.'

She relaxes as she sees that Margaret is just intent on removing a tiny spot of fluff that has dared to land on the sleeve of her navy suit.

Hannah exhales. 'I'm happy to be back.'

She hears a muffled scream from the classroom.

'Honestly.'

Margaret doesn't smile.

'Good.' A sharp frown line cuts even deeper between her eyes. 'We've got a lot to achieve this year, and I need to know I can rely on you.'

So that's what this is really about.

'You know you can, Margaret.' Hannah feels like adding that she cares about the students and does everything she can for them. However, since arriving at Queensdale Margaret has made it abundantly clear that students aren't her priority. She just cares about results. A to C grades. Statistics.

Margaret purses thin lips. 'Now that you're back from your compassionate leave, Hannah . . .'

'Yes?'

'I would be grateful if you could coordinate a presentation on Key Stage 3 results for the parents' options evening tomorrow.'

'Coordinate?' Hannah feels a rush of panic. She is due back at the hospital that night and has a full day of classes. She has precisely no time in which to do this.

Margaret nods. 'It's a key development opportunity. Reviewing the broad range of student ability—'

Hannah nods as panic clenches at her gut. 'I understand that. It's just that I'm still drafting the Year Nine pastoral report, and I'm worried that—'

'If you're saying that you are not able to take this on then just say so, Hannah.'

'I—'

'I know you're very *creative* with your classes.' Margaret makes being creative sound about as desirable as a crack habit.

'But—'

'But we need results, Hannah. And keeping the parents informed is a key part of that, as I'm sure you're aware. I want you to be involved.'

Hannah thought she already was.

She sighs. This job is her life now. She has no Plan B. She has to make the best of it.

'I'd be happy to do the extra work for you.'

'Good.' Margaret nods. 'Now, you'd better get back into the classroom, hadn't you?'

She is already halfway down the corridor by the time Hannah can reply. She stares at the upright figure and clenches her fists, muttering a wide selection of four-letter words at her departing back. Then she re-enters the classroom.

She surveys the class, breathing in the familiar smell of Lynx and illicit fags.

'Be quiet, you lot.'

They ignore her.

'BE QUIET.'

By some miracle they are.

Hannah leans against the desk.

'What kind of sandwich is Lady Macbeth?'

Blank faces.

'Come on. Use your imaginations. What kind of sandwich is Lady Macbeth?'

'What do you mean, Miss?' T'shan folds her arms and slumps back into a classic pose of teenage ennui. Hannah braves eye-watering clouds of perfume to walk towards her.

'Is she peanut butter and jam?'

'Nah, she's not peanut butter and jam. That's rank, Miss!'

'So what sandwich is she then?'

Justin leans forward. 'Well, she's a Waitrose sandwich isn't she, Miss?'

'Yeah, Miss. She's a wrap, isn't she?'

Hannah turns to the new speaker, who has a scar the size of a thumbnail on the side of his face. 'Is she? Why?'

He smiles. 'Cos she likes a bit of posh.'

'Why do you think that?'

A pause. Then a chorus of derision led by T'shan.

'Cos she wears a nightdress, Miss!'

Finally they're off. Gesticulating. Arguing. Laughing.

When the bell goes Hannah realises that she has enjoyed herself.

She had forgotten how good it feels.

As break time starts Hannah stands at the window, watching the students in their black blazers spilling out across the grey expanse of the playground. She hears the crescendo of shouts and squeals as they enjoy their freedom and wishes she could feel that enthusiastic about her own life.

'How unbearable were they today, then?' Steph speaks in a whisper as she enters the classroom, clutching a pile of red exercise books. A Bic biro is tucked into her boisterous ponytail. She dumps the books on the table. 'I've got thirty masterpieces on *Lord of the Flies* here.' She grins. 'Swap you?'

Hannah picks up her pile. 'I wouldn't do that to you. I've got Class 11C on imagery in *Macbeth*. It might not be pretty.'

Steph looks at her sideways as they start to make their way to the staffroom. 'How is it to be back?'

'It's OK, actually. Apart from evil Margaret. She's already started chipping away at my self-esteem.'

'She never rests.' Steph rolls her eyes. 'Now I'm leaving she's obviously retrained her sights. Don't let her get to you.'

'I'll try.' Hannah looks at the new art display arranged in the perspex casing that runs along the corridor. 'Wow. What were they painting? Monsters?'

Steph giggles. 'No you muppet, it's their parents.'

'Oh.' Hannah frowns at a particularly gruesome creature with distorted bloodshot eyes. 'Actually they do remind me of parents' evenings.'

'Sssssh.' Steph flicks her eyes towards a group of students coming down the corridor. 'They'll tell on you.'

'Tell what, Miss?' A girl with hyperactive hair extensions looks up at them.

'Nothing.' Hannah shakes her head. 'Nice hair, by the way. Did you do it yourself?'

The girl grins. 'Nah, Miss. Got my stylist to do it.' She giggles and looks five years younger. 'It's just like that Gok Wan's show at my place.'

Hannah nods. 'Yeah? Can I come round?' She indicates her unruly curls. 'I need a bit of styling.'

'You do, Miss.' The girl puts her head on one side. 'I'll see if we can book you in.'

'You do that.' Hannah turns and walks on as giggles burst out behind them.

'Cheeky gits.' Steph grins. 'Personally I love your finger-in-a-socket hairstyle.'

'Shut up.' Hannah laughs despite herself. 'I'll have you know it takes a lot of insomnia to get it looking this good.'

'It's so great to see you smile.' Steph nudges her with an elbow. 'Maybe things are about to get better. Maybe this is the turning point. Maybe—'

They turn the corner.

And there he is.

'Or maybe not.'

They both come to a standstill.

Steph leans towards Hannah and whispers out of the corner of her mouth. 'What the hell is he doing here?'

'I have no idea.' Hannah attempts to blend into the brick wall behind her. She fails.

'Hello, ladies.'

Hannah looks around desperately for escape routes. Nothing. No fights she can go and break up. No kids lighting up outside the window.

She briefly contemplates setting off the fire alarm. Anything to get out of here.

'How are you?'

He's looking at her.

She opens her mouth. Closes it.

Cool.

'Raj.' Steph's voice is unusually high-pitched. 'What are you doing here? I thought you'd gone to that school in Brighton?'

'I had.' He taps long fingers against a yellow file. 'But then I got the call to come and fill in here. You don't get rid of me that easily.'

'Apparently not.' Hannah dares a look at his face, then flicks her eyes rapidly away.

'Well. It's great to have you back.' Steph has never sounded less convincing.

'Thanks.' He moves a step closer to Hannah. She steps back.

Steph is talking again. 'So who are you covering this time, Raj?'

'Tyler's gone off sick again.'

Steph tuts. 'He's such a slacker. Took a month off a while ago because he had a septic toenail.'

Raj shrugs and a smile crosses his face. 'Well, it's good news for me.'

'If you say so.' Steph walks behind him and puts her hand on the door to the staffroom. 'Are you coming in for a coffee, Hannah?'

'Erm . . . yeah . . .' Hannah looks down and sees that her feet don't seem to be moving.

Raj touches her arm. 'Could I just have a quick word, Hannah?'

God, no.

'I don't think so.' Hannah finally gets her limbs to obey and starts to follow Steph.

'Please?' He blinks big brown eyes. She'd forgotten how long his lashes are.

She halts. Looks at him. Allows herself to think back to the pulsing haze of her thirtieth birthday party. How months of anger and sadness had mixed with the alcohol in her veins until she had found herself kissing him on the street. Not caring about anything but skin and hands and the joy of being wanted again.

Raj's skin. Raj's hands.

Oh God.

Steph is hovering awkwardly. 'I'll see you in there, Han? Soon? OK?'

'Er . . . OK.' Hannah tries to get a grip on herself. She just needs to talk to him. Explain that it was a one-night stand. That it can never happen again.

'So . . .' She turns towards him, cursing the flush that seeps across her face.

He is too close. Too tall.

'How are you, Hannah?'

She drops her eyes. 'You know. Having the time of my life.'

'I heard what happened with Tom. How is he?'

Hannah feels compelled to be positive. 'Oh, he's great. He's coming home next week. He's going to need a bit of help doing—' She stops. Tom is going to need help doing absolutely everything. She bites her lip.

'You look so sad, Hannah.'

She steps sideways. 'Yeah? Well maybe you don't know me as well as you think. This is my happy face.'

She wishes she were better at lying.

His eyes are reproachful. 'You didn't answer my texts.'

'I've had quite a bit going on.'

His voice is low. Eager. 'I was so glad to come back to Queensdale, Hannah. To see you.'

'I don't know why.' She can't restrain the harshness in her voice. 'Anyway, I thought you were getting back together with your old girlfriend?'

'No. I – we – don't fit any more.' He is so close.

She hates her heart for beating faster. She looks down and feigns intense interest in her own shoes.

'Hannah?' He steps even closer. 'I know things have changed for you, but our night together really meant something to me.' She glances upwards as he hits his forehead with the palm of his hand. 'All the poetry in the world, and that's the best I can come up with.' He rolls his eyes. 'Smooth, aren't I?'

For a second she lets herself smile. She remembers how kind he was at her party. How he had calmed her after Tom had failed to turn up – listened to her for hours as she'd talked about how unhappy she was and how she couldn't bear one more minute of Tom's contempt.

He had made her laugh. Wrapped a curl of her hair round his finger when she snuck outside for a fag. Kissed it. Said he was crazy about her. Told her he'd fancied her ever since his first stint of supply teaching at Queensdale six months ago.

She remembers how he had kissed her hurt away.

Then she opens her eyes and sees herself standing in a grey corridor fantasising about a man who is not her sick husband.

She hates herself.

'We can't do this, Raj. I can't do this.' She tries to push the door open but he puts his hand up to stop her.

'No.' Her voice is louder than she thought. 'No, Raj. This isn't going to happen.' She pushes the door. 'Stay away from me. Please.'

He lets her go. 'But—'

'No.' She pushes her way into the stale hubbub of the staffroom. Finds the biscuit tin. Opens it.

It's empty.

A ticket to the London Eye

June 2007

'So you still haven't got a job, Tommo?' Julie slouched against the glass wall of the London Eye, totally ignoring the golden clouds framing Big Ben behind her as they descended towards the Thames. Tom looked at his mum as she stared transfixed at the world's most famous clock, her left hand unconsciously squeezing the safety bar in front of her.

She was drinking in every sight as if it might be her last.

He gulped. After eight weeks of chemo and her mastectomy last month, his mum had become so frail he wondered whether this summer might be the end. He looked down at the inky water of the Thames beneath them and forced the thought away.

He turned back to his sister.

'No I haven't got a job yet, Jules, but—'

Hannah cut in. 'He's got an interview with a great law firm tomorrow, though.' She smiled proudly up at him. 'So I'm sure we'll be cracking open the champagne tomorrow night.'

Julie made a moue of disbelief. 'I can't believe that posh guy Nick got a job before you did, Tommo.'

He sighed. The pod was starting to feel oppressively small. He had been so pleased when they had got one to themselves, but now he wished there were some excitable Italian tourists with them to drown out Julie's negativity.

He reached for the remains of his patience. 'That posh guy is my best mate, you know. And he got me the interview tomorrow via one of his old schoolmates, so . . .'

Julie shook her head dismissively and the stud in her nose glinted in the late evening sun. She stood up straight and her eyes were on a level with his. There was no sign of his little sister. The girl with the wide eyes who would have given him the world if only she had it.

This Julie smelt of fags and looked like she could get served in a pub and flay someone with a single word. He averted his eyes as he realised he could see the black lace of her bra through the thin purple cotton of her top.

'Whatever.' Julie nibbled on a pointed black nail. 'Not like you to come second.' She looked at Hannah. 'He used to punch the walls when I beat him at Monopoly.' She laughed. The sound was dry. Sardonic. She never sounded anything else when she talked to him nowadays.

She pushed away from the glass and padded over to their mum. 'Are you OK?' She put her arm gently round the thin shoulders. Tom saw the tenderness on her face and suddenly she was Jules again. Gentle. Caring. Kind. 'Are you warm enough, Mum?'

'I'm all right, love.' Their mum pulled her thick cardigan closer round herself, even though it was one of London's balmier summer evenings. She stared out at the river and Somerset House and he saw how pale she looked in the soft evening light.

'It's so big, isn't it? London.' Her voice was quiet. 'You'd think that everyone would get lost down there with all those big buildings everywhere.'

'I know, Mum. It's a bit more cosy back home.' Julie

squeezed her shoulder, then put a hand up to her face and viciously dashed away what looked very like a tear. She turned back to the bench at the centre of the pod and sat down, hunching forward and folding her arms, staring out angrily at the thick metal spokes of the Eye. Her mouth was set in a hard line as she inserted headphones into her ears and turned the music up loud.

He knew he should sit down next to her. Talk to her. Try to find some common ground.

He had no idea how. He had thought their mum's illness would bring them closer. Instead Julie's resentment seemed to snare him at every turn.

Hannah went over and stood next to his mum, her bright pink dress bathed in sunset light. 'I know what you mean about the big buildings. I was brought up in the country. Sometimes I love it in London. Sometimes all the noise makes me want to hide.'

His mum looked at Hannah. 'And do you? Hide?'

Hannah nodded. 'Yeah. I hunt down a bookshop and breathe for a while. Makes me feel better. You know?'

The shadows beneath his mum's eyes temporarily disappeared as she smiled. 'I do, love. Like me and garden centres.'

'Yeah.' Tom looked at Hannah's dark curls next to his mum's ill-fitting NHS wig and felt a pulse of love so strong he thought he might burst. He watched as his mum leant close to Hannah, talking in a low voice in her ear. He saw Hannah smile and then lean over and give her a hug.

He turned to look at the dome of St Paul's as they dropped down towards the Thames. He heard a loud bass beat and was spurred into action.

He walked to Julie and gently pulled one of her headphones out. 'Julie, I—'

The look she gave him was so furious it drove the words out of his head. 'What, Tommo?'

He had no idea why she was so angry. All the time. Always with him.

He felt his mum's eyes on them and took a deep breath. 'Nothing. I just wanted to make sure that you've seen all the sights.'

'Of course I have.'

'I was just checking.'

'You didn't have to.' Her mouth was set. Defiant. 'I'm doing fine by myself, thanks. I don't need you looking after me.' She hunched back down and muttered under her breath. 'Just as well, really.'

'What? Jules, I—' He was interrupted by an announcement saying 'You have reached the end of your journey'. He saw the determined set of Julie's shoulders and gave up. He needed to get out. Feel the air. Have a beer.

Julie took their mum's arm and gently led her back onto the walkway leading down to the South Bank. He could see her talking as she pointed to various street performers waiting on plinths along the riverside. Tourists clustered in front of them taking enough photos to bore their relatives into oblivion on their return home.

'Are you OK?' Hannah smiled up at him as she folded her hand round his.

He stepped sideways to let a woman in a wheelchair progress up the ramp, pushed by a sweating man who was clearly struggling to keep a smile on his face. 'Nearly there,' the man puffed as he strained to reach the top. Tom caught the woman's eye for a second and then flicked his glance away. He felt embarrassed. Intrusive.

'Tom?' He felt Hannah's eyes on his face. 'Are you OK?'

'Yeah, I'm fine.' He looked longingly at the pub lit up across the square. Office workers in rolled-up shirtsleeves and dark dresses clustered outside, clutching cigarettes and empty glasses. He could almost taste the cool beer on his lips.

Hannah raised an eyebrow. 'No, you're not.'

'Yes I am.' He frowned and rubbed his eyes. 'Mum just looks so rough. And Julie's so . . .' He ducked out of the way of a little girl attempting to take a picture of the Thames. 'So bloody angry.'

Hannah leant closer. 'She's a sixteen-year-old girl, Tom. Her mum's really ill. And she thinks she's screwed up her GCSEs. Of course she's angry.' The breeze whipped her hair away from her face. 'Maybe you could head down there for a while, once your interview's done. It must be tough for Julie looking after your mum all by herself.'

He felt a kick of anger. 'She's not by herself. I've sorted carers to go in and help. I told you that.'

Hannah nodded. 'I know. I wasn't saying—'

Frustration kept him talking. 'And I need to do more shifts to pay Mum's bills. Her heating's been crazy this month even though it's summer. You'd think it was the bloody Arctic down there in Somerset going by the amount she pays.'

'OK.' Hannah nodded. 'It was only an idea.'

Part of him knew that he wasn't angry with her, but part of him couldn't bring himself to tell her.

'Yeah, well, this isn't easy for me either, H.'

'I know.' She kept her eyes on the pavement.

'And Mum's still got radiotherapy in September, so she won't be able to work for ages, so I have to keep the money coming and—'

She turned her face towards him and the faith on her

face made him want to weep. 'I know, Tom, I'm sorry. I know you're doing everything you can.'

He was still tense. Taut. Spoiling for a fight.

Hannah cupped his face in her hands. 'And she's so proud of you. So excited about your interview.'

He fiddled with the keys in his pocket. 'How do you know?'

Hannah kissed him gently on the lips. 'She told me. Just now.'

He bit his lip hard. It was everything he could do not to cry.

His mum and Julie had come to a halt next to a woman inexplicably dressed as an Ewok. His mum blinked slowly around at the energy and pace of London as it bustled around her. A girl in a bright pink sari blew bubbles into the sky. A clown in thick white make-up smoked a cigarette while sitting on a battered leather suitcase. A little boy giggled as he zoomed past them on a bright green trike, pursued by a red-faced man, presumably his dad.

The words came out before he could stop them. 'Do you want kids one day, H?'

A pause. A sickening lurch in his stomach as he wondered if he'd said too much.

Then he saw the beginnings of Hannah's smile. It could have lit a fire on a dark winter morning.

'Yes.' She squeezed his hand. 'Yes I do.'

He felt a rush of exhilaration and lifted her up in the air. 'Sure?'

She squealed. 'Of course I'm sure.' He whirled her round. 'Put me down!'

He set her feet firmly back on the ground.

'Don't get too excited.' Her eyes were full of mischief. 'I'm not saying I want yours.'

'Oi.' He reached for her but she had already dodged away towards his family.

'Glad to see someone's having a good time.' Julie folded her arms as he approached.

His mum stepped forward. 'Time for us to go, I think, love.' She smiled kindly at Hannah. 'It was lovely to meet you.' The light breeze cruelly pulled her wig to one side, exposing a pale expanse of scalp. She patted it back into place as everyone pretended not to notice.

'You too.' Hannah kissed her on the cheek. 'Let me know if you need anything. Any time.'

'I've got things under control, thanks.' Julie put her arm protectively round her mum's shoulders. 'I've been doing pretty well for the past few months.' She looked pointedly at Tom.

'Now, then, love. Don't let's start that again.' His mum looked like she was about to drop with exhaustion. 'Let's go to the station.'

Hannah stepped forward. 'We can show you the way if you like.'

'No.' Julie shook her head. 'I can manage.' She tucked her mum's arm into hers. 'Come on, Mum.'

His mum held back for a second and looked at Hannah. 'He's a good boy.'

Hannah nodded solemnly. 'He is.'

His mum's mouth twisted at the corner. 'You need to watch him though. If you're not careful he'll just watch the football and eat all your toast.'

Hannah grinned. 'No one eats my toast.'

'Quite right, love.' His mum kissed Tom on the cheek and gently pressed his hand in hers. Tom was shocked to feel how bony her fingers were. He realised she was carrying the navy bag that he'd given her a few Christmases ago. He'd given up asking her when she was going to use it. She had always said that she was saving it for best. Waiting for a special occasion that had never seemed to come.

She pulled the bag up protectively on her shoulder as she walked away.

It scared him that she wasn't waiting any more.

Eight

'Welcome home, Tom.'

Hannah puts his plate down in front of him.

He stares at the food.

'I made your favourite.'

His brow furrows.

She looks at the steak. For once she has remembered to remove it from the grill before charring it to a crisp. The mash is buttery and smooth. The green beans are glistening.

She was so sure he would love it.

Instead he shakes his head.

'Are you not hungry, Tom?' Hannah slumps down next to him at the kitchen table. 'Or have I done something wrong? I'm so sorry. I—'

'No.' Tom's voice is a growl. 'It's not that. It looks great. It's just that . . .' He gestures towards the knife and fork by his plate.

'Oh God.' Hannah hits her forehead with her palm. 'I'm such an idiot.' She takes the cutlery and pulls his plate towards her. She starts cutting the meat into small squares that he can fork into his mouth with one hand. 'I didn't think.'

She looks up but his eyes slide away from hers.

'Here you go.' She pushes the plate towards him again with the fork resting at the side.

'Thanks.' He lifts some steak to his mouth with his right hand, while Hannah starts on her own plate. They both chew in silence. Conversation fails to flow.

Hannah reaches across the table for the discharge pack the hospital had given her when she and Nick had picked him up earlier. 'Let's see what treats they've given us.'

Tom grimaces. 'Can't wait.'

Hannah opens the white paper bag with Tom's name and date of birth stamped on the label. She pulls out industrial supplies of aspirin and a selection of leaflets.

Stroke and incontinence.

Sex after stroke: challenges and solutions.

Cheering. She hastily shoves them back in the bag.

Tom forks up another bit of meat. 'What did they say?'

'Nothing.' Hannah stands up and puts the bag in one of the kitchen cupboards.

She sits down again. 'So, how is it to be back home?'

Tom blinks in the sun that shines through the kitchen window. 'Bloody amazing.' He smiles. 'I've never been so happy to see daylight. And sit in a kitchen. And have a real mug of tea.' His face falls as he looks towards the grey walking frame that stands at his side. 'Wish I hadn't had to bring that with me though.'

'You won't need it for long.' Hannah speaks with a certainty she doesn't feel.

'Look how fast you escaped the wheelchair – you barely use it now,' Julie says as she stalks in from the hall and takes a bit of steak from Tom's plate. She walks over to the radio in the corner of the kitchen as she pops the meat into her mouth.

'S'pose so.' Tom sighs. 'I'll just do a small tap dance to celebrate.'

'Just trying to be positive.' Julie stabs the radio with impatient fingers. 'Why isn't this working?'

'It was working this morning when I left to pick up Tom.' Hannah walks over. 'Have you used it since then?'

Julie shakes her head. 'No.' Her facial expression says yes. Since moving the rest of her stuff in she has deleted everything on Sky+ and crashed Hannah's bike into a wall. If she carries on at this rate Hannah fully expects a house fire by the end of the month.

Julie puffs out her cheeks. 'It's OK. Zac can fix it when he gets here.'

'Yeah? When's he arriving?' Hannah doesn't hold out much hope. Julie's supposed boyfriend is rapidly achieving the status of myth. During Tom's six weeks in hospital Julie has claimed Zac is 'about' to arrive at least twice a week, yet somehow he never quite makes it in the flesh.

'Not sure yet.' Julie's fingers tap against her tight black jeans. Hannah notices the Topshop label. Same as hers. She looks closer. They *are* hers. She opens her mouth to protest but then sees Tom slumping forward over the table and rushes to his side.

She grips his shoulder, fear quickening her breath. 'Tom? Are you OK?'

He opens bloodshot eyes. 'Sure. Sorry. Must have dozed off.'

Julie sits down opposite him and starts helping herself to his food.

'They did say you'd get really knackered for the first few months.'

'I know.' Tom sighs. 'But this is crazy. It's only twelve thirty, for God's sake.'

Julie forks up some mash. 'You're just getting used to

it all, Tom. Just as well you've got your amazing sister to look after you for a while.' She grins. 'It's like that time when you slashed your leg riding your bike into a fence and I played nurse.'

'I remember that.' Tom's face lightens. 'You used up all the plasters in the bathroom cupboard and then thought you'd try Pritt Stick instead.'

'Yeah.' Julie devours another piece of his steak. 'Thought I'd stick you back together.' She swallows. 'We'll have you better in no time, Tommo. I'll be back in Bristol before you know it.'

Tom nods. 'I know.' He tries to smile. 'I'll be the quickest person ever to beat a stroke.'

'Damn right you will be.' Nick comes back in from the living room, where he's been on yet another urgent work call. As she watches him Hannah remembers all the evenings spent waiting as Tom paced up and down in his dark pinstripe suit. She can see him now, pressing his BlackBerry relentlessly to his ear as he talked urgently into the mouthpiece, his work scowl cutting two stark lines between his eyes.

She looks at Tom now in his tracksuit and hoodie. He looks softer. More like the Tom she dated. The Tom she had fallen in love with.

'How are you doing, mate?' Nick sits down on a kitchen chair and undoes the top button of his white shirt.

'Not bad.' Tom's phone bursts into a Spurs football chant. He tries to swipe it with his right hand but the phone slides away across the table. They all watch as he tries to pin it down. Fails. Tries again. Hannah sees Nick reach out his hand. Stop himself. She is the same. Constantly poised. Constantly unsure.

In the end Tom shakes his head and leans back in his

chair. 'Probably no one important anyway.' Hannah sees a muscle flicker in his cheek.

Nick coughs. 'Don't think this is going to get you out of starting our firm, Tom. Think of the PR. "Man comes back from the dead to head up top City law firm Masters and Ellison."'

'Ellison and Masters, thank you.' Tom shakes his head. 'Don't try to take advantage of my weakened state to take all the glamour for yourself.'

'I wouldn't dare.' Nick leans back on the kitchen chair.

Hannah fills the kettle at the sink. 'I'm not sure we should be thinking about Tom going back to work yet. Let alone starting his own firm.' She pulls some mugs out of the cupboard. 'Tea, anyone?'

'Not for me, thanks.' Tom shuffles his chair back from the table. 'I need to . . . you know.' He grips the walking frame with both hands and tries to push himself to stand. Hannah sees how his arms tremble. She knows he wants to do it himself but eventually she can't bear it any more and goes to him to support him as he rises.

'It's OK, H.' He doesn't look at her. 'Jules, can you help me?'

Hannah grips his waist. 'I can do it, Tom. I can help.'

'No.' He won't meet her eye. 'I just—' He exhales and embarrassment is stamped across his face. 'We might as well get Julie started. Seeing as that's what she's here for.'

Hannah nods, surprised. 'Oh. OK.'

'Right, Tommo.' Julie has cleared Tom's plate. 'Let's shimmy.'

Tom inches the frame forward. His right leg steps but his left only drags along the floor.

He turns towards her. 'Thanks for lunch. Sorry I wasn't able to do it justice.'

She isn't used to him apologising.

'That's OK.' All her words feel forced. Like she's playing a part without a script.

'Are you OK, Hannah?'

She looks at Nick as the kitchen door closes.

'I'm better than him.' She gets out two teabags and drops them into two mugs. 'How about you?'

'I'm all right.' He nods. Coughs. Fiddles with his keys. 'I was just wondering though . . .'

'Yeah?' She adds boiling water to the mugs.

'I was just wondering what you talk to him about now?'

Hannah shrugs. 'I don't know.' She sits down and crosses one leg over the other. 'It's difficult.'

Nick fiddles with the gold links on his watch strap. 'I know. I have no idea what to say any more.' He sighs. 'All the stuff we used to talk about, work and cars and stuff . . . it feels wrong now.'

Hannah takes the milk out of the fridge and puts it on the table. 'Well, there's always sport. That normally seems to take up several hundred hours of your time together.'

'I suppose so.' Nick takes the mug of tea. 'He can still watch TV, can't he?'

'Yep. But he probably needs to go easy on the match-day beers for a while.' Hannah's heart aches as she thinks about how much Tom's world has shrunk. She looks out of the window at the garden and sees the bright body of a plane heading away to unknown climes. Unknown adventures. She feels again the thud of opportunities lost.

She looks down at the comedy Santa socks Steph had given her for Christmas. Somehow they don't seem so funny any more.

'What did the doctors say when they discharged him?'

Nick's face is serious. 'I was going to ask you in the car, but I didn't want Tom to hear.'

Hannah feels a familiar nausea start to churn in her stomach. 'They just said that he needs to look after himself. Take it slow. Do his physio. Not put too much pressure on himself.'

'And will he recover fully?'

'It's a possibility, but they aren't sure.'

Nick rests his head on his hands. 'Bloody hell.'

'Yeah.' Hannah sips her tea. 'No guarantees. No timeframe.'

'And might he have another stroke?'

'Apparently that's unlikely. Especially if he's careful.'

'Good.' Nick looks at her. 'Well, thank God he's got you.'

Guilt skewers her. 'I don't know about that.'

'I do.' Nick gulps his tea. 'He's bloody lucky.'

'Hardly. He won't even let me help him.'

Nick shakes his head. 'I'm not surprised. I wouldn't want my wife wiping my arse either.'

Hannah blinks. 'I hadn't thought of that.'

Nick's BlackBerry rings and he snaps back into lawyer mode. 'Right. I'd better get going. Only so long I can pretend to be at the dentist.'

'Bye Nick.' Hannah stands up. 'You will keep coming over, won't you?'

'Of course.' His eyes flick towards his BlackBerry and then away. 'You know I will. Even if it means watching bloody Spurs matches on the sofa.'

Hannah smiles. 'Well, as long as I don't have to.'

She walks him to the front door, and as she closes it behind him she notices a small brown envelope among the cluster of bills that has landed on the doormat. She picks up all the letters and takes them to the kitchen table, where she sits down and rips the envelope open. She reads the letter, something in her wavering when she sees that Teach the World have acknowledged that she can't join them in Tanzania.

She closes her eyes for a second to imagine what might have been.

'What's that?' Julie appears beside her.

'Blimey.' Hannah shoves the letter in her pocket. 'Where did you spring from? Do you have a trapdoor?'

'Nah.' Julie grabs her bag. 'Just Converse.' She looks down at her bright pink sneakers.

'Are you heading out?'

'Yep.' Julie nods. 'He's done his number two and I've got him back on the sofa, so—'

Hannah holds up a hand. 'OK. You can stop there.'

'Why?' Julie blinks. 'You know you're going to have to handle those too, don't you?'

'Yes.' Hannah realises that she shares Tom's feelings about this. 'But that doesn't mean I want to think about it in advance.'

'OK, OK, keep your hair on.' Julie rolls her eyes. 'Maybe it's time you adjusted though. Now he's here. All day. Every day.'

Hannah doesn't want to think about it. 'I'm trying, Jules.'

Julie grabs a denim jacket from the pegs in the hall. 'See you.'

She is out of the front door before Hannah has time to realise that it is her denim jacket in Julie's hands.

She walks to the living room and sees that Tom is lying on the sofa with his eyes closed. She is about to tiptoe away when his eyes flicker open.

'Come and sit with me? If you're not going out?'

'No, I'm not going out, Tom.'

'Are you sure?' She sees fear in his eyes. 'Isn't there anyone you want to see?'

'No—'

'No one from work?' His eyes widen.

'No. I promise.' She wants to reassure him; she pads across the carpet and awkwardly lifts his legs up and slides beneath them. He feels warm. Heavy. She thinks back to the last time they had been on the sofa together. The start of the date night that had turned into hate night. The argument had started somewhere innocuous but progressed towards familiar territory. Tom had called her a selfish dreamer. She'd called him an arse. The evening had ended in stinging drunkenness and mutual recriminations over chips at midnight.

'That's nice.' He is half asleep. 'Anything on?'

Hannah reaches for the remote and flicks on the giant TV that he'd insisted on buying last year. It's roughly as big as their garden. She flicks through the channels, starting to panic as she sees programme after programme displaying healthy people running or playing football or throwing themselves off mountains.

She flicks it off. 'There's nothing I want to watch.'

'Bullshit.' She is surprised to see him smile. 'You love all that action-packed travel-junkie stuff.'

'No.' She shakes her head.

'You're such a bad liar.'

If only he knew.

She raises her hands in surrender.

'Yes. I am.'

Silence falls. His breathing deepens and she thinks he's fallen asleep.

He stirs. 'Do you fancy reading to me?'

'Sure.' She looks at the books and magazines piled on the table by the sofa. 'What do you want me to read?'

'Don't mind.'

'Really? You normally come out in a rash if you come within fifty feet of a novel.'

'Liar.' He rests his head more comfortably on the cushion. 'I read at least two thrillers in Turkey.'

'A year ago?'

'Yeah.' He nods. 'See? Not a philistine.'

'OK, then.' Hannah picks up the latest Sadie Jones. 'Let's give this one a go.'

'Great. Can't wait.' His eyes close again and he reaches out and takes her hand.

She starts to read.

He is asleep before she's finished the second page. She stays on the sofa, turning page after page until she can no longer feel her legs beneath his. Then she eases herself out and stands by the window, staring out into the sunny garden.

This is day one. Of many. And already she feels trapped.

She takes the Teach the World letter out of her pocket and carries it upstairs where she tucks it into a shoebox at the bottom of the wardrobe.

Just in case.

Union Jack lighter

September 2007

'But are you sure it's the right thing to do, Hannah?'

Tom saw Hannah roll her eyes behind the laminated menu that she was holding. She exhaled slowly before answering.

'Yes, Mum.' She lowered the menu and put it down on the polished brown wood of the restaurant table. Her nails were bitten to the quick. The mum effect. Other symptoms included a sustained attack on the sweet stall at Paddington station and chain-smoking throughout the long walk here.

'I *am* sure it's the right thing to do.' Her voice rose and took on an unusually sarcastic note. 'Strangely enough, I did find some time to think it through during the ten-page application form and three killer interviews.' She frowned. 'Thanks for all your congratulations, by the way. So good to know you're behind me.' She stared at her empty wine glass, clearly wishing it was full.

Her mum leant forward and steepled her fingers together. As she surveyed her daughter, Tom saw doubt momentarily cloud the confidence of her expression. It was rapidly wiped away, to be replaced by Jenny Miles: accountant. Her bobbed hair looked as if it would win a fight with a force ten gale, and the gold buttons on her navy shirt were so shiny that Tom imagined her polishing them in front of the ten o'clock news.

127

At the next table, a little girl with mischievous brown eyes was eyeing the buttons longingly. She leant out of her highchair to reach them. Her mother noticed her daughter's intentions and wisely distracted her with an enormous spoonful of ice cream.

Jenny inhaled slowly, and Tom could see the majestic flare of her nostrils.

'Of course you've done well, Hannah, but now you've graduated I thought we'd agreed that you should live at home with us. Do your PGCE and get started on this teaching career of yours.' She shook her head and her chins wobbled as if in disapproval at Hannah's choice.

'No, I think you made that decision for me.' A blotchy flush crept across Hannah's cheeks. She raised her thumb to her mouth and started to nibble the nail. Jenny reached out and stopped her. Hannah rolled her eyes and slumped against the rigid back of her wooden chair.

Her mum seemed to sense an advantage.

'You need to focus, darling. You're not a student now. You can't just wander the world for ever.' She turned to her husband. 'Can she, Harry?'

Hannah's dad cautiously peered at his wife from behind the wine list. He had been hiding back there for at least five minutes, even though there weren't that many wines on offer. His half-moon glasses glinted in the dusty sunlight flooding through the restaurant window.

He blinked in a bewildered fashion. 'Pardon?'

'Harry. It would be so helpful if you could pay atten-tion.' Jenny exhaled heavily and the candle in the middle of the table went out. 'I was telling Hannah that she needs to concentrate on her career.'

'Mmmm.' Harry ran a hand through minimal grey hair,

his tired brown eyes examining his water glass in forensic detail.

Hannah grinned and kicked her dad under the table. 'Dad understands why I want to go, don't you, Dad?' She looked at her mum. 'I mean, he didn't get to be a successful writer by sitting at home, did he?' She gazed adoringly across the table.

'And I'll be teaching when I go to Japan. That's the beauty of it. I'm helping my career. Aren't I, Dad?'

Harry stiffened and his eyes flicked nervously towards Jenny. Then he returned Hannah's smile. 'It certainly sounds like an adventure, sweetie.'

'See?' Hannah looked defiantly at her mum.

Jenny eyed her husband. If looks could kill Harry would be in a body bag by now.

'What are you working on now, Dad?' Hannah looked at Harry eagerly, her face full of pride.

A deep frown furrowed between Harry's eyes. 'Oh, just a biography.'

'Who is it this time?' Hannah leant forward, eyes alight. Tom saw Jenny lean back in her seat, mouth pressed into a severe line.

Harry tapped his nose with his finger. 'Classified information at this stage, sweetie.' He fiddled with the thick black strap of his watch. 'If I told you I'd have to kill you.' He looked at the table. Coughed. Eased his chair back.

'I'll be back in a minute.' Tom could hear the change jangling in his pocket as Harry stood up. 'Just got to . . . er . . .' He smiled affably at Tom. 'You know. Excuse me.'

Hannah's mum looked as if she would like to use the heavy silver cutlery to do some serious damage to her husband. Instead she swivelled her attention to Tom. He forced himself to confront the X-ray of her stare.

'What about you, Tom? What do you think?'

'Erm . . .' He took a sip of water and wished that they had got round to ordering wine. This wasn't exactly the conversation he'd hoped for when first meeting Hannah's parents. Sport, maybe. Politics at a push. But not Hannah's life choices. This wasn't the way to impress the parents.

He looked at the people reflected in the mirror that ran along the wall behind Jenny's head. A man in a blue cable-knit jumper blinked in surprise as his petite girlfriend refused to let him take a bite of her pasta. A family with identical auburn hair appeared to have taken their phones out for a nice lunch. Each face was unmoving, lit only by the glow of a screen.

They were still having more fun than he was.

The restaurant was warm and he felt sticky in his new suit. He took another sip of water and filled his glass from the carafe in the middle of the table.

Jenny sighed impatiently. 'I mean, you must have a view. You must think Hannah's being ridiculous. Going off to Japan to mess around for a year. She'd be far better off—'

He sensed Hannah tensing beside him, and the words came before he had time to think. 'Actually, I think it's a great idea.' He didn't. He was going to miss her like hell. He carried on regardless. 'I think going out there and living in a totally different culture is really brave.'

Hannah cast him a grateful glance and squeezed his hand under the table.

Jenny pursed her lips. He felt the need to convince her. 'I'm really proud of her.'

'Really?' Jenny's voice would freeze lava.

'Really.' He looked at Hannah and smiled.

Jenny sniffed. 'So you won't miss her?'

He met her eye. 'Of course I will. But that's a different thing. It's not about me.'

He wished it was. When Hannah had first told him about her proposed trip to Japan, he had wanted to scream NO from the rooftops. Instead, he had exited rapidly and smoked his way to the corner shop for some beers.

Hannah drummed her fingers on the table. 'Tom's got a great new job, anyway. He won't have time to miss me.'

Jenny eyed him appraisingly.

'Where will you be working?'

'At a City law firm.' He still couldn't quite believe it was true. Amidst all the pain of his mum's illness he had somehow managed to pass the interview Nick had set up for him with a partner he used to play rugby with. He and Nick would be starting there together next week. First year associates. After years of studying, he'd finally be the one in the suit with the paper under his arm heading to a big glassy office in the city. The building had flowers at reception. And its very own café.

Jenny pressed her lips together. 'Which one?'

'Foster, Smith and Weissburg.'

'Oh.' She nodded. 'I know it. One of my friends worked there.'

He wondered for a second if she was giving her seal of approval.

'But she left when they represented a chemical company who were responsible for that huge oil spill in the Atlantic.'

Maybe not.

'Mum.' Hannah rolled her eyes. 'It's his first job. We need to celebrate, not tell him it's shit.'

'Don't swear, Hannah.'

'Oh, come on, Mum. I'm twenty-two, not twelve.' Hannah was tangling her fingers in and out of each other. He had never seen her this tense.

The waiter finally deigned to arrive.

'Good afternoon, everyone.' He pulled his pen from a pocket of his long white apron with the kind of flourish normally reserved for the West End stage. His dark hair was feathered delicately across his forehead and his white shirt was spotless enough to star in a Persil campaign.

'Would you like to hear the specials?'

Hannah smiled. 'Yes please.'

The waiter had clearly spent a lot of time memorising them and was determined to show off his prowess. His list of lamb and truffle oil and caponata and pecorino was so overwhelming that by the end all Tom wanted was a pie and chips. The black ceiling seemed to be pressing down on him and the incessantly cheerful background music was starting to give him a headache.

The waiter twirled his pen between elegant fingers. 'What would you like, sir?'

Tom felt pressure to go for something exotic, so opted for the same kind of swordfish pasta as Jenny. He felt vaguely aggrieved when Hannah chose the burger.

Harry arrived back just in time and ordered a burger too. He glanced at Jenny's rigid profile. 'Now, let's all have a lovely lunch, shall we?'

Tom could see where Hannah got her optimism from.

'Sorry about that.' Hannah leant against Tom's shoulder as they sat on the train from Oxford back to London.

Fields rushed past the window, scattered with cows who seemed entirely oblivious to the rain that was starting to fall.

'Don't be stupid.' Tom cuddled her closer to him. 'The food was amazing.'

She looked mischievously up at him. 'Yours was a bit small.'

He wondered whether to deny it. The five bites of pasta on his plate had left his stomach grumbling for more.

'Maybe.' He stared out of the window. 'But it tasted great.'

She was giggling at him openly now. 'Your face was so funny when it arrived.'

'You mean you knew I thought it was a bit small?'

She was shaking with laughter. 'Of course I knew. That little girl on the next table knew. Your whole face fell. It was the saddest expression I've ever seen. Like the time you dropped your ice cream on that weekend in Brighton.'

'Oh, that was an amazing ice cream though.' He shook his head at the memory. 'Two Flakes. *Two.*'

She hit him on the shoulder. 'OK, OK. It was a tragic loss.'

'It was.' He kissed the top of her head. 'Anyway, I hope I did OK.'

'You were great.' She clasped his hand in hers. 'Sorry about all the bad vibes though.' Her voice dropped. 'Sometimes I wonder if it would have been better if they had split up ages ago.'

Tom shook his head. 'I doubt it.'

'Do you?' Her eyes were huge.

He nodded. 'Yep. Splitting up isn't exactly fun either. And they seem OK to me.'

She looked at him askance. 'You're kidding me. You

mean you didn't notice all the put-downs and the sighs and the disappointed looks she gave him?'

'Nope.' Tom had noticed all of these things, but only directed at Hannah. Somehow he didn't think that was the thing to say.

She gently traced the back of his hand with her forefinger. 'What was your dad like? Before he left?'

He swallowed. He never talked about his dad. Did his best not to think about him either.

Hannah squeezed his fingers. 'I'd love to hear a bit more about him.'

Tom sighed. 'He wasn't very happy.' He stared out of the window at a flock of sheep surrounding a trough in a damp green field.

'No?'

'No.' Tom shook his head. 'And I don't think he really liked anyone else being happy either.'

Her fingers were warm round his. 'How do you mean?'

'I dunno.' He kissed her hair. 'He just didn't like life much.'

'What did he do?'

'He ran the local newsagents. It's where he met Mum, actually.'

'Yeah?'

'Yeah.' He smiled. 'Apparently he used to let her have free Mars Bars.'

'Wow.' Hannah raised an eyebrow. 'Smooth.'

Tom thought of his dad in his old leather jacket and tattered jeans. Smooth was not a description that came to mind.

'But I don't think he ever really enjoyed our family. He used to go out a lot. Didn't ever really do anything with us. You know?'

Hannah patted his leg. 'That must have been hard.'

'No.' Tom shook his head. 'It was just how things were.'

'But you must have been angry with him.'

'Only for Julie's sake. She was so small when he went. Only six.' Tom shrugged. 'She didn't understand where he'd gone. So I just looked after her, really.' He swallowed down the lump that came to his throat whenever he thought of the sweet determination on his sister's face as she carried on laying a place at the table for her daddy for months after he'd gone.

'And later? Were you angry then?'

Tom nodded. 'For a while. The last day I saw him I'd got a really good result on an essay, and I told him all about it.' He remembered how excited he had been. 'And then he just looked at me and said it was a shame I wasn't doing better at maths.'

'That's so mean.'

'Yeah, well.' Tom didn't want to talk about it any more. 'Maybe that's why I worked so bloody hard.' He smiled down at her. 'But it doesn't matter what he thought any more. And it hasn't done me any harm, has it?'

She kissed him on the cheek. 'Apparently not.' She put her head on one side. 'Although I do think you have weird taste in chocolate. Maybe that's his legacy.'

He rolled his eyes in mock anger. 'Just because you don't like Snickers.'

'Peanuts? And chocolate?' She mimed vomiting. 'It's just *wrong.*'

'So you say.' He punched her gently on the arm. 'But you're *crazy.*'

They kissed so fiercely he could barely breathe.

Eventually she pulled away. 'Are you sure it's OK for me to go? To Japan? With your mum so ill?'

'Of course it is.' He felt panic churning deep in his gut. 'Just write to me. Please?'

'OK.' She squeezed his hand and kissed the back of it. 'Deal. And I was wondering if you could look after something for me? While I'm gone?'

'Of course.' He hoped it wasn't her terrible DVD collection.

She opened her bag and took out the Union Jack lighter he had used to light her cigarette all those months ago. 'Look after this for me. It's my lucky charm. I thought it might keep an eye on you while I'm gone.'

'I will.' He nodded, fingering the cool metal in his hand. 'Though I seem to remember it was mine once.'

'Nope.' She shook her head and smiled. 'Never.' She looked up at him. 'I'll come back for it, Tom.'

'You'd bloody better.' He took a deep breath. 'And when you're back you'd better move in with me too.'

Silence. One beat. Two.

Maybe it was too fast. Maybe . . .

He heard her giggle. 'Or what?'

He spoke in a low growl. 'Or the lighter gets it.'

She held up her hands. 'OK. Then I will. I promise.'

He sat back in his seat, wishing the next year away.

Nine

'Hannah.'

Hannah jumps so violently she drops the stack of exercise books that are piled in her arms.

'Margaret.' She reaches down to pick them up.

'Waiting for someone?' Margaret arches an eyebrow that has been viciously plucked to the width of a paperclip.

'Just . . .' Hannah looks around for inspiration. She had in fact been staring out of the window across the car park wondering whether her personality was ever going to reappear. She vaguely recalls a time in her life when she didn't feel like she belonged in a morgue, but can't remotely remember how it felt.

She had been up marking till 1 a.m. and then was woken at 3 when she heard Tom fall over on his way to the loo. She had just closed her eyes when Julie had come home and leant on the doorbell, having lost her keys. Again. Hannah had found them in the morning hanging off a rose bush above a lurid pool of puke.

Nice.

'Just thinking through a Year Ten lesson plan, Margaret.' She picks up the final book and stands up straight again.

'I see.' Margaret's frown tells Hannah she doesn't. She smooths her straight black skirt and the gold band on her ring finger glints in the light. Hannah wonders what

Mr Margaret is like. She suspects that the key require-
ments on Margaret's husband-hunting checklist would
have been abject obedience and absolutely no sense of
humour whatsoever.

Margaret presses her lips together. 'I hope you're still
planning to get me those spreadsheets by the end of the day.'

Hannah feels a jolt of panic. She had thought she was
enjoying a rare moment of being up to date with
Margaret's constant stream of 'career opportunities'.

'What spreadsheets?'

Margaret sighs. 'The Year Seven, Eight and Nine ones
outlining each student's spelling age, reading age etc. I
sent you an email this morning.'

'I've been in classes all day.'

'That's not quite true, is it?' Margaret shakes her head.
'Seeing as you're finding time to daydream out of the
window.'

'I wasn't daydreaming.' Hannah's voice is so feeble she
barely believes herself.

Margaret doesn't stop. 'So please get them to me by
tonight. I need to review them for a senior management
team meeting in the morning.'

'But I don't really have the time.'

Margaret glares at her. 'It won't take long, will it?'

Yes.

'Well . . .'

Margaret shakes her head. 'I was hoping for more from
you, Hannah.'

Hannah is stung. 'It's just that you seem to be giving
me a lot of extra things to do at the moment. And—'

'Well, you did say you were keen to help the
department.'

'Yes. And I am. But—'

'If it's too much for you, just say so.'

Hannah deflates. She is too tired for this. Negotiating with Margaret is as much fun as negotiating with a construction ball.

'No. I'll get it done.'

'Excellent.' Margaret nods in satisfaction. Another problem solved. Another task delegated. Now her mouth twitches with something that might indicate enthusiasm. 'Have you read the latest Howard Jacobson? From last year's Booker shortlist?'

'No.' Strangely enough Hannah hasn't found the time to fit that in.

'You should. Wonderful imagery.'

The only image Hannah can think of is that of her own bed. Climbing in and pulling the sheets over her head until Tom is better and she can start living again.

She sighs. She has no idea when he'll be better. No idea when she'll be free.

Margaret is still enthusing. 'We have to keep up, you know. Lead by example.'

Hannah blinks. Currently the only example she is setting her students is how to be too tired to start her laptop up in the morning.

'Right. Thank you, Hannah.'

Hannah stares after her as she walks briskly off. Whenever she thinks life can't get any worse, Margaret always steps in with another morale-boosting encounter. She is sure that she used to think she was good at teaching, but now she is starting to think Big Reg the book-hating caretaker could do a better job than her.

She sighs and starts to walk towards the English department office, hoping to ingest enough caffeine to ensure she is vaguely capable of keeping her eyes open during tonight's spreadsheet delights. She's turning the corner when she remembers she needs to pick up some new folders from the stationery cupboard, so she piles her exercise books on top of a bookshelf and unlocks the battered blue door.

As it shuts behind her she switches on the light and breathes in the quiet and the smell of paper and photocopier ink. It's lovely being alone. It's so rare nowadays. She's always in the classroom or in meetings or at home trying to cheer Tom on through his latest setback. Fingers locking into a claw so he can't put his razor down. Tipping water over himself when he tries to fill the kettle to make a cup of tea.

Whenever she talks to him she feels guilty for feeling so sorry for herself. But every morning she gets up and knows that her day will be exactly the same as the one before. Work. Tom. Work. Tom. She's been written out of her own life.

It's not surprising that she feels about 103.

She leans her hands on the cool metal shelves by the far wall, wondering if there's room for her to curl up underneath them for a small nap.

The door opens behind her.

'Hannah. There you are.'

Oh God. She squats down and attempts to hide behind the photocopier.

'Hannah. I can see you, you know.'

Damn.

'Oh, hi Raj.' She tries to sound casual. She's not entirely sure she pulls it off, as her sleeve appears to be caught in the paper feed tray. She pulls hard and it suddenly wrenches free, so that she stumbles forward towards him.

That wasn't the plan.

He reaches out to catch her arm. For a second she lets him hold her, then she steps back.

Professional. She is keeping things professional.

He looks at her reprovingly. 'You've been avoiding me.'

'No.' She can't meet his eyes. She really is a terrible actress. There's a reason she had always landed the plum role of Third Sheep in school nativity plays. 'I've just been busy.' She can feel herself start to blush.

'Come on.' He frowns. 'You've barely said two words to me since I came back to Queensdale.'

She folds her arms. 'Raj, I've barely got time to say two words to anyone.'

'Yeah, but . . .' He bites his lip. 'I thought we were friends.'

'But—'

'And you're never in the pub any more.'

Her ragged patience unravels. 'Come on. That has nothing to do with me avoiding you. I'd bloody love to go to the pub. But instead I'm working full-time while looking after my sick husband in any spare nanosecond I have. OK?'

'OK, OK.' He holds up his hands. 'I'm sorry.'

'You should be.' She turns and picks up a pile of violently green cardboard folders. When she turns round again he is right in front of her.

She steps back. Or tries to. The stationery cupboard isn't exactly the ideal place to keep her distance.

He drops his voice and she can smell the tang of mint on his breath. 'I just want to help, Hannah.'

Part of her feels like wrapping herself around him.

Part of her is conscious that the photocopier is digging into her bum.

He puts his hand on her arm again. She knows she

should shrug it away but somehow she can't find the strength.

'Why don't you come out with me?'

She has to physically bite her tongue to hold back her hysterical laughter. She barely has time to go to the loo, let alone go out on a date with a man who is not her husband.

'No.' She forces herself to push his hand away. 'No, Raj.'

'Look me in the eyes and say it.'

'For God's sake.' She raises her eyes to meet his. 'Stop this.' She pushes him in the chest with the folders. 'I'm married. And *knackered*. Any spare time I have is spent doing wildly unexciting things like brushing my teeth or checking my overdraft hasn't gone too far over its limit.'

'I know.' He moves closer. 'But—'

'But nothing, Raj.' She has to get out of here. She pushes past him and almost makes it to the door.

'Come out with me, Hannah.'

She looks at him in exasperation. 'Are you crazy?'

'No.' He shakes his head. 'I just remember how it felt. Being with you.'

'Yeah, well, I can pretty much guarantee that if we spent a night together now you would spend the time gazing at me dribbling onto your pillow while snoring my head off.'

He grins. 'You sound sexy when you snore. Like a—'

She can't take this.

'I'm leaving now.' She has her hand on the door.

'Don't think I'll stop trying.'

She stops. 'Listen to me. Stop. Please. This isn't going anywhere.'

She grasps the door handle.

His voice is full of mischief. 'Stop? Never.'

The sheer madness of the situation makes her smile. 'Well, maybe try a more romantic venue next time. Lovely though this place is, it's still just a cupboard.'

'What, like the canteen? The library? Or . . .' He laughs suggestively. 'The loos?'

'Watch out.' Hannah feels her phone vibrate. 'If you're not careful you'll . . .' She gets it out and reads the text. 'Fuck.'

'Well, that's going a bit far. Not till we've at least been out on a date.'

'No, Raj, not that. Fuck as in I have to go home. Right now.'

'Oh.' He blanches. 'Is there anything I can do?'

'Yes.' She nods. 'You can leave me alone. OK?'

'But—'

'Just give it up, Raj.' She opens the door and runs.

'And I thought things couldn't get any worse.' Tom lies face down on the cold tiles of the bathroom floor.

'What happened?' She hooks her hands under his armpits and starts to pull him upwards.

'Doesn't matter.' He hangs heavy in her hands and her back starts to protest. She grits her teeth. Ignores it.

'It does matter.' She struggles to keep hold of him as he slumps forward. 'We don't want it happening again.'

'I tried to walk without the frame.' He is sullen. Disappointed.

'But the physio said you still weren't ready.'

'I know what she said.'

'Then why did you try?' Her shoulders start aching as she finally manages to prop him up against the bath.

'Because I wanted to see if I could.'

She hears the sadness in his voice and bites back her reply.

'And then my muscles just went cold and I couldn't push myself up.' His face is lined with frustration. 'Just went round and round on the floor like the useless bastard I am.'

She wishes she had something to say to make him feel better.

She redirects. 'Thank God you had your phone with you, anyway. And where the bloody hell is Jules?'

Tom shakes his head. 'I don't know. She keeps disappearing.'

'It's not bloody good enough. She's meant to be looking after you.'

'Yeah. Well, it's not that much fun hanging out with me at the moment.' His voice is thick with self-pity.

'That's not the point, Tom.'

'So you're not denying it?'

She is so tired. 'Oh, come on, Tom.'

'What do you mean, "come on?"' His voice is rising. 'This is a bloody nightmare for me, you know.'

She puts her hand on his. 'I know.'

'You don't know.'

She exhales. 'OK, so I don't know. Of course I don't know how you feel. But all the time . . .' She tries desperately not to sob. 'All the time I just want you to get better. Every day. That's all I want, Tom. I hate what's happened to you. And all I want to do is fix it.'

His face has stiffened.

'So please, Tom.' Hannah feels tears running down her face. 'Please know that I'm trying. Every day. To help.' She stands for a minute as her breathing slows. 'It's all I can do.' She turns towards the door, and as she does so her foot slips on a wet tile and she falls, cracking the back of her head against the sink.

'Hannah?'

She's in so much pain she can't speak.

'Hannah?'

OUCH.

'Shit. Damn. Bugger.' She hears him frantically scrabbling along the tiles.

She blinks. Once. Twice. She doesn't appear to be dead. She's sure there wouldn't be a crack that big on any ceiling in heaven.

'Owwwwww.' She reaches upwards.

'Hannah?' The panic on his face moves her. 'Are you OK?'

'I think so.' She rubs the back of her head.

'Oh, thank God.' He breathes deeply. 'I was brewing up some amazing MacGyver-style rescue, but it might have taken me about five hours to get it started.'

She finds herself smiling. 'It's the thought that counts.' A giggle builds up inside her until she has to let it out.

'So they tell me.' She hears him laughing too.

He slides awkwardly across and rests his head on her belly. 'Talk about the crippled leading the crippled.'

'Yeah.' She starts laughing again. 'We could start our own TV series.'

'Good idea.' He snorts. 'Let's win ourselves a Bafta.'

'Or an Emmy.'

Their laughter dies down and they lie quietly for a minute.

Tom looks up towards her.

'So what are we going to do now?'

'Well, one of us is probably going to have to get up at some point.'

'And after that?'

'I don't know.' Hannah rests her head more comfortably. 'But maybe we need to remember how to have fun again.'

'Fun.' She can feel him nodding. 'What's that?'

'Exactly my point.' She thinks back to the last time they both had fun at the same time. She reckons it was over a year ago. And involved large amounts of alcohol. 'How about we start by making Hantinis?' She stops. 'Shit. Sorry. I mean, we can make non-alcoholic ones. I know the hospital said you shouldn't . . .'

'I can have one or two.' He whistles. 'Wow. Hantinis.'

'Yeah.' She feels herself cheering at the prospect. 'What on earth did you put in them, can you remember?'

'It was so long ago. But Amaretto. Definitely. And pretty much anything else that was in the drinks cabinet.'

'I can't believe you're still calling that crappy cupboard over the sink a drinks cabinet.'

'Of course I am.' She hears the smile in his voice. 'It was my favourite place in the whole flat.'

'Well, there wasn't a lot of competition.' Hannah shakes her head as she thinks of their first tiny rented flat next to an all-night garage. 'What was it the estate agent called it? "Bijoux"?'

'Yeah. Meaning there was barely room for a double bed.' He pauses. 'We had fun though, didn't we?'

'We did.' She levers herself out from under him and stands up. 'So let's go and try to have a bit more. Sound like a plan?' She holds out a hand.

He grins and takes it. 'It does.'

She braces herself and takes his weight as she pulls him up, wrapping her arm round him as they move towards the stairs. Towards their evening.

At midnight she sits bolt upright in bed. She is drunk.
Hazy. In need of a pint of water and several slices of
toast.

The spreadsheets.

Shit.

She drags herself out of bed and starts to type.

Order of service for the funeral of
Mrs Rosemary Jane Ellison

WESTHAYES CREMATORIUM, SOMERSET

November 2007

'Hannah. You came!'

He pulled her out of the drizzle into the shelter of the hallway leading to the chapel. 'I can't believe it.' He stroked her face. It was tanned and soft, and sympathy brimmed in her big brown eyes. She reached her arms round him and hugged him as if she would never let go.

Tears stung his eyes. After all the pain of his mum's final weeks, Hannah's arrival was the thing that threatened to make him cry. Seeing her again pierced him. He wanted to curl himself around her and weep all the tears that were locked in his heart.

'Of course I came.' She pulled away and slid her hand into his. Her slender fingers lifted his palm to her mouth and kissed it. 'You should have asked me to come sooner.' She traced a line along his face with her forefinger.

He looked away, worried her sympathy would dissolve the fragments of his self-control. 'I knew you were having a great time out there.' He swallowed as he saw his cousin Adam walk in with a stack of orders of service in his hands. His mum's name on the front. Her favourite hymns inside.

He looked back at Hannah. Focusing on her was easier than thinking about his mum. 'I didn't want to ruin it.'

He stared at the plaques on the wall behind her. A small blue oval saying DAVID SPELLMAN 1976–1998, WITH ALL OUR LOVE, MUM AND DAD. A large black square with IN MEMORY OF GLADYS SMITH – WE'LL NEVER FORGET YOU spelled out in golden letters.

'Tom.' Her voice was urgent. 'I love you. You're more important than anything else.'

'Really?'

'Really. Nothing's changed. Not for me, anyway.'

He couldn't look at her.

'I promise, Tom.' Her voice was so clear that she woke up his Auntie Sue, who had been snoring gently on a bench behind them just by the chapel door.

'*Bingo!*' Auntie Sue was clearly a little confused about where she was.

'Are you sure?' Tom dared to look at Hannah and saw sweet determination in her eyes.

Hannah took a deep breath. 'I want us to be together. OK?'

He nodded. 'OK.' He squeezed her hand. 'I missed you so much.'

'Me too.' She kissed him. 'Now, is there anything I can do to help?'

'Not really.' He looked around the crowd of mourners who were waiting patiently for the chapel doors to open. 'I think I've got everything sorted.'

'Where's the funeral car?'

'Should be here any minute.' Tom checked his watch.

'And Julie?'

'Same. She said she'd be here at ten thirty. If we're lucky she'll beat the vicar.' He looked outside just in time to see a taxi door being flung open and Julie stepping out. She was hand in hand with someone Tom had occasionally seen chain-smoking in the park opposite his mum's house. He was wearing tight grey jeans and a tattoo snaked up his neck above his black T-shirt.

Tom felt his teeth clench as he walked towards her with Hannah's hand clasped in his.

'Hello, hello.' Julie's voice was too loud as she weaved her way through the subdued group of family and friends grappling with umbrellas as the rain seriously started to fall. One of his mum's fellow volunteers at the local youth club rested her hand on Julie's arm for a minute, but was rapidly shaken off.

'What on earth is she wearing?' Auntie Sue had ventured outside and was staring indignantly at her approaching niece. Uncle Joe did his best to calm his wife, but as usual he lost the battle. Auntie Sue's chins wobbled indignantly. 'I can practically see her knickers. And what's that on her neck? Is it a . . .?'

Uncle Joe coughed so loudly that Tom was mercifully spared the embarrassment of hearing Auntie Sue say 'love bite'.

'Morning.' Julie arrived in front of them and gave him a perfunctory kiss on the cheek. She smelt of stale cider and Marlboro and her hair was lank around her face. Her black top had a white stain on the collar and was badly tucked into her minimal black skirt. Her grey cardigan slid off her shoulders as she tried to light a cigarette. Her hands were shaking so badly that Tom stepped forward to steady the flame.

The cigarette sparked into life. 'There you go, Jules.'

Her face was shuttered. 'Thanks.'

'Why are you so late?'

She rolled her eyes. 'Bloody taxi got stuck in traffic. I told him to go the other way. Didn't I, Si?'

Si was so busy inhaling nicotine he didn't seem to have an answer. Tom suddenly wanted a cigarette too. Anything to kill time.

'Hi, Julie.' Hannah leant round Tom to say hello.

Julie looked her up and down. 'Oh. You came.'

Hannah flushed and looked at the ground. 'I came as soon as I heard.'

Julie inhaled. Exhaled in Hannah's direction. 'Good of you.'

Tom watched Hannah struggling for something to say and felt a rush of protectiveness.

He stepped in. 'How are you, Jules?'

Julie arched an eyebrow. 'I've been better.' She shifted from foot to foot as she finished her cigarette in about three breaths.

Hannah held out her hand to Si. 'I'm Hannah.'

Julie's companion removed a hairy hand from his pocket and held it out. 'Si.'

He ground his cigarette butt into the gravel with his heel and stared into the middle distance. Tom wondered how old he was. Whether he knew that Julie was only sixteen.

Julie lit another fag from her first. 'Si's a truck driver.'

'Oh yeah?'

Julie puffed smoke into his face. 'Yeah.' She looked at the entrance. 'Nice flowers.'

'Thanks.' Tom nodded. 'Wish you'd helped me choose though.'

She shrugged. 'It's not like she's going to see them, is it?'

He searched for words to narrow the gap between them. 'So where have you been, Jules? These last few days?'

'With Si.'

'And at school?'

Julie shook her head. 'No.'

'Well, I hope you're going to get back there soon. You can't miss too much or—'

Her voice was light. Casual. 'Actually, I'm not going back.'

'What?' He had spent hours persuading her posh school to let her board for free. She was so damn smart. Straight A stars at GCSE.

Julie sighed. Kicked the ground with a stained red ballet pump. 'I'm not going back to school.'

'Why?'

'Gonna get a job.'

This was news to him. 'Since when?'

'I decided a while ago.' She ground her cigarette into the floor. 'While I was looking after Mum. While you were making it big in the City.'

He ignored the jibe. He'd heard it before.

'And you didn't want to discuss it with me?'

'Why?' Her insolence was a slap in the face. 'You weren't around.'

'Jules, that's not fair.'

'No?' Her voice was sharp with anger. 'Because the way I remember it, I was the one injecting her and taking her temperature and cleaning up her bedpan. I was the one there, trying to feed her and get her to drink and changing her sheets when she puked. Just me.'

He lowered his voice and leant closer to her. 'I had to work – to pay her bills as well as mine. And I came whenever I could.'

She shook her head and crossed her arms. 'You tell yourself that, Tommo. But I could have really done with . . .' She falls silent.

'With what?'

Julie's face has slammed shut. 'Nothing.'

'But where will you live, Jules? You know the council won't let you live at Mum's any more. Not on your own.'

'Don't worry about it.'

He hated her petulance. 'But of course I worry. I mean, you can come and live with me if you want.'

'Really?' For a second her face was open. Approachable.

'Of course.' He smiled. 'Hannah will be there for a bit, but—'

She looked away again. 'No, thanks. I'll stay with Si. He's got a flat. Haven't you, Si?'

Si grunted and checked his phone.

'But—'

He felt Hannah's hand in his. It was cool. Calming.

'Tom?' She gestured behind him. 'I think you need to go now.'

He turned and saw the funeral car. Long. Black. Final.

A hush fell over the mourners. Tom walked through them, fighting back the tears as two liveried staff expertly removed the coffin and set it on its stand. Its brass handles gleamed. The light wood was polished. A solitary wreath of lilies was laid on top.

It was exactly as his mum had wanted it.

He turned back to see his sister dissolving in Si's arms. He wanted to go back and hug her and help her, but he didn't think she would let him. Instead he stood waiting for the other pall-bearers to join him. Uncle Joe. Adam. Aziz, his mum's boss from the cleaning company. While they gathered Tom looked down at the coffin and thought about the woman inside. The woman who always took the smallest piece of cake. Who cackled at every joke

Bruce Forsyth had ever made. Who always worried she was in the way.

He wished he had made more time. To talk to her. To say thank you.

Too late now. He bit his lip savagely to stop the tears.

As he bent down and took the weight of the coffin on his shoulder, Hannah appeared at his side.

She whispered so only he could hear. 'You're being so brave, Tom. You're amazing.'

He put his hands up to hold the coffin steady.

He was glad he was fooling Hannah.

He wasn't even beginning to fool himself.

Ten

'Oh come on, Han.' Steph's voice pleads down the line. 'You haven't been out in ages.'

Hannah looks out at the garden. The patchy grass looks about as alive as she feels and the rose bush has keeled over entirely and seems ready to go to the big garden in the sky.

She rubs the carpet with her toe. 'I know, Steph, but I can't. Tom needs me.'

'But these are *great* tickets. Gold dust.'

'I know.' Hannah turns round and picks up the cluster of mugs and plates that seem to gather on every cupboard and table during the week. 'But I really can't come. I'm sorry. Tom's still Googling "stroke survival odds" on the iPad whenever he thinks I'm not looking. I have to be here.'

'Well, why can't Julie look after him?'

'She does weekdays, when she can be bothered. I'm with him at weekends.'

'Can't you bribe her?'

'I'd have to find her first.' Hannah puts the mugs in the kitchen sink and starts to head to the spare room, now Tom's bedroom. 'I'm sorry, Steph. I've got to go.'

'Damn.' Steph exhales loudly. 'I really thought it would be good for you to enjoy yourself. I'm worried about you.'

'Me too.' Hannah picks up a jumper and a sock from the bottom stair.

'How's he doing?'

'OK.'

'Meaning crap?'

'Meaning OK.' Hannah sighs.

A pause. 'I miss you, Han.'

'I know.' Hannah climbs the stairs. 'I miss me too. Now, go away. I've got to get on. Have a wild night. And for God's sake don't tell me how amazing it was on Monday.'

She hangs up as she walks into the bathroom, blinking in the sunlight streaming through the window.

'Who was that?' Tom is sitting in his wheelchair wrapped in a towel.

'Just Steph.' She puts her phone in her pocket. 'Nothing important.'

'Oh.' Tom points his right hand at his chin. 'How did I do?'

Hannah examines him carefully.

'Well, it's a bit less Sweeney Todd than last time.'

'Result.' He peers into the bathroom mirror. 'Only two cuts.'

'Nice.' She rips up a tissue and covers the two tiny nicks in his skin. 'Soon you'll be able to get a T-shirt on by yourself too and the awards will really start flooding in.'

'I will, won't I?' He nods his head and looks so proud of himself that she reaches down to give him a hug. There is a clash of cheekbones as he misreads her intentions and raises his mouth to meet hers. She lets their lips touch for a second and then pulls away, hating the disappointment on his face.

'OK.' She makes a big fuss of taking the towel and hanging it over the rail. It gives her a second to breathe. She turns back. 'Now, as a reward for such great shaving I'm going to treat you to one of my finest breakfast specials.'

'You are?' His eyes gleam. 'This is my lucky day.'

Hannah pulls his walking frame across the tiles towards him. 'Well, the hospital did tell us to celebrate every achievement, so I think we're cleared for some serious bacon and eggs, don't you?'

He nods eagerly. 'Absolutely. And will you . . .?'

'Will I what?'

'Will you make your special mushroomy thing? With tomatoes? And that cheese?'

'Feta?' She gets the frame into position so he can pull himself up to stand. 'You remember that? I haven't made it in years.'

'Of course I remember it.' She is constantly surprised by his ability to remember the good times. The times when they still had sex and went out on dates and knew how to make each other laugh.

She can't forget the unhappiness in between.

'OK, then. It's on the menu.' She picks up a blue T-shirt with a picture of Captain Caveman across the front. 'Though actually, come to think of breakfast, Julie's broken the coffee maker.'

'Oh yeah.' He sighs. 'And eaten all the bread.' She holds the right sleeve open for him and he pushes his arm through.

'So maybe we could head out?' She picks up his left arm and pulls the sleeve gently over his skin.

'I'm not sure about that.'

'But it's a gorgeous day. We could go to the Junction?

It's not far. And their bacon sarnies are the best.' She is seized by the desire to get out. To remember what the sun feels like against the back of her neck. To be part of the weekend world.

Doubt crosses Tom's face. 'But we can have bacon sarnies here.'

'Not without bread.' She looks out of the window. Tries again. 'Come on, Tom, we have to get out of this house. It's really warm for March. Let's break out. Make the most of it.'

Silence.

She pulls the T-shirt down over his head.

He emerges nodding. 'OK. Let's give it a try. But only if I can use my stick. I'm not taking this bloody chair.'

Uncertainty needles her. He hasn't walked that far before. 'I can get it downstairs, Tom. Easily. I know how to fold it up now, and—'

'No.' He shakes his head. 'I hate this thing.'

'But are you sure you're ready? I can always drive down—'

'Let me try.' She loves the determination in his voice. 'And you'll just have to give me a piggyback if I get stuck.'

'Yikes.' She knows the effort it costs him to joke about his condition and sets aside her misgivings. 'OK then, let's give it a try. And breakfast is my treat.' She picks up his boxers. 'Now, time to get your underwear on.'

'OK.'

The traditional awkward silence descends. No matter how many times she does this for him it still feels wrong. Intrusive. His grim expression tells her he feels the same.

She untucks the towel from his waist and he uses his right arm to lift himself lopsidedly so she can pull it away. His skin is still flushed from the warmth of the water and it smells of the musky shower gel that she remembers breathing in so happily the first time he held her.

Her hand hovers over his naked thigh. She sees the familiar fur of dark hair on his long legs and the mole near his right hip. She really looks at his body for the first time in months. Normally she's in such a hurry to get dressing him over with that she whisks clothes on and off, as if Tom were a shop mannequin with a new collection to display. Yet today there's sun and his smell in the air and . . .

She hears the resounding rumble of a snore from the study next door and the moment well and truly passes.

She giggles and drops the towel to the floor. 'Who's that?'

'Julie's been making another new friend, I expect.' Tom sighs. 'I have no idea what's going on with her. Or with Zac.'

'If Zac ever existed.'

He looks surprised. 'That's a bit mean.'

'Not really.' She shrugs. 'She's been here a couple of months now and I've yet to see any evidence that Zac's not a figment of her imagination.'

Tom's voice is low. 'I don't get it. I've tried to talk to her but she just changes the subject.'

Hannah stays silent.

'I just worry about what she'll do. With her life. I can't imagine her sticking with anything long enough to see it through.'

Hannah kneels down. 'She might surprise you, you know.' She pulls the boxer shorts gently over his feet. 'I can talk to her if you like.'

'That would be great.' Tom's eyes light up. 'Thank you.'

'No worries.' Hannah pulls the boxers up over his calves, and hooks her hand underneath his left thigh as he helps her by lifting his right from the chair.

'And now the big finale.' She walks behind him, lifting him up with one hand while pulling the boxer shorts up with the other. Her hand gently coincides with his thigh as she pulls the cotton straight.

As she settles the waistband into place she sees something.

Something that's very pleased to see her.

They certainly didn't cover this in the hospital discharge pack.

Tom's shoulders are rigid and her initial embarrassment rapidly becomes sympathy. He is cupping the uninvited arrival with his right hand, and leans lopsidedly forward in his chair.

She searches for something to say. Her mind doesn't oblige.

Tom starts to apologise and she snaps back into action.

'No need to say sorry.' She sounds like a severe ward sister from World War Two. He remains silent, braced forward in his chair.

'Besides . . .' She walks round to face him. 'It's nothing I haven't seen before.'

She sees the start of a smile. 'And nothing you won't see again, hopefully.'

She forces herself to hold his eyes. He needs to believe in their future. 'Of course.'

He shrugs. 'And it's good to know my mojo's still intact.'

'Exactly.' She leans forward and kisses him quickly on

the lips. 'Now let's get a tracksuit on you and get out of here.'

She zips him into it and gets them both out into the fresh air.

'Made it.' Tom looks exhausted as he finally manages to drag his left foot up the big stone step leading to the door of the Junction café. He removes his right hand from Hannah's shoulder and leans heavily on his cane. 'I'd forgotten how far it is from our house.'

Hannah doesn't comment. It's a three-minute walk when she grabs a coffee on her way to work in the mornings. Today it was more like twenty.

Tom is panting quickly. 'Can I just have a second? Before I go in? Need to get my breath back.'

'Sure.' Hannah stands beside him, staring out at the cars on the street in front of them. She hadn't realised how hard it would be. Walking with Tom reminded her of taking her grandpa out to the park just before he died. She used to hold onto his frail arm to guide him over crumbling kerbs and paving stones till they reached the bench where he and Granny had sat and fed the ducks for over forty years.

Tom looks at her. 'So how would you say that went?'

She smiles. 'I think you did brilliantly.'

'Really?' She is relieved to see some colour returning to his cheeks. 'Sorry I said I didn't want to talk on the way. Everything was too bright. Moving too fast.' He frowns. 'And that toddler calling me "Wobbly Man" as soon as we left the house wasn't a great start.'

She shakes her head. 'No. It wasn't.'

'And as for getting my cane stuck in that gutter while those girls were going past . . .' He rolls his eyes. 'Bad.'

'Yes.' She waits. He's building up to it. The explosion. She can feel it.

'Well.' He shrugs. 'Wonder what I can get up to on the way back?' He looks at her. Grins.

She keeps forgetting how brave he can be.

She squeezes his shoulder before swinging the door wide. The bell jangles merrily and she is enveloped in delicious smells of coffee and bacon.

'Double helpings of breakfast for you, Tom. You've earned it.' She ushers him in.

He limps into the heat and noise of the café and gamely starts to navigate a narrow gap between two tables. He is nearly there when his cane catches in the handles of an enormous red handbag. He nearly falls, but catches at a tablecloth to save himself. A woman's coffee flies into the air and splatters across the wooden floorboards.

Tom looks mortified. 'Oh God, I'm so sorry.'

The woman looks up, her face aggrieved. Her eyes take in the cane and Tom's pallor and her expression turns to pity.

'That's OK.' A smile warms her narrow face.

Something flickers in Tom's eyes. Pride. 'I can pay for another, if you like.'

'No.' The woman's tone is sickly sweet. 'That's OK.' She shakes her head. 'It's really not a problem.' She looks as if she is about to stand up. 'Would you like some help?'

'No.' Tom's voice is sharp. 'I'm fine.' He turns and slowly proceeds to a table by the window. He props his cane in the corner and sinks gratefully onto a sturdy wooden chair.

Hannah sits opposite him, facing the huge window that opens on to the street.

He leans forward. 'That was so bloody patronising.'

'I know.' Hannah glances back at the woman. 'But she was just trying to help.'

His face is pure frustration. 'They just don't understand.'

'Of course they don't.' Hannah picks up a menu. Puts it down. Her order hasn't changed since she first came here five years ago. 'No one can understand what it's like.'

'I just feel so . . .' He fiddles with a spoon. 'So bloody out of step with everyone else.'

'I know.' Hannah takes his left hand, lying still on the wooden tabletop. 'But you'll be back. I know it.'

'Do you?' He looks tired and unconvinced.

'Yes.' She searches for the words he needs to hear. 'You're strong, Tom. From what I've read online most stroke survivors go into hiding for months, but here you are having brunch with the rest of south London.'

'Go me.' He arches an eyebrow. 'Though I'm not sure that having brunch was one of my key rehab goals.'

'Who cares?' Hannah grins. 'Might as well enjoy it now you're here.'

He smiles. 'True. Now for God's sake order a coffee. Nobody wants to spend a morning with a caffeine-deprived Hannah, least of all me.'

'Cheeky sod.' Hannah gives him a menu. 'You'd better order some food then. You're about as much fun as an STD when you're hungry.'

'Thanks very much.' He rolls his eyes. 'Bloody charming.'

Hannah waves at the waitress, who has bright orange hairclips and a tight T-shirt that shows the outline of her bra. She comes over and takes their order.

Tom leans back in his chair.

'Do you remember when we used to do this all the time?'

'What, about a hundred years ago?'

Guilt darts across his face. 'Yeah.' Then he smiles. 'Before you got so busy with work.'

'*Me*?' She shakes her head. 'That is *outrageous* coming from the man who took his own pillow to the office.'

'Fair enough.' He shrugs.

She puts her head on one side. 'So, do you think you'll want to go back? To your firm?'

'Maybe.' He picks up a sugar packet and taps it against the table. 'I can barely unlock my BlackBerry at the moment. But I know I want to work again.'

She feels her stomach tighten.

'You do?'

'Of course.' He frowns. 'Why wouldn't I?'

'No reason.'

He puts the sugar down. 'Nick is still talking about starting a firm together.'

'Really?' Hannah tries to keep her expression neutral.

'Yeah.' Tom picks up his left hand and places it carefully on his lap. Out of sight. Never out of mind, Hannah suspects.

'And do you want to?'

'Yeah.' Tom runs a finger along the dark grain of the table. 'It's what we've always dreamed about. World domination.' His eyes glint with mischief. 'You know.'

Hannah looks at him. A thin man in a baggy tracksuit dreaming of the life he had before.

Part of her is scared for him. Part of her is proud.

He smiles at the waitress as their coffees arrive. 'I'm just a bit . . .'

'What?'

'Nothing.' He shakes his head. 'I just need to keep doing the exercises. Taking the tablets. Getting better. You know?'

'Yes.' She sips her latte. 'Sounds good.'

'How's your job, H?'

'Fine.'

'Meaning what?'

'Meaning fine.' She doesn't want to talk about work. She has started getting the Sunday-night blues at Saturday lunchtime. Bad sign.

'OK.' He holds up his hands. 'How about your colleagues? How's Steph?'

'Oh, you know. Loud. Disillusioned. Same old same old. She's heading off to Tanzania soon though, so she's pretty excited.' She sips her coffee to stop herself saying any more.

'And the rest of them?'

Tom never asks about her colleagues. Hannah stares at him, puzzled.

'Like that guy . . . Raj, was it? The one I met at the pub once. How's he doing?'

Hannah nearly drops her coffee cup. She darts a look at him to see what lies behind the question, but Tom's face is smooth. Interested.

She attempts to breathe. 'He's OK. Came back this term for a bit but he'll be off again soon.'

'I see.' Tom's mouth hardens.

She's finding it hard to breathe and leans towards him. 'Are you OK?'

He stares at his teaspoon.

'Tom?'

His mouth twists and then straightens and he looks up and his face clears. 'And are you enjoying it?'

'What?' Her mind is stuck on panic and for a second she thinks he means Raj being around. 'Work?'

'Yes.' He nods. 'You used to love it so much you practically skipped out of the door on a Monday morning.'

'Yeah, well, that was a long time ago.'

'So tell me how it is now.'

Misery clutches her. Work used to mean so much to her. Now school is just a slightly less depressing place than home. 'I don't want to talk about it.'

'Why not?'

'I don't feel like it.'

'Seriously, H. Why not?'

She is stung into a reply. 'Look, I've just got used to dealing with things by myself, OK?'

His face falls. 'OK. I'm sorry. Didn't mean to pry. I was just . . . interested.'

'Well, maybe it'll take me a while to adapt.'

'Fair enough.' He nods. 'OK.'

Hannah tries to regain her composure as the waitress brings their food. Tom doesn't know about her and Raj. Does he?

No.

Definitely not.

She inhales and looks at the plates in front of them.

Breakfast special for her. Bacon and maple syrup pancakes for him.

She touches the smooth yolk of the fried egg with her fork. She is ravenous, but she cuts his food up for him before she starts eating.

'Thanks.' He takes a mouthful and closes his eyes with delight. 'Mmmm. That beats boring Weetabix any day.'

She bites into a hash brown. 'This is amazing.' She chews and swallows. 'Do you want to try it?'

He looks at her askance. 'You never share food.'

She grins. 'Maybe I've changed too.'

'Wow.' He leans forward eagerly. 'I'm going to take full advantage of this.' He points at her bacon and her black pudding. 'Some of those please.' She obediently piles them on her fork and aims it at his mouth.

He chews. Smiles. 'Amazing.'

'I know.' Hannah cuts the bacon with her fork. 'Never fails.'

'No. I mean you actually letting me have some.'

'Oh, shut up.' She scowls. 'I'm not that bad.'

'There are death row prisoners having their final meal who are more willing to share food than you are.'

She rolls her eyes. 'Whatever.' Then she giggles. 'Though I do remember the time you tried to steal some of my salted caramel brownie and I genuinely wondered how I could kill you with a spoon.'

They both laugh and their eyes meet for a moment.

'This is nice.' Tom reaches his fingers towards hers. She quickly picks up her fork. 'Isn't it?'

She feels uncomfortable. Hot.

'Er . . . yeah.' She stares at her plate.

'It's good to hear you laugh, H.'

'I laugh all the time.'

'No you don't.' He sips his coffee. 'You used to. I used to love your cackle.'

'I believe you mean my ladylike chuckle.'

'Whatever.' He raises his eyes to the ceiling. 'People could hear you streets away. Cities away.'

'Shut *up*.' She flicks him with her hand.

'I just want you to be happy again, H. To get your bounce back.'

'I'm not bloody Tigger.'

'I'm serious.' He dabs a stray blob of maple syrup with his finger and pops it in his mouth. 'I want you to be happy. Like you used to be.' He grins. 'Do you remember that weekend in Paris?'

'What? The one where we managed to see precisely none of the sights?'

'Yeah. I loved just staying in bed and eating room service. Laughing at the bidet and at that receptionist who kept appearing at random times with bottles of champagne. It was brilliant.'

'It was.' Hannah had forgotten all that. All she can remember is the hellish row when they got back and Tom got called in to work straight from the airport. He was meant to be helping her with interview preparation for a job she really wanted. Instead she had been forced to sweat all the way home with the luggage before making ferocious coffee and trying to prepare while resenting him with all her heart.

She hadn't got the job.

Now his face is earnest. 'Let's get you cackling again.'

She looks at him. His eyes are wide. Sincere.

'Sounds good, Tom.' She has never felt less like laughing.

'Good.' Tom munches a piece of bacon. 'I'm worried about you.'

Not half as worried as he would be if he knew about Raj. And Tanzania.

If he knew the truth.

'So are you seeing Nick later? For the football?'

'Supposed to be.' Tom stops for a second. He is visibly out of breath after the walk back. 'I might need a rest first.'

'Well, I've got marking to do, so feel free to do whatever you like.'

'Marking? Again?' Tom nudges her. 'Watch out, or you'll be the workaholic in this relationship.'

'Ha ha.' Hannah grimaces and then stands up straighter as they approach their gate and she sees a stranger walking down the path from their front door.

'Hello?'

The stranger towers over her. 'Hi.' His voice is unexpectedly soft. A gentle West Country burr. 'Is Julie around?'

'I don't know.' Hannah looks at him. His cheerful red jumper is at odds with the sadness on his face. 'And you are . . .?'

'Zac.' The man rubs dark stubble with his fingers. 'I thought Julie was staying here, but she's not answering the door. I just want to . . .' He exhales. 'I just want to say hello.'

Hannah gets out her keys. 'She's probably out but we'll double-check for you.'

Tom leans against their garden wall. 'I'll keep Zac company.'

'OK.'

'Thank you.' Zac digs his hands deep into the pockets of his baggy jeans.

Hannah unlocks the front door and closes it carefully behind her. 'Julie?'

'Ssshhhhh.' Julie's head appears from behind the kitchen door. 'I'm not here.'

'What do you mean?' Hannah puts her bag down. 'Zac's here.'

'I know that.' Julie frowns. 'Why do you think I'm hiding?'

Hannah folds her arms. 'But I thought you wanted to see him?'

Julie's eyes are puffy and Hannah sees how pale she is. 'Well, you thought wrong. So just get rid of him. Please?'

'But why? He's come all this way to see you.'

'He's just going to have to go all the way back again, OK?' Julie is speaking in an exaggerated whisper and a vein stands out on her forehead.

Hannah doesn't understand. 'But you could just say hello. I mean, if your . . .' She looks up the stairs towards the study door. 'If your guest has gone?'

'Oh, don't get all judgmental.' Julie draws herself up to her full height. Her attempt at dignity isn't helped by the fact she has a yellow clump of something in her hair.

'But—'

'Please?' Julie's face cracks into vulnerability. 'I just can't see him right now. I feel really ill.' She presses her temples with her fingers.

'Seriously?' Hannah feels a rush of impatience. 'Another hangover? Poor Zac. He's waiting out there. For you—'

'Yes. I know. I'm a complete bloody cow.' Julie sounds bitterly sarcastic. 'Letting myself down again.' She takes a deep breath. 'Just proving that you're right to think the worst of me.'

Hannah shakes her head. 'Well, you can't blame me. You're meant to be looking after Tom but you're never bloody here. What the hell's going on?'

'Nothing.' Julie ties her green dressing gown tighter around her. Hannah sees that she is shivering. 'Look, just get rid of him, OK?'

'OK, OK.' Hannah holds up her hands. 'I'll tell him you're not here.'

'Will you?' Julie swallows. 'Thank you.'

'But I want to know why. Afterwards.'

'OK.' Julie nods. 'Later. OK?'

Then she disappears into the kitchen and slams the door.

Map of Ashdown Forest

Summer 2008

He blamed the Japanese tourists.

He heard them just as he had finally managed to distract Hannah from finding a stick big enough to win at Poohsticks. Cameras whirring. Voices exclaiming. Eyes blinking eagerly behind sunglasses as if expecting to see Winnie the Pooh himself emerging from the bushes searching for a pot of honey.

He wanted this to be perfect. Sun-dappled. Peaceful. Heartfelt. Exactly the way he was sure she had always imagined this moment.

Instead he had a sore knee from an overenthusiastic football practice and was entirely surrounded by camera flashes. He had to get her on her own. Away from the crowds. Somewhere she could hear him. Somewhere he wouldn't end up on YouTube or on a Japanese stranger's holiday slideshow.

Hannah was hanging over the bridge, staring down at the water bubbling in the stream below. Her hair exploded from her head in a corkscrew cloud and the rays of sun cutting through the leaves above their heads lit the pale skin of her arms. He touched her on the shoulder and when she turned to him her eyes were shining. 'Just think, Tom. This is where A.A. Milne must have been when he thought of it all. Right here.'

'I know.' He tried to smile but could feel that adrenaline had frozen his face into some kind of death mask.

'Thank you so much for bringing me here.' Sunlight picked out the auburn highlights in her hair. 'Amazing to see where Eeyore came from.' She had a tiny speck of pollen on her cheek. He gently brushed it away.

Forget the tourists. He was ready. He inhaled.

'*Sumimasen.* Excuse me.' He felt someone touching his arm. 'Photo please?'

He briefly contemplated murder but then turned and smiled into the enormous glasses of the young Japanese man at his side. 'Sure.' His hands were shaking so much he could barely hold the camera. He felt a hysterical giggle begin in his throat when the man got a little Winnie the Pooh toy out of his rucksack and held it next to him as he posed for the photo.

As he handed the camera back Hannah tugged at his elbow. 'Do you think he knows that's not the real bear?'

'Nope.' He took her hand. 'Let's get out of here.'

'But we haven't played Poohsticks yet.'

'Hannah, we've played Poohsticks at every single river we've ever crossed since we met.'

'Slander.' She reached into her pocket and he heard the crackle of a crisp packet.

'I'm starving.' She pulled the packet open. 'All this fresh air.' She pulled out a luminous orange Wotsit and put it into her mouth.

'Maybe you could save the rest till later, H? We only had breakfast a couple of hours ago.' He was trying desperately to preserve the moment. The feeling that had filled him this morning when he woke up. Excitement. Today was the day he was going to propose to the girl he loved. Two years to the day after they'd first met. Or rather since he'd first managed to talk to her. He had a ring. He had the perfect place. He even had sunshine.

She ignored him and rammed three more Wotsits into her mouth, crunching enthusiastically.

'God, these are so good.' She was reaching for more.

Now. It had to be now.

'Come this way.' He grabbed her hand and dragged her into a bank of trees just to the right of the bridge.

She wiped her mouth and spread Wotsit dust up to her nose. 'But what about snakes?'

'Snakes?' Twigs and leaves snapped and crackled underfoot as he propelled them forward.

'Yes.' She started to dig her heels in and resist their progress. 'It said in the guidebook that there might be snakes in the forest.'

Any remaining fragments of romance were rapidly escaping him.

'What kind of snakes?'

'Adders.' She nodded knowledgeably as she came to a halt next to a large patch of what smelt like dog shit.

One enormous forest, multiple stunning vistas and she had chosen this spot to stop moving.

Sod it.

He went down on one knee. He took a deep breath, noting that Hannah was entirely engrossed in fishing another Wotsit out of the bag. A small but determined band of twigs was attempting to dissect his ankle. He felt a dampness penetrating the leg of his jeans and wondered what he was kneeling in.

'Hannah.'

'Or it could be grass snakes.' She turned her eyes to him and froze. The Wotsits dropped to the ground. 'Oh. My. God.'

He looked at her, opened his mouth and then suddenly realised he hadn't thought of anything to say. Nothing to live up to her Mr Darcys or her Heathcliffs or the countless other romantic heroes who galloped through her dreams.

Ah well. He'd keep it simple. 'Hannah, will you marry me?'

Her hands flew to her mouth.

He waited in agony. 'Hannah?'

'Yes please.'

She dropped to the ground beside him and they kissed and they kissed and they kissed.

Afterwards they walked together to the car park, knees covered in shit and hearts full of forevers. Hannah was babbling about weddings and friends and calling her parents, when something she said reverberated in his head.

'Damian said what?'

'Said I was mad to come back from Japan when I had such a great job out there, but I knew it was the right thing. That you were the one for me.'

'Great job? You never said that. You just said you were having fun.' Hannah had never gone back to Japan after the funeral. Instead she was teaching groups of foreign students to speak English in a school in Holborn while she waited to start her PGCE. He had never questioned her decision. He loved having Hannah in his flat every night, telling him about whatever book she was reading or the latest instalment in the melodramatic affair of Cosima and Alberto – two of her Italian students who were worthy of an opera of their very own.

She shrugged. 'Oh, it was nothing really.'

'Tell me, H.' He squeezed her hand.

'They'd promoted me, so I was coordinating the curriculum across a couple of schools in Tokyo. It wasn't really a big deal.' She smiled up at him. 'It was much more important to come back and be with you.'

'But—'

She wrapped her hand round his. 'It was where I wanted to be, Tom. OK?'

'OK.' Part of him knew he should question her more, but another part was scared of what he would discover. He was so happy she'd come back to him.

They reached the hire car and he unlocked the door and opened it for her. 'Let's go celebrate, fiancée.'

She hesitated and her face fell. 'That's the one problem.'

'What?'

'I much preferred being known as your bit of stuff.' She grinned and he realised he had a lifetime of that smile to look forward to.

He couldn't wait.

Eleven

'Your face looks funny, Miss.'

Hannah looks up from her marking.

'More than usual, T'shan?'

The girl considers this point far too seriously for Hannah's liking. She gives a slow nod. 'Yes, Miss.'

'Great.' Hannah puts down her pen. 'Thanks for the heads-up.' She smiles. 'I'll make sure I sort myself out before my glamorous evening of marking in front of the TV.'

'You're welcome, Miss.' T'shan runs her fingers through her fringe. 'Nice dress.'

Hannah smiles as she looks down at the shiny black material. 'Thanks, I—'

T'shan is still talking. 'Think I'd have gone for different shoes though. Those ones are—'

'Stop.' Hannah cuts her off. Any more of this and her ego was going to throw itself under the nearest tube. 'Time for you to go and do whatever you normally do after school.'

T'shan's eyes dance. 'Wouldn't you like to know, Miss?'

Hannah raises an eyebrow. 'Actually I'm not sure I would.'

'You're funny, Miss.' T'shan gleefully undoes the top buttons of her shirt as she walks out into the corridor, revealing the luminous pink camisole beneath. The latest

Queensdale craze. She blends into a sea of covert oranges and greens as Hannah stares after her. Those were the days. The days when all she had to worry about was what top to wear or what shoes to buy.

'How did it go today?' Steph appears in the doorway, wearing a bright red dress and with her hair piled on top of her head. She makes Hannah feel tired. Drab.

'Fine.' She stands up and starts piling copies of *Lord of the Flies* on the white shelves at the corner of the classroom.

'Fine, hey?' Steph sits on one of the desks in the front row and swings her legs.

'Yeah.' Hannah can't be bothered to say any more. Days come. Days go. Nothing changes.

'That's the seventh day in a row you've given me that answer.'

Hannah picks up the last of the books. 'You're keeping score?'

'I certainly am.'

Hannah dumps the books on the shelf with a satisfying thump.

'Well, I don't know why.' She rubs the heels of her hands into her exhausted eyes. 'I'm doing fine. Nothing to worry about.'

Steph frowns. 'There's that word again.'

Hannah feels a stab of frustration. 'Look. It's just a word. I could have said "OK." Or "pretty good." You know?'

Steph shakes her head. 'You could have done, Han, but you didn't. You said "fine". Just like you've said "fine" ever since the night you found Tom.'

Hannah starts to protest but Steph holds up a hand. 'Look, I know it's been a nightmare. And I know it's really hard for him. But you were going to *leave* him, for God's sake, and I don't see—'

'Steph!' Hannah looks around nervously. 'Stop.'

'I'm just trying to help.'

'Well, don't.' Hannah feels cornered. Prickly.

Steph drums her fingers on the desk. 'And another thing while I think of it. Why on earth are you running around for Margaret all the time doing all her shitty jobs?'

'That's not fair.' Hannah feels like she should be wearing a flak jacket. 'This job is all I have now. You know that. I have to try to make the best of it.'

'Han, you hate this job. You were dying to leave.'

'No. Don't say that.' Hannah's tongue feels thick. Dry. 'I don't hate it. I don't hate the students. Or the books.'

'Yeah, but all the other crap from Margaret is grinding you down.'

'Steph.' Hannah shakes her head. 'Everything's grinding me down.'

Steph nods. 'Things with Tom must be so hard.'

Hannah feels an urge to defend him. 'We're doing OK.' As she says it she realises it's true. 'He's being really brave.'

'Yeah, but if you were having problems before—'

'Stop!' Hannah starts wiping the whiteboard clear. 'I told you. I don't want to talk about this. There's no point.'

Steph exhales. 'God, you're stubborn.'

Hannah turns towards her. 'Look, can you just leave it? I'm doing the best I can. You know?'

'I know.' Steph presses her lips together. 'But no, I can't leave it. You're doing it again, Han.'

'Doing what again?'

'Fixing *his* future. Not yours.'

'Steph, how can I do anything else?' Hannah starts

throwing exercise books into her rucksack. 'He's had a *stroke*. Of course it's all about him at the moment.'

'I know, Han, but I'm just scared for you. What happens afterwards?'

'After what?'

'After he gets better and goes back to work?'

'He might never get better.'

'OK, so what happens then?'

Hannah starts biting her thumbnail. 'I don't know. It's not like I've had a chance to think it through yet.' The truth is that thinking about the future terrifies her.

'I know I'm being pushy, Han, but I just want you to think about *you*.' Steph's face is determined. 'You're being so superhuman. Working so hard. Looking after him. Giving up your dreams. Never complaining. You need someone to look out for *you*.'

'No I don't!' Hannah feels tears prick her eyelids. 'I'm not the one who has to walk with a stick. Or be helped out of bed. I'm still *whole*.' She pushes in the final books, full of a wild angry energy. The rucksack's zip protests but she yanks it closed.

She looks up again at Steph. 'Why are you attacking me? You're meant to be my friend.'

'I'm not attacking you. I'm trying to help you. I just can't see you go there again.'

'Again?' Hannah tries to pick up the rucksack. It appears to weigh several tonnes. 'What do you mean, again? And go where?'

Steph sighs. 'Do you remember what happened a year ago? The first time you were going to leave him? The morning after you were meant to tell him you called me instead, saying that you were arranging a holiday to some sailing place he wanted to go to in Turkey?'

'Yes.' Hannah feels herself flush. 'So?'

Steph is swinging her legs faster now. 'And then there was the time when you were coming to the Edinburgh Festival with me and the PGCE crowd, and instead you stayed in London so you could go to some boring partners' dinner?'

'That was different.'

'Not really.' Steph shakes her head. 'It's you doing the same thing. Putting Tom before you.'

'No.' Hannah clenches her fists. 'It's not the same. He's still in shock, for God's sake.'

Steph drops her voice. 'I know.' Hannah hears the sincerity in her friend's voice, but can't open up in response. If she lets her real feelings out she can never unsay them. Her pure panic about her future. Her doubts about Tom. About his recovery. About how to do the right thing and still feel alive.

She breathes in. Controls herself.

Steph is still talking. 'I just don't want you to stay lost, Han.'

'It's not that bad.'

'Bollocks.' Steph shakes her head. 'Your biggest excitement of the week is watching *Nashville*. That's not a life. That's a travesty.'

'I . . .' Hannah opens her mouth. Closes it.

Steph crosses one leg over the other. 'And then there's Raj.'

'What about him?'

'He's still got the hots for you.'

Hannah starts shoving her papers into her handbag. 'No he hasn't. He's just . . . a colleague.'

Steph's arched eyebrow speaks volumes. 'I don't think so. He's always eyeing you longingly across the staffroom.'

Hannah's patience has run out. 'Why are you telling me this? How is this helping?'

Steph's voice drops. 'I'm just trying to get through to you. To my friend.'

'I'm right here, Steph.'

'No.' Steph shakes her head. 'Not this version. The real Hannah. The one who tells Margaret to piss off and teaches crazy classes on *Lord of the Flies* by locking herself in the cupboard and seeing which kid becomes Piggy. The Hannah who laughs. Who tells terrible jokes and dances like a maniac. I want to see her again.'

Hannah sticks her chin out. 'Well, tough. This is me now. OK? I'm being responsible. Working. Trying to get a promotion. Tom might never work again, you know. I need to be ready.'

'Hannah. Listen to me. You can work your arse off and Margaret is still not going to promote you.' Steph shakes her head. 'She's a cow. She doesn't work like that.'

Hannah's fury needs a target. 'Are you saying I'm not good enough?'

'Of course not.' Steph rolls her eyes. 'You know I think you're brilliant. That's why I nick all your lesson plans.'

Hannah hefts her bag onto her shoulder. 'I'm just getting through the days, Steph. It's all I can manage.'

'I know. And I love you for that. But—' Steph stops. 'Sod it. How about we head to the pub? Have some unwise midweek tequila for old times' sake? Are you in?'

Hannah shakes her head. 'I can't.'

She watches as Steph visibly bites back her reply and holds up her hands. 'OK.' She pushes off the desk and walks to the door. 'Just make sure you're not so busy thinking about Tom that you wake up in ten years wondering where your life's gone.'

'It's not like that.' Hannah presses her lips together. She will not cry.

'I bloody hope not.' Steph holds her eyes for a second before walking away.

Later, Hannah walks dejectedly towards her bike, where it stands locked to a tree at the edge of the deserted school car park. It is dark and cold and she can see a car with a smashed window in the lonely street outside. She draws her jacket tighter around her, spine tingling as she hears footsteps on the gravel.

A shot of adrenaline jolts her. Queensdale is in a particularly unfriendly part of south London and she looks round for the mugger who is going to make her utterly crappy day complete.

'I'm armed.' She shoves her hand in her pocket and tries to mime a gun.

'Well, that's good to know.'

She tenses her body still further.

The voice continues. 'But you're also half the size of me, so I'm not sure your lethal finger-gun is going to help.'

It's his laughter she recognises. 'Raj?'

A lean figure emerges from the shadows.

She breathes a sigh of relief. 'You cheeky git. What are you doing here? Stalking me?'

'You wish.' He gently touches her shoulder. 'Steph said I should try to persuade you to come to the pub. Thought I'd give it a go.' He grins. 'Seeing as you've been a bit evasive recently.'

Bloody Steph.

She shakes her head and takes a step back. 'I've got to get home.'

'Really?' He raises his eyebrows. 'Are you sure?' His eyes are wide in the murky light.

'Yeah.' She fiddles with her bag, conscious of his intense focus on her face.

'Want me to walk you home?'

'*No.*' It comes out more violently than she'd intended.

'OK, OK.' He holds up his hands. 'Sorry the idea is so horrible.'

'It's not horrible.' She meets his eyes and all the frustration and the sadness of the last few months makes her want to weep.

Instead she unlocks her bike and wheels it between them. 'It's just that a lot's changed since my birthday.'

'I haven't.' He says it so quietly she can barely hear him.

'Well . . .' She fiddles with the strap on her helmet. 'I'm sorry, but there's nothing I can do about that.'

'Hannah. I miss you.' Part of her hates the distress in his voice.

Part of her is flattered.

'I'm sorry.' She pulls the straps of her rucksack up on her shoulders. 'I'm just letting everyone down at the moment.'

He puts a hand on hers.

'That's not true.' Her skin warms to his touch. 'You just need some fun. Come to the pub.'

'No.' Her fingers seem to be entwining with his. 'I—'

'Just for an hour.'

His lips are so close. It would be so easy to kiss him and forget reality for a minute. Forget the ride home. Forget the evening meal. Marking. She could do something different. Something for her.

'Hannah.' His voice is low. 'I—'

'HANNAH!'

Hannah leaps, turns and peers across the car park to the fence that runs along the street.

'Julie!' She quickly steps away from Raj but he's still holding on to her hand.

He speaks quickly. 'Meet me.'

She pulls her hand away, hoping that Julie didn't see it in the darkness.

She adopts a tone of utterly false cheer. 'Hey Jules. What can I help with?'

He reaches for her again.

'Meet me.'

She pulls away and glares at Raj as Julie rattles the fence. 'I lost my keys again. Can I have yours?'

Bloody typical. Hannah wonders if she should just hand the locksmith a cheque for the meagre contents of her savings account and be done with it.

'Sure. Won't be a minute, Jules. I'm just heading home.'

She turns back to Raj. 'Stop it.'

'No.' His voice is determined.

She speaks in an exaggerated whisper. 'Stop. It.' She places both hands on the handlebars, ready to move away.

Julie's voice is clipped. 'Hurry up.'

Hannah shouts over her shoulder. 'Just sorting out a work problem.'

'Raj.' He is holding on to the bike. She pulls desperately. 'Please?'

'Meet me.'

It seems she has no choice if she ever wants to take her bike home with her. 'When?'

'Saturday.'

'Where?'

'I'll text you.'

'OK. But why? We meet every day at school.'

He squeezes her fingers before unclasping them. 'You know why.' For a second she sees herself through his eyes and her heart lifts.

'Come on!' Julie rattles the fence.

Hannah turns to Raj. 'OK. I'll be there.'

The smile on his face stays with her.

She shouts over at Jules. 'Coming.'

As she walks towards her she looks back and sees Raj staring after her.

'Who's that?' Julie meets her at the exit to the car park.

'Oh, he's no one.' Hannah shrugs. 'Just a colleague.'

She thinks of her and Raj. Of Saturday night.

She'll go, and tell him that nothing can ever happen between them.

That's all. One drink and she'll be gone.

Simple.

Order of service for the wedding of Tom Ellison to Hannah Rose Miles

SUMMERFIELDS BARN, OXFORDSHIRE

11th July 2009

'This is the last time you'll ever get me to do this, you know.'

Hannah's hand was in his, tugging him irresistibly towards the place he least wanted to go. He came to a determined halt just before they reached the corner of the barn and encountered their increasingly merry guests again. He wanted a second to breathe. A second alone with his beautiful wife.

Hannah turned and smiled up at him. The love in her eyes made his heart dance. Unfortunately his feet didn't want to do the same.

'Come on, you big chicken.' She stood up on tiptoe and kissed him gently on the lips. 'Five minutes. That's all. A bit of swaying and a couple of twirls. Then I'll never ask you to dance again. Promise.'

He heard laughter from round the corner and drew her further back into the shadows. Throughout the ceremony, the champagne-fuelled reception and the wedding breakfast he had longed for this moment. Him and her. Tom and Hannah. Husband and wife.

He brushed a strand of hair from her cheek. Her curls had been tamed into relative obedience and there were little white flowers laced into the dark bun at the nape of her neck. She looked beautiful, but part of him wanted to take off all the make-up and the jewellery and set his Hannah free.

He dropped a gentle kiss onto her glossy red lips. 'But you're so good at it.'

She leant closer and dropped her voice seductively. 'At what?'

He smiled as he anticipated what would happen later when he finally got to release her from the golden layers of her dress. 'Dancing.' He gently ran his hand across the bare skin of her upper back. 'Though obviously you have a long list of talents to choose from.'

She grinned. 'So true. What a very lucky man you are to have married me.'

'I know. Apart from this whole first dance thing. I told you I'd be quite happy for you to go out there and do a solo.'

She rolled her eyes. 'That would slightly defeat the point.' She turned her head as a peal of laughter exploded behind them. Then she looked him full in the face. 'And you'd actually be a pretty good dancer, if only you'd take that ruler out of your arse.'

He shook his head. 'I don't believe you.' He shrugged. 'But I'll give it a go. If you make it worth my while.'

Her eyes glinted with the mischief he loved. 'Oh, I wouldn't worry about that. My underwear is *way* better than this dress.' The way she whispered the words made him want to investigate. Now. Right now.

She kissed him and pressed her body against his. He felt the rough concrete wall through the thick material of his suit and wondered if he could somehow whisk her away for an hour and have his wicked way. He knew she would let him. It was one of the many reasons he loved her.

'Get a room, mate.'

They broke off to see Nick peering round the corner, shaking his head at them. 'I can always give a second best man's speech, you know. With added visuals.' He held up his camera, finger poised over the shutter.

Tom reluctantly pulled away from Hannah as his friend approached and leant against the wall of the barn. Nick got out some cigarettes and lit one. 'I can't believe you'll be in the Caribbean this time on Monday.' He inhaled deeply. 'Jammy bastard. Just think of us slaving away without you on the Lindersson deal.'

Tom felt a twang of nerves. It wasn't a good time to be going away.

There was never a good time.

'No way, Nick.' Hannah looked horrified. 'He won't be thinking about you and your bloody deal. It's our honeymoon, you know. Tom won't think about work for a second.'

'Lucky him.' Nick downed the remainder of his glass. 'Meanwhile the rest of us will be working our way through endless due diligence.' He sighed. 'And you'll be lounging on an island drinking a girlie cocktail and getting a tan.'

He ran a hand through his blond hair, then leant over and kissed Hannah on the cheek. 'Congratulations again. You look stunning. God knows why you're throwing yourself away on this idiot.' He smiled and clapped Tom on the shoulder. 'Seriously mate. Nice one. You've done well for yourself.' He raised his empty glass. 'To you two.'

'Where's . . . ?' Tom tried desperately to remember the name of Nick's latest girlfriend.

'Elise?' Nick shook his head. 'I finished with her. I thought I'd told you.'

Hannah shook her head. 'Do you mean you pulled a Nick and stopped talking to her until she finished with you?'

'Yes.' Nick looked impossibly pleased with himself. 'Works every time.'

'You're such a git.' Hannah smiled but Tom heard the reproof in her voice.

'That's why you love me.' Nick grinned and flicked his ash to the ground. 'I'd better head off to hunt down a new lady.'

'Great.' Tom wanted to be alone with Hannah again. 'Just don't touch my sister, OK?'

'No problem.' Nick turned and started to weave his way back towards the wedding party. 'She's vomming into a bush right now,' he called back over his shoulder. 'She can barely stand up.' He disappeared round the corner of the barn.

'Bugger.' Tom rolled his eyes. 'Why does she always have to get so wasted? I really thought going back to college was going to calm her down.'

Hannah put her hand on his arm. 'It's not her fault, Tom. I puked at every single family wedding I went to when I was younger.' She grinned. 'It's a teenage rite of passage.'

'Well, she's eighteen now, so that excuse won't work much longer.' Tom frowned. 'I should go and check up on her.'

'Any excuse to avoid the dancefloor, eh?' Hannah smiled at him. 'Don't worry. Her mates will be keeping an eye on her.'

'I doubt it.' Tom's encounters with the girls Julie shared a flat with were best described as 'difficult.' He'd only invited them today because Julie said she didn't know any of his friends. Which had started yet another argument.

Him saying she could come and meet them. Her saying they were all up themselves and she wouldn't fit in. He wished she would try. Just once. For him.

Hannah kissed him and he forced his Julie worries away as she started speaking. 'It's not as if my family is being the easiest either.' She shook her head. 'Mum's hat blocked the view of about five rows, for starters. And my dad must be the first dad in the world to use crossword clues as a basis for the father of the bride speech.' She giggled. 'It was very sweet though.'

'It was amazing, H.' Tom squeezed her hand. 'I nearly cried.'

'Really?' She grinned. 'Good. He was secretly trying to take you down.' She looked suddenly shy. 'I loved *your* speech, Tom. Thank you.'

He brought her hand up to his mouth and kissed it. 'My pleasure.'

He was about to kiss her again when they heard the piercing tones of Hannah's mum. 'Where are they, Harry? The DJ is ready to start. It's just like Hannah to disappear and get things off schedule.'

'Right on cue. You'd think she might want to spend the day actually being nice to me.' Hannah laughed bitterly as she took a step back and straightened her dress. 'It's not as if she hasn't spent enough time criticising me in the run-up to today.'

'Not you.' Tom shook his head. 'Us.' During the past year of wedding planning he had frequently found himself wishing they had opted to elope. He covered his anger with a joke. 'I mean, we were *very* slack about napkins.'

He was pleased to see a smile warm Hannah's face again. 'Weren't we? How outrageous of us. I mean, calico or linen?'

'Cotton or silk?' He laughed.

A formidable figure appeared wearing a salmon pink suit and a cream hat so big that it blocked out the remaining daylight.

'Ah! There you are.' Jenny waved an imperious hand. 'Time for the first dance.'

'Yes Mum.' A dimple flashed in Hannah's cheek. 'Come on, soldier. You can't back out now.' She took his hand again.

He took a deep breath, nerves kicking in his gut. 'Are you sure we have to do this?'

She shook her head. 'It's just once. I know you hate dancing. I get it. But just today. For me. Please?'

'Come on, you two.' Her mum was practically clicking her fingers. Yet as Hannah walked past her she raised her cupped hand as if to usher her daughter forward. She dropped it as Hannah marched on. Tom saw her face stiffen.

He wished again that his mum was there. To be kind. Quiet. Proud.

Hannah stopped and looked back at him. 'You're thinking about her, aren't you? Your mum?'

'Yeah.' He nodded. 'I just wish she could be here.'

Hannah nodded. 'She is, you know. She's wafting around somewhere. Smiling. And thinking she could have made a better wedding cake.'

'Do you think so?' He bit his lip. 'Really?'

She nodded. 'I'm sure of it. And she's so proud of her boy.'

He swallowed. Squeezed Hannah's hand.

Hannah smiled. 'Ready?'

He nodded. 'Yes. I think I am.'

She led him round to the front entrance to the barn.

Past the bunting and the balloons. Past clusters of pink and cream flowers. Past fairy lights, red faces and warm smiles. Past his Auntie Sue trying to force a chunk of wedding cake into her handbag.

The disco lights bathed the floor purple. Hannah led the way, hands raised as she got the crowd to clap in time to their song. She looked towards him and all he could see was her.

He took a deep breath and followed her onto the dancefloor.

Twelve

'Can I borrow this handbag?'

Hannah jumps and pushes her laptop screen shut.

'Sure.' She hopes Julie didn't see anything.

Julie picks up the silver bag from the floor. 'Why were you looking at those pictures of monkeys?'

Damn.

Hannah feels herself blush. She decides to tough it out. 'Why are you wearing my top?'

'This?' Julie blinks and her eyelids glint silver. 'Thought it was mine.'

'It might as well be.'

Julie frowns. 'What do you mean by that?'

'Nothing.' Hannah can't face another argument. 'You look great in it.'

In fact Julie doesn't look great. Her boobs are busting out of the black lace of the top and her skin is unusually shiny beneath the harsh line of her new fringe.

'Thanks.' Julie smooths her hands over her jeans.

'Out on another date?'

'Yeah.' Julie hesitates in the doorway, a flicker of uncertainty crossing her face. 'Why?'

'Nothing.' Hannah shrugs. 'Just wondered.' Julie seems to have spent most of the month since Zac's appearance out pursuing the opposite sex. Every time Hannah tries to talk to her Julie's reaction is to pull on a jacket and sprint out of the front door.

She tries again. 'Is everything OK, Julie?'

Julie's eyes soften for a second, but then she folds her arms across her chest. 'Look, I'm just enjoying myself, OK?' Her lip curls into a sneer. 'You should try it sometime.'

She stalks out, leaving Hannah alone with her laptop and a familiar sense of failure. She takes a sip of tea and opens up the screen again, gazing at the golden hues of the sun setting over the Tanzanian landscape. She cups her chin in her hand. Ten years ago she'd have been packing her rucksack whenever she even began to feel this sad. Now it's her first Saturday off in months and she is spending her day in the company of an inanimate object.

Julie is right. She should get a life.

The doorbell rings.

'DOOR!'

'Yes thank you, Jules.' Hannah sighs. It would be much more helpful if Julie actually bothered answering it rather than acting as a human doorbell.

She goes downstairs and opens the front door, preparing her finest detention expression for whoever's trying to sell her something today.

'Nick.' She breaks into a smile.

'Morning, madam.' He pretends to salute. 'One driver for Mr Ellison.'

'Good to see you.' She reaches up and kisses him on the cheek. 'How's it going?'

'Not bad.' He steps into the hall, which seems instantly smaller. His teeth flash white against his tan. 'Wheeling and dealing.'

'Cutting and thrusting?' She leads him through to the living room, where Tom is lying on the sofa doing his physio exercises. Lifting his left hand. Closing his fingers. Opening them. Putting his hand down.

As soon as he sees Nick he stops. 'Hello, mate.'

'Ready for some football?'

'Damn right I am.' Tom leans on his right hand and swivels his legs round to meet the floor. 'How are you?'

'Good.' A mysterious smile hovers around Nick's lips. 'Very good, in fact.'

Tom reaches forward for the cane that's propped against the armchair.

'What's going on, mate?'

'Nothing.' Nick looks like he's about to burst with untold tales.

'I don't believe you.'

'Come on, Nick. Put us out of our misery.' Hannah looks at him pleadingly. 'We could do with some good news.'

'Well . . .' Nicks looks at the carpet. 'I may have just found some offices for the new firm.'

'Wow.' Hannah looks at Tom's face. He is smiling, but there is something wounded in his eyes. 'Congratulations.'

'Thank you.' Nick makes a small bow. 'They're just behind St Paul's. Nice spot.'

'I didn't realise you were going to do it so soon.'

'Yeah, well.' Nick looks at his friend. 'Carpe diem and all that. Nothing's confirmed yet, but it's a big step forward.'

Tom is staring at the carpet.

Nick sits down next to him. 'Now all I have to do is persuade my best mate to come and work with me.'

Tom looks up, his expression a mix of confusion and delight. 'Don't be stupid. Look at me.' He gestures to the stick. 'There's no way I can work like this. I can't even type.'

'Bollocks.' Nick puts his arm round Tom. 'I've been researching.'

'Oh God.' Tom leans back against the cushions. 'Last time you did that you ended up buying that crazy robot that totally refused to clean your house.'

'Yeah. Well.' Nick grins. 'This time I've done *much* more research. You can use voice recognition software. Your secretary can type everything up. You'll be back to full speed in no time.'

'Yeah, but I'm still so knackered all the time. I don't want to hold you back.'

Nick sighs. 'No buts, Tom. I need you with me. And you need this, mate. A reason to get better.'

Tom shakes his head but Hannah sees his eyes gleam.

She quietly walks away and goes into the kitchen. She feels sick at the thought of Tom going back. Sick at the thought of all that pressure. At the thought of it causing another stroke. Even though his doctor says it's unlikely, she still worries. Every day.

She wonders when she became so scared of the future.

She hears the front door slam and knows that Julie has gone out. She fills up the kettle and makes a cup of tea, leaning against the kitchen island as steam curls out of her mug. She stares out of the window at the cloudy skies, her pulse quickening at the thought of her drink with Raj later.

She tells herself not to be stupid. To calm down.

It's only a drink.

It'll be fine.

She takes her tea to the bottom of the stairs, meaning

to head up and settle down with her laptop again. Then she hears her name.

Tom is speaking in a low growl. 'The thing is Nick, that Hannah's just been so amazing about all this. I can't do this without discussing it with her.'

She stiffens.

'I mean, if I hadn't had Hannah with me I couldn't have got this far. I'd still be stuck in that chair wanting to roll it off the nearest roof. I can't thank her by making such a big decision without her, can I?'

Nick's voice is urgent. Determined. 'Yes, but this is our chance, Tom. We need to do it now. The clients are ready.'

'To move with *you*.' Tom sighs. 'Not me.' Hannah tiptoes to the door and through the gap she sees Tom shaking his head. 'I need to talk to her. And we need to work out if it's right for us both. Not just me. Things are different now.'

'OK, mate. OK.' Nick stands up and Hannah leaps into action. She runs to the bottom of the stairs and starts to climb. She looks down at them as they come out of the living room. Nick so tall. Tom so lopsided.

'Have a great time, guys. Go the Spurs.' She raises a fist lamely in the air.

Tom shakes his head. 'God. Such a long time together and that's the best you can do. Blimey.'

'Sorry.' She shrugs. 'See you later.'

Then on impulse she walks down the stairs and kisses him on the lips. She heads back upstairs without allowing herself to think about why.

On the way to the pub Hannah realises she wasn't made for subterfuge. Every time she sees a man with dark hair she ducks behind a lamp-post or into a shop doorway. She sees fake Toms everywhere – in cars waiting at traffic lights, by postboxes, in football gear walking across the park. Before she is halfway there she wishes she had invested in a balaclava.

She stands at the level crossing by the High Road, looking at the throng of shoppers making their way along the street, bearing colourful bags containing their Saturday shopping spoils. One couple have grim faces, teeth bared in what Hannah is sure must be a fight. A little girl clutches a Primark bag proudly to her chest as if it contained the world's most precious treasures. A young woman with dark hair and slumped shoulders crushes her cigarette beneath her shoe, before taking her black McDonald's hat from her pocket and putting it on her head.

Hannah stares at her, watching as she goes back into McDonald's to take on the Saturday evening queue.

It's Julie.

Hannah feels a rush of pure anger. This must be why Julie is so unreliable. She has another job. A secret job.

Julie disappears inside the green and cream interior of the McDonald's. Hannah is about to rush in and confront her when she sees her again. She is behind the counter now. Standing unseeingly by the milkshake machine as people yell out orders around her.

She looks so lonely.

Worry replaces anger as a sharp breeze cuts along the street. Hannah shrugs deeper into her jacket and debates what to do. Finally, she puts her head down and crosses the road and walks towards the pub. She will talk to Julie. Tomorrow. Find out why. Get some answers.

She walks past cackling girls wearing minimal dresses and men lining pints up on pub windowsills. London has taken to the streets despite the fact it's not even warm enough to wear a T-shirt.

As Hannah approaches the Dog pub she feels nausea brewing in her stomach. The pub's bright blue sign is festooned in Union Jacks and through the window she can see a tall dark figure amidst the throng at the bar. Hannah breathes in. She smells burgers and beer.

It's her first night out for months. She expected to feel excited.

Instead she just feels guilty.

One drink. Just one.

She steps inside. Thinks about running. Then she hears her name.

'Hannah.'

Raj has seen her. He pushes through the crowd, his bright blue shirt stretched tight across his chest. Baggy jeans. Battered Converse.

He looks great. Yet she feels . . . nothing.

'I didn't think you'd come.' He tries to kiss her on the mouth but she ducks away. He leans in again. She attempts to step back but instead is jolted forward by a group of hens in sparkly cheerleading outfits who have clearly hit the cocktails early.

Hannah starts to sweat and wriggles out of her jacket.

She looks up at Raj. 'Of course I was going to come. You did make me promise, you know.'

'Yeah, but you didn't have to follow through. You could always have stood me up.'

She's starting to wish she had. There's something different about him tonight. Swaggery. Pushy. 'Yeah, but—'

'But you just couldn't resist me, eh?' He tries to kiss her again.

'Raj!' She pushes her hands gently against his chest. 'What are you doing?'

His lips still hover in front of hers. 'I'd have thought that was obvious.'

Hannah looks around for some space. There is none. The hen party crowd have pushed her to the left and her leg is pressing against the rough bricks of the bar. Behind her a man has started singing 'Rule Britannia' and the hens join in, rustling their pompoms in time to the tune.

Hannah can feel how tense her shoulders are. She feels edgy. Unnerved.

Raj shouts to be heard above the noise. 'Shall I get you a drink, babe?'

Babe?

She nods. 'Sure.'

Alcohol. That's what she needs. She is tempted to lean over the brass bar, grab one of the bottles of spirits and pour it down her throat.

'What'll it be?'

'White wine please. Large.'

'Sure.' He turns to the bar.

Music thumps through the speakers as the DJ in the corner starts his set. He is wearing a beanie and an expression of intense excitement.

Hannah's temples start to ache. She sees a table become free and heads across before it can be claimed by a staggering girl whose boobs are just about to escape from her purple top. Hannah clambers up onto the wobbly wooden stool and leans her chin on her hands as she stares at the lamp above her. A brown poodle holding an umbrella. The purple and pink walls of the pub are festooned with dogs' tails and collars and the kitchen in the far corner appears to have been modelled on a kennel.

The Dog. She can understand why.

She looks around her. She sees people eating crisps. Flirting. Starting to sway to the DJ's tunes.

She had been so looking forward to a night out, but now she feels disconnected.

Old.

A minute later Raj joins her, carrying the drinks, a bag of crisps between his teeth.

'So.' He sits down opposite her.

'So.' She drinks half her wine at once. It's sharp. Acidic. Gateway to a morning of Anadin Extra and full-fat Coke.

Sod it. She gulps some more.

'So what have you been up to today?' She summons her brightest smile.

He rips the crisps open and takes one. 'Oh, you know. Got up at midday.'

'Nice.' Her own personal alarm clock had gone off at 7 a.m. when Julie had tripped on the way to the loo and sworn at full volume. 'Were you out last night?'

'Yeah.' He nods. 'Went to a gig. A mate of mine was playing at Smoke. Do you know it?'

Hannah briefly considered faking a yes, but she's done that before and it always ends in frantic lying and a lot of sweat. 'No. What is it?'

He laughs at her. 'It's a club.'

'Oh.' She feels like she should have false teeth and a bus pass.

'I guess you're not that into music?'

'I wouldn't say that.' She struggles to think of any music that doesn't feature in a show with a glossy programme and overly expensive ice creams. Billy Joel springs to mind. Not helpful.

'I like . . . house music.'

She doesn't like house music. But his face lights up. 'Wow. House. Retro.'

Oh God. If he thinks house is retro then her music collection belongs in a time capsule.

The question she is dreading is forming on his lips. 'What do you like then?'

'Oh, loads of stuff.' She has managed to finish her wine in record time. 'Another?'

He is only halfway down his pint. 'Sure.'

As she gets up she realises that this evening is rapidly starting to resemble the terrible blind date of 2003. The one where she'd woken up on the carpet in her dress and heels surrounded by her childhood cuddly toys.

She digs into her wallet and heads to the bar, where she is treated to the delightful sight of a cheerleader and a sunburnt rugby player vigorously intertwining tongues. At one point they stumble backwards and the cheerleader elbows Hannah in the ribs. Hannah swears. The cheerleader doesn't notice.

Ten minutes later Hannah finally gets served and decides to get them two drinks each while she's there. She weaves back through the crowd with the glasses held aloft on a tray.

Raj blinks. 'Wow. You're going for it.'

'Yep.' She sits on her stool and resolutely takes a big mouthful of wine. 'Why not? It's Saturday night.'

'True.' He leans forward and tries to take her hand. 'But you know you don't need to get me drunk to have your wicked way with me.'

She moves her hand smartly away. He is annoying her now.

'Raj, what's going on?'

'What do you mean?' He frowns.

'Why are you being like this?'

'Like what?' He sips his beer. 'Surely that's why you came out tonight?'

'What is?' The wine is making her mind slow. Clumsy.

His eyes are bold. But there's something behind them. Desperation? 'So we could sleep together again.'

Oh God. She drinks more wine. It doesn't help.

She looks up at the poodle. Then back at Raj. 'To be honest I don't know what I'm doing here.'

He blinks. 'But I thought that . . . that we . . .'

She slumps forward on her elbows, feeling incredibly tired.

'Look, Raj. You're great, and I like you . . .' As she says it she realises she doesn't really know him. 'But I shouldn't be here. I knew it when you asked me and I absolutely know it now.' She sighs. 'The wine is grim and I am really starting to hate that poodle.' She jabs her finger at the light fitting. It doesn't care. 'But also . . .' She feels a sickening lurch of guilt. 'There's Tom.'

'You don't love him.'

'You don't know that.'

'But you said you didn't.'

'That was months ago.' Hannah frowns. 'A lifetime ago.'

'But, Hannah, I really like you.'

He sounds teenage. Unconvincing.

'No.' She shakes her head. 'You don't. You just think you do because I'm married and you have some weird thing going on about chasing people you can't have. The fact is—' Tom's face appears in her mind, grinning triumphantly as he made his first successful cup of tea since the stroke. They had sat together at the kitchen table to drink it, dunking Hobnobs and debating whether they were better chocolate-coated or plain.

The image makes her guilt burn. 'Look, Raj. We have nothing in common. You go to gigs. I put the dishwasher on.' She takes another mouthful of wine. 'You sleep in till midday. I'm lucky if I get to seven thirty.' She realises she's finished her second glass. 'You don't want me, Raj.'

More to the point, she doesn't want him.

He tries to reach for her again. 'I do want you, Hannah.'

'No, Raj.' She sighs. 'I'm sorry. I shouldn't be here.'

His head drops into his hands. 'This is the worst day ever.'

She watches him.

Then she sees something running down his face.

Tears?

Oh God.

'Raj?' Hannah reaches out and puts her hand on his arm. He imprisons it beneath his own. 'What's wrong?'

'Amelia got in touch today.' His voice is high and tight.

'Amelia?'

'My ex.'

'Oh.' Hannah extracts her hand and leans back in her seat. Now things are starting to make sense.

He looks up at her, wiping his eyes on his sleeve. 'She told me she's with someone else now.'

'Oh.'

'And that I was crap in bed.'

'OK.'

He blinks. 'I wasn't crap in bed, was I?'

'Of course not.' Hannah can't actually remember, but now is definitely not the time to share that information. She shakes her head vigorously. 'You were great.'

'Really?' He watches her with terrified eyes.

'Really.' She nods as authoritatively as she can.

Tonight really isn't panning out the way she had expected.

'That's good.' He drinks his beer. Eats a crisp.

Hannah looks at him. Sees the sadness. Sees the need. She knows what she has to do.

She leans forward. 'Why don't you tell me all about what happened with you two?'

'No.'

'Come on.'

'No.' His eyes say yes. 'No. You don't want to hear about her.'

'You're obviously still in love with her.'

'No.' He juts out his lower lip.

'Oh, give it up, Raj.' He looks so childlike she feels like giving him a glass of milk and a biscuit. 'Tell me about Amelia.'

So he does.

Two excruciating hours later, a tequila-fuelled Raj has decided to return to Brighton and see Amelia. To declare his love. To win her back. Meanwhile, Hannah has decided to go home and bang her head against a wall.

As she walks down her street she realises Steph is right. She really does need to stop putting other people first.

She wearily opens the front door.

'H?' She is surprised to hear Tom's voice. Normally he's asleep by ten.

She walks in and sits down beside him on the sofa. Despite the lack of romance in her night with Raj, she still feels guilty. She reaches out and pats his legs. 'How was the match?'

He shrugs. 'A draw. We had a few missed chances. You

know.' He's wearing the green hoodie that she loves. 'What about you? Were you out with Steph?'

She tenses. Maybe she should just tell him about what happened with Raj. Now. Get it over with.

Then his hand reaches for hers and she knows she can't.

'Yeah.' She nods. His fingers feel warm. Comforting. 'It was fine.'

She feels his eyes on her face. 'Good.'

She settles back into the cushions and glances at the TV screen, which is flickering out images on mute. 'Hang on a minute. Isn't that . . .?'

'*Casablanca*?' He nods. 'Yep. Thought I'd see what you've been raving on about all these years.'

Hannah sees Humphrey Bogart standing by the piano. 'Oh. I *love* this bit.'

Tom grins. 'Then settle in.'

Hannah sits with him. Watches the screen.

And keeps holding his hand.

Receipt: £600 Westview Clinic

July 2010

'I don't know what to read.' Hannah reached forward and flipped through the numerous sections of the Saturday paper. She held up the magazine. The front cover showed a girl in a party dress holding a cocktail and a silver ticket. 'Somehow learning the top ten secrets of crashing celebrity parties doesn't seem that helpful right now.'

Tom shifted in his plush grey chair and looked up at the leaflets hanging in the rack on the wall above him.

Contraception: a beginner's guide.

STDs: the facts.

Great.

He looked back at Hannah. 'I know what you mean.' He peered half-heartedly at the Sports section lying on his lap. 'Even Spurs doesn't seem that important, when . . .' He tailed off as he looked around the waiting room. He was still unable to say the words out loud. He could barely even think them.

Hannah took his hand in hers. 'I know.' She lifted it up and kissed his palm. 'This isn't exactly the wedding anniversary we were hoping for.'

He pulled his hand away and stood up. 'That's not the point, is it?' He started walking but then realised he had nowhere to go. He stared angrily at a glossy pot plant that was basking in the sun streaming in through the open window. He looked at the holiday sky outside and tried to breathe.

He should have seen this coming. He should have done something.

'Sorry, Tom. I didn't think.' Hannah put her hand on his arm.

He hunched his shoulders. 'Yeah. Well, this isn't easy, you know.'

'I know.' She wrapped her arms round him and rested her head against his chest. 'I'm just so worried. I make bad jokes when I'm worried. You know I do.'

He relented and closed his arms around her. 'Was that thing about our anniversary meant to be a joke? You really are losing your sense of humour.'

'Shut up.' She butted him gently with her head. 'Just because we're spending the hottest day of the year holed up in a family planning clinic, there's no need to be rude.'

He kissed the top of her head, breathing in the lemony scent of her hair. He wished they could be outside – eating ice cream and contemplating a leisurely Saturday lunchtime pint. He looked around at the water cooler and the white walls and the pale girl working her way quietly through a packet of Kleenex in the far corner. She looked so alone. So young.

He released Hannah and went back to sit in his seat. 'Do you mind if I check on some work while we're waiting?'

'Sure.' Hannah sank into the chair next to him, crossing her legs underneath her. She reached for the Arts section and spread it across her knees. 'It's not like there's anything better to do.' She flicked a page.

'Thanks.' He pulled his BlackBerry out of his pocket and saw that its red light was blinking yet again. He'd been up half the night doing due diligence and now the queries were pouring back in from the client.

Hannah turned a page and sighed. 'How's the deal going?'

'Not bad,' he lied.

'Meaning what?' Hannah was clearly not in the mood for reading.

'Well, it's pretty complicated but we're making good progress.' He frowned as another urgent email landed in his inbox. His boss was unfamiliar with the concept of a weekend. He tried to think of a response – to lose himself in legalities and technicalities as he normally could – but his mind wouldn't function. He could barely spell, let alone concoct a carefully crafted rebuttal to a complex legal argument.

The glass door swung open and a man in a white coat walked in and quietly called a name. The crying girl wiped her eyes, got up and followed him. Her flip-flops slapped against the white tile floor. Once she had disappeared the waiting room was oppressively quiet, with only the tap of the receptionist's keyboard in the corner to break the silence.

'God, this is awful.' Hannah flung the paper down onto a chair. 'I feel sick.'

He put his BlackBerry away. 'Me too.' He slumped forward. 'Looks like neither of us is going to be trying those amazing biscuits over there.'

Hannah looked towards the coffee table in the far corner. 'I bet no one ever eats them.'

'Probably not.' He put his arm round her and she leant her head against his shoulder.

'Once this is over . . .' Her voice was tentative. 'Maybe we could head out tonight. Have dinner? See a film?'

'I'd love to.' He swallowed. 'But . . .'

Her voice was resigned. 'But what?'

'But I think I'm going to get called into the office.'

'*Again?*' He hated the disappointment in her voice.

'Sorry. Like I said, this is a pretty complicated deal I'm working on.'

Her voice was low. 'What's new? They always seem to be complicated.'

He was tired of feeling guilty about this. 'Look, I just can't. Not this weekend.' He kissed her on the cheek. 'We'll do something soon though. To celebrate our anniversary. I promise.'

'Really?' She traced a pattern along his arm with her forefinger.

'Of course.'

'And to celebrate my new Queensdale job?'

He nodded. 'Definitely.'

She looked up at him. 'Though we could still go to Nairobi, you know.'

Impatience pulsed through him. 'Hannah, we've talked about this.'

'I know. But you could still apply for a transfer to work on that big deal out there.' She kissed his cheek. 'And I could work at the school I told you about. The one where—'

'No.' He tried to swallow his frustration but his voice was harsh. 'It's not the right time, H. Not for my career. And for God's sake, you've just got a great job. Right here. In London. We don't need to go away.'

'I just thought it might be exciting. For both of us. You'd be under less pressure out there, and we could spend more time together and—'

'I don't *want* less pressure.' He wished she would understand. Wished she would grow up. 'I need to be here. Building my career. My contacts. My experience. Not buggering off for an extended holiday.'

'I'm not talking about a holiday. I'm talking about living life a bit differently. It's the kind of job I've always dreamed about.' She folded her arms. 'I just thought you might want to consider it.'

'But if I want to be a partner it makes no sense. I can't just disappear into some international dreamland of yours.' He slumped back in his chair. 'Why can't you see that?'

'It's not a dreamland. You haven't been listening—'

Exasperation gripped him. 'Why are you mentioning this now? It's hardly the ideal time, is it?'

'Because we never see each other.' He heard the sadness in her voice. 'This is the first Saturday we've spent together in ages.' She folded her arms. 'But don't worry. I get it. Sorry for bringing it up.'

Her head was down and he felt a savage stab of victory.

He leant forward in his seat and looked at the steel clock on the wall. It had barely moved.

Hannah drummed her fingers against her arm. 'God, it's taking ages.'

He looked towards the glass doors. 'I know.'

'You don't think something's gone wrong?' Her eyes were huge.

'No.' He sounded more confident than he felt. 'More likely Julie's having a strop about something. Bed too small. Drugs too weak. Doctor not fit enough.' He tried to laugh but it stuck in his throat.

'Probably.' Hannah's fingers carried on their relentless movement. 'Poor Jules.'

Anger pounded through him again. 'She did this. Just as much as him.'

'Sure, but—'

'But nothing. Jules should have known better.' His voice

was louder than he had intended. The receptionist cast him a disapproving look and then went back to her typing.

Hannah shifted in her seat. 'At least we got her in here fast.'

'It should be fast at the price I'm paying.'

He felt Hannah watching him. 'Julie says she loves him, though. So at least—'

He was tired of Hannah defending his sister. 'Today she says she loves him. Tomorrow she'll have moved on to someone else.' He spoke in a fierce whisper. 'I really tried, you know?' He hated the tears that stung his eyes and blinked them back. 'I tried to help her to get somewhere. To get the education she always used to want. To . . .'

Hannah stayed silent.

'All I want . . .' He sighed. 'All I want is for her to show some tiny sign of taking life seriously. Of using her amazing brain for something more than downing shots or flirting with boys.'

He could feel Hannah's eyes on his face, but he didn't want to meet them. Her voice was quiet. 'I'm guessing she's feeling pretty damn serious right now.'

He thought of the little sister he had spent his childhood with. Book in hand. Mouth opening to tell him about her favourite band or her latest short story.

All week these memories had choked him.

He stretched his arms above his head and then reached for Hannah's hand. 'Thanks so much for coming with me.'

'You're welcome.' She kissed him. 'I wouldn't be anywhere else.'

'Tom Ellison?' A nurse in a dark purple uniform was standing at the door.

'Yes?' Tom jumped to his feet and practically ran

through the doors and down the long beige corridor that followed, Hannah close behind him. They reached a door labelled REST AREA and the nurse pushed it open.

'Here she is.' The nurse pointed towards a plump armchair by a French window that opened onto a tiny rose garden. Julie was sitting hunched under a cream blanket, cradling a mug of tea in her hands. Her nails were still defiantly purple. Her skin was white. Her eyes were lost.

'Afternoon.' Her voice was braver than her expression.

Hannah sat down on the arm of the chair and put her arms round Julie. Tom envied her instinctive kindness. He didn't know how to stand. How to look. What to say. He reached out towards her but then dropped his hand before she could see.

'We've come to pick you up.' He sounded gruff. Like a policeman about to make an arrest.

'No need.' Julie continued to stare out into the garden. 'I'm fine.' Her voice was level. Calm. 'Ben's coming to get me in a minute.'

'Ben?' Tom's pulse spiralled. 'You're going back to that bastard? After this?'

'He's not a bastard.' Julie's mouth pressed into a thin line. 'Don't you dare judge him. You don't even know him.'

'He was your teacher, Jules.' Tom found his hands clenching into fists. He wanted to make her see. He needed her to understand. 'You were his student. He got you pregnant. That makes him an arsehole.'

'No, it doesn't.' Julie's hand shook as she raised the mug to her lips. '*I* chased *him*. OK?'

'What?' Tom stared at the girl who had once written a whole book of stories starring him as the hero. She now felt as fictional as her tales of Sir Tom and his merry band of knights.

214

Julie's eyes dropped to the floor. 'And it's not his fault he didn't have the money to pay for this.' She gestured around the room with its soft chairs and glossy magazines and the colourful haven of garden outside. 'He has a lot of commitments.'

'Yeah?' Tom ran a hand through his hair in sheer frustration. 'You mean he's shagging lots of other students too?'

Julie's face froze. 'You bastard.'

He felt his fists clenching. Ever since his sister had told him she was pregnant he'd been constantly biting back fury. On the tube when people wouldn't move down the carriage. In the queue for his morning coffee when the person in front of him insisted in paying in painfully elusive change. At the cashpoint when it dared to fail to have the notes he needed.

He knew he had failed his sister.

Yet he still felt so angry with her that every conversation became a fight.

Hannah spoke. 'So you're heading back to Bristol, Jules?'

'Yeah.' Jules drained her tea. 'Ben'll be here in a minute. I know he will.'

Hannah saw that Tom was about to speak and raised a hand to stop him. 'We'll wait with you.'

Julie shook her head. 'I'm fine.'

Hannah's voice didn't change. 'I know you're fine. But we're staying here. Just in case.'

'If you insist.' Julie's voice wobbled.

'We do.' Hannah stared out of the window. 'You'll be OK. I promise.'

'I know.' Julie surprised Tom by leaning towards Hannah and tentatively resting her head against her shoulder. He watched Hannah's arm wrapping round his sister. Watched as Julie started to cry.

Hannah looked up at him. Smiled a sad smile.

They waited in silence.

Ben never came.

Thirteen

Steph pokes her head into Hannah's classroom.

'So, have you recovered yet?'

Hannah looks up from her latest unsuccessful skirmish with her interactive whiteboard.

'Have I recovered from what?'

'You know what.' Steph strides into the room, puts her bag on the floor and kneels down beside Hannah's chair. She puts her elbows on the desk and frowns up at the laptop screen. 'From your Saturday-night date.'

Hannah rolls her eyes. 'For the millionth time, it wasn't a date.'

'Whatever.' Steph reaches out and presses a key with a luminous orange nail. 'Well, I don't see Raj here today, so either you've spent all weekend tiring him out, or—'

Hannah cuts in. '*Or* he's gone back to Brighton to declare his love for his ex.'

'Oh.' Steph pulls a face. 'That wasn't what I was expecting.' She presses another key. 'That's nearly as bad as when I turned that rock star gay.' The screen goes blank.

'What rock star?' Hannah puts her head in her hands.

'Before your time.' She hears Steph pressing more keys. 'So sexy. But never very keen to take his leather trousers off. When he came out I finally understood why.' She types some more. '*Yes*. Done it.'

'You have?' Hannah looks up, holding back her curls with her fingers. The lesson is loading.

'Thank *God*.' She gives Steph a hug. 'You're brilliant.'

'So they tell me.' Steph nods and stands up. 'Are you OK? About Raj?'

'Of course I am.' Hannah nods, glad of the certainty she feels.

'Good.' Steph picks up her bag and an envelope drops out. Papers spill out across the floor. 'Oops.'

Hannah looks down and sees the Teach the World logo.

'Tell me you didn't just do that on purpose?' She glares at her friend.

'No!' Steph shakes her head. 'If I'd really wanted to show these to you I'd just have waved them in your face.'

'True.' Hannah slumps forward again. 'What is it? Your placement info pack?'

'Yep.' Steph starts picking the pages up and putting them back in the envelope. 'Do you want to see it?'

'No. Put it away.' Hannah puts her fingers over her eyes but can't resist peeking through. She glimpses tantalising phrases like '*Zanzibar Archipelago*' and '*Make a Difference Every Day*' and wants to cry.

'Are you sure?' Steph hesitates before putting the envelope back in her bag.

'Yes.' Hannah nods. 'Call me a misery but I don't really want to read about how much fun my best mate is going to have on the adventure of a lifetime.' She sighs. 'The adventure I still *really* want to go on myself.'

'*Finally*!' Steph punches the air in triumph. 'Finally we get the truth.'

Hannah shakes her head. 'Calm down, bird. You're not Poirot in a Regency drawing room announcing who poisoned who with the arsenic.'

'Maybe not.' Steph claps her hands together. 'But it's taken me ages to get the truth out of you – let me at least enjoy the moment.'

'Fair enough.' Hannah nibbles her lip. 'Though obviously it doesn't change anything. Next year you'll be bonding with buffalo and I'll be here moderating GCSE coursework for miserable Margaret.' She sighs. 'I'm absolutely dreading your postcards.'

'Then I won't send you any.' Steph walks to the window and looks out across the playground. 'The perfect excuse.' She leans forward. 'Wow. New graffiti. Already. They only just got rid of the last lot.'

Hannah comes and stands next to her and admires the enormous cock and balls on the far wall. 'I quite like it. It makes me smile.' She sighs. 'Oh Steph. What am I going to do?'

Steph puts an arm round her. 'I don't know. But I'm very happy I haven't heard you say the word "fine" today.'

They hug for a second before Steph pulls away. 'Come on. We'd better stop this public display of affection or the rumour mill will say we're having a lesbian affair.'

'Didn't it say that a year ago? Do you remember that kid in Year Ten coming up and asking which of us wore the strap-on?'

'Oh yeah.' Steph giggles. 'When I said it was me he nearly exploded on the spot.'

'Teenagers.' Hannah shudders.

Steph eyes her appraisingly. 'How's Tom doing?'

Hannah considers. 'He's a bit better. A bit more positive.'

'You're smiling, Han.'

'Am I?' Hannah flushes. 'Well, I'm just pleased for him. You know?'

Steph speaks quietly. 'Is that all? Are you two . . .?'

'No.' Hannah walks round behind her desk. 'Nothing like that. I'd hardly be wanting to go to Africa if I was falling for him again, would I?'

Steph shrugs. 'I suppose not.' She claps her hands together. 'Now. Are you coming to the pub?'

'No.'

'Is Julie doing another shift in Maccy D's?'

It would be easy to lie but Hannah doesn't want to any more. 'Nope. Tom and I are having dinner. He's cooking.'

'Right.' Steph nods. 'I see.'

Something in her tone makes Hannah prickle. 'I'd love to come to the pub, but Tom's not really up for big nights out yet.'

Steph bites her lip. 'He never did really want to come out with us, anyway.'

Hannah feels a rush of defensiveness. 'Well, he was busy. I didn't exactly rush out to the City every night to glug champagne with his lawyer buddies either.'

'I know.' Steph folds her arms. 'I wasn't having a go at him.'

Hannah's just opening her mouth to reply when Margaret appears with her black glasses perched on the end of her nose.

'Hannah – a word?'

'Of course.'

Hannah catches sight of the corner of the Teach the World envelope sticking out of Steph's bag as she goes.

Somehow Margaret's office doesn't have quite the same allure.

'So you see, Hannah, I do need your help.'

Hannah looks behind Margaret's head and sees that

someone has scrawled the words 'Jane Austen is shit' on the beige blind that is rolled halfway up the window. Through the glass Hannah can see that the world outside this office is enjoying the first proper day of April sunshine. On the street in front of the school, girls are in cotton dresses, men have their shirtsleeves rolled up and one little old lady struts past with a bright pink shopper and Ray-Bans. Hannah grins.

'What's so funny?'

Hannah remembers where she is. Margaret's office has all the spring atmosphere of an igloo and the books on the shelves behind the desk are arranged in ferociously alphabetical order. Hannah imagines Margaret carefully moving each book along when a new arrival appears. In today's grey dress, black flats and glasses, she looks like someone who actively enjoys doing her tax return.

Hannah sits upright in an attempt to wake herself up. 'I was just thinking what a lovely day it is, Margaret.'

'I see.' Margaret clearly doesn't. She leans forward, tucking one hand neatly into the other as she rests her forearms on her desk. 'Look, Hannah, I'm hoping for your support on this.'

Hannah has no idea what she's talking about.

'Mmmm. Sure.' Hannah knows she needs to kick her brain into gear, but the sun outside is lulling her into a delicious daze.

'Good. So you can cover his classes?' Margaret is looking at her expectantly.

'What?'

'Mr Harat's classes.' Margaret pushes a folder so that it is at perfect right angles to the edge of the desk. 'You can cover them? As I suggested?'

Hannah is so surprised she nearly falls off her chair. 'Raj's classes? Are you being serious?'

Stupid question. Margaret is always serious.

'Of course.'

'But, can't you get another supply teacher? To replace Raj?'

'Our budget's been cut, I'm afraid.'

Of course it has.

'Then . . . why me?' Hannah feels a wild urge to laugh. 'I already teach flat out most days of the week.'

'Well, I'm not asking you to take on all of his classes. Obviously. Only two.'

'That's ten extra periods a week.'

'Yes.'

'Leaving me with precisely two periods a week where I actually get to plan my classes.'

'Hannah, we all have to do some work out of hours, you know. It's part of the job.'

And how. Hannah is gritting her teeth so hard they are starting to ache. So far she's done everything Margaret's asked of her, but the point of no return is looming. If she carries on like this she'll soon be working harder than Tom did. And for a fraction of the pay.

She shakes her head. 'It's too much.'

'Hannah, if you want to progress in this school then you're going to have to make some sacrifices.'

Through the window Hannah sees a small boy licking an ice cream. She wants to dive out there and have some too.

She wants to feel free.

Just for a second.

No chance.

She sighs. Reminds herself that she has precisely no

options at the moment. 'Well, I've got most of my revision classes planned already, so maybe—'

'Excellent.' Margaret moves her mouse and her screen flickers into life. 'I know you won't let the students down.' Margaret brushes a tiny speck of dust from the screen.

'No. I won't.' Hannah can feel tears starting to form as hopelessness overwhelms her. 'I've got to go.' She gets up.

'Of course.' Margaret eyes her beadily. 'Finally, could you just pull together a GCSE coursework update for me? Tonight?'

'I . . .' Hannah's mouth clogs with swear words.

'Thank you.' Margaret pushes her glasses up her nose and starts to type.

Hannah leaves the room. Walks to the end of the corridor.

Then she starts to cry.

Half an hour later she becomes aware of an insistent knocking at her classroom door.

'Hannah?'

She lifts her head. Pulls out a make-up mirror. Wishes she hadn't.

'Who is it?' Most of her eye make-up is on her cheeks. She tries to repair the damage but only manages to smear it down to her chin.

'It's me, H.'

'Tom?' She leans on her desk.

'Yes.'

Oh God. He mustn't see her crying. 'What are you doing here?'

'I thought I'd take you out to dinner.'

'But . . .' She frantically tries to brush her curls into some kind of order. As usual, they refuse to obey.

'Come on, H.' He sounds worried now. 'Let me in. I took the bus. All by myself. I'm knackered. At least let me into the classroom.'

'OK.' She wipes her eyes again and walks towards the door. She puts her hand on the lock. 'But if you laugh at me I'm throwing myself out of the window.'

'You're only on the first floor.'

'Shut up.'

'I won't laugh. Promise.'

She unlocks the door and holds it open.

'As you can see, Tom, I don't think I'm in a fit state for dinner.'

He looks at her, taking in her tearstained face. 'Bollocks.' He kisses her on the cheek and limps in, sitting down heavily in the first chair he sees. 'I'm not exactly an oil painting.' He brandishes the present Nick had given him for his birthday. 'Though my new cane's looking pretty good.'

She puts her hands to her eyes as she feels the sobs starting again. She doesn't have the strength to stop them.

'Come here, H.'

She walks towards him and kneels down at his side. He puts his arms round her and she allows herself to thoroughly drench his shirt.

'What's wrong?'

'Everything.'

'OK.' He hugs her until her sobs start to ease. 'If this is what me turning up at school does to you, then I might not do it again.'

She gives a feeble laugh.

'Do you need a drink, H?'

'I'm not sure that's a good idea.' She takes the tissue he holds out to her.

'I know it is.' He pulls away from her. 'Let's get out of here.'

'So what was all that about?' Tom pushes Hannah's glass of wine towards her. 'Drink.'

She obediently tips the glass upwards and takes a mouthful.

'More.'

She drinks again.

'So.' He leans back against the black leather banquette. 'Our food is ordered. We have wine. Unless you need the loo again I think you're out of excuses. Talk to me.'

She opens her mouth. Closes it. Tries again.

'It's all fine really.'

He holds up a finger. 'H. You were sobbing behind a locked door. That's not fine.'

Hannah drums her fingers against her glass. 'Yeah, but I'm just being stupid.'

'Says who?' Tom looks around. 'I don't see anyone else saying that. Look, I know how much that job means to you. So talk to me.'

'OK.' She takes a breath and looks down at the dark wooden table. She is so unused to sharing things with him.

She raises her eyes. 'I suppose the first thing to say is . . . I hate my job.'

He stops his glass halfway to his mouth. 'You're kidding.'

She holds his eye. 'No. I've hated it for months.'

'But I thought you loved it?'

'I used to love it. But recently it's been horrible. Partly my new boss. But partly . . .' She searches for the right words. 'I can't remember why I'm teaching. I don't feel like I'm helping anyone any more.'

A vein pulses in his forehead. 'Is it my fault?'

'What do you mean?'

'My stroke. It's put so much pressure on you.'

'No.' She shakes her head. 'If anything, what happened to you has made things clearer. Seize the day, you know? I've just realised I've had enough of all the shit about pass marks and pressure – I love the kids and I still want to teach but I don't belong at Queensdale any more. And I want to feel that . . . passion again. That I used to have. You know?'

'Yeah.' He nods. 'It's how I was feeling before the stroke.'

'Really?' Hannah takes another glug of wine and looks up at the elegant lampshade that hangs above them. It looks like it's been retrieved from the set of a 1920s movie. Long fringes of cream silk drop down towards their heads. 'You never told me.'

'No.' His mouth lifts at the corner. 'Obviously I was too busy weeping behind my office door.'

'Don't take the piss.' She realises she is smiling. Her mouth starts to water as she inhales the smell of the food that sizzles in the open kitchen behind them. Ginger, garlic and the tang of lemongrass.

'So what are you going to do about it, H?'

Tanzania. She has to press her lips together to stop herself saying it.

'I don't know.' She pulls a pair of chopsticks out of their paper wrapping. 'I just need to do something . . . different.'

Tom points at her glass. 'Focus please. Keep drinking.'

'Yes, boss.' She raises her glass to her lips. 'I feel bad

moaning like this, though. You've got much more to deal with.'

'To be honest it's good talking about something that isn't my stroke.' Tom gives a wry smile. 'I'm bloody sick of it.'

'Yeah.' Hannah sips her wine. 'That makes sense.' She puts her glass down. 'Though when you got flu you used to milk it for all you were worth.'

He looks outraged. 'No I didn't.'

'You did.' Hannah grins. 'You used to leave forlorn packets of Lemsip in the kitchen to make sure I knew you weren't well. As if you groaning on the sofa wasn't enough of a clue.'

He laughs. 'Slander.'

She catches his eyes resting on her face, and feels a flash of something like excitement. She gulps her water and tells herself not to be silly. It's just Tom.

His forehead furrows. He's planning something.

'Nick has a mate in that private school – Beaumont College?'

She raises her eyebrows. 'Nick knows someone everywhere.'

'True.' He nods. 'Maybe he could get you an interview there.'

Hannah feels a thud of anticlimax at the thought. She doesn't want to be in a private school. She wants to feel useful. She wants battered books. Bright eyes.

She wants Tanzania.

But Tom looks so excited . . .

'That sounds great.' She exhales. 'Thank you.'

'Pleasure.' He raises his glass to hers.

As they drink she looks around to avoid his gaze. It's

too understanding. Things might come out that can't be unsaid. To their left she watches a young couple who are clearly having the worst blind date of their lives. They are engrossed in texting people who aren't there and consuming as much alcohol as humanly possible. Every now and then the man looks at his companion and resolutely downs another half pint of beer.

Tom is watching them too. He looks amused. Contented.

'Your turn now, Tom.'

He turns to her. 'Sounds serious.'

'It is.' She takes a breath. 'Do you think you'll join Nick? Start a firm?'

Tom shrugs. 'Would you like me to?'

The question unnerves her. She has too much power. 'I don't know.'

'Then I don't know.'

'What do you mean?'

He takes her hand. 'I mean that I want us to be a team again. A proper team.'

'Really?' This is moving too fast for her.

'Really.' His face is open. Earnest.

She drops her eyes, feeling suddenly shy.

'Too much, H?'

She looks up. 'A little.' It's so strange being honest with him. Feeling that she can tell the truth.

'OK.' He leans back in his chair and waves at the waitress. 'Then I suggest we have a proper night off. Banned topics include my stroke. Jobs.'

Hannah starts to smile. 'Politics.' She tops up their glasses.

'Absolutely.' Tom nods.

Hannah raises her glass. 'To our night off.'

'Cheers.' They clink glasses and he grins just the way he used to grin when they first met.

Hannah forgets about the past. Forgets about the future. She's going to have a damn good night.

She doesn't care about what comes next.

She's staring into wine glass number four when she looks up and notices that ten minutes have gone by since Tom went to the loo.

Her alcoholic buzz dissipates fast. Even with his cane Tom doesn't usually take this long. Fear jolts her. Maybe he's had another stroke.

Her pulse spirals. She gets to her feet and then sits down again. She knows he loves to feel independent. Like his old self.

She's being silly.

She nervously pushes her pad thai around her plate with her chopsticks. She glances towards the toilets, panic tugging at her breath.

Then she hears footsteps. Running.

One waiter. Then another.

Oh God.

Hannah gets to her feet, not caring that she's dropped her napkin on the floor. She must get to Tom. She must see if he's OK.

She joins the runners and sprints past tables of bewildered faces. Past the chefs with sweat on their brows and big sizzling pans in their hands. Past all the people eating and arguing and laughing their way through a normal Thursday night out. She sees their eyes following her for a surprised second, before they take another mouthful and forget what they've seen.

Hannah launches herself against the white door to the

toilets, and narrowly avoids colliding with the larger of the two waiters. She catches herself just in time and inches past his bulk before the other waiter blocks her path. He is sweating through his white shirt and uses his red apron to mop his forehead before continuing to pull ineffectually on the disabled toilet door.

'Is he OK?' Hannah can barely breathe.

The waiter turns his head. He has tired red eyes and flecks of grey in his beard. 'You can't go in there, Miss. Someone's pulled the emergency cord.'

'Of course I can.' She reaches past him and rattles the door. 'It's my husband in there. He's been in there for ages.'

She rolls up her sleeves, ready to break in if she has to. 'Tom? Are you OK in there?'

She hears a high-pitched keening.

Oh God. No.

'Tom? We're going to break the door down.'

She hears a piercing squeal.

'Shit.' She bangs her shoulder against the door. It entirely fails to give.

'SHIT!' She takes the tiny run-up the space will allow and succeeds only in hurting herself more.

'Come on!' She turns to the two waiters. 'Do something.'

'We could always use this.' The larger one holds up a key.

Hannah grabs it. 'Why didn't you bloody tell us you had that?'

He rubs his eyebrow repeatedly, as if waiting for a genie to appear. 'I dunno, I . . .'

'For God's sake.' She inserts it in the door. It opens first time.

Tom is collapsed on the floor, the emergency cord in

his hand. His hair is dishevelled, his face red. One leg is stretched along the floor while the other is pulled up towards his body.

It's happened again.

Everything in her narrows to a heartbeat.

'Tom!' She rushes to his side.

'Are you OK?'

She reaches for his hand. And sees that he's . . .

Laughing?

'Sorry.' He can barely speak as spasms of hilarity rock his body. 'I got a bit tangled up.' He holds up the emergency cord in explanation. 'And then I couldn't get back up. And I kept thinking . . .'

'Yes?' She feels her pulse start to slow.

'How bloody romantic this all is.' He erupts into peals of laughter.

She looks at his face and then sits down beside him and joins in.

The laughter dissolves their past and breaks their future wide open.

The waiters watch them in mute disapproval.

It only makes them laugh more.

Set of house keys

Summer 2012

'Shit. The Wi-Fi hasn't been switched on yet.' Tom stabbed his BlackBerry with angry fingers as he stepped through the front door. 'They bloody promised it would be.'

Hannah jangled a set of keys in his face. 'Focus, Tom. New house?' She nudged him in the shoulder, right in the spot where he'd injured himself on the football field a week before. He'd told her a hundred times.

She didn't notice him wince. She had already slipped off her sandals and was padding across the wooden floor of the hallway in her bare feet. She ran a hand along the white paint of the banisters. 'This is meant to be exciting. Remember?' She turned and walked towards him.

'Sure.' He frowned as he concentrated on his email rant to the internet provider. 'Nearly finished.'

She groaned and then pushed open a door at the bottom of the hall. 'Wow. I'd forgotten how huge this kitchen is.' He glanced up and saw her running a hand over the blank white walls as she walked towards the dark granite surface of the island in the middle. She ran her toe over the black and white tiled floor. 'Our poor old kitchen table is going to get a serious inferiority complex next to all this stainless steel.'

'We'll get a new one.' He was still typing.

'I don't want a new one.'

He pressed send and shoved the BlackBerry back in his pocket. 'Well, our old one is going to look like a postage stamp in here.' He gestured towards the glassed area that led towards the garden. 'And a pretty knackered one at that.'

'But I love that table.' Hannah wandered around the room, opening cupboard after cupboard, running her fingers along the glossy white shelves.

He felt a beat of irritation. 'Get real for a second, H. That table was a piece of shit from a charity shop. It has a dodgy leg and we have to keep it propped up with a paperback.'

She came to a halt underneath the skylight. A beam of sunlight highlighted the stubborn set of her face. 'You said you liked it when I bought it.'

He ran a hand over his eyes, annoyed to feel a familiar ache creeping across his temples. 'I know I did, H. But we've moved now. More space.' He pointed towards the floor-to-ceiling window leading into the garden. 'More light. Remember?'

'Bigger mortgage.' She nibbled on a fingernail.

He struggled to find a patience he didn't feel. This conversation had been playing on repeat ever since they had exchanged contracts a month before. 'I've told you we can handle that now. I've got my pay rise.'

He sounded more confident than he felt. His boss was not his number one fan. He had been visibly holding a grudge ever since Tom had dared to switch off his BlackBerry during a weekend away with Hannah. Naturally that was the weekend that the clients had gone ballistic about a banking discrepancy and when he'd switched it back on he had 600 emails and a voicemail telling him he was going to be fired.

He had talked his way out of it, but since then his workload had trebled and every day he had less time in which to do more. Most of the time he coped, but every now and then he cradled his aching head in the small hours and wondered if takeaways and naps at his desk were all life had to offer.

He wanted to tell Hannah. To share. He just didn't know how.

One day he'd figure it out. Soon. He walked across to Hannah and put his arms round her. 'We needed more space, H.'

She sighed. 'I miss our flat.'

He felt a familiar irritation. He exhaled and kissed the top of her head. 'This is so much better than the flat. It's a whole house! And if we have kids . . .' He waited a second, hoping for a word of encouragement.

She stayed silent. Since starting at Queensdale she always did. She was too busy now. Too dedicated to her career.

He sighed. 'And here you can get all your books out of storage and out on the shelves. We can make a bit of a library in the study upstairs.'

'I suppose so . . .' Her arms gently folded round his waist. 'And at least we're still close enough to the Junction to get my morning coffee.'

'Exactly. Three minutes to your favourite café.' He smiled. 'What more could you want?'

She giggled. 'Well . . . We do have a lot of rooms to christen.'

He gently pushed a curl behind her ear as she raised her head towards him. 'You bet we have.' He touched his lips to hers.

Her eyes glinted. 'What time's Jules coming up to help us unpack?'

He shook his head. 'God knows. She just texted saying she might not come till tomorrow. Her shift's been changed. At the shop.' He frowned. 'Or the swimming pool. I keep forgetting what she's doing at the moment.'

Hannah snuggled closer to him and he noticed how much thinner she had become since starting at Queensdale. 'She's been working at that trainer shop since January. She says she loves it.'

'Stop dreaming, Hannah.' He frowned. 'She never lasts long. In about a month's time she'll have resigned for some mad reason and will be asking me for money again.'

'Maybe not.' Hannah pressed her body to his. 'Maybe this job is the one. Maybe she'll be running her own international trainer empire by the time she's thirty.'

He grinned. 'And maybe you're a crazy optimist.'

'Maybe I am. And what's wrong with that?' She leant closer. 'I mean, I was wondering whether I might get lucky before the removal van gets here.' She gave him a coy smile he remembered from dates past. 'Just to pass the time, of course . . .' She ran a hand over his bum.

'Oh well.' He leant down and kissed her. 'If it's just to pass the time . . .'

'Our bed hasn't arrived yet, so it might be tricky.' She looked pointedly at the kitchen island. 'But I can think of another way of doing things.'

'You can, hey?'

'Yeah.' She nodded.

'I like the sound of that.' He rested his head on hers, then lifted her up into the air and carried her to the island. He placed her down gently, and she wrapped her legs around him and they kissed. Hungrily. Passionately. Like two people who'd been eyeing each other in a bar all night wondering how to say hello.

He ran his hands over her thighs. 'The good news is we can keep doing this till dawn.'

She was pulling her dress over her head, so her voice was muffled. 'I'm out tonight.'

'What?' He stopped. 'But I thought we were celebrating our first night here.'

She finally won her battle with the dress and her face reappeared. 'You said you were going to be working tonight, so I made plans.'

Irritation flared. 'I didn't say that.'

'Yeah, you did.' She threw the dress on the floor and he nearly forgot his grievance in the glory of her cleavage in its pink lacy bra. 'You said you'd be working tonight because the deal was closing this Monday.'

'But the deal closed early. I told you.'

'Yeah, but I assumed you'd still be working.' She leant forward and bit his lower lip with tantalising gentleness. 'There's always a deal on. Isn't there? That's why you work till midnight five days a week.' Her eyes challenged him. 'Isn't it?'

He felt petulant. Angry. 'Yes, but not today. Today's meant to be special.'

She shook her head. 'Sorry. I'm seeing Steph and Stu and Mike. Steph's just broken up with Tony so we're taking her out to cheer her up. I can't let her down.'

'But . . .' Hannah was always out with her mates from work. Steph in particular. Blonde. Bossy. Blunt.

Hannah grinned. 'You can come with me if you like? They'd all love to see you.'

He doubted it. As soon as she heard that he was a lawyer, Steph had clearly filed him in her 'City git' folder, which activated endless stories of how the bankers had brought down Britain. Not to mention the fact that all they talked about was teaching. They were all so bloody enthusiastic with their talk of changing lives and transforming futures. It made him feel sick. Or jealous. Or both.

'No thanks.' He'd rather unpack the cutlery.

'OK.' Hannah nodded. Fingered the top button of his shirt. Gave him a wicked grin. 'Then let's make the most of the time we have now.' She slowly undid his buttons.

He wrapped his arms round her and drew her close.

But everything felt different. A little less vivid. A little less true.

It was almost a relief when the removal van arrived early.

Fourteen

'Surprise!'

Hannah slides her heavy marking bag off her shoulder and lets it drop to the floor.

'Is that a disco ball?' She blinks at the new arrival on the hall ceiling.

Tom grins. 'It is.' He beams. 'Nick put it up.'

'Nick?' Hannah starts to wriggle out of her denim jacket. 'It's a bit early for him to be on the loose, isn't it? It's only four o'clock.'

'Hannah!' Nick appears from the kitchen and kisses her on both cheeks. 'Great to see you. I hope you're in party mood?'

'Erm . . . sure.' Actually Hannah had been hoping to have a cup of tea and a sneaky watch of *Deal Or No Deal*. She leans down to pull off her shoes. 'What are we celebrating?' She realises Nick is wearing jeans and a T-shirt. On a weekday. 'Are you on holiday or something?'

Nick grins. 'Or something.'

He is clearly so excited she can't help smiling back. 'Meaning what?'

He looks like he might attempt a somersault at any moment. 'I've done it. I've started my own firm.'

'*What*?'

Nick's rubs his hand over his hair. 'Yeah. Finalised it

238

today. I just felt like . . .' He looks at Tom. 'I've been feeling a bit mortal recently – for obvious reasons – and I just knew I couldn't wait any longer.'

Tom claps his friend on the back. 'Amazing, isn't it?'

Hannah feels a plunge of fear.

'Tom. Are you . . . ?'

'Don't worry.' Tom comes over and puts his right arm round her. 'This is Nick's firm. I might go and work with him one day, but not now. Didn't think I was quite ready. Yet.'

Nick looks at Tom. Grins. 'You won't hold out for long, though.'

Tom shrugs. 'We'll see. Not sure I'm quite as ballsy as you.'

'Bollocks.' Nick shakes his head. 'You're the one that made me take the plunge.'

Tom's eyes drop to the floor and he prods the carpet with his cane. 'Yeah. Well.'

'Don't be modest, mate.' Nick grasps his shoulder affectionately. 'You must know how bloody brave you've been.'

Tom examines the carpet in minute detail and Hannah sees his cheeks flush.

'That's enough, Nick.' She takes Tom's arm. 'The new boss of a shit-hot law firm can't come out with that kind of soppy crap. You'll be out of business in weeks.'

'Good point.' Nick slaps himself on the chest. 'Enough. From here on in I'll be all man.' A mischievous expression appears on his face. 'Just as soon as I've blown these up.' He waves a packet of violently pink balloons and disappears into the sitting room.

Hannah walks with Tom into the kitchen, where she

is touched to see a pot of tea steaming on the table, next to her favourite mug and a plate of Jaffa Cakes.

'Aw, thanks, Tom.'

'You're welcome.' He shrugs. 'I only dropped one plate this time. And I made sure it was one of those ones your mum gave you. The horrendous orange ones.'

'Well done.' Hannah shudders. 'I hate them. Feel free to drop the whole lot if you want to.'

They both sit down at the table.

'So. Nick's done it.' She pours the tea.

'Yeah.' Tom swallows. 'I'm sorry I didn't tell you. I wanted it to be a surprise.'

'It's certainly that.' She takes a sip of tea. 'Are you sure you don't want to be in on it?'

'Yes.' He nods emphatically.

'What made you decide?'

'That night out we had.' He picks up a Jaffa Cake.

'Really?' Her stomach plunges.

'Yeah. You know.' He bites into it. 'We had fun. And I want us to keep doing that.' He drops his eyes and looks hesitant. Shy. 'If you'd like that, I mean.'

'Of course I would.'

They look at each other and smile. It feels new. Precious.

'So you thought your own firm would be too much?'

His fingers are wandering towards hers.

'Yes.' He takes hold of her hand. 'But it's not only that. I just . . .' He looks at her and the hope on his face makes her pulse spiral. 'Please don't think I'm going to morph back into who I was before, H. I love spending time with you. I love seeing you smile. I don't want to be that workaholic guy any more. Instead I want to be

this guy. The guy who has impromptu parties.' He grins.
'Remember our New Year's Eve party the year we got
engaged?'

'Oh God. Yes.' Hannah shudders as she remembers
how close Nick had come to falling off the roof while
trying to prove he had 'Spider-Man hands'.

'And that Halloween party when I was living with Nick?'

'Oh my *God*. That was the one where I was sick on
Nick's duvet, wasn't it?'

'It was.' Tom nods. 'Just before he pulled that underwear model.'

'Ha ha.' She wrinkles her nose. 'And that bloody duvet
cost about fifty quid to dry-clean.'

He laughs. 'It did.'

She shudders.

Tom finishes the Jaffa Cake. 'Anyway, I want to be
that guy again. What do you think?'

'I think . . .' She feels his fingers around hers. He is
so close. 'I think . . .'

Then his lips meet hers.

It's not the kiss she remembers from before. The
perfunctory peck at the beginning or end of a day.

It's soft. Kind. Gentle.

'Now we just have to make you happy too.' He kisses
her again.

'Am I interrupting something?' Nick is standing in the
doorway, holding some shiny silver ribbon in one hand.
He shakes his finger at Hannah. 'I hope you're not
distracting my party planner, Mrs Ellison?'

'No.' Hannah shakes her head. 'Wouldn't dream of it.'

'Good. Because I need vital advice on where to put
the stereo.'

'Why?' Hannah stares at him suspiciously. 'How many people have you invited?'

Nick won't meet her eye. 'A few.' He looks at Tom. 'Come on. Get up and help me. Don't think that cane is an excuse.'

'OK, OK.' Tom levers himself up. 'See you on the dancefloor, Hannah.'

'You hate dancing.'

He turns, leaning lopsidedly. 'That was the old me.'

'Wow.' Hannah folds her arms. 'You really are a new man.'

'You'd better believe it.'

He limps after Nick, leaving her touching her fingers to her lips, longing for another kiss.

'Are you finished in there yet?' Hannah bangs on the bathroom door. 'You've been in there for ages.' She presses her ear to the door and hears violent retching. Nick's fruit, aka rum, punch is having an impact. She pauses for a moment, only to hear another bout beginning.

It sounds as if whoever it is might puke up a lung.

Hannah bangs again. 'Are you OK in there?'

Silence. Then more retching.

'Hello?'

More retching. Then, over the thumping bass of the music downstairs, Hannah hears it.

Crying.

She turns the handle but the door is locked.

'Let me in.' She drops her voice, the way she has in a million similar situations at school.

'No.'

A woman's voice. Julie?

'Jules, let me help.'

'You can't help.' There is prolonged nose-blowing from behind the door.

'I can try.'

'No point.'

'Look, just let me in, Jules. I need a pee and the downstairs loo is probably jammed with City boys who can't aim straight any more. And I've got bare feet.'

A muffled giggle.

Then the sound of the lock being pulled back.

Hannah walks in and heads straight for the toilet. 'Look the other way.'

'All right, all right.' Julie averts her eyes while Hannah makes use of the facilities. 'And I always thought you were classy.'

'You're kidding me, right?' Hannah zips up her jeans. 'I was eating baked beans out of a can the first time I met you.'

'Yeah, but they were reduced sugar.'

Hannah giggles as she washes her hands. 'Clearly one of my very rare attempts at a diet.'

'Whatever.' Julie stares miserably at the tiled floor. She reaches into her pocket and brings out a packet of Refreshers. She opens it and starts to crunch them gloomily.

Hannah closes the lid of the loo and sits down, feeling the chill of the tiles on her bare feet. 'So what's going on?'

'Nothing.' Julie sighs.

'I don't believe you.'

'Not surprising.' Julie shrugs. 'People generally don't.'

Hannah notices that she's not slurring her words. Considering there's a party going on, this is extremely unusual.

Frankly, it's pretty rare for Julie on a quiet night in.

'Jules?' She watches her. Sulky mouth. Pale. So far, so normal.

Yet there's something else.

'What?'

Everything clicks into place. The moods. The weight gain.

'Jules, are you pregnant?'

'Why, do you think I'm bloody fat or something?' Julie looks down at her body. 'I thought you were here to make me feel better.' She starts crying again.

Oh God. 'I'm so sorry.' Hannah is mortified. 'I just wondered—'

'I mean, am I that bloody HUGE?' Julie fiercely dashes the tears away.

'I'm sorry.' Hannah feels like banging her head against the wall.

'It's rude, making comments like that, you know.'

Hannah has a sudden yearning for a time machine. 'I know.'

'You could really offend someone.' Julie has two bright spots of anger on her cheeks.

'OK. I'm sorry.' Hannah leans back against the loo. 'I will never call you pregnant *ever* again. OK?'

'OK.' Julie exhales.

Silence falls. Hannah looks up at the big mirrored cupboard on the wall and sees that someone has sprayed *C woz here* on it in shaving foam. Original.

Julie sighs. 'I bloody am, though.'

It takes Hannah a second to catch up. 'What?'

Julie rolls her eyes. 'Listen, will you? I AM. Bloody pregnant.'

Hannah breathes. Twirls a curl round her finger. Panics. She has precisely no idea what to say.

The silence is too long now. She forces some words out. 'Congratulations, Jules.'

Julie's face is stony. 'Very funny.'

'I'm serious.'

'No you're not.' Julie practically spits the words out. 'You're thinking, oh, poor Jules, she's messed up her life all over again.'

'No.' Hannah puts a hand on Julie's shoulder, but it is firmly pushed away. 'I'm not thinking that.'

The truth is she's so shocked she can barely think at all.

'Really?' Julie snorts furiously. 'You think becoming a single mum is really going to work for me?'

'I—'

'See?' Julie's face shuts down. 'You think I'm going to screw this up. You two always think I'm going to fuck stuff up.'

'No.'

'YES.' Julie pushes her hair behind her ears with her hands.

God. There were landmines everywhere in this conversation.

Hannah tries to calm her. 'What does the father say?'

Julie shakes her head. 'Haven't told him.'

Worry swirls through Hannah's mind. 'Why not?'

'He wouldn't care.'

'How do you know?'

'Well, he hasn't exactly been in touch recently.'

Hannah keeps her voice soft. 'Is it Zac?'

Julie's eyes cloud with tears again. 'Wow, you really do think I'm a slag.'

'Sorry.'

'Never mind.' Julie shakes her head. 'And yes – it's his.'

Hannah remembers the panic on Julie's face as she hid from Zac in the kitchen. 'Is that why you wouldn't speak to him when he came up here?'

'Bloody hell, Hannah.' Julie folds her arms. 'No need to make me feel like even more of a bitch. I was panicking. I'd just found out. And I knew it was too soon for him – that he'd run – and I couldn't stand it.'

'Sorry.' Hannah looks at the swell of Julie's belly above the waistband of her jeans. 'I can't believe how long you've been hiding it. Nice work.'

Julie produces a glimmer of a smile. 'It's just as well you have so many loose tops, isn't it?'

Hannah grins. 'How thoughtful of me.'

She keeps trying to think of something to say. Something positive. Something helpful.

'When is the baby due?'

'Early October.' Julie's face darkens again. 'But seriously. I don't know how to do this. I'm crap with babies.'

'Are you?' Hannah frowns. 'I didn't know you'd spent much time with them.'

'Yeah, well, there's a lot you don't know about me.' Julie scratches her leg and Hannah sees that her nails are bitten down to the quick. 'I've spent loads of time with my mates' babies and I know they're tiny and they cry all the time and they're too stupid to hold up their own heads.'

'Right.' Hannah nods slowly. 'But I do hear they have other pluses. It's not all bad.'

'All very well for you to say. What with you being married and not carrying round a little person in your belly.'

Hannah puts her head on one side. 'Well, if you're really not sure, have you thought about your options?'

Julie unconsciously places her hands protectively over her belly. 'Yes. And I can't go through that again. Not after last time.'

'OK.' Hannah feels a rush of concern. 'Then are you taking folic acid? Eating lots of oily fish and vegetables?'

Julie gestures to the Refreshers packet. 'No.'

'Then you should think about starting. You're what . . . four or five months along now? Have you seen a midwife yet?'

Julie pops another sweet in her mouth. 'Yes. And how come you know so much about it?'

Hannah shrugs. 'People at school keep having babies. They like talking about it. A lot.'

Julie's face crumples again. 'See? I'm going to be BORING.'

'No.' Hannah leans forward, folding her arms round her knees. 'You're not. You're many things, Jules, but boring isn't one of them'

Julie smiles properly for the first time. 'Really?'

Hannah nods emphatically. 'Really.'

Julie leans back against the bath. 'You know this wasn't exactly my plan.'

'You have a plan?'

'Ha ha.' Julie looks at Hannah and shakes her head. 'I

know you two think I'm rubbish but I've been working at McDonald's. To get some money together.'

'I know.'

'*What?*'

'I saw you.'

'And you never said anything?'

'I meant to, but you were pretty good at disappearing whenever I was about to try.'

Julie's face twists. 'You didn't tell Tom, did you?'

'No.'

'Thank God.' Julie weaves her fingers in and out of each other as she explains. 'He always says how smart I am. He would hate to think of me working in there. But I was desperate. For cash. For the baby. But then they fired me. For being sick during a shift. They thought I was hungover. I wish. I was just trying to do the right thing, you know? I didn't want to let everyone down again.'

Hannah puts her hand on Julie's shoulder. This time it isn't pushed away. 'No one thinks you've let them down.'

'Bollocks. I've been crap and you know it.' Julie hangs her head forward. 'Since I found out about the baby, I keep thinking back to when I was little. When Mum was alive. I used to keep a diary and I wrote down all the books I read and mapped out the amazing career I was going to have.' Her face is pinched with bitterness. 'What a load of crap.'

'What were you going to be?'

Julie's face looks somehow younger as she remembers. Lighter. 'Well, at first I was going to be a politician.'

'Obviously.'

'And a movie star.'

'That's a unique combination.'

'No.' She shakes her head. 'Arnie did it. And Ronald Reagan.'

'True.'

Julie carries on. 'But then I worked out that I really wanted to be a doctor. But then Mum died and then I got pregnant by that teacher, Ben, and – well, you know what happened then . . .' Julie sighs. 'And I never really got started again, did I? Now I'm just a big old screw-up with no job and really bad split ends.'

'Not quite the spin I'd put on it.' Hannah squeezes her hand.

'What if this little one ends up like me?' Julie's eyes are full of fear.

'Then he or she will be very feisty.'

Julie snuffles. 'That hasn't exactly got me anywhere, has it?'

Hannah thinks hard. She must come up with something positive. Something true. 'And they'll be brave.'

Silence.

'And bloody clever too.'

Julie's head stays down.

'Come on, Jules.' Hannah squeezes her shoulders. 'Look at the way you looked after your mum. You were brilliant.'

'Yeah but with Tom I sucked.' Julie wipes her hand across her eyes. 'I was totally unreliable. My usual self.' Her mouth hardens. 'But I was still so angry with him. For what happened with Mum. For not being around more.'

At last. Hannah's been waiting years for her to say that.

'Well, why don't you give him a chance now? To help?'

'No.' Julie's head jerks up. 'We can't tell him. He'll kill me.'

'He won't.' Hannah shakes her head. 'He's different now.'

Julie is weeping. 'Is he? I don't know.'

'Yes.' Hannah feels a confidence she hadn't expected. 'He is.'

'But he's having such a hard time. And . . .' Julie grimaces. 'Part of me thought he deserved it. The stroke. I'm such a cow.' She grabs a piece of loo roll that is way too small to soak up her tears.

'You were angry.' Hannah stands up. 'And if you ask me you had every right to be. Now.' She passes Julie more loo roll. 'Clean yourself up a bit. I'm going to go down there and get Tom and you are going to tell him about all this. OK?'

'No.'

'Well, I'm doing it anyway.'

She's halfway down the stairs before Julie can stop her.

She finds Tom in the garden, sitting on the bench with some of his old colleagues, talking about Christmas parties past. He smiles when he sees her and pats the space beside him.

'You know, it's really strange being the sober one.' He lifts his can of low-alcohol beer. 'I'm going to be that annoying git who tells you what you got up to at three a.m.'

Hannah squats down on her haunches next to him and puts a hand on his arm. 'Tom, Julie needs to speak to you upstairs.'

He looks at her and takes in the gravity of her expression. 'What is it?'

Hannah takes his hand. 'You need to talk to her. Right now.'

'OK.' He pushes up and starts to follow her past Nick's very inelegant attempt to start a conga. He stops her at the bottom of the stairs, speaking loudly over the music. 'Is she OK?'

'Yeah.' Hannah nods as she realises it's true. 'Just talk to her.'

She hopes Tom will do the right thing. Be the new Tom. Not the old.

He enters the bathroom. Looks at his little sister crying on the floor. And before Julie can say anything he lowers himself awkwardly down and folds his right arm round her.

Julie leans against him. 'Please don't be angry, Tom. You're always angry.'

'I won't be, Jules.' He strokes her hair. 'I promise.'

Hannah gently closes the door behind him.

New Tom is real.

She walks to the top step, gazing at the pictures of what she had thought to be the happiest day of her life. Her gold dress. His endless smile.

Today is sweeter.

She goes into her bedroom and looks at her phone. She has a new picture message. From Raj.

Her stomach tightens.

It's a picture of him and a girl with amber hair and huge green eyes. Amelia. The text says Mission accomplished. Thanks Hannah x

Raj.

She thinks of Tom. The trust in his eyes.

And she knows that she has to tell him. If they're really going to start again.

She has to tell him what happened with Raj.

Invitation to a
Winter Wonderland Christmas soiree
December 2013

She looked so beautiful. And she was trying so hard. She was standing in a far corner of the room, only just taller than an enormous reindeer made of fairy lights and tinsel. She scratched her back surreptitiously through her unusually demure black dress while taking a hearty gulp of the champagne that had been flowing freely all evening. Her curls were tamed and glossy as she smiled at the man next to her, and she shifted from foot to foot in the high heels that he knew she hated.

She was doing it all for him.

She turned her head and flashed him a smile. He raised his glass in return and noticed that some fake snowflakes had attached themselves to his sleeve. The bar was covered with glitter and snow and chubby Father Christmases smiled smugly at him from the barman's bowtie.

He wasn't in the mood. He drained the remains of his champagne and slammed it down on the bar.

'Hannah's doing well, isn't she?' Nick appeared beside him, bearing a very welcome bottle of whisky. 'She's doing a great job on old Smith over there.'

'Yep.' Tom grabbed a heavy tumbler from behind the bar and held it out. 'Isn't she just?'

Nick was too full of booze to pick up on the sarcasm in his voice. He ran a hand through his thick blond hair and filled Tom's glass. 'The partners seem to love her.'

Tom took his first mouthful and winced as the liquid warmed his throat. 'It's a bit late for that.'

'What are you talking about?'

Tom downed the rest of the whisky and grabbed the bottle. 'You must have heard by now.' He poured until the tumbler was half full.

'Heard what?' Nick threw two ridiculously small prawn canapés into his mouth and leant against the bar.

Tom could hardly say the words.

'I've been . . .' He forced the words out. 'Let go.'

Nick nearly choked on his prawns. 'What?'

'You heard me.'

'Why?'

Tom didn't want to talk about it. 'Doesn't matter, does it?'

Nick frowned. 'I'm so sorry, mate.'

'Yeah? Me too.' Tom downed the whisky in one and reached for more.

Nick put his large tanned hand over the bottle. 'Slow down.'

'Why? What have I got to lose?'

Nick shrugged. 'Fair point.' He poured more into Tom's glass.

Tom looked at him. 'I take it you've survived? Still on the payroll?'

'Yep.' Nick nodded. 'Don't know why.'

Tom rubbed his eyes. A fierce headache was starting to slice through his temples, but he downed another mouthful anyway.

'It's not fair.' Nick put his hand on Tom's arm.

Tom saw the pity in his eyes. He couldn't bear it. 'It's fine. Really. I was getting a bit bored here anyway. You know? Time for a change.'

'Sure.' Nick looked unconvinced. 'But it really doesn't

make sense. You've done more billable hours than anyone. Worked your arse off.' He shook his head. 'Bloody recession. It's killing us.' He sipped his drink.

'Yeah.' Tom stared at everyone downing free booze in one of the plushest hotels in London. 'Obviously.' He looked at their smiles. Their smart suits.

Bastards.

His boss had only just told him. He was on his way in to the party when he'd been pulled aside. Told that he wasn't 'quite the right fit'. That it was time for him to 'seek new opportunities'. That the firm was 'so grateful for all his hard work'.

Funny way of showing it.

Nick was watching him. 'At least you've already bought that house. Got the mortgage, I mean.'

'Yeah.' Tom wondered how the hell he was going to pay for it. And the car. And their forthcoming holiday. It wasn't as if Hannah's salary brought in much, apart from vast quantities of moral high ground.

Nick chinked his tumbler against Tom's. 'Bastards.'

'I'll drink to that.'

Nick reached for the bottle again. 'Let's drink them dry. Free bar.'

'Now that is a damn good plan.' Tom gestured to the bottle. 'Pour me another.'

He took the replenished glass and glanced over towards the Christmas tree. One of the junior associates appeared to be trying to climb it. 'That new paralegal you like is just over there.'

'Oh, I know.' Nick nodded. 'I'm just biding my time.'

Tom shook his head. 'I would say good luck but it would be a complete waste of breath.'

Nick grinned and raised his glass.

Tom walked over to Hannah and slung his arm round her neck. He felt alcohol rushing to his brain and had to concentrate to stand up straight.

'Hi Tom.' She turned back to the cluster of partners. 'Marcus was just telling me about what you get up to on your big City boy nights out.'

Her smile was wide but something in him heard criticism beneath her words. She giggled. 'It sounds – amazing.'

Now he knew she was laughing at him. Laughing at them all. She was safe – she was changing lives and all that shit. Her nights out involved eating crisps and downing cheap wine at poetry slams in scruffy pubs. Tonight of all nights he should sympathise with her, but instead he felt anger needling his heart. He took a slug of whisky to try to fight it off. He felt a piercing urge for a cigarette and wished he hadn't nagged Hannah into giving up a few months ago.

'Can you excuse us for a minute?'

Marcus nodded assent and turned back to his wife, who was waving her hands around enthusiastically as she told some kind of story involving wrapping paper and a donkey.

Hannah leant up and kissed him on the cheek as he marched her away. For some reason it infuriated him even more.

He found a quiet corner and stood in front of her as she leant against the wall.

'Are you trying to take advantage of me?' Hannah raised an eyebrow. 'Because the ladies' loos are just over there.'

'No, Hannah, I—'

'I'm game if you are.' She put a hand suggestively on his thigh.

'For Christ's sake, Hannah!'

Her face fell and he hated himself for being the cause. It only made him more furious.

Her voice was tiny. 'What?'

'I can't shag you at my firm's Christmas party. Even you must understand that.'

She frowned. 'I was joking, Tom.'

'It wasn't very bloody funny.'

She folded her arms across her chest. 'Obviously.'

A horribly familiar silence grew between them, mocked by the jolly music of a string quartet playing a medley of Christmas hits.

She cracked first. She always did.

'What's the matter? I thought you'd be happy that I'm here.'

He would have been. Another day. Another time.

She kissed him gently on the lips. 'Talk to me.'

He looked left. He looked right.

Then he told her.

When he'd finished there was pity in her eyes. And something like relief.

'Maybe you could do something else, now. Maybe it's time.'

'What?' He was wrong-footed. Misunderstood.

'If you've worked so hard and this is the thanks you get then maybe you could try something else. Retrain.'

His tongue felt thick. 'Wouldn't you just love that?'

'What do you mean?'

He saw the sincerity on her face and something in him wanted to crush it.

'Well, it's your dream, isn't it? Having me at home more. Giving you all the attention you feel you deserve. Telling you how wonderful you are and how bloody special you are. All that crap.'

'Tom.' He heard the sob in her voice but he couldn't stop.

'I'm not giving up my career for you, Hannah. Just stop dreaming that particular dream. I'm not going to move to sodding Ethiopia or wherever it is you want to go.'

'I—'

He could taste whisky on his tongue. 'Not going to happen.'

A tear slid down her cheek. 'I'm not asking you to do that.'

'And it's not like your job can pay the bills.'

She flushed. 'I know. But we could downsize. I'd be fine if—'

'Yeah, right.' He felt anger rampaging through him. His head felt like it would burst. 'Hannah in her bloody garret. Like you'd really be happy without all the things I give you.'

He felt a savage satisfaction at the hurt stamped across her face. She dropped her eyes. 'I don't know why you're so angry with me. I just want you to be happy.'

'Yeah?' He was snarling. 'Well, I'm not.' The anger was draining away leaving only alcohol and overwhelming failure. 'I'm not.' His head dropped to her shoulder. He didn't want her to see his tears.

'I know.' She cradled his head in her hands and he heard the sympathy in her voice.

Somehow it only made him feel worse.

Fifteen

Hannah stares at the peeling blue door, willing it to open. Or to collapse. Or spontaneously combust. Anything to get her out of here.

Margaret looks pointedly at her watch. 'Do you have somewhere to be, Hannah? Because we've only just got started.'

Hannah looks despairingly around the airless grey armpit of a room. She is sure the departmental office would never have inspired any of the writers whose works they teach. She can't imagine even Keats would have managed to come up with an ode to the dilapidated bike sheds she can see from the tiny window.

'Of course not, Margaret.' She shifts in her paralysingly uncomfortable chair.

Margaret leans forward and places her pen at perfect right angles to her notebook. 'The head is very concerned about the department's projected pass rate.'

Hannah looks at the sun reflecting off the battered metal railings around the shed. Above it she knows the sky is its most uplifting shade of blue.

If only she could see it.

She crosses her legs and tries to feel any kind of interest in what Margaret is saying.

She fails.

'So we need to come up with an action plan.'

Margaret is looking at her expectantly.

'Really?'

'Yes, Hannah.' Margaret's voice acquires a note of irritation.

Hannah finds she doesn't care about that either. She notices a piece of yellow thread on Margaret's sleeve. It's weirdly hypnotic. She wonders how long it will survive before being ruthlessly removed.

She keeps staring as she speaks. 'But isn't that your job, Margaret?'

'Pardon?'

Hannah meets her eyes. 'Correct me if I'm wrong, but isn't it your job to fix things like that?'

'I'm just trying to give you opportunities, Hannah.' Margaret tries to smile but her mouth is clearly out of practice.

'Are you?' Hannah thinks of all the extra classes she's taught and the spreadsheets she's created.

She thinks back. Margaret has never said thank you. Not once.

Margaret gives a curt nod. 'Yes. Of course I am.'

Hannah looks at Margaret's pinched face. Her tired eyes. It's how Hannah looks in the mirror every morning.

She is aware of an end approaching.

Enough.

Life is too short for this. She's tired of looking out at the world she wants to live in. It's time to get out there and be part of it.

She speaks in a kind of trance. 'Well, Margaret, I'm sorry but I think I'm going to have to turn this opportunity down.'

'Excuse me?' Margaret's mouth falls open and Hannah is pleased to see some spinach stuck in her back teeth.

'You heard me.' Hannah gets up from her chair. Stretches. Feels roughly a hundred years younger. 'I can't help you.'

'But it's your job to—'

'No, Margaret.' Hannah shakes her head. 'It's my job to teach the kids. To get them to read. To try to help them to be enthusiastic about life and stories and aspire to be something themselves. And you know what?'

Margaret doesn't speak. She seems to be shrinking. Hannah wonders how she'd ever been scared of her.

She speaks calmly, full of a confidence she hasn't felt in months. 'I think if you spoke to my students they might say I'm OK at what I do. Yeah I'm small and stubborn and occasionally I sound like a Jack Russell, but most of the time I put my heart into it. And you have never once thanked me. Not once.'

'I . . .' Margaret's mouth hangs open. Hannah rather hopes a fly will appear and pop in for a visit. As usual in this office, she's disappointed.

Hannah puts her hand on the door as Margaret rouses herself into action.

'Where are you going, Hannah? We're not finished here.' Her cheeks are flushed and her movements jerky.

Hannah sees it now. Margaret's not a monster. She's just a woman with a pinched heart and a serious case of OCD.

'I know that you haven't finished, Margaret. But I—' She feels lightness surge inside her. 'I think I'm done here.'

'No, you're not.' Margaret lowers her voice. Normally a dangerous sign.

'Really?' Hannah shrugs. 'I don't agree.'

'But—'

Hannah finds herself smiling. Properly smiling. 'Because you see, Margaret. I resign.' It sounds so good that she says it again. 'Yes. I resign.'

Margaret whips her glasses off and stands up. 'I think you'll find your contract says that you have to give a term's notice. And as it's May already, I—'

Hannah stays calm. Margaret can't upset her any more. 'And I think *you'll* find that if I send all your emails and notes and voicemails to the education authority they'll find you guilty of bullying. And I don't think you want that on your record, do you?' She feels a stab of vindication as Margaret drops her eyes first.

Margaret picks up her notebook. Tucks her pen into the spine.

Then she meets Hannah's gaze. 'Look, you seem a bit upset. If it's a little hot for you in here we can always rearrange this meeting.'

'No.' For once the words Hannah wants come at the right time. Not five minutes later. Not in the pub when she's three glasses of wine down. 'It's not too hot for me in here. It's too cold. I can't think like you, and I don't want to. I don't care about statistics. I care about my students loving books. And I'd rather take a job plucking chickens or putting the sodding cherries on Bakewell tarts than turn into a spreadsheet obsessive like you.'

She turns and opens the door. 'I'll work the rest of the term. Not for you. For the kids. You'll have my resignation letter in the morning. Meanwhile . . .' She sees Margaret slump back in her chair. 'Have a lovely evening.'

As the door closes behind her she texts the first person she thinks of. Tom.

TOM. I'm FREE. Pub. Now.

Then she goes and finds Steph.

As she turns the corner she bumps into T'shan.

'Hey Miss.' The girl grins. 'You look happy. Like you're about to do something naughty, Miss.'

Hannah smiles. Ear to ear.

'Maybe I am, T'shan. Maybe I am.'

'What's the answer then?' Steph stares intensely at her shot glass.

'Dunno.' Hannah leans her head on the bar and subsequently realises it's too far away. Tom reaches out his right hand and catches her for the third time tonight. His fingers linger as he sets her straight in her chair.

Hannah catches Steph staring at them curiously. She catches Hannah's eye and looks away, grabbing another handful of peanuts from the packet.

'What would you do, Steph?'

'It's easy.' Steph misses her mouth with yet another peanut. The purple pub carpet is covered in fallen casualties.

'Does it involve Botox, by any chance?' Hannah picks up her shot glass, trying and failing to remember how many she's had so far. She remembers the first bottle of prosecco, but has no idea how she got from there to downing tequilas on a Tuesday night.

Steph's eyes gleam. 'Maybe. You see, I'd hire the best person in the world, and then I'd—'

'No, no, no!' Hannah hits her hand against Steph's knee. The rest of the peanuts slide to the ground. 'You don't need Botox, Steph. You're beautiful. It would be a *crime*.'

Tom blinks. 'I don't think she likes your idea, Steph.' He shakes his head. 'Though I have to say I think Hannah's right.'

'Oh, shut up.' Steph rolls her eyes. 'Now that I'm . . .' She leans forward and speaks in an exaggerated whisper. 'Now that I'm *in my late thirties,* I think it's time to invest in a little help. You know?'

'Nope.' Hannah shakes her head. 'Besides, that's a really boring thing to do if you won the lottery.'

'Says who?'

'Says me.' Hannah folds her arms. 'And I am *right.*'

Steph laughs. 'You should resign more often. It's nice to have feisty Hannah back.'

Hannah nods. 'It is, isn't it? I'd forgotten how much fun she is.' She gestures to the barman for another round. 'All I know is I couldn't stand working with Margaret any more. Life's too short.' She looks at them both. Shrugs. 'Now on to important things. Like what *I'd* do if I won a million quid.'

Steph's voice has a hint of steel. 'So, come on then, Little Miss Adventurous. While I'm freezing my face with poison, what would you be up to?'

Hannah thinks of the battered map of the world she still has stuck up in the study.

'Well, I think I'd start with a steak breakfast in Brazil.' She smiles as she imagines the juiciness of the meat on her tongue. 'Tom and I always said we'd go there one day, didn't we?' Their eyes tangle. She finds it hard to look away. 'Then I'd go and see the Iguaçu falls and look at toucans and party at Carnival.' She sighs. 'Later I'd shimmy over to Vietnam for lunch and a quick bit of beach time, then a Tanzanian safari for tea, and then maybe I'd go to New Zealand for some skydiving over Queenstown or a swim with some dolphins.'

'Wow. Have you discovered time travel as well as winning the lottery?' Steph looks sceptical.

Hannah shrugs. 'Maybe I have.' She giggles. 'And then I'd come home and have cocktails at one of the Junction's theme nights.'

Steph wrinkles her nose. 'That café? Round the corner from your house? That's hardly millionaire territory.'

Hannah wags a finger at her. 'Not the point, Steph. It's the place I'd most want to go to celebrate the start of something new.' She turns to Tom. 'Best mojitos in the world, you know. The *best*.' She thrusts her arms wide for emphasis as the tequila burns through the remains of her stress and sobriety. 'They can turn a day from cloud to sunshine. From dark to light.'

Steph groans. 'Oh God. She's getting poetic. She'll be launching into her Wordsworth quotations next. I'm going to the loo.' She slides off her stool, only for her heel to get tangled in her handbag. 'See?' She struggles up again. 'Late thirties. It's all downhill from here.' She pats her skin. 'I feel all hot.' Her face falls. 'Oh my God. MENOPAUSE.'

'Oh, shut up.' Hannah pushes her towards the loo. 'Menopause? Or the fact you've just downed a load of tequila?' She shakes her head. 'I know which I'd vote for.'

'So unsympathetic.' Steph shakes her head dramatically. 'Some best friend you are.' She weaves her way unsteadily towards the ladies.

'What else would you do? On your millionaire day?' Tom leans close and watches her intently.

She feels oddly shy under his scrutiny and sits up straighter. 'Oh, I don't know. It's silly really.'

'Why?'

'Well, it's never going to happen, is it?'

'Why not?' He sips his pint. 'You probably didn't think you were going to resign this morning, but now you have.'

He puts his arm over her shoulder. 'You can do anything you want to.'

'I suppose so.' Hannah shrugs. 'But I'm not sure fixing the lottery is within my power.'

'Fair point.' He lowers his hand to his knee, next to hers. 'But what else would happen during your day? If you could have anything?'

She moves her legs away. Something is changing between them and it makes her nervous. She still hasn't told him about Raj. She needs to. But she doesn't know how to start.

She doesn't want to break this before it's started.

Tom's looking at her. Waiting.

She jokes her way out of the intensity on his face.

'Well, obviously at some point I'd manage to bump into David Tennant.'

He nods. 'Of course.'

'Who would be so wowed by my conversation that he would ask my advice on his next TV project.'

'Naturally.'

'And then I'd write it for him and be a superstar.' She sips the pint of water that has been sadly neglected for the entire evening. 'Plus he'd leave his wife and marry me.' She sighs. 'It would all be very sad and tragic but utterly romantic at the same time.'

Tom looks at her askance. 'And what about me?'

'Well, I'd keep you in the mix too. Of course.'

He leans towards her again. 'That's good of you.'

Hannah pulls away again. Looks around for distraction. Sees only two old men having a particularly slow game of chess. Most of the other punters have sensibly gone home.

He puts his hand over hers and grasps her fingers in

his. She tries to pull her hand away but his grip is too tight.

'Hannah, I—'

Oh God.

Panic rises. She breaks free and slides off her stool. Wobbles for a second. 'Back in a minute.'

'OK.' His face falls again.

Guilt makes her blush and she turns and follows the faint smell of toilets to the back of the pub. She pushes on a heavy brown door until she stumbles into the harsh glare of the ladies' loos.

'Steph?'

No answer. She walks forward and carefully negotiates the three steps that have led to numerous ankle injuries for drunken Queensdale staff.

'Steph?'

She hears a groan and turns the corner to see her friend. One of Steph's high heels is inexplicably in the sink, while the other sticks out of her handbag. There is a large hole in her tights and her hand is clutching a clump of toilet paper.

'Steph?' Hannah reaches her friend and removes a strand of hair that has got stuck across her face. 'You OK?'

'Yesh.' Steph puts her thumb in her mouth. 'Never better.'

'Steph, you're lying on a toilet floor with your head against a Tampax dispenser. I really think we can safely say that it's much nicer at home.'

Steph absorbed this. 'Maybe.' She held her hand up in front of her face. 'Look. I have two right hands.'

Excellent. Hannah puts her arms around Steph and heaves her onto her feet, grateful for all the practice she has had with Tom. There is a moment of dangerous swaying before they establish any kind of forward momentum.

'Ouch. I'm not a bloody crutch, Steph!' Hannah squirms away as Steph plants a hand firmly on her head. Somehow Hannah manages to navigate them both to the sinks running along one side of the room. They stand for a second, gazing at themselves in the deeply unflattering mirrors.

Steph stares with the sudden clarity of the truly drunk.

'How did we get so old, Han?' She runs a finger along a wrinkle in the mirror. 'I mean, seriously. How?'

Hannah notices how well the light brings out her eye bags. 'I'm not sure.' She sighs. 'But maybe you were right about the Botox idea.'

Steph laughs and nearly falls over. 'I just feel *so* old.' She leans forward against the sink with an uncharacteristically defeated slump of the shoulders.

'Honestly. Sometimes I just wonder where it's all *going*. You know?'

Hannah nods. 'I know exactly what you mean.'

'What are you going to do?' Steph wrinkles her nose. 'Now that you've broken out? Now that you're free?'

'I don't know. Panic about the mortgage . . .?'

Steph isn't listening. 'Sometimes I just want someone to shag.'

'How romantic.'

'And I wonder if he's out there.' Steph sighs. 'I mean, I would move on to women if only I could get round the whole boobs issue.'

'What about them?'

'The fact I don't like touching them.'

'Right.' Hannah nods.

Steph turns and studies her with deep concentration. 'Seriously Han, what's your plan? Now?'

Hannah stares back at her.

She finds that she's thinking of Tom's smile.

'I have absolutely no idea.'

'Really?'

'Really.'

Steph puts her arm round her. 'Because Teach the World are still looking for people, you know. For this summer.'

'Are they?' Hannah closes her eyes for a second. Imagines packing her bag. Stepping onto the plane. The excitement in her belly as it takes off.

'Come on.' Steph squeezes her harder. 'Come with me. Suntans. Kids who actually want to learn. *Elephants.*'

Hannah opens her eyes. 'Oh, well, if there are elephants . . .'

'So you'll come?'

Hannah feels a pulse of regret as she shakes her head. 'No.'

Steph's face darkens.

'It's Tom, isn't it?'

'What?'

'That's why you won't come.'

'No. I—'

'Don't lie to me, Hannah. I've seen the way you look at him. You've fallen for him again, haven't you?'

Hannah doesn't understand the accusation in Steph's voice.

She shakes her head. 'No.'

Steph narrows her eyes. 'Still a crap liar.'

Hannah hears her phone and checks it.

It's from Tom. Nice bum.

She flushes and then looks up to see the worry in Steph's eyes. Her pleasure turns to irritation.

'What is it now, Steph?'

Steph shakes her head. 'You know what it is. You're going to go back to exactly how you were before. It's like you've forgotten everything that happened. Everything he said to you. How crap he made you feel.'

Hannah feels a rush of anger. 'Steph, that's not fair. He needs me.'

Steph glowers at her. 'Talk about denial.'

'What do you mean?'

'You say he needs you, but really I think you're in love with him again. And I know that you're married to him and, believe me, I want you to be happy.' Steph attempts to put on some lipstick. It does not go well. 'And I know you think he's changed.' She throws the lipstick down and tries to wipe the pink goo off her nose. She gives up and leans against the sink. 'And I really hope he has changed, Han. I really do. But you know what? You know what really kills me?'

'I expect you're going to tell me.'

'That you're going to sacrifice what you want for him. *Again.*'

'What do you mean, "again"?'

'Oh, come on. You told me about Japan.'

Hannah gasps. 'His mum was *dying*, Steph. I had to come back.'

'Sure, but you didn't have to stay in the UK afterwards. And anyway . . .' Steph washes her hands. 'There was that head of department job in Manchester you turned down because of him.'

'Steph, I'm married. These decisions aren't just about me.'

'They're not ever about you. Every time you've asked him for something he's turned you down. And then he's made you feel so crap about yourself, you stop trying.'

'I . . .' Hannah mouths words but none come out.

'Look, Han. It all boils down to one question for me. When's he going to give anything up for you?'

Hannah drops her voice as a group of giggling girls come in.

'He's ill. He can't give things up at the moment.'

'I get that.' Steph shakes her head as one of the girls teeters into a cubicle. 'But I just don't know if he'll ever want to. That's what worries me.'

Hannah holds on hard to the sink. Her heart beats fast and she feels an anger that scares her. Through the pounding in her head she becomes aware that one of the girls is talking. Her voice is high. Superior.

'Did you see that guy with the walking stick?' She combs her long red hair with her fingers.

Her mate is powdering her upturned nose. 'Yeah?'

Redhead pouts in the mirror. 'He'd be really hot if he could walk properly, wouldn't he?'

'Yeah. Looks like Jake Gyllenhaal.'

Redhead clicks her fingers. 'Yeah. That's who it is. I couldn't quite work it out.' She plumps her boobs higher in her low-cut top. 'I wonder what it would be like to shag him.'

'Doubt he could manage it.'

Cold fury pulses in Hannah's veins.

'Yeah. Probably can't even get it up.'

That's it. Hannah snaps.

She whips her head round. 'Shut up, you two. That man is my husband. And he's better and braver than you two cows will ever be.'

She picks up her bag in trembling hands.

'All right, all right.' The girl at the sink shakes her head, wide-eyed. 'God. Chill out.'

Hannah feels tears pricking her eyes as she pushes on the door. She turns. 'And for the record, he's fucking dynamite in bed. OK?'

She hears Steph's voice as the door swings shut behind them. 'Han? Han?'

'Steph, just piss off.'

She wants to get away from all of them. Away from anyone else.

She just wants to be with Tom.

Steph leaves without saying goodbye and the rest of the night is like the old days. The two of them. The days of chips and beer in cosy pubs. Of discussing why Maltesers are better than Revels and whether Ant or Dec would be more fun on a night out.

Hannah takes Tom's arm as they walk out onto the street, keeping an eye out for any uneven paving stones that could upset his cane.

'What next?' She points to a thumping cocktail bar across the street. 'Fancy that?'

He closes his right hand round hers. 'Not really.'

'So what do you want to do?' Hannah looks around them, unable to meet his eyes. The night sleepers are finding their corners on the High Road. Across the street the night bus is pulling up.

'We could go home.' He is examining the pavement intensely.

Everything in her wants to say yes. But she must tell him. First. She doesn't want their future built on a lie.

'Tom, there's something I need to say to you.'

'You don't want to?'

'No.' She realises what she's said. 'I mean, yes. I do. But . . .'

'But what?' He prods the pavement with his cane. 'You don't fancy me any more?'

Oh God. 'Of course I do, Tom.' She steels herself, and then puts her finger under his chin and lifts it.

'Tom – something happened – during the bad times. I need to tell you about it. Before . . .' She searches for words. 'Before we start again.'

'Sounds serious, H.' He watches her. 'Let's talk after we've—'

'No.' She feels sick at the thought of what she might be about to lose. But she must do this.

'Tom, I'm serious. I—'

'You're crying, H.' He reaches out a fingertip and catches a tear.

'I know.' She is shaking. Holding on to him for support. She takes a shuddering breath. 'Look, I—'

He holds a finger to her lips. 'I already know.'

She stares at him, tears pricking her eyes. 'What?'

'I already know.'

Horror freezes her. 'What do you know?'

'About you. And him.' She sees the hurt on his face.

She pulls her cardigan tight around her shoulders, but the shaking continues. 'I'm so sorry, Tom.'

'Me too.' The sadness on his face slices through her.

'Then . . . all this time . . . you've known?'

'Yep.'

'Why didn't you say anything?'

Her whole heart hangs on his answer.

'Because I didn't want to lose you.'

'Even though I . . . ?' She can't say it.

'Yes.' He helps her. 'Even though you slept with someone else.'

'But you can't be OK with it, Tom? Can you?'

'Of course not.' Anger flashes across his face and she sees the pain she's put him through. 'But it's happened. Just like the stroke happened. And me being a bastard happened. Yet we're still standing. Together. You and me.' He kisses one of her curls. 'That's what matters.'

She is scared he doesn't mean it. That he's lying to himself. 'But—'

'No.' His voice is gentle. Calm. 'No buts. Let's go home.'

'Home sounds perfect.' She leans into him and circles her arms around him, feeling all the luck in the world landing at her feet.

When they get there the inevitable happens.

They hold hands and walk towards the bedroom.

Birthday card:
'Keep Calm You're not that Old'
December 2014

Tommo. Need cash. Can you transfer? 100 shd b ok. Ta. J x

Pain skewered Tom's temple as he swore under his breath. Julie had promised last time that she would never ask again. Just like the time before. And the one before that. With every amount the distance between them widened and he despaired of ever closing it again.

'Tom.' His boss appeared in the doorway.

Damn. He was desperate to get out of the door. It was 10 p.m. on a Friday and if he didn't get to Hannah's thirtieth birthday party soon, she wouldn't be sober enough to realise he was there. He'd been attempting to leave for hours, but kept being foiled by client requests for amendments to the endless documentation supporting the Imperion deal.

'Yes, Silas?' He smoothed the resentment out of his expression. After six months of unemployment earlier in the year he felt far too lucky to be getting a pay cheque to show any sign of rebellion.

Silas's habitual frown lines were carved deep into his forehead.

'Tom, I was just wondering . . .'

Since arriving at this firm, Tom had learnt that Silas's 'wondering' generally led to sleeping in the office and Red Bull at dawn.

'Yes?' He hitched his bag up onto his shoulder, hoping Silas would take the hint.

275

No chance. Instead his boss held up a hand, while carefully perusing a document that was clearly causing him some consternation. He wasn't a man who liked to be hurried. Tom tried to massage the pain in his temples away with his hands. It was getting worse. If it got any more pressurised in there he was seriously worried his head might explode.

'Yes. I thought so. There's a problem with the due diligence.' Silas looked up and the bright office lights glinted on the mighty pink dome of his forehead. 'To do with charging assets. You need to double-check the figures.'

'Really?' Tom blinked exhausted eyes. He'd gone through them several times already. Anxiety knifed his belly. 'Are you sure?'

'Yes.' Silas gave him an arctic glare. 'I am.'

Tom felt a lurch of panic. He couldn't screw up again. Couldn't take another spell 'between jobs,' sending out CVs and having nightmares about the mortgage. Seeing the pity in his friends' eyes.

Silas walked further into Tom's office and leant his skeletal frame against the heavy black wood of the desk. He twirled his long-suffering glasses in his hand. 'As you know, this deal closes on Monday. And you need to contact all those involved to get this sorted out by then.'

'Of course.' Tom could almost hear a hiss as his party spirit evaporated. 'I'll get on to it right away and call the juniors back in to help.'

Silas stared at him seriously. 'I know I can rely on you, Tom.'

Tom heard the warning behind the words.

'Yes, you can.'

'Good, good.' Silas turned and walked out, his feet making no sound on the thick beige carpet.

'Shit.' Tom heaved his bag back down, hearing the dull thud of Hannah's birthday bottle of champagne making contact with the floor. It reminded him of the resentful slap of Hannah's feet round the kitchen on the rare occasions he made it home for dinner nowadays.

His head was starting to ache all over now. He quickly swallowed a couple more painkillers from the pack in his desk, washing them down with a gulp of Red Bull. He frowned at the offending papers. The firm didn't seem to care that his wife would never speak to him again. Every weekend he intended to take her out and spend time with her. Every weekend he ended up here instead.

He sighed. With every passing moment somehow it was harder to look Hannah in the eye. He tried to talk to her but everything he said offended her. Now he just saved time by not even trying. Tonight he had planned to make a grand entrance. Buy her mates drinks. Dance with her if she wanted him to.

Instead it would be at least three hours of calls tonight. He wished he could make the party. But he didn't have a choice.

Deep down he knew that she wouldn't understand why he wasn't there. It would be yet another reason for her to moan at her teacher friends about how awful he was. How unhappy he made her. He looked at the picture of her on his desk. Greece. A couple of years ago. Hair thick with salt from the sea. Cocktail glass held high.

He missed that smile.

But he couldn't lose this job.

He pulled his phone from his pocket, intending to text her an apology.

I'm sorry, he started.

'Tom?'

He stopped typing and looked up.

Silas was looking ominously at another file. 'It might be a good idea to review all the Imperion documents while we're here.'

'But I need to—'

'Need to what?' Silas arched an eyebrow that had clearly enjoyed a full public-school training in the art of conveying disdain.

Tom continued, despite the ice in the air. 'I need to call to explain . . .'

He petered out as Silas's face furrowed in disapproval. He looked as if his thirtieth birthday had occurred several centuries ago. And had been a teetotal event.

Silas balanced his glasses on the end of his pinched nose. 'We do need to make sure we have this in hand, Tom.'

'Absolutely.' Tom slumped down behind his desk again.

As he found the papers he realised that he had accidentally pressed send. Still, *I'm sorry* seemed to sum his feelings up pretty well. He picked up the file and started to work.

At 1 a.m. his eyes wouldn't focus any more. He downed a coffee from the pot in the kitchen, but it was disgustingly lukewarm and had no effect whatsoever apart from increasing the pain in his head. He stood up, stretched, and ordered a cab home. If he could grab a couple of hours of sleep he might be able to make Hannah breakfast in bed before coming back here again for the rest of the weekend.

When the cab came he leant his thumping head against the window as it drove through raucous Friday-night streets. Everyone in London was having more fun than him. Girls in short skirts milled outside a kebab shop, cackling over chips and cans of beer. A heavyset man laughed uproariously into his mobile phone.

Tom felt totally alone.

He wanted to see Hannah. Now.

He leant forward.

'Could you drive past the Nightingale? On the High Road?'

'Sure.' The cab turned right and they drove past a big group of men staggering their way towards the club on the corner. They were all wearing Viking helmets and devouring kebabs.

Tom remembered being like that once. Nights with no end. Nights when tomorrow didn't matter.

He thought of Hannah's smile. Her laugh.

He couldn't wait to see her.

'Can you speed it up at all, mate?'

The driver grunted and obligingly accelerated through an amber light. Past the bank. Past the cash machines on the corner. Past Sainsbury's.

'Can you just pull over here, please?'

Tom stared eagerly through the window. With any luck she would still be here. Dancing on the bar. Drinking it dry.

Maybe she would be keeping an eye on the door. Watching in case he appeared. Waiting for him.

He hoped so.

He reached for the door handle.

Then he saw her.

Or rather, he saw them.

He watched, frozen, as her hands circled round another man's waist. He was one of her colleagues – he remembered him from a rare night at the pub a few weeks ago. Raj, was it? Tall. Dark. Arsenal fan.

Bastard.

Tom's stomach burned. He saw Raj's arms encircling his wife. Her eyes gazing up at him. The way she stood on tiptoes as they began to kiss.

The pain floored him.

'Are you getting out, mate?'

Tom stared through the window. Stared at the man standing in his place.

His fists clenched. He was going to get out. Going to confront them. Now. Right now.

'Are you opening the door or what?'

Tom pushed the handle. Stopped.

'No.' He collapsed back on the seat. 'God, no. Just get me out of here.'

When he arrived home he put his key in the door and let himself into the silent house. He knew what he had to do. He walked through the kitchen and found the whisky bottle. He filled a tumbler until there was no room for any ice. He downed it in four searing mouthfuls. Winced. Poured more.

He checked his phone. Nothing.

Bitch.

He rubbed his aching temples. Then he turned and grabbed the packet of fags Hannah always kept in the pot on top of the fridge. She still pretended she'd given up. Another lie. He wrestled with the French window and then pushed out into the freezing night, where he gulped air into his lungs and forced himself not to think about what he had seen.

What she was doing now.

Bitch.

He was furious to feel tears on his face.

He hated her.

But he couldn't stop crying.

He lit the first cigarette of what he knew would be many and tried to block out the image of the kiss by pouring whisky into his glass. But with every mouthful her face loomed larger in his mind. With every drag he heard her laugh or felt her hand resting in his.

Eventually all her could see was her. His Hannah. His wife.

Not any more.

He poured the last of the whisky into the glass, thinking of all the things he would say when she finally appeared the next morning. Thinking of the divorce lawyer he would hire. How she would be left with nothing.

Nothing was what she deserved.

But when she crept in the next morning he didn't say a thing. His head was too painful. His heart was too bruised. He lay on the sofa where he'd fallen into a fitful sleep, watching as she walked towards him, her face pale and her mouth opening to speak. He knew that she was about to confess. That she was leaving him.

And he couldn't bear it.

'Got to get to work.' He stood up, unable to bear breathing the same air as her.

And he went to the office.

She was crying as the door slammed behind him.

He was glad.

Sixteen

It's not the stuff that movies are made of.

His lips are on hers. His hands are on her back.

His cane is digging into her thigh.

'Tom.'

'Hannah. Oh, Hannah.' He keeps kissing her.

'Tom. I just need to . . .' She shifts away from the cane and it falls to the ground.

Tom stumbles heavily to his left.

'Oh God.' He grabs her shoulder to steady himself. 'Sorry.'

'Don't worry about it.' Hannah gently starts to unbutton his jacket.

'I can do it myself.' There's a fierce pride in his voice.

'I know that.' She keeps her voice low. 'But let me do it. Please. Like I used to. OK?'

He dips his head in agreement. His breathing is ragged and his cheeks glow in the light from the hall landing. She removes his jacket and places it gently on the bed.

'Shall we get more comfortable?' She smiles.

'OK.' He swallows and she can feel him trembling as he leans on her for support. She kisses him gently and helps him to sit down on the bed.

He gazes up at her as she lies him back against the pillows. He reaches up and runs a hand down her cheek.

'You're so beautiful, H.'

She is overwhelmed by the wonder in his eyes.

She wrinkles her nose. 'Not really. And I'm still wearing yesterday's pants.'

He doesn't miss a beat. 'I might have to do something about that.'

She grins and leans in and they kiss deeply and she aches to be even closer. His right hand wraps round her body, and then he moves it falteringly upwards to the soft V of flesh above the neckline of her dress. As it descends it encounters a button. Tries to undo it. Fails. Tries again. Fails.

'Shit.' He lets his hand fall.

'Don't worry, Tom. We'll work this out.' She feels her confidence growing. She holds his eyes and slowly undoes her buttons. One. Two. Three. His eyes widen as more and more of her naked flesh is exposed. Then she lifts the dress over her head and drops it to the floor.

'Is that better?' She gently kisses his neck. He murmurs and she lifts his T-shirt to kiss the smooth skin of his chest. She can feel his ribs beneath her lips and it makes her want him more. She thinks of how hard he has worked to get this far. How brave he is.

She kisses him all over his chest and then pulls his T-shirt over his head. She takes his hand and reaches over to switch on the bedside light.

'Don't.' His voice is strained.

'But we always have the light on.'

'Not any more.'

'But I want to see you. Properly.'

Silence.

'Tom?'

'I can't do this.'

'But . . .' She can feel his excitement. She can feel how much he wants her.

He gently pushes her away. 'This doesn't feel right. I can't. I just can't. OK?'

She clicks the lamp on and reaches for him again. 'I know it feels new. But that doesn't make it wrong. It's just different. That's all. And we can get used to it. Get used to each other again.'

He sighs. 'I just feel so useless. I can't even undo my own bloody trousers.'

'Tom.' She takes his face in her hands. 'You're not useless. You're amazing. You're the man I used to know. The man I fell for.'

He shakes his head and looks down, running his fingers along the grey stripe edging the duvet.

She keeps trying. 'You have to believe me, Tom. The way you've handled everything – you've been incredible.'

His voice is low and a tear drips from his cheek onto her fingers. 'But I'll always be different. I mean my bloody hand . . . and my leg . . .' He stops and a sob convulses him. 'What if they never get better?'

'They will.' She hopes she's right. 'They are already. They're going as fast as they can.'

'Well, it's not bloody good enough.' His voice is a whisper. 'I'm sick of all the exercises. Sometimes I worry I'll never be the same again.'

'I know.' Hannah never lets go of his hand. She kisses him gently. 'Listen, Tom. Listen to what I'm about to tell you.'

'You're sounding all teachery.'

'Yes I am. And I will be issuing detention to any husbands who don't shut up and listen to me.'

His smile is back. 'It's quite alluring.'

'Well, we've got your cane over there, so it can get a whole lot more alluring if you want it to.'

'Bloody hell.' He raises his eyebrows. 'And to think you look so innocent.'

Hannah looks down at her naked body. 'Hardly.'

He reaches his good hand towards her breast and starts to stroke it in gentle circles.

She pushes him away. 'OK, so now I know you're *not listening.*'

'Sorry.' He is clearly trying to look apologetic but only succeeds in staring at her boobs.

'Right.' She catches her breath as he starts to tease her nipple with his thumb. 'All I want you to think about is how brave you've been. How brave you are. And how brave you will be every day from now on. And because of that . . .'

She leans down and gently bites his chest.

'And because of that . . .'

She moves lower.

'And because of that . . .'

She lets her lips travel downwards.

'Yes?' He can barely speak.

'I want you even more.'

Then she unzips him and shows him exactly how much.

Afterwards they lie together in a warm naked huddle under the duvet.

Tom sighs happily. 'I have no idea why we haven't been doing that more often.'

'I know.' She grins into his chest. 'We're pretty damn good at it.'

'We are.' She can feel him smiling. He shifts his head

on the pillow so he's looking at her. 'When did we last get round to it?'

'Can't remember.' Hannah snuggles closer.

'That's a bad sign.'

'Yeah.' She sighs. 'We weren't in a good way, before. Were we?'

He shivers. 'No.' He exhales. 'We weren't.' He kisses the top of her head. 'I'm so glad you stayed.'

She shakes her head. 'No need to thank me.' She takes a deep breath. Readies herself. 'And just so you know. The other guy.'

He stiffens.

'I hated myself for it. Every day.'

He stays silent.

'I was just so angry with you, Tom.'

Another beat of silence. 'Yeah.' He pulls her closer and she relaxes. 'I know.'

She can feel him breathing. Warming her.

She settles back into the curve of his body. Closes her eyes. She is about to fall asleep when he whispers 'I love you' into her hair.

'I love you too.'

Her eyes flick open as she realises it's true.

She does love him.

She goes to sleep with his arms round her.

Hospital wristband: Tom Ellison

January 2015

He was so terrified she would leave him.

'Tom?' Hannah leant forward. He could see her fingers wrapped around his. But he couldn't feel them. He wanted to feel them. Needed to.

'Water.' He could barely hear himself. His throat felt dry. Thick.

'Here you are.' She reached over and picked up the plastic glass and held the straw to his lips.

He was so useless. Broken. The lights were too bright and even the tea lady moved too fast for him. And he was scared. Every second. With every breath he was terrified it would happen again.

He sucked and swallowed and gazed at the ceiling panels above him. There were ten above his bed and he had spent far more time than he would have liked staring up at them. Grey speckles. Yellow edges. They reminded him of the ones at his mum's house in Somerset and he remembered the way he'd pushed them up and used the space above to hide vodka. Cigarettes. Beers.

He wondered if he'd ever drink a beer again. If he'd ever want one.

Hannah was stroking his hair, her face alive with concern.

He tried to lift his left hand to touch her face. It wouldn't move.

He felt a clutch of terror.

'Other side.' The words sounded clumsy. Heavy.

'What?' He saw the furrow on Hannah's forehead as she tried to understand his slurred speech.

'Other side.'

'Oh. Of course.' She got up and walked round to the right-hand side of the bed. He envied her effortlessness. How easily she could scratch her nose or reach out to pick up a glass.

He envied everyone now. Everyone who could move. Talk. Put one foot in front of the other.

She cleared the chair of bags and coats and sat down. Took his right hand.

And he felt the connection. The warmth of her skin.

It was like a miracle.

He closed his eyes to hide the tears that were threatening to fall, forcing away the image of her outside the Nightingale. Her hands round someone else's waist.

He had to forget. Had to move on. Had to keep her.

Because he needed her. He hated it, but it was true.

He knew that if she left he would never get up again.

The image resurfaced, but this time he pushed it away.

He looked at Hannah.

His Hannah.

And they held hands until he fell asleep.

Seventeen

'Can you two stop snogging for a second and actually order something?'

Hannah reluctantly pulls away from Tom to see Julie rolling her eyes at the barman. 'It's like an episode of *Hollyoaks* round here.'

The barman pours orange juice into a tumbler and pushes it across the bar.

'I've seen you do far worse than that, Julie.' His brown eyes twinkle as he points to a leather sofa in the far corner. 'I think that's your favourite pick-up spot, isn't it?'

Hannah is amused to see Julie blush. 'Shut up, Stefan.' She takes a sip of juice.

Stefan raises a bushy eyebrow. 'Don't want the bump to hear?'

'Something like that.' Julie drinks more juice and pulls a face. 'God, I miss alcohol.'

'Oh well.' Tom entirely fails to suppress a smile. 'Only another four months to go, sis.'

Julie scowls. 'Thanks for reminding me.'

Tom grins at Stefan. 'Pint of Best please. And some white wine for this gorgeous girl.' He kisses Hannah lingeringly on the mouth.

'Euggghhh.' Julie turns away and heads for a table by the window. Red buses rattle down the High Road behind her as she sits down and starts rooting through the cluster of Mothercare bags she has at her feet.

'I really wish she'd talk to Zac.' Hannah leans against the solid grey stone of the bar.

'Me too.' Tom wraps his arm round her waist.

Hannah leans against him, loving his warmth. The last couple of weeks have been as magical as when they first met. They have rediscovered each other. She loves the way his eyes gleam when she walks into a room. The way they laugh together. The way that when she reaches out she is absolutely sure that he'll be there.

'You all right, H?' Tom gently kisses her cheek.

'Yeah.' She is paralysed by an enormous yawn. 'Just a bit tired.'

His eyes glint. 'Can't think why.'

'Ha ha.'

She knows it's not the sex. Or not *just* the sex. During the days she's blissful, but at night she can't sleep. She lies listening to Tom's breathing, wondering what on earth her future holds. She's so happy when they're together, but as soon as she's away from him – at work or on her bike or even just doing her teeth in the morning – she realises she has absolutely no plan for herself. She feels lost. Pointless. And now Tom's going to work for Nick. He's doing reduced hours, but he'll still have a pay cheque and a sense of purpose.

Whereas she has . . . nothing.

She forces the thoughts away and tunes in to the present again. Tom's arms round her. Wine waiting.

Life is good.

'You're looking great, Tom.' Stefan puts the pint on the bar.

'Thanks.' Tom nods. 'You too.'

Stefan laughs. 'Yeah, well. People keep saying that ever since I shaved off that God-awful moustache I grew in February.'

Tom shuddered. 'Yeah. Not your best look, mate.'

Stefan picks up a towel and starts polishing shot glasses. A strand of his long blond hair slips out of his ponytail and falls across his cheek.

'And how are you feeling?'

'Pretty good.'

'So you won't need that cane much longer, then?'

Tom smiles. 'I bloody hope not.'

Hannah feels a needle of fear. He seems so confident since they got back together. 'Let's see what the doctor says, shall we?'

'Yeah.' Tom shakes his head dismissively. 'But my leg's getting much better now, so I'm sure I'll be all sorted by Christmas.'

'Definitely.' Hannah nods. She doesn't mention his left hand. Its erratic grip and freezing fingers.

She doesn't want to discourage him.

He kisses her on the cheek. 'Shall we go and join Jules?'

'Good idea.' Hannah carries the drinks as they walk towards the table. Jules is hunched forward, holding up a strange cone of pale blue cloth covered in aeroplanes.

'What's that?' Hannah puts the drinks down.

'Apparently it's a Peepee Teepee.' Julie frowns. 'It stops you getting wee in your face when you're changing nappies.'

'Does it?' Hannah blinks. 'How?'

'You put it over the baby's . . . bits.'

'Boys only, surely?'

'Yeah.' Julie tucks her hair behind her ears as she delves into the bags again.

'So do you know it's a boy?'

'No.' Julie shakes her head. 'But good to be prepared, right?' She pulls out a white babygro with THE PARTY'S AT MY COT emblazoned on the front in green. 'I love this one.' She grins. 'Thank you Ronald McDonald.'

Hannah smiles. Tom had offered to help out but Julie had insisted on paying for everything herself. She takes a sip of wine. 'What on earth is that?' Julie pulls out a plastic monstrosity that wouldn't look out of place in a medieval torture chamber.

Julie looks at the label. 'A breast pump.' She holds it over her boob. 'Though God knows how you're meant to attach it.'

'This is a bit weird.' Tom averts his eyes until she puts it away. He grips the wooden handle of his chair with his right hand as he carefully lowers himself down onto its squishy brown seat. He wobbles precariously at the last minute and Hannah tenses, ready to help. Then he lands and she relaxes into the chair next to him, reaching out to hold his left hand. It's cold. As always.

Tom looks at Julie. 'When's your next appointment, Jules? I'm happy to come with you. If you'd like me to.'

Julie's face softens. 'I'd love that, Tommo.' Hannah smiles as she sees the trust that's growing between them.

Tom's face is serious. 'I really want to help, Jules. You can stay with us. Or whatever you need.'

Hannah can see tears in Julie's normally resolutely dry eyes. She blinks them away. 'All right, Tommo. No need to get all bloody emotional.'

Tom laughs. 'Am I the one getting emotional?'

Julie finishes her juice with a loud slurp. 'Yeah, yeah, whatever.' She thumps her glass down. 'And guess what? I need the loo again. Shocker.' She pushes up from the sofa. 'I can't believe how much I'm peeing. Fifteen times yesterday. FIFTEEN.'

Hannah and Tom raise eyebrows at each other as she walks away, phone clutched in her hand. Tom sips his drink. 'She's going to tell us every little detail, isn't she?'

'Yep.' Hannah nods. 'No holds barred.'

'Wow.' Tom rolls his eyes. 'I may have to avoid her after the birth, then.'

'Good idea.'

Tom smiles. 'I can't wait till we have kids.' He leans back in his chair. 'Maybe we can have a whole football team?'

She smiles back at him, ignoring the clench of anxiety in her stomach.

'Maybe we can.' She squeezes his hand. 'Think I'll find a job first, though.'

'Oh yeah. That.' Tom leans forward. 'I forgot to say – Nick's contacted his mate at Beaumont if you still fancy an interview there?'

'Oh. OK.'

His face is bright. Eager.

'It's got great facilities apparently. And they take the kids all over the place – New York, Italy. You'd love it.'

'Erm . . . sounds great.' She drops her eyes away from his.

She has never wanted to teach in a private school. *Never.*

Tom should know that.

She should tell him.

Then she looks up again and the sun's shining through the window and Tom looks so excited about his big idea.

She can't say anything.

Instead she leans over and kisses him as the world narrows around her. 'I'll sort something out. Don't worry.'

He squeezes her hand. 'I know you will.'

'I just don't want you thinking that I'm not being responsible.'

'Why on earth would I think that?'

'Well, you used to say that all the time.' She tries to smile, but her mouth is rigid.

He leans towards her. 'How many times do I have to tell you? I'm not him any more. Not that Tom.'

She has to ask more. 'How do you know that?'

'What? That I've changed?'

'Yes.' She feels adrenaline leap in her stomach. They are reaching the big questions now. The 3 a.m. staring-at-the-ceiling questions. She looks him straight in the eye. 'I mean, what happens if you don't get any better and work is too much and all that pressure changes you back again?'

'Is that what you're scared of?'

Hannah holds his eyes. 'Of course it is. I'd be crazy not to be scared of that.'

'I really did make you miserable, didn't I?'

Hannah nods.

'I'm so sorry, H.'

She believes him but she still can't speak. Her hand is shaking and she puts her glass of wine down on the table.

He swallows. She watches his face intently, looking at the deeper lines round his mouth. The furrow along his forehead. Lines of pain. Lines of recovery. A strand of silver glints in his dark hair.

He sighs. 'Do you remember when I was fired?'

'How could I forget that?'

'Yeah.' He looks at his hands. 'I know. But there's something you never knew about that.'

She leans forward, tucking her hands under her knees. 'What?'

He meets her eyes. 'That I blamed you.'

'Me?'

'Yeah.' He nods.

Her mouth is dry. 'Why?'

'For distracting me. For taking me away for weekends where I didn't work and got bollocked on Monday mornings.'

'You what?'

'Yeah.' He presses his lips together. 'They didn't approve of time off.'

'You never told me.'

'No.' He shakes his head. 'I didn't feel I could. I thought you wouldn't have understood.'

'Why?'

'I was wrong. I know that now.' He shrugs. 'But back then I thought you'd resent my job even more if you knew how much fuss they made if I ever dared not to be available. And it's not like you were exactly a fan of my firm to start with.'

'I didn't hate your firm. I hated what it did to you.'

He smiles. 'I'm not sure that's much of a difference, is it? I used to feel like I couldn't really talk to you about anything to do with work.' He exhales. 'About any of the pressure I felt.'

Hannah feels a flush of failure. 'I'm sorry.'

'No, that's not what I mean.' He shakes his head. 'Back then I also didn't really realise how strong you were. I thought that if I told you how hard things were you might – I don't know – break.'

'Why?'

'Honestly?' He sips his beer. 'I don't know. Maybe

because you got so emotional about everything. I thought you weren't . . . able to cope with stuff. So I protected you. But then I got angry because I couldn't share things with you.'

'You could have talked to me.'

'I know that now.' Tom nods. 'But back then I couldn't. I just kept working and hoping everything would get better and that's why I got more and more furious with you. But now . . .'

He reaches forward and takes her hands. 'I know how strong you are.'

She feels tears springing to her eyes.

'You've been so strong for me. I want to be the same for you.' He stares at her. 'Do you believe me?'

She looks at the pink and purple flowers on the rug at their feet. 'Maybe I'm starting to.' She is practically whispering.

'Hallelujah.' Tom's eyes glint. 'I mean, it's not as if we haven't come through some tough stuff already. We can handle a bit of job-hunting.' He takes a gulp of beer. 'Now. Let's get you good and pissed.'

'What about you?'

'Still taking it easy. Early days.' He grins. 'White wine?'

'Yes please.'

He stands up and limps over to the bar.

Two hours later they are both nestled in their seats, the table between them covered in empty packets of crisps and a plate containing the remains of a cheeseburger and salad.

Tom picks up a final sliver of crisp. 'Do you think Julie'll be OK at home? By herself?'

'Yes.' Hannah rolls her eyes. 'She's pregnant. Not sick.'

'Yeah, but—'

'But nothing, Tom. She's fine.' Hannah squeezes his hand. 'She'll be tucked up in bed indulging her Ovaltine craving, watching her millionth episode of *One Born Every Minute*.'

'Ewww.' Tom shudders. 'I can't watch that show.'

'Really? I quite like it.' Hannah looks at a couple in the corner, who are busy pretending they don't fancy each other. They are part of a larger group who are celebrating someone's birthday, complete with silver balloons and an enormous chocolate cake. Hannah watches as the girl leans towards the boy, clearly about to speak, only for him to lean away to talk to one of his mates. She turns back to her friends just as he looks at her.

'How's Steph?' Tom picks up a fragment of cheese with his fingertip. Hannah senses danger. She hasn't spoken to Steph since their fight at the pub on her resignation day. Staffroom encounters have been icy and departmental meetings are even more endless now Steph no longer giggles with her on the back row.

'Don't know.' She starts swaying her head as 'Size of a Cow' starts to play over the pub speakers.

'Really?' He looks surprised. 'Normally you two are thick as thieves.'

'Yeah, well. She's busy. Getting ready for her trip.' She looks towards a group of girls who are giggling over a picture on a mobile phone.

'Tanzania, isn't it?'

'Yeah.' She nods. 'She's leaving in July.'

'Sounds amazing.'

'Yes.' She is still looking at the girls, wondering what kind of picture is causing such hilarity. 'I'd love to go.'

Wait.

She's said it out loud.

Shit.

She looks at him. His eyes are wide with shock.

'Why?'

She might as well be honest now. 'Because I'd feel like I'm doing some good for a change. And I've always wanted to live in Tanzania.'

'I thought . . .' He is pale.

She rushes to calm him. 'But not now.' She swallows. 'Of course I wouldn't go now. Because I want to be here. With you. Because I love you.' She's scrambling now. 'I couldn't just go away.' She laughs. It sounds more like a squawk. 'It would be awful. Who would make my toast in the morning?'

He's still. Watching her.

'My travelling days are over now, anyway.' Hannah can't meet his eyes. 'All I want is to stay here with you.'

'You said "stay here".' She glances towards him. He looks worried. Vulnerable. 'Like you were intending to go somewhere, H.'

Damn. She tries to laugh it off. 'Don't read too much into anything I say when I'm a bottle of wine down. OK?'

'OK.' He nods. 'I won't.'

She senses his doubt, so she leans towards him and kisses him. 'Does that convince you?'

'One hundred per cent.' He cradles her cheek in his hand. 'I'm so happy.'

'Me too.' She tries to lose herself in his smile.

But part of her feels cold. Sad.

Finished.

Teach the World letter

May 2015

'Have you found it?'

'Yeah.' Tom stares at the letter in his hand. 'I'll be down in a minute.'

'OK.' He hears Julie clattering around in the kitchen.

He turns the paper over, his gaze lingering on the Teach the World logo at the top. He reads it again. Just to make sure.

Dear Mrs Ellison,
We are sorry to hear that you are withdrawing your application to travel to Tanzania with us in July.

He checks the date. February this year.

Just after his stroke.

So here it is. The truth.

She had been planning to leave him.

He sits back on the carpet, leaning his head against the bed and staring at Hannah's clothes hanging in the wardrobe above him. The bright red dress she had worn the night they got engaged. The shapeless oatmeal cardigan her mum had given her one Christmas. The gold strappy sandals she had saved from her childhood dressing-up box and which were now officially her karaoke shoes.

So many colours on her side. So many dark suits on his.

He carefully folds the letter and puts it on the floor beside him. He had been trying to pick up a shirt that had fallen off a hanger when he saw it lying crumpled beside a shoebox. He had grabbed it. Seen Hannah's name. Read the first sentence before he had time to think.

Obviously he couldn't stop after that.

He shuts his eyes. He had come so close to losing her. Whatever she might say, he knows the truth now. Part of her wants to go. Wants to be somewhere else.

Away from him.

'What are you up to, Tommo?' Julie appears in the doorway, hands on her hips. 'Thought I'd come and see if you'd got stuck in the wardrobe or something.'

He picks up the letter and waves it in the air. 'Just reading this.'

'Oh.' She sinks down onto the bed, exhaling loudly as she lands. Her bump swells majestically beneath her yellow T-shirt. 'You found it.'

He stares at her. 'You mean you knew about this?'

'Yep.' She twirls a strand of hair between her fingers. 'I found it a while back when I was looking for some shoes to borrow. I meant to put it back in the shoebox.'

'You didn't manage it.' He feels the slow creep of fear in his belly. 'Why didn't you tell me?'

'Why would I?' She shrugs.

He frowns as he thinks of his conversation with Hannah in the pub. The stars in her eyes when she'd talked of Tanzania. 'Because it might have been useful for me to know that my wife was thinking of leaving me?'

Julie treats him to one of her most pitying stares.

'Yeah. Because that was just the morale-booster you needed back then.' She rolls her eyes. 'Pillock.'

'Well, it's not exactly uplifting now either, is it?' He

looks at the letter again. The simple sheet of paper seems to be getting more malevolent by the second. 'This is so shit. I can't believe she was just going to disappear.'

Julie sighs. 'You just don't get it, do you?'

'Get what?'

His little sister puts her hand on his shoulder. Her gold fingernails gleam.

'That this is a *good* thing.'

He feels a surge of impatience. 'How can Hannah wanting to move to another continent be a good thing?'

'God you're dumb sometimes.' She tuts in exasperation. 'Hannah *not* going to Africa is a good thing.'

'What do you mean?'

'Do you really need me to spell it out for you?' Julie flings her arms wide. 'Look around this room. What do you see?'

He has no idea what she's getting at. 'I don't know. A bed. A wardrobe?'

'Not those.' She shakes her head. 'How about that Japanese print on the wall?'

'The owls?' He looks at their faces properly for the first time in months and sees that the smallest one has a distinct resemblance to his Auntie Sue.

'Yes.' Julie points at the thin strip of wall by the window. 'Or the rice painting hanging over there. From Vietnam.'

'So?'

She points at the chest of drawers. 'Or that bowl from China she keeps her make-up in.'

He feels irritated. Prickly. 'What are you saying?'

'That Hannah *loves* travelling, Tom. And she gave this chance up. For you.'

'I . . .' He hadn't looked at it like that. 'She probably felt sorry for me.'

'Of course she did.' Julie rolls her eyes. 'You had a stroke, for God's sake. Everyone felt sorry for you. Even the old man on the corner who can't remember his own name. But that's not the point.'

'It's not?'

'No, you dick.' Her face is flushed with irritation. 'The point is that Hannah did the right thing. *That's* what you need to remember. She stayed. She helped. And then she fell in love with you again.'

Doubts whisper in his head. 'I suppose so.'

He winces as Julie whacks him across the back of the head. 'You're bloody lucky, you know. Most women would have run. Especially as you spent the vast majority of last year being an absolute bastard to her.'

He hangs his head. 'Wow. Don't mince your words, Jules.'

'I'm not.' She inhales slowly and then puts a hand on his shoulder. 'I know I wasn't always a massive fan of hers, but—'

'Really?' He widens his eyes in mock surprise. 'But you were so subtle about it. Even when she came back from Japan for me you still didn't give her a chance.'

She flushes. 'I know. But I had other stuff going on. You know that. Anyway . . .' She glares at him. 'We're talking about you, remember? And now I think she's great. Not because she makes you so happy – though she does. But because she put you first when you needed her. So don't let that stupid letter ruin things, OK?'

He looks at it one last time. He knows Julie is right. 'OK.'

She stands up and stretches her arms over her head. 'Right. Now let's get to the cinema. I want to have enough time to make the most of the pick 'n' mix before we go in.' She pats her belly. 'Only the best for baby.'

He leans forward and tucks the letter back where he found it. 'Is that what they say in those crazy baby books you're always reading nowadays? That pick 'n' mix is the perfect pregnancy diet?'

She shakes her head. 'Nope. This is all my own idea.'

Tom tries to push himself upwards. He falls back.

'How's that leg of yours?'

He tries again.

'It's fine.' He doesn't want her help.

'Are you sure?'

'Yes.' He's not sure at all. Every day his leg is feeling tighter. More awkward. More of an ache with every step.

He doesn't want to think about it.

He keeps pushing and eventually makes it up to standing. Julie is staring at him. Hands on hips.

'Tommo . . .? Is this like the time when we were little and you fell off that roof and broke your leg, but insisted on watching the Cup Final before you admitted it hurt?'

'No.' Yes. 'I'm fine, really Jules. I've probably just overdone the physio.'

She still looks disbelieving. He hugs her. 'Let's go. Those Liquorice Allsorts won't pick themselves.'

As he leaves the room he looks back at the wardrobe. At the sliver of white paper.

He doesn't want Hannah to leave him. Ever.

Now he just has to work out how to make sure she stays.

Eighteen

Hannah looks up from her position on the floor. 'What are you doing in here? I thought you weren't talking to me.'

'Yeah, well, that got boring.' Steph shrugs. 'It turns out there's no one else around who thinks my jokes are funny.'

Hannah looks back down at the book on her lap. She is still angry. She still feels judged.

'What are you reading?' Steph peers downwards.

Hannah covers the pages. 'None of your business.'

'Please, Han.' Steph is rummaging in her bag. 'I brought Minstrels.' A brown disc lands on one of the pages.

Hannah flicks it away. 'You're going to have to do better than that.'

The whole packet lands on the book. 'Is that better?'

Despite herself, Hannah can feel her mouth twitching upwards. She resolutely sets it straight and keeps pretending to read. She pulls a sweet out and crunches into the shell. Might as well. She needs to keep her strength up.

She feels Steph watching her and carries on staring at the words on the page. One more minute and . . .

'Look, I'm sorry, Hannah. OK?' As ever, Steph needs to work on her apologetic tone.

Hannah holds back her forgiveness for a second. 'Are you? Some of the things you said were pretty harsh.'

Steph is looking uncharacteristically flustered. 'I'm just really worried about you, and it all came out wrong, and . . .'

Hannah relents. She pats the floor next to her. 'It's OK. Park your bum down here.'

Steph hesitates.

'It's all right.' Hannah grins. 'It's clean. Your lovely cream dress won't be ruined for evermore.'

Steph eyes her suspiciously. 'You said that when we went to Glastonbury and look what happened to my gorgeous stonewash cut-offs.' She sighs and starts lowering herself downwards.

Hannah rolls her eyes. 'Steph, you were hammered. And it was Glastonbury, for God's sake. Nothing comes out of there clean. Besides . . .' She turns a page. 'You couldn't have cared less about those cut-offs. Didn't you stick them on that flagpole by the yoga tent the next day?'

'Only because they were dirty.' Steph lands on the carpet and sticks her tongue out at Hannah.

'Sure.' Hannah turns another page. 'Or because it's what that guy with the dreads was doing. The one you said you were going to marry.'

'Oh yeah.' Steph stretches her legs out in front of her. 'I thought he was so hot. Until I realised he had head lice. That was a real tipping point.'

'Understandable.' Hannah nods. 'Itching never really does it for me.' She runs her finger down a page. 'By the way, how did you know I'd be here?'

Steph taps her nose with her finger. 'Easy.'

Hannah raises her eyebrows and waits.

'You always come here, Han, when you're feeling crappy. Always Finch Books on Nightingale Road. And always on the bloody floor when there are perfectly good chairs just over there.' She indicates the bright orange armchairs in the far corner.

Hannah looks around her. Multicoloured spines are packed into the shelves all around her. She feels enclosed by books. Safe. She breathes in the smell. Paper. Ink. It reminds her of her dad's study at home. He used to love it when she ran in and hugged him and told him that he smelt of words.

She nods. 'Yes, I guess I do.'

'Though I have to say . . .' Steph reaches out and takes one of the Minstrels from the packet. She crunches the chocolate enthusiastically between her teeth. 'That you're normally in a different section.'

'Which one?' Hannah turns another page. This book's tone is verbose and patronising. She knows that if she ever met the author she would get a strong urge to strangle him with the red silk tie he's wearing in his author photo.

'Travel.' Steph stares at her meaningfully.

Subtle as a brick in the face.

Hannah ignores her and flicks through some more pages, doing her best to look focused and engaged.

'Well, today I'm doing something different.'

'I can see that.' Steph flips up the book's cover and read out the title. '*Education, Education, Education: How to make children aspire.*' Hannah doesn't react. 'Bloody hell, what's this?' She looks at the spines of the books Hannah has piled all around her. '*The Brainy Bunch? School of Hope? Out of Our Minds – Learning to be creative?* What in God's name are you doing? Trying to become prime minister?'

Hannah shakes her head. 'Nope. I've got an interview.' She attempts an excited face. She fails.

'Really? For what?'

Hannah braces herself. 'Beaumont College.'

'What?' Steph's face is exactly as sceptical as Hannah was expecting it to be. 'That crazy girls' school in Clapham where they all wear green blazers and have pointlessly long plaits?'

Hannah crosses her arms defensively. 'I don't think it's quite as bad as that.'

'I bet it's twice as bad.' Steph shudders. 'Don't they all have to learn Latin?'

'I don't know.' Hannah keeps talking. 'But I need a job, OK?'

'You're not that desperate.'

Hannah frowns. 'Steph. Not helping.'

'OK, OK.' Steph eats another Minstrel while Hannah stares up at a man who is torn between two books by Stephen King. Eventually he gives up the struggle and takes both to the till.

Steph looks at Hannah. 'Whose idea was that, then? Beaumont?'

Hannah opens another book. She can't meet Steph's eyes.

'Tom's actually.' She carries on before Steph can get a word in. 'Nick knew someone there and he put in a word for me, and the money's OK and the holidays are great and I just thought I might as well go along.'

She glances up and sees Steph's mouth opening, so she rushes onwards.

'And if I work there then I can be with Tom.' She slams another book shut. 'And I don't want you to argue with me. OK?' She still can't meet her friend's eyes. She knows she'll see only her own doubts staring back at her. 'Because I know what you think and why you think it and the fact is that I love him. Yes, I want to go to Tanzania.' She holds up a hand. 'Don't speak, Steph, please.'

She gulps in more air. 'But I can't have both. So I'm choosing him, OK?' Weeks of worry are pouring out of her now. 'I have to. Because I love him. And I want him to get better. I mean really better. Not just limping with a cane but playing football and carrying me in his arms better. He needs me.' She finally looks at Steph's face. 'And I can't live with myself if I'm not there for him.'

She glances up and hesitates, puzzled, as she realises Steph isn't opening her mouth to speak. Isn't about to shoot her down. Isn't about to contradict her.

Instead, her friend puts her arms round her and hugs her. In the middle of a bookshop. Next to the shelf on sex education.

She mutters into Steph's hair. 'I'll miss you, though.' A big juddering sob escapes her.

'I know.' Steph pulls away and Hannah sees her eyes are red. 'Who's going to share tales of emotional dysfunction while drinking three bottles of wine with you now?'

'It's true.' Hannah shakes her head. 'What a yawning gap you're going to leave in my life.'

'I know.' Steph nods seriously before breaking into a smile. 'I'll annoy you via email though. And Instagram. And I might even join Twitter.'

'Bloody hell.' Hannah laughs. 'Do you mean *the* Twitter? The one that you proclaimed would bring an end to civilisation by the end of the next century?'

'I do.' Steph grins. 'Even *I* realise that living overseas means I'll have to embrace modern technology.'

'Amen to that. You might want to try Skype too.'

Steph rolls her eyes. 'Yeah. Whatever. Don't get carried away.' She looks at the unappetising pile of tomes around them. 'Now. Are we going to get you sorted for this interview then?'

Hannah narrows her eyes. 'You hate teaching books.'

'True.' Steph smiles. 'But that's how much I love you, Hannah. I'll read . . .' She picks one up. '*Putting the "I" in Child* for you.'

Hannah's eyes prickle with tears again. She puts her hand on her heart. 'A noble sacrifice, Steph.' Then she squeezes her friend's hand. 'Thank you.'

Steph holds her eyes. 'Anything for you. You know that.' She flicks the book open. 'Now get that notebook and let's crack on. If we really get motoring we can be at the pub by nine.'

'Yes boss.' Hannah puts her head down and starts to write.

Later, when Steph's left the shop for a fresh-air break Hannah hears her phone bleep. It's Nick. He hasn't texted her since Tom was really ill.

Is T OK?

She answers. Think so. Why?

Bit worried.

She replies. What happened?

He wouldn't leave his seat at the game today and he looked really wasted. Like he did back in January.

Hannah feels nausea start to rise. Tom has seemed different in the last couple of weeks. Sluggish. More unsteady. And his left hand seems to be freezing back into a heavy and unwieldy claw.

But Tom has promised he'll be honest with her now. She's sure he would tell her if something was really wrong.

She sends another text. I think he's just tired. But he's seeing the consultant next week – I'll make sure I get all the info.

Thanks. Keep me posted.

Will do.

She looks at the message again. Sighs.

Then she redoubles her efforts to get the Beaumont College job.

Picture of Hannah covered in tomatoes

June 2015

'Steph.' Tom looks downwards and tries to hitch his towel further up his waist. 'What a surprise.'

'Hi. Sorry I'm here so early.' She pushes her long blonde hair out of her eyes and pulls her bag further up her shoulder. 'Is Hannah out getting her hair cut?'

'Yes.'

'Good.' She smiles. 'Then can I come in?'

He blinks, puzzled. 'Erm . . . sure.'

She has already swept past him.

He closes the door behind her, wondering what on earth she is doing here. She stands in the hallway, an unusually nervous expression on her face. 'I need to talk to you about something.'

'OK.' He has a feeling he may not like what she has to say. 'Great. I'll just go and put some clothes on.'

'You do that.' She kicks off her heels and heads into the kitchen. He hears her picking up the kettle. 'Tea?'

'Yes please.' He goes into what is now the spare room again and grabs a T-shirt from the dirty washing pile on the floor. As he pulls it over his head he hears the bang of cupboard doors being opened and shut. He swears to himself as his left hand refuses to go through the armhole, leaving him groping blindly inside the T-shirt as he struggles to push it through.

When he eventually emerges he hears the hopeful rustle

of a packet of biscuits being opened and tries to calm his panic by stretching and curling the fingers of his left hand. Once. Twice. Then they freeze.

He forces his fear away. One day they will work. He just needs to keep trying.

He finds some tracksuit bottoms and wriggles into them before hopping across to his cane and making his way back to the kitchen. He remembers when getting dressed was something he didn't have to think about. Now he feels like he's completed an assault course before he has his first cup of tea.

Steph is sitting at the table, hands wrapped round a mug. A photo rests on the other side of the table, next to the 'Groom' mug Hannah had given him on their honeymoon. The picture shows Hannah at La Tomatina, red fruit splashed across her white T-shirt. Across her face. Her hair. Hannah had gone to the food fight festival with Steph during their PGCE year. He looks at her face. So open. Her head thrown back in the smile to end all smiles.

He slides into a chair. 'Nice photo.' He reaches for his tea. 'Why have you brought it?'

She shrugs. 'To jog your memory.'

'I see.' Silence falls. Steph is staring into her mug, brows drawn into a frown.

'What are you reminding me about?' He takes a chocolate digestive from the tin and bites into it. 'At nine thirty a.m? It's great to have an excuse to have biscuits for breakfast, but—'

She raises her head and her blue eyes pierce him. 'I'm worried about Hannah.'

'OK . . .' He chews slowly. Waits.

She nibbles her lip. He has never seen her look nervous

before. It's decidedly unnerving. She struggles for a second, then her face clears and she launches into it. 'Look, I'm really sorry for what I'm about to say. I know you're having a totally shit time and this is probably the last thing you need.'

He feels a kick of pride. 'I'm doing OK.'

She nods. 'I know. I didn't mean that.' She takes refuge in her tea. Tries again. 'Hannah's really proud of you.'

'I'm really proud of her, too.'

Steph takes a breath. 'Look, the thing is that I think Hannah's got a bit lost. And I think you need to help her.'

'OK.' He dunks his biscuit in his tea. 'Don't pull your punches, Steph, will you?'

She puts a spoon of sugar in her tea. 'I don't know how else to say it. You know me. Straight to the point.' Confusion crosses her face. 'And the truth is I've spent weeks wondering whether to talk to you.'

'Why?'

'Hannah's just not herself any more. Is she?' She points at the photo. '*This* is Hannah.'

He puts his tea down. 'What are you talking about?'

He knows exactly what she's talking about. Ever since he found that bloody Teach the World letter he has started to notice how muted Hannah is. She is always staring out of windows or gazing into her endless cups of tea – and the more he watches the more he notices the split second of sadness on her face before she realises he is there.

Now Steph is here he can't ignore the feeling any more.

She gazes at him, eyes wide. 'I feel so bad that I have to talk to you like this. I really do. And Hannah would kill me if she knew I was here. She loves you so much.'

She is visibly steeling herself. 'But the thing is, that she

had plans back in January. To go away. Before you . . .'
He sees her wondering whether she can say the word
'stroke' out loud.

He puts her out of her misery. 'Are you talking about
Tanzania?'

Yes.' Steph freezes. Then she nods. 'So you know that
she applied?'

'Yep.'

She frowns. 'Hannah doesn't know that.'

'No.' Tom sighs. 'I didn't want her to feel bad.'

'Oh.' Steph's mouth drops open.

She is silent.

Unusual.

She picks up a biscuit crumb with her fingertip. 'She
was so excited about it. Spent months planning what she
was going to do out there.'

Anger is rising. This isn't his fault. 'Yeah, but circumstances have changed, haven't they?' He tries to laugh
but it sounds harsh. Twisted. 'Sorry to put a spanner in
the works and everything . . .'

Her silver earrings glint as she nods her head. 'I know.
I know everything's changed. Believe me. But I just had
to talk to you. Because she's giving up the one thing she
really wants. For you.'

'Look, Steph.' He hopes that if he can find enough
words he can override the part of him that thinks she
might be right. 'Hannah loves me. I love her. We're
married – we have to do what works for both of us. We
have to compromise.'

The sadness on her face shocks him. 'Sure, but she's
wanted to go to Tanzania for years. You know that. So
when does she get to do what she wants?'

He feels hot. Uncomfortable. He has no answer for her.

314

She takes another biscuit but puts it down uneaten. 'I'm worried that she'll never really be her again if she doesn't go. It's a great chance for her. She'd get her confidence back.'

'She seems pretty confident to me.' He thinks of Hannah's downcast face as she heads out of the front door on a Monday morning. 'So . . .' His voice falters.

'You don't really think that.' Steph leans forward. 'She's so happy now the two of you have worked things out, but at work she's still quiet. Never says stuff in meetings. Doesn't put forward ideas any more.'

'Well, she's leaving. And she hates it there.'

'I know, but still. She used to be non-stop. And now . . . nothing.'

He doesn't want Steph to be right. He is still fighting. 'But maybe Beaumont College might—'

'No.' Steel glints in Steph's eyes. 'Again I'm sorry to say it but she's just going through with that for you.'

'How do you know?'

She looks at him and her mouth curves upwards. 'The same reason you know. She's the worst liar in the world.'

Damn. He knows it's true. Whenever she talks about the interview her eyes are dull. Her smile is for his benefit. Not from her heart.

He is starting to feel sick. He can't even think about Hannah going. His life wouldn't work without her. He wouldn't want to get out of bed. He would miss her face every morning. Her giggle every night.

Everywhere he looked, he'd miss her.

He couldn't bear it.

He closes his eyes. Breathes. When he opens them again he sees that Steph has tears in her eyes.

This scares him more than anything.

He blinks. 'Why Tanzania, anyway? Why not . . .' He tries to smile. 'Brighton?'

'Because it's her dream.'

Yes. It is. He understands that. He has understood it ever since she'd shown him the map on her ceiling back when they very first met.

'But . . .' He stops, thinking of the way Hannah approaches her day now. The way she lines up his clothes every night so it's easy for him to put them on. The way she places his pills on the table with his phone charging next to them. The way she always leaves the remote on the right-hand side of the sofa.

Her world is all about him.

It always has been.

And as he realises this, he looks at the photo and the final protesting remnants of his denial fall away. He wants Hannah to live again. Really *live*.

It doesn't matter if he can't join her. Doesn't matter if he has to stay here and click on images of her adventures from thousands of miles away. Doesn't matter if he's left behind.

Without her.

He can hardly bear it.

But he looks at Steph and nods. Once. Twice. He knows what he has to do.

He just doesn't know if he can find the strength.

Nineteen

'Hello. Can I speak to Hannah Ellison please?'

'Speaking.' Hannah shifts in her seat. The collar of her white blouse is rubbing against her neck and her black interview suit is having its normal effect of setting her sweat glands to ON.

She looks up and sees that the school secretary is treating her to a fierce glare as she taps on her keyboard with perfect red fingernails. The plaque on her desk announces that she is called Joy, but experience so far tells Hannah that she has very little intention of living up to her name.

Hannah mouths an apology at Joy's rigid features, while hunkering down in her seat and putting her hand over her mouth to try to muffle her voice. This place is so different to Queensdale. There the office is so loud that Hannah can barely hear herself speak over the constant ringing of phones and the rattle and slam of the filing cabinets in the corner as the students' latest exploits are filed away.

Here at Beaumont all she can hear is the clock ticking and the odd squeak as the cleaner quietly polishes the windows. The plant on the windowsill looks like it's recently featured at the Chelsea Flower Show and next to it is a wall displaying pictures of students in green uniforms enjoying a mind-blowing variety of school trips. Jordan. Dubai. Australia.

'I'm calling from Teach the World.' Hannah stiffens and her pulse rises. 'We don't normally do this, but we've been told you might be available in July and so we're contacting you about a new opportunity in Tanzania.'

'Pardon?' Hannah uncrosses her legs and crosses them the other way. Her tights continue to squeeze her thighs in a thoroughly unfriendly fashion and she can feel her hair getting more curly by the second.

The voice at the other end is low. Determined. 'We have a new opportunity that's just opened up. Coordinating the curriculum across our Tanzanian education programme. We were hoping we could persuade you to come to an interview.'

'I . . .' Hannah looks at Joy. Joy looks at Hannah.

Hannah decides it would be a good idea to leave the room.

She heads out into the corridor, the phone cradled under her chin.

'Look.' She drops her voice as two girls walk past, eyeing her with chilly teenage disdain. She brushes her curls back from her forehead. 'I don't know where you heard that, but I'm not available in July.'

The voice sounds amused. 'We were told you'd say that.'

'What?' Hannah looks around, wondering if someone is stalking her. 'Who said that?'

Then the penny drops. Steph.

Hannah's going to kill her. Just after she burns this suit.

She is prickly with sweat. She cradles the phone on her shoulder and tries to reach into her shirt and wipe some of it off.

It does not go well.

'The thing is, Hannah, Teach the World desperately needs someone like you.'

Hannah doubts they would think so if they could see her now. Her watch strap is stuck on her top button and it takes her three goes to extract her hand from her shirt. She hears giggling from the far end of the corridor and turns to see that the two girls are watching her. As she looks they flick their hair to one side and strut off in perfect step.

Ah well. At least they didn't record her. That's the last thing she needs turning up on YouTube.

'So what do you think, Hannah? Would you like to come in and talk to us?'

She thinks of Tom and knows she can't.

She forces the word out. 'No, I—'

'The person who called said you were so keen to come and work with us.' The voice rises enticingly. 'And there's no commitment. Just a chat.'

'I don't know.' Hannah sees a dark green door opening along the corridor and someone who is presumably another candidate comes out. Her dark hair is swept into a flawless chignon and she looks like the kind of woman who always has a spare pair of tights in her handbag. She glides down the corridor towards the exit. Back straight. Head up.

Hannah instantly feels small. Messy.

Inadequate.

'Hannah?' The voice continues. 'The kids out there are amazing, you know. They have the biggest smiles and they're so grateful for every scrap of information that comes their way. I was there for two years and when I came back home I had such a spring in my step.'

Hannah can't remember when she last had a spring in her step. Despite Tom. Despite how much she loves him.

'Hannah, the person who called us – they said that you wanted to rediscover your love of teaching. This is the way to do it, I promise you.'

'Who . . .?'

'I can't tell you that.'

'Hannah Ellison?'

The door has opened again, and a man in a pinstripe suit and florid green tie is staring at her expectantly. 'Are you ready for your interview?'

She stands there, phone in hand, the future diverging before her.

She needs to get this job. Needs to be at Beaumont. There's no point going to talk to Teach the World.

Yet . . .

'Please come and meet us, Hannah.'

Sod it. She can just go and see what's involved. That's all. 'When?'

She is told a date and a time and scribbles them on her hand with a biro.

'I've got to go. See you then.'

Her interviewer is staring at her, fingers drumming against the door. It's clear he is not a patient man.

'Are you ready, Hannah?'

'Of course.' She puts on her finest interview smile and walks in.

'What are you doing here?'

'Charming.' Steph walks up the wide stone steps towards Hannah. 'I schlep all the way down here in my free double period, and this is the thanks I get.'

'Sorry.' Hannah is still thinking about the phone call as Steph falls into step beside her. 'How did it go? Did they have gold-plated teacups?' Steph points towards the pond that is next to some fir trees near the distant dining hall. 'Did you know they have koi carp in there? Real ones?'

Hannah shakes her head. 'Didn't quite get the chance to look at the grounds.'

Steph puts an arm round her. 'So? Did you do yourself proud?'

Hannah cringes. 'Honestly?'

'Of course.' Steph walks with her through the wrought-iron gates and back into reality. A motorbike whistles down the road in front of them as Hannah presses the button and waits for the traffic lights to change.

'It was bloody awful.'

Steph eyes her suspiciously. 'Hannah Ellison bloody awful, or the rest of the world bloody awful?'

'Meaning?'

'Meaning you are absolutely terrible at knowing when you've done something well.'

The green man appears and Hannah starts to cross the road. 'That's not true.'

'Oh yeah?' Steph follows her. 'What about the time we had the Ofsted inspection and you were convinced they'd fail you but then they graded you as outstanding?'

Hannah swerves to avoid a guide dog as she reaches the pavement again. 'Yeah, well.'

'Or the fact that the whole way through your PGCE you kept telling me you were the worst teacher on the course.'

'I didn't.' Hannah looks at her reproachfully. 'I'm sure I thought that guy Matt was worse than me.'

Steph shakes her head. 'Hannah, Matt didn't know what an apostrophe was. Even you couldn't feel inferior to that.'

'OK, OK.' Hannah feels a rush of embarrassment. 'Anyway. Today was bad. I came out with such a load of crap.' She steps sideways to get out of the way of a mum with a triple buggy. 'For example, I said my only flaw was perfectionism.'

'Ouch.'

'Exactly. And I forgot who wrote *The Bell Jar*. And I sweated so much I stuck to the leather sofa. It sounded like a plaster coming off when I stood up.'

Steph gives a low whistle. 'All right. You win. Sounds like you had a shocker.'

'Thank you.' Hannah nods. 'Told you so.'

'What happened? You were all systems go for that job.'

'I was a bit distracted.'

'Why?'

'Because just beforehand I got a phone call from Teach the World. Asking me to go and meet them about a job in Tanzania.' She eyes her friend suspiciously. 'But then you'd know all about that.'

'What do you mean?'

'Oh, come on. I know it was you who got in touch with them.'

Steph holds up her hands. 'Not guilty.'

Hannah shakes her head in disbelief. 'Seriously? Who else would have done it?'

Steph holds her eye. 'I don't know. But it wasn't me.' She elbows Hannah eagerly. 'But were you tempted? When they called?'

'No.' Best to shut this down.

'Really?' Steph nudges her in the ribs. '*Really*?'

Hannah resists the temptation to talk about the call for approximately a nanosecond. Then she cracks. 'Yes.' She swallows. 'I couldn't stop thinking about it when I was in the interview. I was barely listening to the questions at all.'

'Well, I never thought you'd like it there anyway.'

'We'll never find out, will we?' Hannah thinks of Tom and feels a stab of guilt. 'Shit. What am I going to do now?'

'I don't know.' Steph clasps her hands together. 'But now you've brought the subject up – PLEASE COME TO TANZANIA PLEASE COME PLEASE COME!'

Hannah shakes her head. 'Can't.'

Steph keeps going. 'PLEASE COME PLEASE COME PLEASE COME!'

Hannah can't help laughing. 'It's a different position anyway. I'm not sure I'd be sharing your mud hut any more. Or even be in the same place.'

'That's OK.' Steph shrugs. 'I was planning to move in some friendly cockroaches instead.'

'Ewwww.' Hannah grimaces. 'I'm not good with them. Remember that hostel in Argentina?'

Steph mimes puking. 'Yes. That was disgusting though. When they took up residence in your washbag.' She steps left as a wizened lady zooms past on a mobility scooter. Then she tugs Hannah's arm. 'Oh my God. You actually look excited. I haven't seen you look like that in *ages.*'

'Yeah. Well. I can't go. Obviously.' Hannah kicks the pavement with her shoes.

'Why not?'

'Don't be a pillock. I love Tom.'

'You can still leave the country. It's legal, so I hear.'

'But who would look after him?'

Steph's face is alight. 'He'll be running up Everest by next week at the rate he's going. He'll be fine.'

'It's too soon.' Hannah checks her watch. 'And— Shit. I'm late.'

'What for?'

'Tom's consultant appointment. Got to rush – see you later.' Hannah sets off down the street at a sprint. 'TAXI!'

By some miracle one stops. 'King's Lane Hospital, please.'

Hannah gets in and slams the door shut behind her. As it rumbles off she sits back and stares out at the scenic view of a battered minibus and the back of a Ford Fiesta.

She can't go to Tanzania. She knows that.

But she can stare out of the window and dream.

Clinic letter

June 2015

Tom sits in the waiting room, praying that Hannah doesn't walk through the door. He's told her the wrong time for his appointment, but he has no back-up plan if she chooses this as the one time in her life she's going to be early. He needs to be called in to see the doctor before she gets here. That way his plan will work.

He rubs his left arm and wonders whether it will ever truly feel like a part of him again. It currently seems to be waging some kind of campaign against his every waking moment.

He knows that Hannah notices. He knows she worries. Which is why he can't let her anywhere near Dr Malik right now. One look from her could break his resolve and he's not going to let that happen. However much it might hurt.

He looks around and sees that the whiteboard at the front of the rows of seats is now telling him that the clinic is running half an hour late. Damn. He leans back in his bright yellow chair and breathes in the fetid smell of the toilets outside, which are clearly experiencing some kind of plumbing issue.

The chairs around him are full of people infinitely older than he is. People with hearing aids and white hair, faces pleated with a lifetime of experience and laughter. He sees an old woman walking without a stick and feels resentment rise. Then he sees the tears running down her face and hunches further down in his seat, ashamed.

Nurses in blue uniforms appear from behind various doors, calling names that aren't his. Occasionally they talk and laugh together while dangling a list from their hands, ignoring the questioning looks and impatient sighs of the patients around them. The young receptionist ferries notes into various rooms and occasionally consults the mobile phone sticking out of the back pocket of his trousers.

'Tom Ellison?' Tom looks up.

'Yes.'

The nurse by the whiteboard gives no sign of having heard him and disappears again without a word.

Helpful. Tom sits up in his seat, unsure whether he's meant to follow her.

Two minutes pass before she reappears. 'Tom Ellison?'

'YES.' His reply is practically a shout. Tom apologises to the woman next to him as she jumps in surprise and spills coffee down her blouse.

'Come this way.' The nurse indicates a door behind her.

Tom does one last check for Hannah. She's nowhere in sight.

Stage one of his plan is complete and he limps towards the door alone. As he moves he sees a tall man in stained blue pyjamas shuffling past the clinic. He drags a drip behind him and his steps are slow and hesitant. His shoulders are hunched. His eyes glazed.

Tom shudders.

'Hello Tom.' Dr Malik walks forward, giving him a

hearty handshake. He is taller than Tom remembers. 'How are you?'

'Oh. You know.' Tom indicates his cane. 'Could be better.'

'I see.' Dr Malik sits down behind his narrow desk and flicks through the yellow folder of notes in front of him. Tom sees a picture of three small children in a grey frame by the phone. They look so healthy. So carefree.

'So, how have you been feeling in yourself?' Dr Malik steeples his long fingers together and eyes Tom over red half-moon glasses.

'I'm OK.' Tom nods. Now that he's here he suddenly doesn't want to voice his doubts. If he does then he has a horrible feeling he's not going to like the doctor's reply. Better to carry on. Hoping.

No. It's time for the truth. He starts slowly. Weighing his words. 'I'm working really hard at my physio programme and it seems to be paying off. My left hand has more movement. I can grip again.' He looks downwards. Searches for the honesty he needs.

'But sometimes I can't hold anything at all. And I'm a bit worried about my leg – it seemed to be improving too. At first.'

'But . . .?'

He steels himself. 'But sometimes it seems to have a mind of its own. And it does this thing when I yawn. It kind of – tightens.'

'I see.' Dr Malik narrows his eyes. Frowns.

It's not a promising facial expression. Tom's heart starts to thud unpleasantly.

Dr Malik leans forward. 'Well, I have your physio notes here and I see that you've met a lot of your original goals. Making a cup of tea. Walking to the shops.'

'Yes.' They sound so trivial. Things he could do in his sleep before.

'I also see that you're planning to go back to work.'

'Yes.'

'Soon?'

'Yes.' Tom is starting to sweat.

'I see.' The doctor nods slowly. 'And do you really feel that you're ready?'

'I hope so.'

'You hope so?'

'Well, of course. But . . .' He inhales. Tries to calm himself. 'But I still get really tired. And I get a lot of pain. In my arm. And my shoulder.' He feels a rush of self-pity. 'I just really expected to be doing better by now.'

Sympathy warms Dr Malik's tired face. 'It has only been six months, Tom. It's still very early days in terms of your recovery.'

'Is it?' Tom shakes his head. 'It feels like it's been years.' He thinks of Hannah. 'And I need to get back to normal. To how I was before.'

Dr Malik compresses his lips. 'The thing is, Tom, that you might have to find a new normal.'

'What do you mean?'

Dr Malik runs a hand over his stubble. 'I mean that it may be that your function will never return to exactly how it was before – we can't know what's ahead. Your hopes are understandable – everyone wants to get back to being the person they were. But sometimes that's just not . . . possible.'

Tom stares at him, his brain fighting the words with all its might.

'Not possible?'

'Sadly not.' Dr Malik's gaze is unwavering.

Tom can't accept it.

'But—'

Dr Malik cuts in. 'Tom, the fact that you're walking independently and using your left hand at all are signs that there's hope. There's always hope.'

'So I might get totally better? Back to how I was?'

Dr Malik sighs and runs a hand through his greying hair. 'It's unlikely, Tom. Not what you mean by better.'

Tom feels a kick of fury. 'So you're saying I should just give up?'

'Of course not.' Dr Malik shakes his head. 'I would never say that. I just think it may be wise to adjust your expectations. And I'm worried that if you rush back into your old job you may set back your recovery.'

'But I need to work.' Working is the one thing he has to cling on to. Once he's talked to Hannah. The only thing that will keep him going. 'I feel so . . . useless.'

'I understand. But maybe wait a bit longer. You need to keep making these marginal gains – the fact your leg jerks may be a sign of some kind of late reconnection. You need to take the time for your therapy now or you might miss chances to regain function.'

Tom clenches his fists. Or rather clenches one of them. 'I'll be fine.'

'Tom.' Dr Malik shrugs his shoulders. 'I'm really not trying to be discouraging. And you've done incredibly well so far. But your left-hand side may never be the same again. We could try a cast for you. Or maybe some Botox to help the movement in your hand and arm. But it's unlikely you'll move with as much freedom and flex-ibility as you used to. I'm sorry.'

'But I can do more physio.' He must fight this. 'I can try harder.'

'It's not entirely a question of trying harder. If you push yourself too hard you may do more damage.' Dr Malik shakes his head and Tom feels a desperate stab of anger.

Dr Malik's eyes are gentle. 'Please, Tom. Please listen. You need to take more time. Adjust. Tell your family to make allowances for you. To help you. You have to let them support you.'

Tom thinks of Hannah. The furrow on her forehead as she organises his days.

The sacrifice she's made.

No more.

He's decided now.

'OK.' He nods. 'I'll think about when to go back to work a bit more.' He sits up as straight as he can. 'But I'm not giving in. Never. I know I can get a whole lot better than this.'

'That's great.' Dr Malik breaks into his first real smile. 'Now, let's talk about your options.'

'Good idea.' Tom nods and leans forward to listen.

Half an hour later he walks out of the room, needing a second to breathe. A second to compose himself.

No chance. He hears his name and turns to see Hannah sprinting towards him. Her green bag is slung across her shoulder. Her hair is wild. Her tights have a large hole round the knee.

The love on her face makes him catch his breath.

'I didn't know you could run in heels.'

'I got lost.' Her shoes squeak as she skids to a halt. 'Ended up in paediatrics. You'd think I'd know this place well enough by now after spending all that time here with you.' She fans her face with her hand. 'But apparently not.' She reaches up and kisses him on the lips.

'How did it go? What did he say?'
Her eyes are so eager. So full of faith.
Tom pauses. Reaches inside himself.
Then he starts to talk.

Twenty

Tom is pale. He starts to speak but rapidly falters. He takes a breath.

Nerves kick inside her. 'Tom? Is everything OK?'

She sees emotions dancing across his face. Then they settle. Clarify.

He smiles. 'He said I was well on the way to getting back to my old self.'

'Really?' She closes her eyes. She doesn't trust this news yet. It's too positive. Too much.

She opens her eyes again. He is still smiling. '*Really*?' she asks again.

'Yeah.' He nods. 'Amazing, isn't it?'

She gives herself a quick shake. Just to check.

No. Not dreaming.

Tom kisses her. 'All that physio is paying off. He says my arm and my leg will soon be totally back to normal.'

At the words the sheer determination that has sustained her since the stroke finally starts to ebb. Tears form in her eyes but she blinks them away.

'That's so great!' His joy makes her heart sing. 'So you'll walk like you used to?'

'Yep.' He beams at her.

'And your arm will be better?'

'That's what he said.'

'And your hand?'

'Yes!' He kisses her again.

'That's incredible.' She hugs him. 'Bloody well done.'

'Thanks.' He squeezes her hand. 'Shall we go and celebrate?'

'Definitely.' She walks beside him towards the exit, swerving to avoid a doctor in a light blue robe and clogs covered in spots of blood.

She raises her arms as she feels all the worry and pressure of the past six months starting to lift from her shoulders.

'I can't believe it.'

'I know.' His right arm rests round her. 'Me neither. And he said that I can go back to work as well.'

'That's amazing.' For him. She wonders what she'll be doing while he is at the office. Then she starts to feel guilty. Selfish. Now is not the time to think about her. This is *his* day. She does a skip of happiness and narrowly avoids colliding with a woman in a purple dressing gown being wheeled towards the garden by a nurse.

'I'm so sorry.' The nurse clucks disapprovingly. Hannah turns back to Tom. 'I can't believe I did that. I remember how much I used to hate people not paying attention when you were in your chair.'

'Me too.' He coughs and looks away as they approach the exit and something in his voice makes her wonder.

She comes to a halt and turns to face him. 'Tom? Are you sure you're telling me everything?'

He holds her gaze. 'Yes.'

She's still not sure. 'Really? It just all seems a bit too good to be true.'

'Yes.' He nods solemnly. 'I'm going to get better. Just like I was before.' He grins. 'But maybe even better at football.'

'Not possible.' Hannah kisses him. 'Wow. What a day. And the sun's even shining for you.' They walk through the hospital doors and stand staring up at the sky. 'You're amazing, you know that?'

'Thanks.' He kisses the top of her head. 'I couldn't have done it without you.'

'Yeah, you could.'

'No.' He shakes his head. 'I couldn't.' The love in his eyes overwhelms her. 'Thank you.'

'Excuse meeeeeeeeeee.' A little boy with blond curls speeds towards them, clutching a water bottle to his chest. His mum is in hot pursuit, ponytail streaming out behind her as she struggles to stop him before he hurtles into the car park. She shouts an apology over her shoulder as she runs on.

Tom and Hannah look at each other and smile. She has never felt so close to him. Never felt so loved.

It's enough. To make up for Tanzania. He can make her happy. She's sure of it.

Her ears prick up as she hears a nursery-rhyme tune blaring across the car park. She scans around until she sees a white van parked by the fence that circles the hospital grounds.

'Ice cream!' She pulls on his arm. 'Let's go and get some.'

He crinkles his nose. 'I was hoping for a pint.'

'Oh, come on. Just one ice cream. Please?'

'All right, then.' He starts to move towards the van. 'I'll get them.'

Doubt creeps in. 'Are you sure? They might be a bit difficult to carry.'

'Hannah.' He holds up a hand. 'I can do it. OK? I've got a medical seal of approval now.'

She nods. 'Sorry. Still adjusting.' She points towards

the narrow garden in front of the A&E sign. 'I'll be over there.'

She stares after him for a second as he limps off. Tall. Dark.

Brave.

Her Tom.

She walks towards the grass, hugging the good news to her like a charm. Hospital staff are taking off ID tags and putting on sunglasses as they lay claim to minimal strips of green and start to sunbathe. She spies an unoccupied patch and heads towards it.

As she sits down she wonders why no one has colonised it yet.

A drill starts to whine behind her.

So that's why.

She settles back anyway, savouring the smell of roses from her left and trying to ignore the yellow dust blowing towards her from where the drill is attacking the pavement. She leans back on her elbows, watching an elderly man carefully driving the wrong way round the one-way system. The sun glints off the silver bonnet of his car as he comes face to face with a pedestrian crossing the road with a stethoscope round his neck.

Workers in high-vis jackets pick up rubbish and a red crane swings sleepily above the green and black building where Tom had stayed all those months ago. Hannah remembers staring out of those windows, craving air. Craving hope.

She is so lucky.

She knows that.

She can work out what she's going to do, now Tom's better. She can rethink things now. Make a plan. Build her life again. With him.

'99 Flake?' Tom looms over her.

She reaches out her hand. 'Thank you.'

Tom teeters down to sit beside her. She puts her hand on his knee and takes a lick of her ice cream.

'Yum.' She nibbles on her Flake. 'This is the life, isn't it?'

He dispatches his Flake in one bite. 'It is.' A fragment of chocolate lodges on his chin.

The drill starts up again.

'OR MAYBE NOT.' He puts his hands over his ears.

Hannah giggles.

The noise stops again.

'So, how was your interview?'

Oh.

'Erm . . .' She kicks the grass with her toe.

'Tell me.'

Hannah can't meet his eyes. She knows how happy he would be if she got the job. How much he wants her to love her work again.

No. She can't lie.

'Not great, actually.'

'No?' He calmly licks his ice cream. 'Why?'

Because I was hopelessly distracted.

No. That won't do.

She focuses on her ice cream. 'I don't know. It just didn't fit. I don't think it's the right place for me, really.'

'Why not?' He crunches his cone.

'I just don't think that Beaumont is going to be the place where I can make a difference. The kids there are probably all going to rule the world anyway.'

'But surely you can be *more* useful there?' He darts a glance at her. 'Smaller classes? Better resources?' He shrugs. 'Nick's mate loves it.'

'I know.' Hannah finishes the ice cream and gets to work on the cone. 'And I am so grateful to you and Nick for getting me the interview. But I'm just not sure my heart's in it. Maybe it's time to . . .' She reaches out and plucks a lone daisy from the lawn. 'To do something different.'

He looks at her. Full in the face. His expression is probing. It makes her uneasy. 'What is it, Tom?'

'There's something I need to say.'

She shivers despite the heat of the day. Tries to joke away the seriousness on his face.

'What is it? Have you been stealing my Hobnobs again?'

'That's more than my life's worth.' He grins as he shakes his head. 'I wouldn't dare.'

'So . . .?'

He is pleating the edge of his T-shirt with his fingers. His voice is low. 'I called Teach the World today.'

She blinks. 'You what?'

He glances at her. Quick. Tentative. 'I called them, H. For you.'

She can't compute it. 'It was *you*?'

He attempts a smile. 'Yep.'

Her mind is fizzing. Excited. Confused. 'But why? How did you know? When . . .?'

He reaches out and takes her hand. 'I found the letter they sent you. A few weeks ago.'

Oh no. She feels sick with guilt. The ice cream is threatening to reappear.

'I'm so sorry.' She presses his fingers in hers. 'I'm so sorry that you found out like that.' She must reassure him. Let him know she's not going anywhere. 'But it's nothing to worry about.' She lifts his hand and kisses it. 'I applied before your stroke. Before we – before we fell in love again.'

'I know.' He nods. 'You have nothing to feel bad about.'

Tears form. 'But I do. I feel horrible that you even found out.'

He looks peaceful. Resolute. 'It's a good thing I did.'

She shakes her head. 'No it's not.'

'No. I needed to know.' He turns to her and his eyes are clear. Determined.

'I want you to go, H.'

She stares at him, her heart on pause, unable to believe what he is saying.

He takes her hand. 'I want you to get on that plane.'

Daisy chain
June 2015

His words don't quite have the effect that he's expecting.

Her face crumples. 'You mean, after everything we've been through, you've suddenly decided you want to get rid of me?' Her eyes well up and the tip of her ice cream cone drops to the ground.

Bad sign. Hannah never throws away food.

'God, no.' He puts his arm round her as she starts to sob. 'No. I would never want to get rid of you.'

If only she knew how much he wanted her to stay.

'Then why . . .?' Her eyes are bright with tears. 'Don't you love me?'

He grits his teeth. 'You know I love you. These past few weeks have been the best we've ever had. You know that.'

She stares at him, face full of confusion. He kisses her cheek. It's salty with tears.

'Then why are you saying this?' Her eyes search his face.

'Because I want you to be happy.' He looks at the mascara dripping down her cheek. 'Though it isn't really going according to plan.'

'But I am happy. I want to be with you. It's all I want now.'

He squeezed her fingers. 'It's not, though, is it?' He searches for words. 'That's why I think you should go.

339

We know now I'm definitely going to be OK. It's *your* time now.'

'That doesn't make sense.'

'Yes it does.' This is killing him. He had really wanted some alcohol to power him through this conversation. A Cadbury's Flake just isn't the same.

He swallows. 'I think you want to go. If you're really honest with yourself. If you look beyond our life together I think you need more. I think a large part of you wants to head off and do this job.'

'But I can wait, Tom.' She is picking at the hole in her tights. It is rapidly approaching her ankle. Her shoulders are so tense beneath his arm that they feel like they might snap. 'I can wait till you're better. We could go together.'

She diverts from her tights and starts picking daisies. One. Two. Three.

His heart is leaden. It'll probably be years before he can do a trip like that.

'No. I want you to go now.'

He doesn't. Oh, how he doesn't.

'But why?'

He feels a horrible temptation to tell her the truth. To tell her what Dr Malik really said.

No.

'Look, I hate the thought of being without you.' His words come with difficulty. 'But I want you to be happy.'

Her mouth is pressed in a stubborn line. 'Good. Then I'll stay here.'

'No.' He is running out of words. 'You're happy with me. But you're not happy with your job. Or lack of one.'

'I'm OK.'

'I know you, remember, H? I've seen the signs.'

'What signs?'

He feigns an amusement he doesn't feel. 'The way you go all misty-eyed when you see safaris on TV. The way your eyes light up whenever Steph talks about her trip. You want to go too.'

'No.' Hannah shakes her head. 'I don't want to give you up.'

'You're not giving me up. It's only a year. Maybe I can visit.' He knows he can't, but he needs her to say yes. He may be broken but he wants to do something good. Something for her.

'But—'

He cuts in. 'Hannah, I can't live with myself if you don't go. OK?'

'Well, I can't live with myself if I do.'

Her voice says no. But her eyes are saying yes. He can see the gleam beginning.

She shakes her head. 'No, Tom. No. It's not going to happen.'

He has to persuade her. *Has* to.

He leans closer. She is focused on her daisy chain. Making holes in the thin green stems. Stringing the flowers together.

'Your life can't just be about me. There has to be more. Something that's yours.'

She makes a hole in the final stem.

'Just think about it, Hannah. Please.'

She stretches the chain across his palm.

He pushes on. 'I love you, H. But take a year. Go and get your Hannah back. The giggler. The bubbly madwoman who wears bright red and never stops talking.'

'Excuse me.' She frowns. 'I do stop. Every now and then.'

He sees her start to smile.

He's nearly there.

He wants to weep.

'And I can stay here and carry on getting better.'

Or not.

She blinks up at him. 'But Julie? And the baby? And you? Who'll look after all of you?'

He has no idea.

'I don't need looking after. I'm getting better. Remember?'

'Yes.' He sees belief beginning in her eyes. 'But—'

'What now?' He can't keep this going much longer.

'But I'll miss you.'

And then he hears it. The note in her voice.

Acceptance.

He has done it. She is going to go.

For a dangerous second he wavers. He could change her mind. So easily.

But he doesn't. He won't.

'Then let's celebrate.'

'Let's.' She traces his lips with her fingers. 'Thank you, Tom. I love you.'

'I love you too.'

He bites his lip to stop himself crying.

Twenty One

Hannah looks at her phone. The texts are arriving thick and fast.

Shit. Zip has given up the struggle. Got any spare rucksacks I can borrow? Only needs to hold half my house.

Hannah giggles as she texts Steph back. Erm . . . sure. My little silver one I used to take dancing. Will fit your wallet and some chewing gum if you REALLY squeeze.

She pulls open the door of the big Ikea wardrobe in their bedroom. It scrapes slightly, and she runs a finger along the wood as she remembers the day Tom assembled it from what seemed to be several hundred parts. It had taken five hours and many beers longer than proclaimed on the instructions. She grins as she remembers marking GCSE mocks that afternoon to an explosive backing track of his fluent swearing.

Another text arrives.

Thanks for nothing. That's you off my in-flight Malteser list.

Hannah skims her hand over the clothes in the wardrobe as she tries to decide what to take. She pushes her grey skirt and black suit gleefully to one side. She won't be needing them now. She pulls out summer dresses and shorts in bright pinks and blues. A long purple skirt. A silver scarf. She grabs green flip-flops and her turquoise sarong and throws them all in a big heap on the bed.

Right. That's her packing sorted.

Another text from Steph. However I might forgive you if you pick up a coffee and a cake for me when you head over later.

Hannah sits down on the bed as she replies. Deal.

She puts her phone in her pocket and gazes around the bedroom that she and Tom have shared for the last four years. She buries her toes in the thick white carpet and looks at the spot where she found him lying that terrible morning.

It was only half a year ago, yet everything has changed. She thinks of waking in his arms this morning. Of watching his sleeping face before slipping out of bed to make them both a cup of tea. His slow grin as he sat up to drink it. His wave as Nick drove him off for his first day back at work.

Every moment is precious now.

As he got into the car he seemed so much better. So himself. Tom the lawyer again. Dark suit. Bright eyes. Hair that looked like it might actually have encountered a brush.

He looked strong. Self-sufficient.

He'll be fine without her.

After all these weeks spending so much time together, part of her feels a wrench of sadness at the thought.

Yet part of her can't wait to get on that plane.

She lies back on the bed and breathes in the room. Their room.

Her phone vibrates. Steph again. You OK, bird? Not getting sentimental on me?

Hannah blushes. Maybe.

Get your arse to the doctor then. Jabs time. I'm not having you catching typhoid and ruining all my fun.

Hannah checks her watch. Steph is right. She needs to get out of here. She heads down to the hall and takes another look around. She sees Tom's coat hanging on its peg. His battered trainers on the floor. His beloved record bag leaning against the radiator. Hannah smiles as she remembers the day she first saw it. Frith Street. So many years ago.

Steph texts again. Han? Are you on your way to the doc's yet? If not then wipe your eyes and get out of there.

Hannah smiles but something still makes her linger. The tang of Tom's aftershave. The memory of their first and greatest food fight – involving squirty cream and lemon meringue pie. She remembers their laughter. The shower they took together to wash it off.

She hears a key in the lock and hope surges through her. Maybe Tom's come home early. They could go for a drink. Talk. Make the most of every second.

She moves quickly to the door.

'Fancy meeting you.' Julie's bump enters the house several seconds before she does. Her face is flushed and she stands fanning herself for a moment before putting her bag down.

'Hey.' Hannah feels a pang of disappointment that it's not Tom. 'How's it going?'

'Not bad.' Julie pats her belly. 'Considering I'm lugging this human medicine ball around.'

'Great.' Hannah feels uncomfortable. Stilted. Julie's reaction to the news of Hannah's departure has been muted to say the least.

Hannah taps her keys against her leg. 'I'm just heading out to get some jabs for Tanzania.'

'Sure.' Julie shrugs. 'So you're still going then?'

'Yes.' Hannah crosses her arms.

'OK.' Julie nods and walks towards the kitchen.

Hannah turns and follows. 'Look, Jules, are you worried about me going away? It was Tom's idea, you know.'

Julie calmly puts the kettle on. 'Yeah. I know.' She looks at Hannah. 'Tea?'

'No thanks.' Hannah realises she is rattling her keys like a hyperactive toddler. She shoves them in her pocket.

Julie takes a teabag from the cupboard. Something about the set of her shoulders makes Hannah feel defensive. Judged.

'Look.' She stops as Julie puts some sugar in her tea and stirs it at breakneck speed.

'What?' She glances at Hannah over her shoulder.

All the words Hannah had intended to say stop on her lips.

A tear is dripping down Julie's cheek.

'Jules?' She walks towards her. 'Are you OK?' Her pulse spirals. 'Is the baby OK?'

'Yes.' Julie's shoulders heave. 'The baby's fine.' She starts to sob.

'Why don't you sit down?' Hannah puts her hand on Julie's arm. 'I can finish that for you.' She looks at the mug. 'Though I have to say you've done a pretty thorough job on the stirring.' She guides Julie over to the kitchen table.

Julie sits down with a groan, and starts fanning herself with her hand. More tears fall and Hannah moves the biscuit tin away to prevent serious damage to the digestives.

Hannah pulls out a chair and sits in front of her. 'What is it? What's happened?'

Julie's answer is drowned out by her wails. All Hannah can distinguish initially is the word 'blood.'

It's not a good start. She takes Julie's hand.

'Hey, can I just check again, is the baby OK?'

She thinks she sees a nod.

'Thank God for that.' Hannah exhales. 'So what happened?'

'My. Blood. Pressure. High.' Julie forces the words out between hiccupping sobs. Then she looks at Hannah and her face crumples. She looks about fifteen. 'I'm SCARED.'

Hannah thinks of Tom's stroke and fear knifes her. She puts her arms round Julie and holds her, stroking her long hair until the sobbing starts to subside.

'Have they given you any medication? For the blood pressure?'

'Yes.' Julie's voice is high. Strained.

'Good.' Hannah pulls away. 'They know what they're doing, you know. Look how much they've helped Tom. He's going to be as good as new.'

Julie opens her mouth. Closes it. More tears spill from her eyes. 'Still scared.'

Hannah offers her a balled-up tissue from her pocket. 'Of course you are. You've got a little person in there.' She touches Julie's belly. So hard. So warm. 'I'd be terrified.'

Julie relaxes a little. She blows her nose, and eyes Hannah. 'How about you? Are you scared? About going away?'

'Yes.' Hannah nods. 'I'm terrified.'

'Why?'

Hannah sighs. 'I'm scared that going away and leaving Tom is the wrong thing to do.'

Julie dabs her eyes with the tissue and doesn't speak.

Hannah carries on. 'I'm worried he's hiding something

from me.' As Hannah says it she realises it's true. 'That maybe he's not doing as well as he says he is.'

'Why would he do that?' Julie takes a long gulp of tea. 'That would be crazy.'

'I know, but . . .' Hannah searches Julie's face for any sign that she's correct. Not a flicker. She hangs her head. 'I just feel . . . wrong. Selfish.'

Julie stares at her, her mouth pressed into a hard line. Then her lips curve upwards. Hannah had forgotten how infectious her smile can be.

'Just enjoy it, OK? That's what Tom wants. That's what'll make him happy.' She laces her fingers round her mug. 'It might not be the normal thing to do after five years of marriage and a stroke, but who cares? I don't believe in normal any more.' She gazes at her bump. 'I mean, I'm having a fatherless baby while living in my big brother's house.' She looks up. 'What's normal about that?'

'And you're still sure you don't want to contact Zac?'

'Yeah.' Julie nods. 'That ship has definitely sailed.'

'But if you haven't told him—'

'I can't.' Julie rubs her forehead with the back of her hand. 'Not now.'

Hannah remembers Zac's face the day he'd come to visit. Hurt. Closed.

'He's probably still angry. About when he came up here.'

'Doesn't matter, does it?' Julie's eyes glint defiantly. 'It's too late.'

'Jules, you . . .'

'Look.' Julie holds up a hand. 'I don't want to talk about it. It's not good for my blood pressure. OK?'

Hannah sighs. 'I'm just worried about you.'

'Well, stop.' Julie rolls her eyes. 'Stop bloody worrying about everyone else. And go and have some fun. Make a difference, or whatever it is you teachers do.' Her eyebrows arch upwards. 'And no. That wasn't me being sarcastic.' She stretches her arms above her head and her coloured bracelets jangle. 'Maybe one day me and Teenie will head out there. Really teach them something.'

'Well, feel free to visit.' Hannah stands up.

'Really?' Julie's face lights up. 'That would be amazing.'

Hannah has a brief flash of fear about babies and tropical diseases. She decides to ignore it. 'Good. Well, let me know if you really want to. I think we have the internet out there. Most of the time.' She smiles at the thought of being somewhere so remote. So new. 'Either way, time for me to go and get jabbed.'

'See you later.' Julie waves. 'And Hannah . . .'

'Yes?'

'Don't worry about Tom.' Julie's eyes meet hers. 'I'll keep an eye on him.'

For the first time in months, Hannah believes her.

Work pass: Sutton Associates

July 2015

'Say that again?' Nick bangs his head gently against his brand-new 'I'm the boss now' desk. It is made of dark mahogany and stretches intimidatingly across the office. 'Today was a "fake" day at work? To make Hannah think you're nearly back to normal?' He pushes up and leans on his elbows. 'What on earth are you playing at, mate?'

Behind Nick's head Tom can see the dome of St Paul's reaching into the darkening sky. He wants to run back out there and inhale the evening. Have a drink. Have a laugh. Hold Hannah's hand as the sun goes down.

Oh God. He feels weakness overcome him and slides into a brown leather chair.

'Tom?' Nick is watching him with concern. 'Are you OK?'

Tom tries to breathe. 'Yes. I think so.' His heart rate starts to slow. 'Apart from the fact I don't know what the hell I'm doing.'

'Well, I do.' Nick's BlackBerry buzzes. Once. Twice. He ignores it. 'You're going completely bloody mad.'

'Maybe.' Tom is horrified to realise he's about to cry.

'And you're not going to change your mind, mate? About sending Hannah away?' Nick wheels his chair back and stands up. 'I mean, that would be the sane thing to do, but knowing you that's not going to happen.'

'Damn right.' Tom rubs his hands over his eyes. One day in an office and he's beyond shattered. Every bone in his body aches to be horizontal. 'Not going to happen.'

'Of course not.' Nick leans against the desk. 'So, just let me summarise here. You love Hannah. Hannah loves you. Right?'

'Right.'

'So because of some crazy guilt about what you put her through last year, you've decided to send her to Africa to play with elephants?'

Tom huddles down defensively. 'She's not playing, Nick. She's going to teach kids. It's not for a bloody holiday.' He feels a beat of wry amusement as he realises he is echoing words Hannah has said to him many times over the years.

'I see.' Nick's folded arms tell Tom that he doesn't. 'And even though you've just heard that your arm and leg may never be the same again, you still think this is a good idea?'

'Yes.'

'So you haven't told her the truth?'

'No.'

'God.' Nick rolls his eyes to the ceiling. 'Like you haven't been through enough this year.'

Tom stays silent.

Nick drums his fingers against the desk. 'And you're doing all this as some mad gesture of love in the hope that she'll come back in a year and tell you she still loves you and wants to have your babies?'

'I'd settle for the "I love you" bit. But yeah. That's

the plan.' Tom squirms in his seat. He is so exhausted he can barely see. 'It's better when you don't say it out loud.'

'You bet.' Nick rubs the thick cream carpet with the toe of his very shiny shoe. 'And you didn't think about discussing any of this with me? Beforehand?'

'Nope.'

'Because I'd have told you that you were *insane*?'

'Pretty much.' Tom nods. His leg aches and he rubs it slowly with his hand.

'So why are you telling me now?' Nick gazes at him intently.

Tom sighs. 'Because I need a drink. And you're my number one pub companion.'

Nick flicks a glance back at his screen. 'Right now?'

'Right now.'

Nick grimaces. 'I'm meant to be—'

Tom feels desperation surge. 'Please?'

Nick glances at his watch. 'What about Hannah?'

Tom shakes his head. 'I think me drinking around Hannah is a very bad idea indeed right now. I'm sorry mate. I know you've got a lot on. But—'

'OK.' Nick snaps into action. He walks round behind his desk and logs out.

Tom watches him. The focus. The energy.

He wonders if he'll ever feel like that again.

'And mate . . .'

'Yes?' Nick eyes him warily.

'While I'm being honest, I don't think I'm quite ready to get back to work yet.'

'Really?' Nick's voice is sharp. Surprised. 'Was today too much for you?'

Tom swallows. 'It's just a bit soon for me to be here.'

He looks at the green and black legal tomes packed along the bookshelves. Thinks of the phones ringing outside. The emails squeezing into overcrowded inboxes. 'It's too hectic.'

'But you were great today. I'd never have known that—' Nick stops. Looks at the cane propped against Tom's chair. 'I mean—' He looks unusually confused. 'Apart from when your voice recognition mixed "kickstarts" with "kicks tarts" it's gone pretty well.'

Tom shakes his head. 'I didn't really do that much. Just helped you out a bit.' He smiles. 'And one day I'll definitely be back.' He stops. 'For now, though, I just need to concentrate on getting better. Stretch my savings a bit more. But don't worry.' He nods. 'You've convinced me. When I do start law again, I'll be working for you.'

'Damn right you will be.' Nick nods.

'Turns out you're quite a nice boss, for a Man City fan.'

'Watch it.' Nick wags a finger. 'You know you promised to keep our bitter football rivalry out of this office.'

'Sorry.' Tom looks at his friend.

'No worries.' Nick puts his BlackBerry in his pocket. 'OK. Ready. We have drinking to do.' He holds up a finger. 'There's one condition though.'

'What's that?'

'That you promise to talk to me before doing anything *really* dumb, like giving your money away to a cult or something. Seems like you're in some kind of Good Samaritan zone. Keep hold of your house, at least, OK?'

'I will.' Tom grins. 'I have to. Julie's moving in permanently. With the baby, when it comes.'

'*What?*' Nick looks like he's just ingested an iPad. He mouths nothings for a few seconds, and then visibly gets a grip. 'Oh my God, you really are going for a sainthood. Are you sure that's a good idea?'

'Yeah.' Tom nods. 'I am.'

'Bloody hell.' Nick peers anxiously out of the window, as if expecting to see a pig flying across the sky. 'I need to take you in hand. Before you start playing the violin or writing bloody poetry.'

'No chance of that.' Tom's leg protests as he levers himself up to stand.

Nick is staring at him.

'What?' Tom checks his shirt for stains. Nothing.

Nick reaches across and clasps him briefly on the shoulder. 'I just hope it works out, mate. With Hannah.'

'Me too.'

Nick picks up his wallet. 'And you're absolutely sure this is the right thing?'

Tom nods. 'Yes. I know what she's given up for me. Now it's her turn.'

'If you say so.' Nick shrugs on his jacket. 'But aren't you worried? That she might—' He stops.

'Meet someone else?' Tom feels a kick of pain as he thinks of Raj. It still feels raw. Jagged. He expects it always will. 'I'm bloody terrified.' He shrugs. 'But I've got a pretty fine line in one-handed emails, you know, so I'm sure that'll wow her from hundreds of miles away.' He tries to laugh but it's not funny.

Nick puts his arm round Tom's shoulders and guides him towards the door. 'Beer o'clock.' He holds the door open. 'But make sure Hannah knows. That you . . . you know.' He peters out.

'That I love her?'

'Exactly.'

'Of course I will.'

Tom grins to himself. He has something pretty special planned.

For Hannah.

For their last day together.

Twenty Two

'Right. There's only one rule for today. No talking about tomorrow. OK?'

'OK.' Hannah reaches out and gently touches his face.

He is so warm. So real. She can't believe that tomorrow she'll be thousands of miles away. Unable to touch him. Kiss him.

She wants to make the most of every second.

He turns his head and kisses her fingers. 'No looking mournful either.'

She swallows her emotion. 'No problem.' She puts the luminous pink straw in her mouth and sucks her raspberry milkshake. It's thick. Creamy. Addictive.

'I can't believe you brought me back here.' She taps the end of the straw against the glass and stares at the thick pink gloop dripping from the end. 'Were the milk-shakes always this . . .' she drops her voice, '. . . this sugary?'

'Yep.' Tom takes a sip of Coke. 'I lost a couple of teeth while I was pursuing you.'

'Poor Tom.' Hannah leans back. 'It must have been so much simpler in the days when men just had to risk death in order to get their girl. Fighting. Jousting. A bit of light duelling first thing in the morning.' The thought of leaving him intrudes again and her stomach skewers.

She runs her hand along the silver rim that edges their

table, remembering how Anton the manager used to subject them to extended polishing sessions when he was in a bad mood. 'Instead you faced hours of sitting on your bum growing love handles.' She loves making him smile. 'So noble.'

Tom nods. 'I know. Though I have to say the view was pretty good from where my ever-increasing arse was sitting.' He looks towards the corner table where he had spent so much of that summer trying and failing to summon up the courage to talk to her.

'Glad to hear it.' Hannah peers at their waitress, taking in the minute skirt and clingy pink blouse. 'I used to think I looked hideous. I hated that bloody baseball cap.' She shudders and points at her exuberant curls. 'Took me half an hour to persuade my hair into it and then about ten washes to get it back to life again.'

'Well, I always thought you looked hot.' Tom snakes his right hand across and squeezes her thigh. 'So there.'

The pride on his face makes her want to cry.

She digs her nails into her palm in an attempt to get a grip, pulling a napkin out of the red chequered dispenser as the waitress puts their food down in front of them. Big white plates. Portions that would feed a family of five.

Perfect.

Hannah's stomach rumbles as she admires her hot dog and crispy onion rings. She steals a fry from Tom's plate and takes a bite.

'Cheeky.' Tom holds out his hand. 'You owe me an onion ring for that.'

'HOT.' She waves her hand ineffectually in front of her mouth. 'Ow.'

'That'll teach you.' Tom rolls his eyes. 'Or maybe not.'

Hannah gulps some iced water and her eyes start to stream. 'Excuse me.' She forces the fry down her throat. 'Just choking to death. Don't worry about me.' She finally swallows it and sits quietly. Breathing deeply. Tomorrow looms again. She must keep talking. Block out the parting to come.

A new song comes on the jukebox to help her out. She turns to Tom. Grins.

'It's our song!' She taps along on the counter. '"Everyday".'

'Yeah.' He takes her hand. 'I lined it up while you were in the loo earlier.' He drops his eyes and a faint flush appears on his cheeks. 'It's part two of our day on memory lane.'

She squeezes his fingers as Buddy Holly starts to sing.

'Our memory lane day?' She feels a beat of excitement. 'Is that the plan?'

'It is.'

'Amazing.' She kisses him. 'Thank you.'

'My pleasure.' He looks so surprised and delighted that she kisses him again.

He grins. 'So, we have peanuts and pints at that dive near London Bridge next, then Borough Market pies, then a grand finale mystery activity tonight.'

'Wow.' She nibbles an onion ring. 'It sounds perfect.'

'I'm so pleased.' He puts ketchup on his plate and Hannah cuts his burger in quarters for him. 'I did wonder if it was classy enough for our final day together.'

'I love it.' She picks up her hot dog. 'You know, it might sound weird but I always preferred the things we used to do before you started earning your megabucks.'

'You did?' He looks sceptical.

'Yeah.' She nods. 'Crisps and chardonnay are much more me than caviar and Veuve Cliquot.'

'Really?'

'Really.' She reaches for another of his fries. 'Not that I'd say no to the Veuve, obviously.'

'Obviously.'

She chews thoughtfully as the song continues.

'I just think I always felt more relaxed in the old days.'

'The old days?' He laughs. 'What are you? A hundred?'

'You know what I mean.' She takes another bite of hot dog. Chews. 'The early days.'

'They were the best, weren't they?' He grins. 'I couldn't believe I got to hold your hand.'

She drinks in the love on his face. A memory to treasure. When—

She stops herself. Regroups. Smiles.

'Can you still remember our dance moves? For our first dance?' She sings along under her breath. 'What did we do again?'

He chuckles. 'I think our "moves" consisted of sway, shuffle, sway, shuffle.' He signals for another Coke. 'Or mine did, anyway.'

'Don't do yourself down.' She wipes her mouth with her napkin. 'I'm sure there was the odd twirl in there too.'

'Nope.' Tom takes a bite of burger. 'Definitely no twirling. I was far too manly for anything like that.'

'Bollocks.' Hannah glances at him sideways. 'I've seen you when the *Match of the Day* theme tune comes on. The toe tapping. The cautious attempts at a sway.' She laughs at the indignation on his face. Once it would have intimidated her. But now she knows him again. Knows how much he loves her.

'Right.' He puts down his burger. 'That's it. If you don't stop taking the piss out of me I'm going to make you dance with me. Right now.'

She narrows her eyes. 'Maybe it's more of a *Match of the Day* sofa sashay . . .'

Tom starts to move out of his chair. 'I warned you.'

She shakes her head, not wanting to pressurise him. 'You don't have to do this, Tom. I don't want you to hurt yourself.'

'Hurt myself?' He stands on two feet and holds out his right hand. She notices it has ketchup on it. She finds she doesn't care. 'Why on earth would I do that? You only weigh about a kilogram.'

She stands up and faces him. 'Well, with romance like that in the air, how can I resist?'

Somehow he closes his left arm round her waist and starts to rotate her around with his right. He staggers for a second and she feels them both waver in a way that would earn precisely no points from the *Strictly* judging panel. A family of five behind them look up from their fries and the little boy at the end gives them an enthusiastic toddler clap.

It's all the encouragement they need.

Tom steadies himself and Hannah attempts to twirl with some kind of grace. She turns round and round in the cramped floor space between tables, and she looks into his eyes and smiles with him and knows that this is the happiest they have ever been.

The song ends and they stand staring at each other. Laughing.

He shrugs. 'I think that might have gone better if I'd tried it before I had a stroke.'

'Maybe.' Hannah pouts for a second. 'Though I doubt it somehow. You weren't *that* coordinated.'

'You cheeky cow.' Tom glares at her and then grabs her round the waist. 'Now shut up and kiss me.'

So she does.

And as they embrace she feels the tears come.

Tomorrow is looming. Time is running out.

'Do you remember when we came here with Mum?'

Hannah licks her caramel ice cream and looks up at him. The evening breeze is rippling his hair and his green eyes are dark and serious. She thinks of that day. The London Eye. Julie.

'I do. It was the last time I saw her.'

'Yeah.' He shoves his hands in his pockets. 'I wish you could've spent more time with her.'

'Me too.' Hannah takes his arm as they stroll along the river. His left foot is starting to drag. The first sign that he's tiring.

'I wish *I'd* spent more time with her.'

She guides him over to a bench and they both sit down, gazing out at the Thames. A speedboat carves white foam through the water. A mum blows bubbles for her daughter, who completely ignores them in favour of the boats. A man pleads into a mobile phone, asking the person at the other end to give him more time. Just a day. An hour.

Hannah knows how he feels. Their day has whisked by and now there are only a few hours left. A few hours of him.

She takes his hand. 'I think she was happy that you moved away and made a life for yourself in London.'

He turns to her, eyes searching her face. 'Why do you think that?'

Hannah kisses him gently. 'Isn't that what every mum wants?' She leans back again. 'It's what my mum wants, I think.' She gently flaps her flip-flop against her foot. 'In her own way.' She smiles. 'I'm sure that's why she sent me a first aid kit as a going away present today.'

Tom groans. 'I can't believe she did that.'

'I can.' Hannah raises an eyebrow. 'The good news is it didn't send me screaming to the off licence as it would have done once upon a time.'

'Well, that's good.' She hears the affection in his voice and nestles closer to him. 'Much as I love holding your hair back while you puke.'

She chuckles. 'Also, I didn't want to waste one second. Not one second of being with you.'

His eyes cloud and he presses his lips to hers. 'I know what you mean.'

Eventually he pulls away and they sit side by side, her head on his shoulder, like a couple who have all the time in the world.

She leans into him. 'So what else do you wish?'

'How do you mean?' He draws her even closer and she kisses his palm.

'Things you wish we had done. Or . . .' She thinks of Raj. 'Or things you wish we hadn't.'

He stays silent as a chattering group of male students file past them. They're all sporting bright yellow tour T-shirts and appear to have universally decided to attempt One Direction hair.

Hannah looks back at Tom. At the hurt on his face.

Finally he speaks. 'I wish you hadn't slept with him.'

Guilt pierces her. She wonders when the pain will lessen. If it ever will.

'Me too, Tom.' She stiffens, expecting him to move his arm. Instead he pulls her closer.

Tom continues. 'And I wish we hadn't got lost.' He kisses her hair. 'I wish we'd realised what was happening and done something about it sooner.'

'Me too.'

'And . . .' She sees the light in his eyes. Knows that whatever is coming is important.

Then he stops as his phone starts to ring. 'Sweet Child of Mine.' The song Julie has programmed into Tom's phone as her signature ringtone.

'Sorry.' Tom pulls out his phone. 'I have to answer this. Just in case.'

'Of course.' It's probably just Julie demanding chips. Or pickles. Or whatever incredibly desperate pregnancy craving she is suffering from today. Hannah settles back and watches the evening. The lights that twinkle in the trees above them. The boats bobbing along the Thames. The distant rush of skateboarders.

She wonders what Tom had been about to say. Feels a twist of excitement as she waits to hear it. As she waits for the night ahead.

Then she feels Tom pull away from her. She turns towards him. He is pale. Worried.

'What is it? What's wrong?'

He is scanning the walkway frantically. 'We need a taxi. Now.'

'Are we late for something?' He still hasn't told her what he has planned for tonight.

'No.' He pushes himself up on his cane and starts to move back towards the National Theatre and Waterloo station.

Fear knifes her.

'What is it?'

'It's Julie.' His face is set. 'We need to get to the hospital. Right now.'

Then he turns and does his best to run.

Unused tickets for Matilda the Musical

July 2015

Tom curses his left leg even more than usual as he limps down the grey hospital corridor behind Hannah. Her hair flies behind her as she runs, weaving nimbly round a yellow cleaning sign that has been left by one of the big windows to her right. He drags himself along in her wake.

By the time he catches her up she is bent over by the red doors to the maternity unit, trying to catch her breath.

'Come on.' She reaches up and presses the buzzer. Nobody answers. Frustration is stamped across her face as she tries again.

Nothing.

'Why aren't they answering?' She leans on the buzzer and he puts out his hand to stop her.

'Sit down for a sec.'

She pulls away. 'No, I—'

He takes her gently by the shoulder and steers her over to some plastic chairs that are roughly the colour of diarrhoea. Tom wonders why anyone has bothered to bolt them to the wall. As if anyone would want to steal them.

As she sits down he moves back and presses the buzzer again, worry fizzing in his veins.

Nothing.

He drops his head and stares at the battered blue floor. His mind is seething. Julie. The baby. The future.

'I hope she's OK.'

'Me too.' Hannah's voice is tight. 'What if she'd hit her head when she fainted?'

'I know.' Fear churns inside him at the thought of Julie lying on the floor. Unconscious. Alone.

He gives up on the buzzer and walks across and collapses next to Hannah. She puts her arm round him and they cling together. He can feel her heart beating just as fast as his own. He loves how much she cares.

'I don't know what I'll do if something happens to her. Or the baby.' He stares at the double doors. They remain resolutely closed.

Hannah strokes his back. 'I'm so sorry.'

He feels a prickle of cold, even though the corridor is heated to the temperature of the earth's core. The flaking metal radiator beside them is pumping out heat despite the balmy temperatures outside.

'I'm sorry too.' He reaches into his pocket. 'I was planning to take you to see this tonight.' He pulls two tickets out and passes them to her.

'*Matilda*.' She looks at him and beams. 'Wow. I've been wanting to see that for ages.'

He shakes his head. 'Well, it hasn't really worked out, has it?' He stares at the enormous painting on the wall opposite him.

'Yes it has.' She squeezes his hand. 'I've had an amazing day. And right now . . . ?' She snuggles closer. 'I wouldn't be anywhere else.'

'Thank you.' He leans back and looks at the painting on the wall opposite them. He sees a sea of browns and greens. 'What on earth is that—' He puts his head on one side. It doesn't help. 'Is it someone having a crap?'

Hannah snorts. 'I think it's meant to be a cow.' She

leans forward. 'Or maybe someone's dinner.' She kisses him on the cheek. 'Either way it should be burned.' She smiles. 'Seriously. Thank you. For our day on memory lane. I loved it.'

He nods. 'Me too.'

'And the tickets were such a lovely thought.' She eyes him. 'And don't think I don't realise what a sacrifice it would have been for you to go and see a musical.'

Tom wrinkles his nose. 'I don't know about that. Now that I've seen *Casablanca* I feel it's the natural next step.' He looks at the doors again. Nothing.

Worry stabs. 'God, I hope the baby's OK.'

'It will be.' Hannah nods decisively.

'I'm not so sure.' He folds his arms. 'Our guardian angel appears to have pissed off on a pretty committed tea break for the past six months.'

'I know.' She starts biting her thumbnail. 'But listen . . .'

'What?'

Her voice is low. 'I'm happy to stay.'

It takes him a second to catch up. 'What?'

He is moved by the love on her face. 'I'm happy to stay here. With you. To help. If Julie—'

'No!' He is surprised by the strength of his reaction. 'No. You're going.'

'But—'

'No, H.' He shakes his head. 'We'll be fine.' He reaches for some humour. 'Besides, you need to keep an eye on Steph.'

She giggles and he knows that he has persuaded her. It's bittersweet.

He sighs. 'God, I hate this. It brings it all back. You know?'

'Your stroke?'

He nods. 'Yeah, and . . . last time. When Jules was at that clinic to . . . you know.'

'That was terrible.' Hannah rests her chin on her hands. 'I don't think she was ever the same after that.'

'No.' Tom is struck by how much his sister has fought through. 'With that and Mum she had a pretty tough time.'

'At least she had you to look after her.'

Shame stings him. 'I didn't do a very good job.'

'Stop it.' Hannah's eyes are full of faith. 'She's moving in with you, for God's sake. You're giving her a home. She's lucky to have a brother like you.'

'No.' He exhales. 'I could have done more. I—' A cleaner huffs into view at the far end of the corridor, dragging a bucket behind her. She heaves towards them at funereal speed until she comes to a halt just in front of their chairs. She wrings her mop out painstakingly against the side of the bucket, squeezing as if it's the neck of someone she's fully intending to kill.

Tom raises his voice as the cleaner emits a crackling cough, seemingly immune to the emotion of the moment. 'I . . .' He watches, fascinated, as she sniffs and wipes her bulging nose with her hand, smearing the results down her bright orange uniform.

He sighs. Closes his mouth.

'What were you going to say, Tom?'

Words rush through his mind, but none of them fit. 'Doesn't matter.'

He jerks his feet away as the cleaner slops the mop towards them. She pulls out a dank grey cloth and starts to wipe the back of the chair Hannah is sitting on. Hannah takes the hint and stands up.

The cleaner clanks her bucket on down the corridor

as a doctor finally comes through the double doors. She has a white coat and a frown that makes nerves swoop in Tom's stomach.

'Are you Julie Ellison's family?'

'Yes.' Tom stands up. 'How is she?'

The doctor pushes a grey strand of hair behind her ear. 'She's doing well now.' She gives a half smile. 'Quite chatty, isn't she?'

Tom shares a silent glance with Hannah.

The cleaner decides now is the moment to bang her trolley into the wall.

Perfect.

The doctor gives the cleaner a weary stare and pushes her thick brown glasses up her nose. 'You can come through and see her now.'

Tom takes Hannah's hand as he follows the doctor. Past a waiting room where a man watches helplessly as his wife braces herself against the wall. Past doors to rooms full of screams and howls. Past worried men downing coffee as they brace themselves to go back inside.

This is hardly the evening Tom had been hoping for.

The doctor opens a door and there she is, sitting up in bed. Jules.

His little sister.

Love surges within him and he walks towards her and hugs her close.

He finds he can't let go.

'All right, Tommo.' She gently pushes him away. 'Calm down.' The irritation in her voice gives him hope. 'Give a girl some room.'

He pulls away. Her hair is scraped back from her pale face. The white sheets are pulled up over her chest and a black monitor is fixed to the wall. He hears the rapid pulse of the baby's heartbeat. It sounds fierce. Strong.

Determined.

Thank God.

Hannah walks over and kisses her. 'How are you doing?'

'Better now.' Julie's tone is defiant, but Tom can see her hands shaking as she reaches for a glass of water. 'I shouldn't have been carrying so many baby clothes. Bloody Primark.'

'Yeah, because obviously it's Primark's fault.' Tom pats his sister's arm. He wants to stay close. Just in case. 'Let me help you out next time. OK?' He starts to feel shaky himself, and sits down hastily on the edge of the bed.

'You? In a clothes shop?' Julie giggles. 'You must be kidding.'

'I could try.'

Julie looks at Hannah. 'I don't think so. Do you?'

'Nope.' Hannah's expression leaves no room for argument. 'He has palpitations if I take him into M&S to get a sandwich.'

'Exactly.' Julie nods.

'OK, ladies, I think we're getting off the point here.' He needs to know more. 'How's the baby?'

Julie grins. 'She's doing fine. Heartbeat like a horse.' Tom can see the pride in her eyes. 'But I expect you've already noticed.'

'It's so loud there are probably people in Scotland who've noticed.' He pauses. Rewinds. 'Hang on a sec. Did you just say you're having a girl?'

'Well spotted.' Julie beams.

'I'm going to have a niece?' Joy spirals through him. A little niece.

New beginnings.

He has to check again. 'Really?'

Julie rolls her eyes but her smile is wide. 'Really. It's a girl.' She points a finger at him. 'Just don't start buying her loads of pink stuff. No bloody frills.'

He raises his hands. 'OK, OK.' He nods. 'No pink.'

'Good.' Julie smiles. Satisfied. 'And before you ask me yet again, yes I have texted Zac.' Her face is suddenly serious. 'After today I thought it was the right thing to do.' She exhales and Tom thinks he sees a glint of hope in her eyes. 'He's coming up tonight. But we're not together or anything.' She shakes her head. 'So don't get all excited. OK?'

'OK.' Tom catches Hannah's eye. She's beaming.

Then suddenly her eyes fill with tears.

He knows why. Hannah has always been terrible at goodbyes. Once the crying starts there's no way back. The night before she left for Japan she had even disappeared in the middle of a meal, texting him straight away to apologise and say that she'd gone home to cry.

This time won't be any different.

He sees her sneaking a look at him as she turns and surreptitiously dabs her eyes with a tissue, trying to hide her tears from Julie.

Julie isn't fooled. 'I can see you, Hannah.'

'Sorry.' Hannah turns round again. 'It's just—'

Julie's voice is unexpectedly gentle. 'It's just that this isn't exactly the place you thought you'd be saying goodbye?'

Hannah wipes her nose. Her voice is low. Husky. 'Kind of.' She musters a smile. 'But it's more than that.' She looks around. 'I think I've just realised that I'm really leaving. Hearing about the baby . . .' She swallows. 'It makes me realise what I'll be missing.'

'We can Skype, you know.' Julie's tone is jokey but Tom can see the emotion on her face.

'I know.' Hannah smiles at his sister and seems to come to some kind of decision. He sees her hands are shaking as she puts the tissue in the bin. Sees how pale she is as she leans down towards Julie.

'I'm really happy for you, Jules.' She's looking away from him. Deliberately. 'And I can't wait to meet Zac again. Or the baby. Next—' She doesn't finish the sentence. Her shoulders spasm and she puts her hand to her mouth to suppress another sob.

Next year.

An age away.

If he's not careful he'll start crying too.

Julie is speaking. 'Look, you two can go. Please. It's your last night. You don't have to stay here, Tommo. You don't have to—'

'Yes.' Hannah's voice is clear. 'He does. That's what big brothers do. Isn't it, Tom?'

He looks at his sister. Looks at Hannah. At her hair. Her beautiful face.

Longing pierces him.

But she's right.

'Yes.' He nods. 'It is.'

Julie rolls her eyes but he can see the relief beneath. 'Well, at least go outside to say goodbye. I really don't need to see *that*.'

Hannah gives Julie a long hug and then takes his hand as they head outside.

A woman in the next room is clearly in the final throes of labour, bellowing so loudly he can hardly hear

Hannah speak. She leads him round the corner and gazes up at him. A lump forms in his throat as she cups his face in her hands and stands on tiptoe to kiss him gently on the lips.

'Goodbye, Tom.' Her voice catches.

He has so many things to say. So many hopes to share. 'Hannah, I . . .'

He stares at her face and all his words disappear.

He swallows. 'I love you.'

She holds him close. 'I love you too.'

She pulls back and she's trying so hard to smile it breaks his heart. Her mouth trembles as she gives him one final kiss. It's so soft. So gentle.

So final.

'Goodbye.' She turns and presses the exit button. He prays for the door to stick. For an alarm to go off. Anything to keep her here. With him.

No such luck.

The door opens and Hannah pushes her way through, already taking another tissue from her bag. He watches as she walks away, unable to believe she won't turn back and steal another minute. Another moment. But she keeps moving, getting smaller and smaller until she reaches the end of the corridor and disappears.

And she is gone, leaving him leaning on his cane as he starts to feel the piercing ache of her absence.

Twenty Three

'Here you are, madam.' The barista places a red coffee cup on the glass counter in front of Hannah. 'Enjoy.'

His smile becomes a frown as a little girl with dark plaits reaches behind the glass and grabs a particularly tempting Danish pastry from the bottom of the pile.

'Santana. *No.*'

'What, Mum?' The girl turns and takes an exultant bite out of the soft dough as the rest of the display slowly collapses behind her.

The mum struggles to be heard over the constant flight reminders on the tannoy. 'You know you shouldn't do that.'

Santana contemplates this logic for all of a nanosecond. 'I was HUNGRY.'

Hannah starts to move away as the mum rubs a thin hand over tired eyes. It was clearly going to be a very long flight for Santana and family. Hannah hopes they're not heading for Tanzania.

She weaves her way back through the tables and chairs occupied by people with carrier bags full of purchases inspired by sheer relief at having survived the security queue. She climbs up onto a stool that faces out across the airport concourse and places her small canvas rucksack on the counter in front of her.

She still can't believe this is actually happening.

She looks out at the hundreds of people all rushing somewhere that isn't here. People in T-shirts and tracksuits. In dresses and designer sunglasses. Couples arguing or laughing or wandering around in circles searching for departure gates. Travellers chewing gum or changing money or checking their documents for the hundredth time.

People going places.

And at last she is one of them once more.

Her big rucksack is off to the hold. Her passport and boarding pass are in her bag.

She is finally on her way.

She thinks of Tom's face as they said goodbye and takes out her phone to type a final text. Her thumb hovers over the screen for a second as she wonders how to say so much in so few words. She imagines it arriving and suddenly finds tears in her eyes. Again. Damn it.

She taps her phone against the counter for a second and then decides to call. It's quicker. And she wants to hear his voice one last time.

No answer from his mobile, so she calls the number he's given her for his new secretary instead.

She answers on the first ring. 'Hello. Sutton Associates. How can I help you?'

'Hi Winnie. Is Tom there please? It's Hannah.'

'Hello, Hannah. I'm so sorry, but Tom's in a meeting.'

'Can you get him out please?'

'Sorry. I can't.'

Hannah tries again. 'It's just that I'm about to get on my plane and I really want to talk to him.'

A short pause. 'He's out of the office.'

Hannah frowns. 'But you just said he was in a meeting. Didn't you?'

Another pause. 'Winnie?'

'I—'

Hannah feels a clutch of fear. 'Winnie. What's happening? Is Tom OK?'

Silence.

'Winnie?' Hannah is standing up now, ready to run to wherever Tom may need her. What if he's had another stroke? Or worse.

'He's not here.'

Hannah sits down again. 'What do you mean? It's a Monday. He must be there.'

Silence.

'Winnie. I'm about to fly halfway across the world. Tell me what's happening.'

An intake of breath. Hannah turns the volume up on her phone, struggling to hear above the shrieking children to her left.

Winnie sighs. 'Hannah. I'm probably going to get fired once Nick finds out I told you, but the truth is that . . . Tom's not really working here. Yet.'

'What?' Hannah feels dizzy. She sinks back onto her stool, holding her hand to her forehead. She had *known* something was wrong. That he was hiding something. 'Why?'

But part of her knows why.

'He's not quite ready yet.'

'But—'

'Oh dear.' Winnie coughs. 'Look, you weren't meant to find out. Not until you'd gone. But apparently Steph has a letter for you. Just in case. OK?'

'What? Steph? She knows about this?' Hannah looks frantically round the concourse but can't see Steph's long blonde ponytail anywhere. 'I'll bloody kill her.'

'Talk to her.' Winnie is about to hang up. 'Please. Tom wants you to. And have a great trip.'

There was no way she was going to go now. Hannah searches the crowd. Steph could be anywhere. She loves airport shopping, spending hours in stores that she walks past every day without a second glance.

'Hannah?'

She looks up to see her friend.

'Are you ready for an adventure?'

'No.' She blinks back tears. 'I'm not.'

'What's wrong?' Steph tries to shove an enormous Toblerone into a tiny carrier bag. She fails.

'What the hell's going on?' Hannah is raging. 'I just called Tom at work. He's not there. Doesn't work there at all, apparently. And his secretary said I should talk to you. That you have a letter for me?' She picks up her little rucksack, about to run back through security and get home. To him.

'Yes.' Steph puts a hand on her arm. 'I'm so sorry, Han, for not telling you. It was all Tom's idea.'

Hannah is starting to shake. 'Just give it to me please.'

'Of course.'

Steph rifles through her bag and pulls out a thick cream envelope from her bag. She holds it away from Hannah's eager fingers. 'Now, I want you to promise me not to freak out and run home once you read it – because that's exactly what Tom doesn't want you to do.'

'What about what I want?'

'Seriously, Han. Listen to what he says.'

Hannah is jangling with worry. She snatches the envelope and turns it in her fingers.

'I'll just be over there. Buying even more chocolate.' Steph walks off into the crowds. 'I think you might need it.'

Hannah rips the envelope open and smooths out the paper inside. The writing is spidery. Uneven. His.

H

 Damn. You found out. I should have known I couldn't fool you and that all your years of Sunday evening Poirot *would pay off just when I don't want it to.*

 So. First things first. Don't you dare turn round and come home. I will set Julie on you. Or the baby. Once it arrives. Either way it would be a Very. Bad. Idea.

 You may think I'm being noble but the fact is I'm not. I think we need to be apart for a while. Honestly. I need to work out who I'm going to be now. And you need to do the same. I don't want us to fall back into that pattern – working and sad and never looking each other in the eye. We can be more than that. I know it.

 The stroke might have changed me, but I'm still crazy about you. I love you when your curls are spread out on my pillow. When you spill red wine on the carpet and move the furniture to try to hide it. When you dance to cheesy pop songs with a piece of toast in your hand and the sun on your face.

 I love your giggle. I love your heart. I love your bravery and I love how much you care. I wish I could make you see the Hannah that I see. If you could, I know that you would love her as much as I do.

 My stroke isn't going to hold me back, and I don't want it to hold you back either. So don't you dare turn round. Don't even think about it. Just put on those insane turquoise sunglasses of yours and get on that plane. Have a glass of champagne for me as you take off. And don't let that Steph girl anywhere near the loos

*when there are any hot men nearby. We don't want her
being arrested before you even get there.*

*But most of all, my gorgeous Hannah, don't you
DARE worry about me.*

I love you,
Tom

'Han?'

Hannah wipes away the tears that are rolling down her face.

'Han?' Steph's eyes are dark with worry. 'Are you OK?'

Hannah stands up.

'You're not going home, are you?' Steph's forehead creases in concern. 'Because Tom has given me full permission to rugby tackle you if you try.'

'You don't know how to rugby tackle.' Hannah slides her bag onto her shoulder.

Steph sticks her chin out. 'I do. I've spent a lot of time watching Jonny Wilkinson, you know.'

'Ooh. I'm terrified.' Hannah stares at her friend. Weighing things up. Testing her heart.

She has Tom's words in her head when she decides.

'Time to go, Steph. We've got a plane to catch.'

Steph grins and Hannah knows that this is when the adventure begins.

'This way.'

Hannah turns and leads them towards the departure gate, clutching Tom's letter in her hand, carrying his love with her as she walks away.

Silver box

July 2015

Hannah has left notes everywhere. On the kettle. On the fridge. Post-its and cards reminding him of places they've been. Food they've eaten. Songs they love.

He follows the trail of memories all round the house. Through the kitchen and the living room. Up the banisters and into the study. In his sock drawer. On his bag. In his coat pocket. There's even one stuck to his shower gel. He adds it to the top of the pile he has collected.

Waking up on the beach next to an unfriendly seagull, Spain, 2006.

He grins, remembering the warmth of the sun on his face and the ferocious glint in the seagull's eye. The music festival. Their first trip together.

For a second it's as if she's next to him again, laughing up at him and daring him to dance as the waves break at his feet.

Then he looks around and sees a gap where her toothbrush used to be. Sees that her hairband isn't occupying its usual place on the windowsill. Her pink dressing gown is no longer hanging on the back of the door.

She's gone.

He closes his eyes and allows himself to stop fighting. Just for a second. Loneliness hits him like a fist and he clutches the edge of the sink with his good hand, squeezing the porcelain until it hurts.

Then he turns the tap on and splashes his face with cold water until he can't feel his skin any more.

He straightens up and lets the water run down his cheeks. He looks at himself in the mirror and he looks so terrible he almost laughs.

Day one. Cold. Wet. Sad.

He shakes his head and tries to find the energy he needs. Life goes on.

Hannah has taught him that.

He heads downstairs, his leg stiff and unwilling as he moves. In the living room he turns the key and opens the French windows, stepping outside and inhaling the sunlit air. The sky is clear and later Nick has invited him to one of his legendary Test Match barbecues. The cricket is purely background. The main event is seeing how many steaks Nick can cram onto the barbecue at once without inciting a 999 call.

Tom sits down on the bench that his mum left him in her will. Her one extravagance in the tiny back garden where he'd spent so many summers kicking a football against the long-suffering fence. It now sits next to a tub containing a few brave clumps of parsley and the chipped Jane Austen mug that Hannah has been hunting for every morning for the past two weeks.

Tom runs his hand along the rough wood of the bench, thinking of the rare occasions his mum would let herself take ten minutes off to sit on it with a cup of tea and the biscuit tin. He remembers her nibbling slowly on a fig roll or a piece of shortbread, prolonging the treat until it was only crumbs in her fingers. He wishes he could talk to her. Tell her how scared he is. Scared that Hannah will never come back. That he will never get better. That he has just made the biggest mistake of his life.

He pushes the thought away.

And then his fingers find it. Another note. Taped to the side of the bench under a protective layer of cling film. He had to hand it to her. Hannah had been organised.

He rips off the note with eager fingers.

> *Tom. Get off that lazy bum of yours and check out the silver box in the wardrobe. My collection. Things that remind me of our highs. And our lows. Just to make sure you don't forget me, H x*

He levers upwards, and goes through the living room and slowly up the stairs. He forgets about the pain in his leg. Forgets about the future. For now, she's here again. His heart beats faster as he goes into the bedroom, pulls open the wardrobe and props his cane against the door as he searches for the box.

He can't see it. Panic rises.

Maybe she forgot. Maybe . . .

There it is. An edge of silver, covered by a blue shirt that has fallen from a hanger. He reaches down and extracts it from its position next to a pair of boots and a terrifying device Hannah had unsuccessfully bought to straighten her hair.

He clutches the box to him and sits on the bed. On the top Hannah has stuck a white card, with the word '*Us*' written in black. He traces the word with his fingertip. Even when she was about to leave, she was still thinking about him.

He puts the box on his knees and holds his breath as he opens the lid. It is full to bursting. Objects. Mementoes. Their past.

He slowly starts to take them out. A coaster from Coco's. A map of Ashdown Forest. A picture of a birthday cake. The Union Jack lighter that she had used so often just after proclaiming she was giving up smoking for ever. He grins broadly as he flicks the wheel and – in keeping with tradition – it doesn't spark.

He digs through the collection. House keys. A Batman mask. He presses it to his face, thinking of the parties and the laughter and the extra shots they have shared. Then he sees his thirtieth birthday card to her. He sighs. The night they will both regret for ever. Then his fingers graze the thick card of the order of service for his mum's funeral. He closes his eyes.

He hopes she'd be proud of him today.

'Oh God, you're not getting all weepy, are you?' He opens his eyes to see that Julie has appeared in the doorway.

'No.' He snaps the box shut and surreptitiously wipes his eyes.

She puts her hands on her hips. 'You really are a shit liar.'

'Yeah.' He tries to stand up and his cane snags in some fairy lights that are trailing out of the box and he is jerked downwards. He manages to catch himself on the bed and steers himself down till he's sitting on the duvet. He disentangles his cane from the wire and runs his fingers along the tiny clusters of bulbs. He remembers them so well. Hannah draped them over the fireplace when she moved into his flat, and somehow they never went away. He always claimed to hate them – too girlie – but somehow he missed them when they moved here and Hannah packed them away in the attic.

There's a note attached to the plug.

Something for the future, maybe? H x

He smiles. Looks around. Towards the spot where he fell all those months ago.

He points. 'This is where it all started, Jules.'

'What?' She cradles her bump in both hands. 'The nightmare?'

'No.' He shakes his head. 'The second chance.'

'If you say so.' She shakes her head. 'You're still a doofus though.'

'True.' He pushes himself up. 'But at least I know that now.' He stretches. 'And what are you doing up, anyway? The doctor said bed rest. So get back in there. Now.'

'All right, all right.' Julie rolls her eyes. 'But only if you make me some tea.'

He shakes his head. 'Oh, so that's how it's going to be, is it?'

'Yep.' She giggles. 'You're my bitch. Deal with it, Tommo.'

'If I must.' He feels a rush of affection for her and goes across for a hug.

'What's that for?' Her voice is muffled by his shirt, but the strength of her embrace tells him that she's happy he is there.

'Just making sure you earn your tea.' He releases her.

'Well, get on with it then. The kettle won't boil itself.' She looks at him expectantly.

'OK.' He feigns grumpiness, but secretly relishes having someone else to look after for a change. Someone needs him. It feels like a miracle. 'Tea it is, then.'

Julie watches him for a second, then steps forward and gives him a quick kiss on the cheek.

'Thanks, Tommo.' She turns at the door. Gives an impish smile. 'And I'll have some biscuits too, please.'

'Just call me slave.' Tom rolls his eyes. 'Until Zac gets here, at least.'

'If he gets here.' She waddles back towards her room. 'Oh come on, Jules. The guy is clearly mad about you.'

'Or just mad.' She keeps moving. 'Who can say?'

He suspects she is rather less casual than she pretends. He saw her smile at the hospital. Saw the way she clung onto Zac's hand.

She clicks her fingers. 'Tea!' She dips her head to one side. 'Maybe I should get a bell?'

'God forbid.'

He leans on his cane and starts to head for the stairs. At the top he looks through the landing window and sees a plane arcing its way through the sky. He imagines Hannah curled up in her seat, chin on hand, staring out at the infinite blue. Dreaming of what's to come. Of her adventure.

And he knows this year will be worth it. Whatever happens.

He moves forwards. One step. Two.

He'll get there.

He knows he will.

Epilogue

S he watches him through the window, wondering when he'll realise she's there. The evening air feels pleasantly cool against her skin after the heat of the Tanzanian dry season and she is pleased to feel some light drops of rain against her skin. The perfect welcome home.

She stands on the front path, absorbing the pulse of London around her. She hears a siren rising above the thrum of the traffic on the High Road and smells onions from the barbecue outside the new pub that's opened on the corner. She smiles. She feels buoyant. Confident. Ready.

She looks back through the window again, enjoying every detail. The battered white paint of the sill. A corner of sandwich abandoned on Tom's Spurs plate on the floor. The curve of his shoulder. The way he scratches his stubble as he reads. Everything is so achingly familiar even after so many months apart.

Tom is sitting on the sofa with *The Times* sports section spread out on his lap, sipping occasionally from the Maltesers mug on the table to his right. A classic Saturday. His face looks fuller and his expression is relaxed. Comfortable. Her eyes land on a new cane resting at his side. Light brown. She narrows her eyes to see it better and spies the three footballs clustered together at the head. A present from Nick, she suspects. It has to be.

She is about to knock on the window when she sees a small figure in a turquoise dress appear in the doorway of the living room. Big blue eyes peer carefully into the room and settle delightedly on Uncle Tom.

The baby crawls determinedly towards him, coming to a halt just by the cane. It is clearly a favourite plaything. Her pudgy arms reach out and her lip juts in concentration as her fingers close around the wood.

Hannah grins as Tom reaches down and hooks the girl up onto his knee with his right arm. He starts tickling her and her blonde hair sticks up in a lopsided mohican as she writhes in sheer delight. Tom stops to take a breath and she raises her arms, clearly desperate for him to do it again.

He does.

Little Rosie. Nearly ten months old and already very much in charge of her uncle.

Hannah gazes, transfixed, as he pulls a brightly coloured picture book from a pile on the table and settles the little girl on his knee. She feels a beat of anticipation as he points at the pages patiently while Rosie sucks her fingers as she examines the pictures. Hannah can't drag her eyes away from the two of them. Away from the image of what she hopes may lie ahead. One day. Soon.

He's just turning the final page when he looks up. Through the window. Straight towards her.

She stands, caught in his stare, pulsing with hope.

His face doesn't change.

She can't breathe. She raises a hand. Drops it again. Maybe it's too late. Maybe . . .

Then he smiles and the months of distance dissolve. She stands on the path, caught between the familiar and the unknown. Waiting for whatever comes next. Waiting for him.

Slowly the door opens. She looks inside.

Then she walks forward into the future.

Author's note

A stroke occurs every three and a half minutes in the UK and so, sadly, it will affect many of our lives. While I was researching this book, I found Different Strokes, Headway and the Stroke Association to be extremely useful sources of information and support. The advice and stories I read made me even more impressed by the work that charities, clinicians and individuals undertake to help those facing life after stroke, and, of course, by the bravery and tenacity of stroke survivors themselves.

Acknowledgements

First of all, a lifelong thank you to George and Ann – aka Mum and Dad – for filling my childhood with stories. Thank you for bedtime reading, weekly trips to the library and for making me think the local bookshop was the eighth wonder of the world. I am also lucky enough to have a brother who has encouraged me from first word to final page. Richard, thank you for your unquestioning belief in me – it made a world of difference.

Huge thanks to my wonderful agent, Hannah Ferguson, for your eagle eye, your faith in me and for always making the time to support me through every stage of submission and publication. I am also very lucky to have such an incisive and creative editor in Francesca Best – thank you for your boundless energy and for working so hard to make this book as good as it could possibly be. Many thanks are also due to the wider Hodder team – especially to Anna Alexander and the brilliant rights team, to Emma Knight and to Naomi Berwin – I am so appreciative of your enthusiasm and dedication.

Many clinicians gave up a lot of their time to talk to me while I was researching this book. I owe a huge debt and several large drinks to Anthony and Karen Padgett, Dr Geoffrey Cloud, Dr Omid Hulse, Rachel Sibson, Alex Harling, Alyson Warland, Claire Edmonds and Helen Mann. An extra big thank you to Gill Cluckie for hours spent filling in the gaps in my knowledge and for wielding your red pen so tactfully as the scenes took shape. Any clinical mistakes or inaccuracies are entirely my own work.

I am grateful to Angela Jackson for your insights into working in schools, and to Rhian Fox, Louise Robinson and Vicky Lester for explaining the pressures and joys of teaching to me. Thanks too to my early advisors – Al Walmsley, Andy Kocen, Refik Gökmen and Robert Allcock.

Thank you to everyone on Team Novel for your advice, support and for strategic cocktails when required. I am indebted to Jo Rose, Myoung Rhee, Helen Winterton, Rza, Maria Nicholson, Sandra Iskander, Alice Jarvis, Nijma Khan and Rhona Muir for being so enthusiastic about early drafts. I am constantly thankful for Kate Holder's shining encouragement, and am also very grateful to Louise Forbes, Andrea Marlow, Adam Cayley, Katie Jarvis and Diana de Grunwald. I owe many thanks to Henry Sutton for first draft advice, and am sending an extra big hug to Kim Curran – you have no idea how much your kindness and conviction spurred me on.

Most of all, thank you to my husband, Max, for keeping me in my writing chair and for believing so wholeheartedly in me and in this book. I would never have reached The End without you. And extra love to Evie for always knowing when to make me smile and for resisting the urge to colour all over the pages as they grew.

Finally I am indebted to the stroke survivors and families who were so honest with me about their experiences. Thank you to Jim Currie, Shumi and Nelesh Jeyadevan, Angela MacLeod and Viv Black. I am a little in awe of you all.

- Tom is very young when he has his stroke. Do you think it's more or less challenging for him to cope with the issues that face stroke survivors at such a young age?

- Tom doesn't like to be pitied when he goes out and about – do you think he comes to terms with this by the end of the novel? How do you feel society treats those with physical disabilities?

- Who do you think is bravest, Tom or Hannah?

- How do you think becoming a carer can affect a marriage? How do you balance caring with being a couple in the more romantic sense? What are the key challenges?

- Both Tom and Hannah make mistakes. Who do you think is to blame for the breakdown of their marriage?

- Do you think Julie is right to blame Tom for the way her life has turned out? Could he have done more for her as she grew up?

- How does Tom and Julie's absent dad affect the way they have lived their lives?

- Do you think Hannah is right to make the decision she does at the end of the novel?

- Where do you think Hannah and Tom will be a year after their story ends?